Blue Keltic Moon

Children of the Keltic Triad
Book One

*lizzie starr

Book Layout © 2014 BookDesignTemplates.com

Cover Design by JinGraphix, Dokopot Books

ISBN 978-0-9977542-4-7

Dokopot
Books

Authors cherish their fans.
And so, my darlin's,
This tale is for each and every one of you!
Sparkles!

ONE

"Yield."

"Never." With the clang and ring of faerie steel against faerie steel her opponent's sword slipped the length of hers and he twisted away. "Ha."

Silent, Breanna advanced, the tip of her weapon swaying slightly, a slow, mesmerizing dance meant to lull an opponent into complacency. A seasoned fighter would hold the tip steady, ready for a thrust, slice or defense. This was a new trick Granda recently taught her. One she hoped hadn't been passed on to her opponent as well.

He took a backward step then stood his ground. Eyes calm, he watched her advance, his own sword gripped lightly but steady in his hand. She allowed herself a half smile and his eyes narrowed with confusion though he remained still.

Lunge. Parry. Slice. Sounds of battle filled the glade quieting the birdsong. The metal clangs echoed off the ancient trees, and dropped heavily from the overhanging branches.

"You *will* yield."

He danced away and shook his head. One eyebrow lifted in a cocky arch. "Shouldn't waste your breath talking. Need it for fighting," he panted.

Knowing she gave him an advantage, she glanced at the sun. Time passed too quickly and she had somewhere else to be. Unlike others of her clan, she wasn't able to manipulate a time portal.

As she knew he would, her opponent took the bait.

A quick sidestep. Crouch. Swing one leg. Connect.

Flailing his arms for balance, he went flying forward and crashed to his knees. Then he ate dirt. Breanna leaped to his side and planted one knee in the center of her brother's back. "Yield?"

He angled his head to spit out a mouthful of dirt and dried leaves. "No."

A low growl vibrated in her throat. She wrenched his free arm back, angling it high between his shoulders. "I don't have time for this."

He struggled against her weight and laughed. "Sorry to keep you. Yikes!"

The tip of her sword dug deep into the soft ground an inch from his nose. She yanked the shining steel from the dirt and planted it again, this time a half an inch closer. "Yield."

She grinned when he slid his hand from his sword hilt, flexed his fingers then pressed his palm flat against the ground. "Okay."

"Say it." She tugged, just a little, on his arm.

"Okay, Bree, I yield."

In one lithe movement she stood to the side and held out one hand. Chance rolled away from her sword and lay on his back staring up at her. Finally he shrugged, took her hand and hung heavily making her strain to help him to his feet.

Chance scrubbed a hand through his short, white-blond hair. "Geez, sis. This was just supposed to be practice." He moved his hand to his shoulder, cast her a disgruntled look, and rubbed. "Man, Bree. Did you have to pull so hard?"

She shook her head. He was never serious about practice. "You know how important this is, Chance."

"Yeah, yeah. But there hasn't been anything to fight against since Jayse and Lucidea killed Fiedhlim." An odd, distracted look passed through his expression and Bree wondered how often he thought about the evil Faerie who had fathered him. All her life she'd struggled to keep that taint of evil from her beloved baby brother. Now he was nineteen, almost a man. And like any man, he wouldn't let her into his thoughts.

"We never know when or where a new threat will appear. I want to be able to keep both of our worlds safe."

"Ever since Granda handed the leadership of the Alastriona over to you, you've been nuts. What? Are you on some sort of power trip? Granda left the Alastriona because there wasn't enough to keep him busy. Where are you finding all these threats? Where have all these dangers been hiding? Think they were waiting just for you?"

It was an old argument. She didn't know why she felt there was something lurking, some evil power waiting until the protectors of mankind were lackluster and lazy. Deep in her bones she knew, she understood, a power waited. And that power would soon become impatient.

Chance waved a hand then moved toward the thick tree trunk where they'd left their scabbards. He wiped his sword on the hem of his tee shirt then sheathed the blade in the plain, worn leather. "Whatever. I know you'll make me practice. And I will." He turned to her, the laughter gone. A dark, serious light shimmered in his blue eyes. "I feel a gathering of some power, too. If my... if Fiedhlim wasn't dead, I'd say he was gearing up for another attempt to take over."

Eyes wide, Bree stared at her brother. "You... feel it?"

He gave her a typical adolescent eye-roll and snorted. "I'm not stupid. I'm half-Faerie, too, ya know."

Interesting. She'd never suspected Chance had any inkling of the vibrations she felt in the dark night, much less honed the powers he'd exhibited so strongly when he was a baby. Having fully human parents in a clan made up of a multitude of Fey peoples hadn't been easy for any of them. She'd been pretty precocious herself. Much to her father's dismay.

"Why haven't you said anything before now?"

"I wasn't sure." The darkness left his eyes and the clear blue sparkled with mischief. "Besides, I knew you'd really hit my training hard then. It's bad enough now."

"We need to talk about this. Do Mom and Dad know? Granda or Jaysson?"

"Nope, nobody but you. But..." He glanced at his hands and spread his fingers in a helpless, beseeching gesture. "I don't suppose you'd keep this quiet. At least for a while. At least until I understand a little more about what's going on."

"Until we understand this, baby bro, I'll keep your secret." She sheathed her sword and wrapped one arm around his shoulders. His broad, well-developed shoulders. She paused in surprise. *When had her little brother gotten so muscular?* Must be all the training she put him through. "But you and I are going to talk about it. And soon."

He opened his mouth, but she stopped his speech with a shake of her head. "Not now. I've got to be somewhere and I'm running late."

His sly, knowing grin and waggled eyebrows made her groan.

"Off to the library again?"

"As a matter-of-fact, yes. Gowthaman's found some new old manuscripts."

"Since when are you interested in old manuscripts? Oh wait. I know. Since Gowthaman has something to do with them." Chance laughed, holding his stomach as if trying to hold in the glee. It didn't work.

Drawing back her fist, Bree punched his arm. Instead of laughter, a harsh oomph of air burst past his lips.

"Geez, sis. Did ya have to hit so hard? Good thing we're grown up or I'd have to run and tattle to Mom."

"Grown up? The way you tease?"

He danced a jig around her then bowed. "Part of my Faerie heritage."

"Honestly, Chance. I've been helping Gowthaman..."

"Got the hots for him more like."

Heat blazed in her cheeks but she refused to fall prey to Chance's effective teasing. "Like I *said*, I've been helping him with research. You know Lucidea's determined to get her uncle back from the World Between Worlds."

"Yeah, she's been trying for what... oh, since I was born? I know that's a serious concern and everyone's main focus now. But come on, Bree. Just admit it. You go to the library for the librarian."

There was no getting around his astute statement. He was right. Although, as the leader of the Alastriona, it was important she knew and reasonably understood anything that could be harmful to Faerie or to the human world. She did spend more time at the library than she probably needed to. If only Gowthaman would admit he loved her. She knew he did. At least, she thought he did.

From Chance's wide grin, she expected him to start skipping around her like he had when he was eight. *Bree an' Gowthaman sittin' in a tree...* The singsong taunting had merely annoyed her then. If he broke into song now, she'd deck him. Maybe a low blow that would have him singing soprano for a while. She'd never really do that, but just thinking about the possibility made her giggle.

"I don't like the sound of that." Chance sidestepped away from her, then joined in her laughter. "You were just thinking about when I used to tease you."

"Used to?"

He stopped and scuffed his toe in the dirt, looking like he was eight again, before lifting an innocent expression to her. "I'd never--"

"Uh-huh." She rolled her shoulders to ease the remnants of battle tension. "Never mind. I've got to run. Will you take my sword back for me?"

"No sweat, sis. Give Gowthaman a kiss for me--oh wait--I take that back. Give him one for you. Just say hi from me." Laughing he took her sword and jogged along a narrow path toward the Faerie armory.

Breanna shook her head. *Irrepressible.* She loved him dearly and couldn't imagine her brother any other way. Still, a darkness seemed to haunt his eyes at times and the odd expression she'd witnessed before he'd hidden his thoughts away behind laughter or smart-ass remarks concerned her deeply. With luck, someday soon, she'd get him to open up to her like he had when they were younger. Once he'd reached puberty, his confidences had become few and far between. She supposed that was the way it was with teenagers, but she missed their closeness.

Of course, she hadn't exactly been an open book with him, either.

Books. She was due at the library and she really needed a shower. She wanted to appeal to Gowthaman, not offend his sensitive Faerie nose with the stench of mock battle. Forming a portal back to her apartment, she rushed through, leaving her concerns over her brother behind.

White hot, the desert sun blared down from a crystal blue sky. Gold and copper sand stretched in undulating dunes into the distance, ending at a hazy horizon. Gowthaman dragged his sandaled feet through the sand as he walked, relishing the warmth, willing the heat to seep into his cold, cold body.

He'd had another dream, or perhaps it was a memory. He no longer knew the difference. He wished the legends that the Fey didn't dream were, in fact, truth. Fate had not been kind to him over the past twenty human years. He had been able to hold back the memory and keep the debilitating pain at bay for only so long.

He reached the oasis and sat cross-legged in the shade of a trio of palm trees. Clear water bubbled from a rock outcropping and splashed into a small pool. He dragged his hand through the water and shivered. Before long he would be forced to swallow his reluctance and ask for help--again.

Requiring assistance was not a bad thing. But there was only one who could chase away the pain and fill the emptiness left by the mind rape. Only one who held the skill to ease his suffering. *Only one.*

At first, each time she touched his mind to take away the agonies, he'd carried guilt nearly as intense and debilitating as the pain. She had been so young, only five, the first time she'd offered him healing.

Only five the first time she'd told him she loved him.

"Ah, Breanna." The few birds inhabiting the oasis lifted in flight at his agonized cry. "You should not love me."

He stared unblinking at the sun and whispered, "As I should not love you."

Humans would find a relationship between them a matter of gossip for he was uncountable years older than she. But as Faerie, age held no meaning once she had reached adulthood. As a child she had been adorable and charming. Now she was a beautiful, vibrant woman. He should feel honored she cared about him.

The love shining in Breanna's startling blue eyes when she looked at him was as painful to his heart as the dreams. The fact she was the only one who could comfort him, take the agony from his mind and return him to a functioning being tore through his soul. No one should have such responsibility for another. Or witness the extent of his pain and still love him unconditionally when he put harsh conditions on himself.

He pushed to his feet. She would arrive at the library soon to look over the latest information he'd discovered for the Zeroun clan. He suspected the information had initiated the onset of his dreams. The young lord's uncle by marriage had been imprisoned in the World Between Worlds and once the immediate danger to the clan had been eliminated, most of their resources had been focused on finding a way to rescue him.

Gowthaman shivered and moved from the comfort of the shadows into the sunlight. The family was careful around him, knowing each mention of the gray nothingness reminded him of his time there. But more than that, the memory of the faerie witch who had forced her way into his mind and stolen his knowledge, his... self, that caused him deep and abiding anguish.

Shoulders hunched he stared into the golden distance. He should have remained in the World Between Worlds when the others escaped. His damaged mind would have had no stimulation and he could have forgotten.

He shook his head. He would never forget the torment of another clawing through his mind, taking his memories, his hopes and desires. Never forget the hopelessness left in the witch's wake. The World Between Worlds may have been the kindest fate. At least there it wouldn't matter if he couldn't forget.

No one would hear his nightly screams.

Gowthaman inhaled deeply. The desert air heated his lungs, but the warmth refused to spread to the rest of his body. Forgetting was not his destiny. Most days he didn't much care, knowing he would survive as he had over the past years, little more than a shell.

He glanced again at the sun and steeled himself. No more moments remained for self-recrimination. Instead it was time to put on a face to show the world, at least those few who visited the ancient Fey library of Alexandria. A calm, untroubled face for Breanna's sake. She had taken to the responsibilities as leader of the Alastriona with joy and determination yet arranged her duties so she could frequently assist him in the library. A smile relaxed his face. He was proud of her.

He quickened his steps as he crossed the hot sands. Hidden from human eyes in the guise of yet another unremarkable mountain of sand and extending far beneath the ground, the library held the Fey texts of many races. In his aimless wanderings through the maze of hallways and tiny alcoves, Gowthaman had discovered scrolls and tablets he had yet to announce to any others.

Had these been discovered only twenty human years previously, the importance of the extremely ancient writings would have been overlooked. Or dismissed as fiction. Until he understood the vague references and hidden meanings relating to happenings in the Faerie and Alfar worlds, he would hold the knowledge close.

He drew a deep breath before passing into the cool library. This new information, the clues to helping the Zeroun clan, had precipitated the intensity of his dreams and the unintelligible voice. His steps slowed.

Temptation whispered into his mind. Perhaps it was time to allow Breanna to touch his mind, to heal...

He flattened his palm against the cool wall and knew he would not. Years had passed since the last time he accepted her offer of comfort and a short time of peace. He would not burden her further with his failings. Nor could he allow the woman she'd become access to his thoughts. If she touched his mind that intimately he would not be able to disguise his feelings for her. Then she would know how much she truly meant to him. How he loved her. Desired her.

He froze in the doorway of the small chamber he used as work space. Breanna stood to one side, her profile lit by the flickering soft candlelight he preferred to the harshness of mechanical lights. She studied a heavy stone tablet, angling it toward the flame to peer at the faint notches of carving.

Gowthaman avoided thinking about how the flame brightened the golden strands of her short hair. He pushed away thoughts of the intensity of her bright blue eyes when she concentrated. When she traced the angled cuts of words with her finger he shuddered as if that finger touched him. He swallowed heavily.

"That... that is a recording of a curse."

She turned a wide smile to him. "Then I shouldn't try to read it out loud, should I?"

He drew his eyebrows together in confusion, then relaxed when he remembered the movie she had made him watch with her a month ago. She'd explained then it was a common device to have the innocent hero or heroine read a chant or incantation they didn't understand, speaking the words out loud and thus releasing the danger. He struggled then found his own smile. "No, you should not. Unless you wish a sand demon from Bard's world waiting on your doorstep."

"I don't think I'm in the mood for that today." Replacing the stone rectangle on the table, she tilted her head to one side and studied him. "How about you, Gowtham? How are you?"

Gowtham. She was the only one to use the shortened, personal form of his name. A familiar, pleasant heaviness filled his chest. "I am fine."

"Uh-huh. I don't think so. But don't worry, I won't press. This time. So, what do you have to show me today?"

He wished he could show her the worlds upon worlds he'd been discovering in the ancient writings. Expose her to the amazing places described in the scrolls and volumes hidden deep in the library. Experience those worlds through her innocent eyes. To show her feelings, his feelings... about her.

With a tightening of his fist at his side he brought himself back to the reality of this world.

"You've been having dreams again, haven't you? Nightmares." Her bold statement startled him. He hadn't been hiding the pain deep enough. What more did he need to do to keep his agony secret?

"I can always tell. It's your eyes, Gowtham, surrounded with lines of pain. Let me--"

"No." He retreated two steps and lifted his hands before him to keep her at a distance. "No," he said more softly.

"Why won't you accept what I offer?" She sat and watched him, the sadness stark in downward turn of her full lips and the dimming of her eyes.

Did she realize she offered herself along with her healing touch? Of course she did, she was a woman grown. A woman who had offered him her love when but a child and who had never retreated from that offer. "No, Breanna." *Sweet Breanna, my love.*

Ignoring her wounded expression, he lightened his tone and steered the discussion to a safer topic. "I have added to the family trees."

Instantly, her expression brightened. "You've discovered more?"

Waving one arm to indicate the huge parchment covering an entire wall, he nodded. "Nothing new for the Zeroun clan, but I have discovered ancestors for others related to the rulers, including one of my own."

She clapped her hands once, and he was struck by her youth. There was too much time between them but still her enthusiasm tugged at his heart. "Wonderful."

"Yes. Many families have been entwined again and again for untold ages. Look." He pointed to a branch of a small ornate tree set to one side of the large, multi-branched Zeroun genealogy.

Breanna felt her eyes go wide. "It's me."

Gowtham's easy smile erased some of the pain from his face. The tight lines of his dark eyebrows eased to a slight arch. Tiny strands of black hair twisted into curls at his temple. Bree restrained the impulse to smooth them back, because then she'd want to touch his face. Nothing would delight her more than to trace the angles of his straight nose or the firm line of his jaw. She loved the contrast of her pale skin against the golden brown of his. In a wistful moment she'd once written in her diary that his skin reminded her of rich, cream-lightened coffee.

A dimple, barely beyond his lips, deepened. She tore her attention from his mouth to gaze into his eyes. A twinkle danced in the dark depths. This was the Gowtham she wished he could be with her help in healing.

He spoke softly, the words a caress. "Remember when you insisted you were to play Mustardseed?"

"I was determined, wasn't I? That was the first time I performed in *A Midsummer Night's Dream.*" She chuckled at the memory. At seven she'd astounded all the adults in the production by knowing every character's lines perfectly. She couldn't help if she followed the Zeroun clan's obsession with the play.

"Follow the trunk to the roots."

Tracing her fingertip down the parchment, she discovered a barely pronounceable name with a notation below it in a gilt edged rectangle. She read silently then gasped. "He was the inspiration for Shakespeare's Mustardseed?"

Gowthaman gave a rough chuckle. "You know better than that. He *was* Mustardseed."

"Amazing." She swept her hand over the wall of family trees. "I see what you mean about families being intertwined. Guess we just can't get away from each other."

Gowthaman stepped back. "There is another addition to the ancestries."

"Hmm, I see." Next to the thin tree of her family history was another newly labeled tree with few branches. She easily found Gowthaman's name on a top branch. Smiling to herself, she wondered if he realized he'd drawn their families so close together. And that his branch reached toward hers. Maybe there was hope for them. "You've discovered your ancestors?"

"Ah, yes. And look..." He leaned over her shoulder making her ache to lean into the heat of the sun he'd brought in with him. Or maybe it was the heat of the man. She squelched the longing and glanced at the tree's roots.

"The kidnapped Indian prince?"

At one point in his life, Morghan had counted time in human years. His age, the passage of centuries, the brief moments a companion remained with him. Even here he'd begun by keeping account of the years. *In the beginning.* But his efforts ended when he could no longer determine time.

In the beginning he had been able to use small puddles to watch the human world and communicate with the place where he'd been pulled through. But the water had dried and an impenetrable haze thickened around the place he had called home.

Then, in the beginning, he'd raged against fate, and constantly sought out the being who had wrenched him from life. But after a few fruitless battles, the creature had disappeared into the gray landscape, laughing, taunting, always before him, always heard but never seen.

Then, in the beginning, he'd tried to remember the things he'd read, the spells he'd memorized before his fight with the fire elemental. The mere thought of Brandr Ur and a growl would rise from deep in his chest, a sound of hatred and determination. Then, he'd ached to finish what his spells should have done--completely banish the elemental from all worlds. Then...

When was then? Morghan shrugged and turned in a circle surveying the gray, mist-shrouded landscape. Rare now were the times he wondered how long he'd been held here. Rarer still were the times he cared.

A flash of light blinded him. When he stopped blinking and the bright balls of fire disappeared from his vision, the shadowy form of a comely wench swayed before him. The shadows grew colors. Intense, vibrant, unbelievable. He shook his head knowing he should remember this woman, then smiled. She'd come for him. Finally.

He took a step forward. The uneven gray ground sucked at his feet, holding him back. He struggled to reach for her. Thin clothing fell from her orange skin. The bright yellow waves of her hair flowed down and curled intimately against her body. A brief memory surfaced in his consciousness then fluttered away. He ached for her, startled by the feeling.

She moved closer, not walking, but floating. As she disturbed the gray, tendrils swirled from her body, coloring the mist blue, purple, green. He pulled his feet from the stony ground and the sucking pop echoed, coloring, adding swirls of violet and fuchsia. Twirling, twisting, merging then flowing away, the colors drew him to her. He strained, called to her, watched his words float away on iridescent dragon wings.

Close. So close. He smelled sea flowers in the colors, felt the cool of her body, tasted how she would feel to his mouth. The sound of her voice sang to him in pure crystal hues. Fingers twitching, curled as if to hold her, he leaned forward. The tip of one finger touched her.

Bursts of light, aroma, sound and color flared outward then collapsed, imploding, and rapidly disappearing. Into the gray. Into nothing.

Morghan collapsed to his knees and dug his fingers into the ground. He lifted the dry gray mass into the colorless air and cried out his frustration. No colorful sound escaped from his mouth and he sank back on his heels.

Had she been real? Imagination? Hallucination? Morghan let the dust trail from his open hand then scrubbed his fingers over his face and speared them back through his tangled hair. The sharp tugs caused pain and that pain gave him the illusion of life. He howled in anguish, the sound muffled by the thick air. What was life--he didn't even ken if he'd ever lived. Mayhap his memories were only the dream of some sadistic being.

Was this hell? No, he didn't think he believed in the human need for a place of evil. Or did he? He pulled harder, willing the sharp sting at his scalp to focus his drifting thoughts. It seemed forever since a clear thought had remained for longer than a breath.

Morghan curled into a ball on the cold ground. Taking handful after handful of dry earth, he let it sift through his fingers, the dust merging with the gray, misty air. *This was real.* An unreality had become his reality. *Or was it reality that was truly unreal?* He clutched a handful of dirt to his chest when a soft sound captured his attention.

Sound was unusual in this gray world, so any instance was cause for investigation. Frowning, he strained to hear the continuing sound. At least he should discover the source, shouldn't he? He rolled to his hands and knees and crawled forward. He knew this sound, a knocking as if on a door. No, not knocking... speaking. No, not words... moonlight.

He clamored to his feet. He heard moonlight. Stumbling forward he followed the sound. There was a reason for the light and the moon. He stopped. If only he could remember.

Faster, then, he ran on until he moved beyond the small patch of the gray earth and rock he'd claimed as his own. Heated anticipation burned through him. Something was happening. Something important. He needed to be there. In the moonlight.

Rhythmic pounding sounded behind him. He touched his face, curious at the rise of his eyebrows. *Another followed the call of the moonlight? Who of the damned would sense such a call?* A flash of fire. He struggled to capture the thought then shrugged as the memory blinked from his mind.

Morghan paced in a small circle. Why had he been running? There was nothing different in this world of sameness. After another slow circle Morghan found his direction. Slowly he moved across the barren landscape until he found his chosen place. Cross-legged, he sat, rested his chin on his fists and stared into the dim, hazy distance.

Breanna perched on a bird-splattered picnic table at the edge of the park across the street from her parents' home. Though the sun blazed down on the green expanse before her, it was cool in the shade. A breeze ruffled the pages of her journal, denying her the chance for long, rambling trains of thought. That didn't matter, she was having difficulty concentrating anyway.

Finally she closed the book and escaped into the Sunday afternoon entertainment. It was a busy day at the park, with all the shelters and picnic tables filled. The shrieks from at least three birthday parties kept the resident birds and squirrels on alert. Freshly washed and polished antique cars filled the parking lot while the promoters of the event scurried to set up a long grill and a cotton candy machine.

The couple directing the set up looked a bit flustered. Bree grinned. Many times she'd assisted Pop-pop setting up events at The Castle, Jaysson's permanent faire site. So she understood all the things that could go wrong. But telling the hot couple, now involved in a low-pitched argument, to simply take a few deep breaths to calm down wouldn't help. She was glad Pop-pop and Jaye had decided to close Zeroun's catering, although they still helped out at the Castle. Sometimes she missed the excitement of a successful event.

She let her gaze wander to the group of teenagers reenacting battles with padded, wooden and plastic pipe weapons. The young people were dressed in an interesting combination of medieval, fantasy and modern garb. Today, there was even a Samurai. Their enthusiasm and dedication were real, though if they fought actual battles, there would have been no survivors. Once when she'd been the same age, she'd tried to join them, and show how battles really would be waged.

She'd been laughed out of the park by a handful of know-it-all boys. Now one of those boys was a banker. Another ran a video store. A third, who had actually listened to her, worked as a knight in the jousts at The Castle.

Chuckling, she shooed a fly with a wave of her hand. She'd seen him practice. He still had much to learn.

And she was the leader of the Alastriona, the defenders of mankind. She proudly equated her faerie warriors to a special ops group--no discernable presence, but on the ready, nonetheless.

A fine irony.

"Hey, baby girl."

"Dad. Come to join my critique of today's battle?"

"Nope. I've got a message for you from lord Jaysson."

Bree's shoulders tightened, shedding the pleasant relaxation of the summer afternoon. Jayse usually just called her. To receive a message like this meant important, official faerie business. Her heart thudded heavily. "Lord Jaysson?"

Bryce sat next to her and shrugged one shoulder. "It's an official request for you to call him as soon as possible. Official requests require the proper titles and officious tones."

"Now you sound like some of the counselors in Lucidea's high court." Bree chuckled and her father joined her for a moment before resting his hand on her arm. "He sounded stressed, so it must be important, honey."

Rubbing her palms together, she watched her father's face trying to determine if he knew more than he was saying. "Is someone hurt?"

"No, I don't think so. They need you as Alastriona, not healer this time."

"He still could have just called my cell."

Bryce bit back a grin. "He did."

"I didn't..." She patted her pocket. "Where did I leave the silly thing this time?"

"Dining room table." With an easy, practiced flourish--the culmination of years as a magician--he waggled his fingers then pulled a tiny phone from her ear. "Call him now, Bree. He was pretty rattled."

They rose together. Bree punched in the overseas number as they crossed the street and they made it to the porch. Her father had stepped inside before the connection went through. "Breanna. Come to Scotland. Now," Jayse said without preamble then disconnected.

Surprised at his terse communication, Bree gave her folks a quick farewell and hurried across two connecting backyards. Jaye's backyard was home to a permanently opened portal to Faerie, well disguised from human view as a rose covered trellis. From there it was but a few short steps to create a portal to her destination.

She stepped from the bright, clear daylight of Faerie into the dark of a Highland night. Without her usual slow enjoyment of the area, she jogged to the manor and pushed open the heavy, scarred wood door. She paused a moment, listening, then followed the faint murmur of voices to the workroom.

The conversing trio fell silent when she entered and stepped back to reveal a tartan covered lump centered on a table. Tall and regal, Jayse, ruler of her faerie clan, motioned her forward. Then his shoulders slumped noticeably and he gathered his wife to his side.

Lucidea, ruler in her own right of another fey race, glanced up at him, shivered, then sat on one of the four chairs placed around the table. She held tightly to Jayse's hand and he sat next to her.

Full of questions, Bree turned to Coralie, who gnawed on her lower lip and gave a single shake of her head. Tears shimmered in the Alfar-Sindhu's eyes. Coralie glanced past Bree's shoulder, took a deep breath and sat.

It didn't take much thought for Breanna to realize this meeting had something to do with Morghan. Lucidea's uncle, and Coralie's lover, the prince of the Alfar-Sindhu had disappeared into the World Between Worlds twenty years previously. But from the concern and sadness on the faces around her, she assumed she wasn't there to hear good news.

"You know the history behind Morghan's disappearance," Jayse stated softly. "Of how he found a skull, a sacrifice, shortly before the fire elemental attempted his escape from the World Between Worlds?"

Bree nodded then turned slightly to look at the bust on a pedestal near the inner door. Lucidea's father, Morghan's brother, had been killed to open the way for the elemental. Morghan had prevented the elemental's escape, but had been trapped in the World Between Worlds himself. A sculpture of him, one of Lucidea's creations, stood at the other side of the doorway.

Jayse continued, "For the first year after Morghan's disappearance, Lucidea and Coralie attempted to bring him home at each full moon. After that they--we--concentrated on the rare blue moons. But we must have always missed some clue, or maybe the timing was never right. I don't know." He stroked the back of his fingers along Lucidea's cheek. "We just don't know."

"No," Lucidea said and covered his hand with hers. She leveled her gaze on Breanna. "We do know there's another blue moon in a week. We need to talk with Gowthaman. He's archived most of the calendars and texts Coralie used... used the last time. We need to see if there's another conjunction of blue moons in all those different calendars."

The reluctance in Jayse's movements as he angled to face Breanna sent a pang of longing into her heart. To love another so much, and to be able to show the world that love...

"You'll bring Gowthaman here, along with his research. We need his expertise."

"Did you send a message?"

Jayse gave her a rueful smile. "As always, he respectfully declined, saying he'd send pertinent materials to us. I want *him* here, Bree. Even if you have to carry him."

"Understood. I'll leave now and--"

"Wait, Bree," Lucidea said. "There's more. We think this time might be... no, this *will* be the time we find Morghan and bring him home to us. There's another part in the equation this time. There's... there's this."

At Lucidea's nod, Coralie rose and carefully lifted the square of tartan from the table. The dark empty eye sockets of a fleshless skull stared toward Breanna. "What's this?"

At Coralie's uplifted eyebrow, Bree waggled her hand toward the table. "A skull. I know that. But whose? Where?"

Jayse took up the telling again. "This was found near the spot Morghan discovered his brother's skull. We didn't find any other parts of a skeleton."

Calling on her analytical skills, Bree leaned forward to study the bones. "Coincidence?"

"Hardly," Jayse said. "The location is in a remote part of the property and the surrounding rocks and ledges are difficult to navigate. So it wasn't an accidental fall. And all we found was the skull."

"Who found it?"

"Coralie."

Breanna turned to Coralie who gave a one shouldered shrug. "I was out walkin' an' for some reason I walked a different path. I ken 'tis strange, but I ken now 'twas where I was supposed to be. 'Twas for me to discover."

"Any idea--"

"Oh, aye. We ken who 'tis." Coralie made a face so filled with disgust, Bree smiled despite the growing unease in her belly. "'Tis Pagas."

Bree jerked her gaze to Lucidea. "The high chancellor you beheaded? Are you sure? How?"

Nodding, Lucidea angled the skull to point at an odd configuration of the bones. "See these? The openings for Sindhu breathers. And this..." She placed a heavy ring next to the skull. "This is Pagas' ring. Before you ask like a thorough investigator, yes, I'm sure. This ring designates his position within the palace and if you look inside you'll see the faint markings of his family crest etched on the back of the stone. It's his. I'd never seen him without it. The ring... was inside the skull. And, I took measurements and drew the face supported by the skull. It's Pagas."

To Bree's relief, Coralie covered the stark bones. "After Lucidea delivered punishment, as was her right, Pagas was no' taken to the Great Sea. Instead his disgrace was unceremoniously tossed into the deepest rift in our world. None should have found his remains."

"No one would," Lucidea agreed. "I'm just taking a guess here, but from the condition of the bones, I'd say they've been out of water about a year." She glanced at Lachlan's bust and her voice broke. "The same time period as... like Daddy."

Silence surrounded the table while Jayse comforted his wife. Bree's mind whirled with the possibilities. The similarities between the two incidents were far too precise to be coincidental. If the events of twenty years ago opened a passage from the World Between Worlds, then this--find--might help them do the same. "But, Pagas died nearly twenty years ago, would it still count as a sacrifice?"

Jayse cleared his throat. "We have no idea how the skull was returned, or why. Unless we consider the timing. Then, yes. I would say this is our sacrifice. We'll understand the truth of this discovery soon."

Rising, Bree straightened her spine. "The truth of now is that opening the veil into the World Between Worlds is highly probable as long as this coming blue moon is confirmed by other calendars. Gowthaman will know if it is. And he'll help discover ways to support the spells Morghan used before, so we can rescue him."

"Very succinct." Jayse smiled wearily. "Our thoughts exactly."

"I'm on my way. I'll have Gowthaman here by this afternoon." She gave Jayse a wink. "Even if I have to knock him over the head to do it."

THREE

Breanna stood before Gowthaman and solemnly voiced Jayse's command. Before she began her own arguments, Gowthaman stood, his slow smile halting anything she might have said.

"Yes, I will come. I, too, believe this may be the propitious time. I am glad you have given me a little time before we must leave. I would like to show you what I have been working on. I have developed theories which may be of benefit."

"And you want to practice them on me?"

Again he smiled that slow smile, one that delighted her to the tips of her toes. "Perhaps."

She pulled out a chair to keep from reaching for him but stopped when he shook his head. "Please come with me." Bree nodded and followed him across the workroom into a smaller alcove.

He'd covered the wall with a huge sheet of paper and begun a drawing in the center of the page. Breanna studied the arrangement of circles then faced him and shrugged. "I don't understand this."

She sensed his hesitation to move closer so she eased back a step. While she expected relief, the flash of regret in his eyes startled her. But he turned toward his drawing before she had a chance to analyze what she thought she'd seen.

He touched the large center circle with a long, square-tipped finger. "This is the human world, as we know it at this point." His hand slid over the circle and Bree shivered. He moved to indicate a neighboring circle. "And this is our Faerie Otherworld. The other circles represent the worlds we've identified. Bard's world, the conjoined worlds of the Alfar, a few others."

"I would have expected the all worlds to touch at some point. It's so easy to pass from the human world to Faerie."

His lip tightened and a flat, haunted expression filled to his eyes. Realizing what she'd said, and the implications for him, she bit at her lower lip. As a child she'd known how he, and others, felt when she'd witnessed their aura. She realized as a teenager purposefully sensing auras was an invasion of privacy. So she'd trained herself to not see unless she made a conscious effort. Especially with Gowthaman's sensitivity to anything barely hinting at an invasion of his personal space or his mind.

Yet, without flipping her mental switch on, she saw his golden aura flare around him. Immediately the brightness dulled to a dim reflection tinged with brown.

"I'm--"

"Do not say anything, Breanna."

"But..."

"Please." His deep, nearly black eyes glistened and she ached to touch him. Even if he wouldn't allow her to heal him, touching him would ease *her* discomfort. More than he realized, she did understand the depths of his agony.

As a child, she had only known that he hurt. She'd taken hurts from him and others and in innocence had diffused the pains without effort. But as she'd gotten older it had become difficult to simply let go. Now, except for common physical wounds or illness, she needed time alone afterward. An agonizing time to shove the remnants of pain from herself, then find and return to her own centered calm.

Because she had no idea how her process worked, she'd never told another how she affected healing. Nor would she ever let anyone see the straining release of those hurts she took into herself. Ever. Once it was understood the way healing affected her, no one would ask her help again. She would not allow her talent to waste away, no matter the occasional cost to her.

Gowthaman took a deep breath and stated in a flat voice, "The World Between Worlds."

"I still don't understand."

"I believe if worlds that are separate now actually touched another world, grand chaos would erupt. The worlds might be totally destroyed. Perhaps the worlds would merge or one world would overtake the other. Timelines could be skewed. There are innumerable possibilities. This..." He swept his hand over the blank space between the circles. "This distance acts as a cushion to protect the worlds from colliding, keeping each world separate, yet accessible."

"But, when we pass from Faerie to the human world, there is no hint of an empty space. There's got to be a direct connection."

Staring at the wall, he spread his hands. "This I do not yet know," he said and turned back to the worktable.

Breanna stood a few moments longer staring at the chart. Each world was labeled in Gowthaman's precise calligraphy. Squinting, she imagined lines connecting the worlds. She only knew of two others who had spent time in the World Between Worlds. Bard had been sent there with Gowthaman. Searlait, the mate of her second in command, had been held there for long years. There were interesting possibilities here.

She whipped around to Gowthaman but the words she prepared to speak died on her lips. With his back to her and both hands planted flat against the wooden table, he leaned heavily, his head hanging.

"Gowtham?"

He shook his head. "I am..." He angled his face to her. "You were thinking about Searlait, were you not?"

"Yes." He often knew her thoughts about matters that didn't concern the two of them. Those personal thoughts, dreams, and hopes, she kept tucked away tightly. Moving to his side, she hesitated then rested one of her hands over his. "I was. The concept and then the truth of the World Between Worlds surprised many in Faerie. For so long no one considered the existence of such a place. Yet, when Searlait was punished the Faerie queen sent her there."

Gowthaman shook his head. "Since we, as a people, have seldom needed places of punishment, it was believed she had been incarcerated in a world similar, yet separate to our own. In our arrogance, we believed in only three worlds." He lifted his free hand and ticked them off on his fingers. "Faerie, the human world and the world of banishment. I do not know if Searlait reached the place of punishment then somehow found her way to the World Between Worlds, or if the Queen mistakenly placed her there. It is not a question I am willing to ask Searlait or the Queen."

"I'd like to know how she was able to make frequent contact with the human world. It's still hard to believe she was Mom's imaginary friend when she was a little girl."

"Perhaps it is time for such questions."

"I think so. Especially with your research into ways to bring Lucidea's uncle back from... there."

He slipped his hand from under hers as he straightened. Bree bit back the sound of dismay that echoed through her mind. He continued to refuse her. If he couldn't love her, at least he could take the comfort she offered freely with... "No strings."

"Pardon?"

Bree ducked her head to hide her guilty expression. She'd spoken out loud. How much of her thoughts had escaped into reality? "Uh..."

"What do you mean by no strings?" Gowthaman's tone was soft and curious.

Relief washed through her. *That was all she'd said? Thank goodness.* She lifted her head and scrubbed her palms against her hips. "Oh, just a stray thought. They slip in and out occasionally." It was a flippant statement and an even more lame excuse. Hopefully he wouldn't press, although the odd, almost speculative expression on his face made her wonder if she'd somehow exposed more of her thoughts.

"Now, you have seen some of what I wished to show you in the hope you will assist in explaining these concepts. There is a wealth of information we must convey to lord Jaysson and his lady."

Breanna grimaced.

A half-smile eased the strain around his mouth. "Yes, I know Jayse dislikes being called lord, but he is who he is. There are times when respect is necessary."

"This is one of those times?"

His smile deepened though the expression didn't reach his eyes. "Perhaps not. But the information *is* important. Will you

assist me in determining the best way to present my findings?" He hesitated then held out his hand to her.

It wasn't often he offered physical contact and she happily
let him wrap the warmth of his hand around hers and lead her
from his workroom.

The crackle of ancient, brittle pages roused the fire elemental from the oblivion of his gray temple. With a negligent
wave of his hand, Brandr Ur ignored the call. Too long had
passed, too many countless eons had crawled like unseen
creatures through the nothing for him to again find interest in
the dim doings of another world. Another rustle intruded on
the silence and despite his disinterest, he cocked his head to
listen.

A memory was hidden in the sound. No. He shook his
head. Not in the sound, but in the direction from which the
soft rustling traveled. The sound teased, tempted, begged him
not to return to the ennui that had been his frequent companion since failing to reach the adjoining world. Even the crazed
ranting of his enemy, trapped now with in the gray of the
World Between Worlds had interested him only a short while.

The unmistakable sound of a turning page. Rising from his
hard, stone bed, he paced forward. Gray mist swirled through
the ruins, parting then closing behind him as though he'd never passed. He reached out one hand as he walked, fingers
spread--to feel, to grasp, to discover... Nothing. Nothing but
the sound.

Brandr Ur moved forward, his feet sure on the uneven
landscape beyond his temple ruins. For too many millennia he
had trod over this ground and dared not count how many

times his had soles touched the stone. He knew every pebble, every inch of dry, cracked soil as well as he knew his own skin. As he walked he searched his mind. If he were to count the time in the short spans the humans of one world called years, how long had it been since the grand confrontation?

Frozen mid-step, he sighed, taking in the oppressive air then expelling with a long breath. The allure of vengeance, paled to gray in this prison, returned to glow faintly around him.

A rustle. The faint scratch of quill upon parchment? The sounds echoed, the clear tones vastly different from the usual muffled movements around him. So rare, he couldn't help the sparks of interest burning to life around him.

Brandr Ur moved quickly, renewing the nearly forgotten incantations used to reach acceptable, open minds in other worlds. Spells that alone did not release him, but brought him knowledge, sacrifice and the power to control the fates of less worthy beings.

The glowing promise of revenge burned rapidly through him, filling his mind with recent communications he'd set aside as unimportant, those touches of denial and acceptance. As he increased his pace he drew residual power from the gray landscape and gathered the tiny sparks into him. The reserve of power swelled and he stopped to inhale deeply.

The time had come again. He would take this opportunity and all that was offered and return to the worlds that had denied and banished him. Holding one hand before his face, he exhaled and a flicker of flame burned at one fingertip. He closed his fist around the heat, strengthened the fire as it returned within and smiled.

He would be denied no longer.

At a loping run he crossed an expanse of dull landscape where the color of the stones merged with sky to create a solid gray prison. There were many here, most forced into the World Between Worlds as punishment. A few others had chosen the oblivion or had been trapped here.

Other than the rare worshiper or one he used for his own pleasure, Brandr Ur seldom encountered any of them. Now he felt a presence a short distance before him. One who moved in the same direction.

A scowl accompanied his narrowed eyes. There was only one who might hear what he had heard, and realize the possibilities. The spawn of his spawn. Blood of his blood. His enemy.

FOUR

The portal opened at the end of a long drive leading to Lucidea's stone manor house. Breanna paused to study the centuries old building. Arched windows, thick, ivy covered walls, a stone drive. Familiar. Maybe this house felt so welcoming, almost like a second home, because she'd spent so much time here as a child. First in hiding while the threat of fey evil hung over her family, then being home schooled. Her mouth twitched to a lopsided grin. Her folks had wanted to integrate her into the human school system, but she'd been more than a bit too precocious with her magical abilities. Chance had been even worse.

So when Jayse and Lucidea had begun fostering children from their differing fey races in an attempt to bring their worlds closer together, she and her brother had joined in the lessons. Coralie had been an excellent teacher, knowledgeable and tolerant of magical mischief.

Gowthaman started forward and she longed to take his hand as she had in the library. That had been just a momentary thrill, and she wasn't even sure he had been aware of grasping her hand. Now, his arms were full of books and a canvas bag of scrolls hung at his hip. Even after she'd insisted, he wouldn't allow her to carry anything but the thin journal crammed with his notes.

She clutched the book against her chest. "Do you really think all this information will be Lucidea's miracle?"

Gowthaman paused and canted his head to look at her. "Do you have reason to believe my calculations are incorrect?"

"No, of course not. But--"

"We approach a time of great magic. A time that is similar enough to when Morghan was taken into the World Between Worlds, the possibility for his rescue increases." Gowthaman continued toward the house.

Focusing on Gowthaman's back, she frowned. It had cost him dearly to research this problem. Knowledge she'd gained from healing his pain was limited. Part of that may have been her fault. When she'd healed his mind the first time, her five year old mind didn't comprehend the extent of the damage done to him. So, she'd innocently reconstructed his mental shields, creating a thick wall to protect his deepest thoughts.

In those rare moments he allowed her to touch his mind now, he kept too many thoughts, and too much of his discomfort and pain behind that wall. Curious as she was, she'd never pressed beyond what he allowed her to see.

Shoulders stiff and tight, his jaw clenched, he showed signs of needing her healing. He needed *her*, though he would not yet admit to either need. Soon, as he had in the past, he would no longer be able to hold back the emptiness and agony and would come to her. Grateful, she would heal him. But this time, she would offer him more. Yet, only if he were willing.

She'd been doing research of her own on the soulfire that sparked between two people when they were destined to be together. Soulfires were strong and easily recognizable in her faerie clan. The colorful evidence of each couple's love and devotion was unique. Rich and vibrant, Breanna saw them all.

Before he'd guarded his emotions, when he believed she was too young to understand such things, she'd seen the soulfire between them. Her adult aura had deepened to a bright red, Gowthaman's danced with gold. Yet the colorful connection with him, with her destined mate, had faded as she'd gotten older, not grown stronger. When they were together, she had often sensed her half of the fire reach out to him, only to be blocked and repelled. In those times, brief sorrow would flash in Gowthaman's eyes or his sensual, full lips would tighten to a thin line. He deflected her love consciously.

She glanced at him when he paused to rebalance his stack of books. "Sure you don't want me to carry some of those?"

"No. We are nearly to the doorway."

"It might have been nice if Jayse would have positioned the portal a little closer to the door instead of at the end of the drive."

He arched one eyebrow. "The distance should not trouble a young one as yourself."

Bree gave an unladylike snort when he stepped forward. He had some hang up about the difference in their ages. She was fully adult now and knew her mind. As Faerie, once a child reached maturity, the aging process slowed to an almost imperceptible crawl. She was only half-fey, but with the amount of time she spent in the Faerie Otherworld, she had no reason to believe she would age any more rapidly than any other of the clan. She and Gowthaman would appear close to the same age all their long lives.

Long lives. Bree stifled a sigh. She would wait all that long life for him, for there had never been another who called to her soul. Someday he would realize the joy to be found in accepting the soulfire. And her. Someday. *Soon,* she begged silently. *Soon, please.*

The heavy front door opened as they neared the stone stoop and Jayse motioned them inside with a weary swipe of one hand. "Dea Annie's in the workroom, but she'll meet us in the kitchen. Hope you're hungry. Coralie's been baking up a storm today."

Gowthaman nodded and moved down the wide hall toward the back of the house. Jayse touched Bree's elbow and she paused, both of them watching Gowthaman's tense back. "Do you think he's discovered anything new?" Jayse asked.

"Yeah, I do. It's amazing. I believe we're on the right track this time." She held the journal flat and placed her palm on the cover. "The information he's culled from so many different sources, from so many different worlds... all in here. I think we'll be able to make a concrete plan and take action. Get Morghan back."

Palpable tension flowed from Jayse's shoulders and he released a long breath. "I hope so, Bree. We've had so many disappointments over the years. I'm afraid we're running out of energy to deal with much more."

He frowned then turned and led the way to the huge kitchen. Breanna watched him sadly. In a clan filled with the joys of many children, Jayse and Lucidea never had any of their own. After numerous miscarriages, they'd been brave and blamed the incompatibility of their two fey races to form a child. But everyone had easily seen through the bravado to their pain. Fostering children, a combination of Faerie and Alfar-Sindhu helped... to a point.

So now Lucidea focused almost exclusively on finding a way to return her uncle either to this world or to the world of the Alfar-Sindhu. She'd only known of him for a week before the night he was taken, but she missed him fiercely nonetheless. Breanna understood her sadness and determination, and as leader of the Alastriona, she had the ability and tools to help.

Coralie welcomed them into the bright, light-filled kitchen with mugs of warm, spicy cider. Breanna smiled her thanks. Cider was Gowthaman's favorite beverage. Bless Coralie for attempting to put him at ease.

After giving Coralie an appreciative nod, Gowthaman stacked his books neatly on the table and sat. He cupped the mug with both hands to tame the trembling and waited silently for the others. Breanna sat next to him and he was thankful for her presence and support.

When he'd explained his findings to her, she'd grasped the concepts easily, amazed at the complexity of occurrences needed to effect a rescue. When she'd added the discovery of an apparent sacrifice, he'd been able to fill in the missing pieces and add to his theory. She would be able to simply explain the theories that still hovered convoluted in his mind.

She slid his notes before him and casually touched his hand. The warmth of the brief contact filled him, spreading confidence in his knowledge through him. He may not be a warrior, and had no desire to fight, but this upcoming battle would need his skills as well. Before her hand escaped, he clasped her fingers and gave a gentle squeeze.

If he could hold her hand, her heart, her body for the rest of his life, perhaps he would never again feel the... No, the horror would always be with him. He had no right to subject her to his defects.

Reluctantly, he released her fingers, but she didn't move her hand from under his. He chanced a sideways glance and she graced him with a small smile filled with understanding.

He looked down at their hands, her fair skin pale against his darker flesh. So different, yet so right. A brief flash of golden-red sparkles made him blink. His heart thudded a harsh rapid beat and he pushed back the flare of joy in his chest. The sign wasn't what he thought it to be. Couldn't be. He was unable to love her in that way. He glanced quickly again at Breanna's face, but she watched the doorway where Lucidea stood talking quietly with Coralie.

Breanna hadn't noticed the sparkling colors so his secret was safe for the time being. Before long they would be so immersed in Morghan's rescue, there wouldn't be time to contemplate the irony of imagined soulfire. Then he would return to the library, his solitary life, and his private pain.

Lucidea turned toward them with a hopeful grin. "So, you've found something?"

Gowthaman felt Breanna's gaze turn to him so he moved his hand to his journal and nodded. "Yes. I believe I have found a final answer."

When Jayse and the two women joined them at the table, a sudden rush of uncertainty kept Gowthaman silent. He fumbled with the edge of the journal and cleared his throat.

As if aware of his discomfort, Breanna spoke. "I should have copied down the drawing you made. The one of the worlds. That might make explaining some of your ideas easier."

"Can you reproduce the drawing now?" Lucidea asked.

After a moment's pause, Breanna shrugged. "It's pretty simple, really. I don't see why not."

Lucidea left the kitchen and returned a moment later with a large sketch pad and a handful of pencils. Breanna nodded her thanks and quickly sketched a series of circles spaced around the page, pausing once or twice to remember exact placements. Angling a pencil, she shaded the areas between the circles with the side of the lead. Gowthaman nodded. *She had done well.*

When she looked at him for approval he smiled. "Would you explain your drawing first? Then I will discuss my other findings."

Tapping the pencil against the pad, Breanna hoped she'd remember and pass on all the important facts. True, Gowthaman sat next to her and could fill in any gaps, but she wanted to prove herself to him, to show she listened and understood what he was passionate about.

"So," she continued after she'd given the basic layout of her drawing. "This is how the worlds could look now. At least those we know of. I don't suppose any of us really know how many worlds there are."

Lucidea traced her finger over the main, largest circle. "An infinite number I'd say."

"Sure, especially since there's so many ways the worlds can connect." Breanna drew a series of circles in one corner of the paper. "I mean, they might not just butt up against each other in long chains, though I'm sure that happens. They could overlap like this. Or if I could draw in another dimension, maybe they'd stack one on top of the other. We know that since there has been some communication between the three, the worlds of the Alfar probably sit close to each other. And to the human world, like Faerie does."

Bree glanced at Gowthaman who sat with his hands folded on the table. Though his head was bowed, she knew he listened intently, ready to add any information she missed in her telling.

"The most confusing thing is what part the World Between Worlds plays in all this. We don't understand yet the full impact of one world on another. Are there simply doorways and portals, or are there more serious consequences of interactions between the different worlds? Or with the World Between Worlds. Or what might happen if the cushion of the World Between Worlds disappeared. From what Gowthaman told me, I'm thinking there could be extremely important implications in what we plan to do now."

To turn the discussion over to him, she angled expectantly toward Gowthaman. The depth of information he continued to find in the far reaches of the library amazed her. Now, she was even more astounded he'd been able to put those scattered bits of knowledge into a coherent theory.

Without preamble, Gowthaman stated simply, "I believe there is a way to return Morghan to this world. However, the window of opportunity is very small. One night only, and in that one night, only at the height of the full moon."

With a lackluster swipe of one hand Morghan destroyed the pyramid of monochromatic pebbles he'd spent minutes building. Concentration drew his mouth to a tight line. *Or had it been days?* He blinked and swiveled his head, gazing at the surrounding landscape.

The soft echoes of distant voices captured his attention and he strained to interpret the words hovering just beyond his hearing. Shrugging, he attempted to ignore the persistent sounds, but the almost-words called him to remember.

Covering his ears amplified the sounds, and unable to resist, he kept his palms flat against the sides of his head. Listening. Remembering.

He closed his eyes. How long had he been like this, his brain as dull and unremarkable as the landscape or the flat gray sky? For a moment, he cared. Then his hands slipped to his sides, falling limply, palms up in the dirt.

Nearer, the clear sound of laughter seemed to suck the gray from the air. When he opened his eyes, he found no colors to taunt him. Morghan tilted his head to one side. He remembered there could be laughter without the colors that danced through his hallucinations. He remembered.

Morghan shot to his feet and lifted his fists high over his head in celebration. He remembered.

He let his fists lower until they rested on the top of his head. What good was remembering when he was trapped and no longer able to even see those he'd left behind? Still, he turned toward the mumbling voices and took a step forward. A single voice separated from the others. The gray of his world lightened. He pressed one palm over the hard beat of his heart. Tattered shreds of the haze that had filled his mind disintegrated. After all this time, he still lived. He knew. He remembered.

Behind him, laughter rang from a high ridge. Morghan tensed at the dark, taunting sound then turned to face the shadowed form, tall against the gray sky. Dragging his nails over his chest he captured the cool fabric of his shirt and curled his fingers into a tight fist. The muscles in his jaw tightened and he narrowed his eyes to glare at the intruder.

Forced past tight lips, his breathing grew harsh. He took one step forward but stopped at a sudden, strange stillness. He no could no longer hear the murmurs that had returned him to life. Struggling to keep the welling of despair at bay, he focused on the laughing figure of his enemy. He let anger settle in his chest and constructed a ragged wall of hate around his heart.

The call to battle, the driving need to protect, this too he remembered.

Gowthaman completed his recitation, satisfied with the silent contemplation filling the expressions of those seated at the table with him. Confident he'd presented the facts and possibilities to the best of his capabilities, he slid his hands over the dry parchment of the last book he'd shown to support his theory. Absently he turned the page.

At Coralie's startled gasp, he froze and shifted his gaze to the Alfar-Sindhu. With her eyes wide and staring at the book, she gnawed on her lower lip.

Wondering what had caught her attention, he slowly bent his head to peer at the partially turned page. A precise drawing covered half of the thick page. "Coralie?" he asked.

"I've seen that," she said, pointing to the book. "In the palace library."

Lucidea leaned closer trying to see the page so Gowthaman turned the volume so the others could see clearly. Jayse and Breanna rose to lean over the others for a closer look. Lucidea turned her face toward Jayse. "What do you think?"

Jayse frowned. "That looks like..." He straightened and left the kitchen. The others continued to study the drawing.

Coralie shook her head. "'Tis no' quite the same, the figurine I remember. But similar enough there could be a meanin' to it. See here?" She pointed to a flat circle suspended between three slender, curving and uplifted supports. "I remember this bein' lower, held closer to the base. An' this looks to be made of stone."

Gowthaman reached for his journal, turned to an unused page and clicked the top of a fine-line pen. As he scratched a rough copy of the drawing with the black ink, he allowed himself a smile. Years ago Breanna had provided him with his first 'gel' pen and now he disliked capturing his thoughts with any other type of writing instrument. Even the smooth flow of a Faerie quill paled in comparison.

Next to the first sketch, he recreated the uplifting supports and base, but drew the circle at a lower position. He turned the journal toward Coralie. "Would it appear as this?"

At her nod, he turned the journal so he could study the two sketches. Possibilities, and probable connections shifted through his mind, but he struggled to focus and verify his thoughts. Breanna returned to her seat next to him and gave him a quick smile.

Jayse hurried into the room and set a small, abstract glass sculpture next to the open book. Coralie's eyes widened further. "That be almost the same as well. Howe're, the one I remember is metal. An' look, here the dish be held high, at the very top of the supports.

Something about the odd art piece sparked her memory and Breanna spoke without thinking. "There's one like it in Morghan's bedroom in the palace, too."

Eyes narrowed, Lucidea leaned over the table. "And you know this how? At my request, that room was sealed by the council until Morghan returns. I didn't even allow myself in there."

"Oh, I..." Breanna took a deep breath. Heat flamed her cheeks. She'd been caught. Glancing around the table didn't help. Coralie's normally calm face bore a scandalized expression. Jayse looked amused and Lucidea frustrated. Unable to read Gowthaman's eyes since he'd immediately turned back to stare at his drawings, Breanna blew out the breath she'd been holding and started again.

"I, uh, did a little exploring when I turned old enough to be allowed to visit the palace."

Coralie leaned back in her chair and fisted her hands at her hips. "Ye betrayed my trust and explored areas of the palace ye were forbidden to go?"

Breanna hadn't had a dressing down in years, hadn't deserved one since she'd stayed out too late on her seventeenth birthday. With a great effort she lifted her gaze to look Coralie in the eyes. "Only that bedroom and some connecting storage areas. I was almost caught in Morghan's room by one of the guards. I wondered what he was doing there, but was really more concerned with not getting caught. I didn't want to face your anger and disappointment. After that, I kept to the places where I knew I should be."

Fighting to keep a frown on her face, Coralie nodded slowly. "I was told ye had been explorin'. I did no' realize ye found milord Morghan's private chambers."

Feeling more and more like a child caught misbehaving, Breanna stared at the table, willing herself not to pull her shoulders forward to make herself appear smaller. "I... I didn't really know where I was. Or, I mean, whose rooms they were. I only stayed a few minutes. But, I do remember a sculpture on the stand across from the bed that I think looked like the one in the book. And I'm pretty sure it was made of stone."

Jayse planted his palms on the table. "Anyone know of any more of these things?"

In the silence, he looked around before continuing. "Okay then. Let's gather all three of these statues here and see if there is some relationship between them or if there's a new clue to help us bring Morghan home. Coralie, would you swim to the palace and bring those two back for us?"

"Immediately." Determination tinged with hope filled her eyes as Coralie rose then rushed toward the workroom. The faint sound of a splash carried back to the kitchen.

Lucidea sighed. "I'll always wish I could do that so easily." Then she rose and busied herself with gathering bread and vegetables for a salad. After another curious glance at the glass figurine, Jayse excused himself and left the kitchen, leaving Breanna and Gowthaman alone at the table.

While Gowthaman picked up the figurine to study it from each side, Bree watched Lucidea. There was something different about her, a slight physical change Breanna couldn't quite distinguish. So, she let her vision blur, narrowed her eyes to a squint and released her magic. Lucidea's distinctive color surrounded her without breaks or invasions. Then Bree traced the flow of the soulfire blessing Jayse and Lucidea. She let her eyes widen slightly. Something about the soulfire was a bit off, a bit disconcerting. Concentrating, she found the disturbance. A concentration of sparkles.

Smiling, Breanna joined Lucidea at the counter and started tearing lettuce leaves into a salad bowl. Even knowing Gowthaman was deep in concentration and wouldn't hear their conversation anyway, she leaned close to Lucidea and lowered her voice. "Have you been to a doctor lately?"

Lucidea frowned but kept chopping at a handful of carrots. "Saw a healer about six months ago for a virus, but otherwise I feel healthy. Why?"

A hint of tension escaped in the single word question. Breanna's healing abilities far outshone any physician, fae or human, and she knew showing interest could cause Lucidea some concern. "I think you might want to visit an obstetrician soon."

"Obsetri--" Lucidea laughed bitterly. "I don't need and obstetrician. I'm not pregnant."

Bree's smile grew. "Are you sure?"

Carefully and methodically, Lucidea placed the knife on the cutting board then turned to Breanna and crossed her arms. "Not funny, Bree."

Tempering her expression, Bree explained. "I know how many times you've been disappointed. You and Jayse. I'd never make light of your inability--I take that back--your past inability to carry a child. Trust me. You show the signs of a soulfire baby."

Disbelief warred with hope in Lucidea's expression. "Even if it were so, I've had so many miscarriages."

"Always early?"

"Yes, almost before we even knew there was a possibility of a child." Lucidea slumped wearily against the counter.

Touching her arm, Bree nodded. "I know. But this is more than just a possibility. From the strength and vibrancy of the indications, I'd say you're over four months pregnant."

Hope won the battle and sparkled in Lucidea's eyes but she worried her lower lip. "It can't... can't be true."

"So, if you don't trust me, check with a healer or a human doctor. In my non-medical opinion you're going to be a mom."

Lucidea snatched her into a hug so fierce Breanna gasped, then chuckled and returned the hug. Lucidea spoke softly into her ear before releasing her. "Don't mention this yet. I want... need to make sure. We've had so many disappointments. I'm old to be having a child." She stepped back and hugged herself. "A first child."

Bree chuckled and Lucidea frowned at her. "What?"

"You're forgetting your family history. Your own husband was born when his mother was in her late forties. His grandmother was..." She paused to calculate. "As near as we can figure, she was over nineteen hundred human years old when Jaye was born."

Joining in the soft laughter, Lucidea swatted Bree's shoulder. "She's Faerie, I'm not. And I'm only half Alfar. But, don't worry, your point is well taken."

"Good. And you'll see a healer?"

"Yes." Lucidea's eyes softened as she seemed to look inward. "Yes," she whispered, then gave herself a soft shake and nodded toward the counter. "Now, let's get this food on the table. Coralie should be back with the sculptures soon.

Now that he'd woken from the lethargy of boredom, and renewed his focus for revenge, Brandr Ur gathered power in a frenzy of determination. Stepping beyond his claimed territory, he discovered others. Most ran, terror of the light burning in his chest stronger than their fear of the unknown gray. A few, some he'd manipulated before, came to him willingly. For, if Brandr Ur made good his escape, he knew they would follow. It mattered not what world they spilled into--the land, the people, power would be theirs for the taking.

Or so he let them believe. He'd waited long enough, had been without strength and ability far too many eons. He itched with the need to burn, to destroy, to conquer. He'd escaped one prison long ago, he would do so again.

The fire elemental stood still and let the memories of his emergence into the world of Dea Anu flush through him. He still desired her, a child born of humans, who became woman and was more than human. He tilted his head to one side. *What had the believers called her?* Not a god. He snorted. There had been few of power even then. Weaklings all. Barely worthy of an elemental's distain.

Ah, yes. His lips twisted. *A demi-god.* Even with that human given title, had she not been Dea Anu, she would not have garnered his notice, being no more than a pesky fly. But even as a newborn babe, she had radiated power. Not a power he could take--though he'd tried--but power that should have merged with his and lifted him to the lording of many worlds.

She had refused him. *Him!* Brandr Ur. The last, the greatest of all elementals. *Foolish girl.* Instead she had chosen a godling with minimal powers.

Even after these long eons, remembering the woman brought new fire to his body and he grew painfully thick and hard. She'd refused him but he'd taken her anyway. First by force, a marginally pleasing experience. Then he'd tried tenderness, but she'd no more responded to him than she would to a tree branch. Finally he'd pounded into her in anger, her tears more satisfying than the release of his seed.

She'd born three children from his seed. He laughed. And none to the upstart godling. The laughter turned to a growl. None of his children worshiped him. Instead they'd joined their mother and her godling in banishing him to this place. Ingrates. Fools. He pounded a fist against his palm. After the human world, the worlds they'd populated would be the next to cower beneath his anger.

Now echoes from other worlds rang with the promise of a new conjunction. Long ago he'd set his plan in motion, a motion now closing the circle of time. From this circle he would burst anew into worlds ripe for his taking. Grinning, he rubbed his palms together generating pleasing heat.

Yet time remained before he could rip free of the World Between Worlds. Time enough to renew his torment of the young water prince he'd pulled into this prison at the last juncture. His erstwhile descendent. He lifted his chin to sniff the wind. How had there come to be such weakness in the blood of his blood?

Then Brandr Ur bent and scooped up a handful of the dry dirt, warming the dust with his power. The gray grains sifted through the elemental's fingers, drifting away on a hot breeze.

By remaining a step ahead of the prince, Brandr Ur could torment, taunt, and destroy any spark of life remaining in the fool. Brandr Ur searched his memory for the upstart's name. Personalizing his torment would make the pleasure more satisfying. After a piercing glance into the distance, he turned and strode toward the temple ruins of his chosen territory. No matter. He would remember soon.

Gowthaman watched with vague interest while Breanna and Lucidea talked. Sure the rise and fall of quiet laughter had nothing to do with him, he attempted to focus his thoughts on the glass figurine and the drawing from the open volume and how they related to the information he yet needed to discover in this quest.

But his gaze kept slipping past the pale, leaf-green glass to Breanna. Her wide blue eyes sparkled and he wondered what made her so happy. His heart pounded and stark emotions lurched in his chest. He closed his eyes. He knew how to put the sparkling glow of happiness in her expression. To do so would be easy. All he need do was love her. The way she deserved to be loved. To give what she silently asked of him every time she was near.

Yes, he did desire to make her happy. Ached for the chance. But with the darkness clouding his mind such a relationship was ill-fated and impossible.

The splash and soft footfalls signaling Coralie's return was a thankful diversion from the morose direction of his thoughts. Gowthaman shifted in his chair. And for his uncomfortable physical reaction to Breanna's smile. Moments later Coralie, wrapped in a terry robe, glided into the kitchen and placed the two carvings from the palace beside the first. She slipped a small towel from her shoulder and blotted water from her curls. Jayse returned and lay a folded parchment on the table next to the sculptures. With its worn appearance, Gowthaman surmised the page had been handled and refolded many times. To complete the circle, Breanna and Lucidea brought salad and thick sliced bread to the table with them.

But the meal remained untouched while they studied the three nearly identical figurines. One of smooth glass, one of well polished, silver-toned metal and the third of roughly chiseled stone. Only the position of the center disk marked any other difference between the three. Gowthaman added to his original sketch then froze with his pen suspended over the page.

Tiny nicks and protrusions in the bases might indicate--

Lucidea gasped and reached for the stone piece. "What if..." Carefully she moved the stone and metal statues close together. "It looks like... yeah, these fit together."

Her thoughts mirroring his, Gowthaman nodded and leaned closer. "Yes, but not in the manner you have them. Place the glass piece in the center."

After switching the pieces, Lucidea held her breath and slowly pushed them together. The tiny indentations and pro-trusions fit and locked with soft clicks.

Breanna rose to lean over Gowthaman's shoulder. Her soft scent teased Gowthaman's nostrils. "Okay, that's nice. What does it mean?"

Everyone's eyes turned toward him. Startled from drawing in a deep appreciation of Breanna's unique spicy-sweet scent, he straightened. A moment passed in silence as he mentally scrambled to gather his straying thoughts. "I do not know. I discovered nothing like these in any of the scrolls or texts. Perhaps--"

A light, melodic hum rose from the glass disk. The light vibration spread to the other disks. The resulting chord rose in volume, paused and restarted twice, then faded. When the last tone died, a tenor, overly-modulated voice began to speak.

"I make this recording to immortalize my role in the glorious new world created by the coming of the fire elemental Brandr Ur."

"Pagas," Coralie hissed in disgust. Her fingers tightened on the table edge and she rose.

"Wait, Coralie. Listen," Breanna said. "Maybe what he's saying will help us bring Morghan home."

Coralie shook her head. With an apologetic glance at the others, she released a long breath and took a step away from the table. Breanna grabbed her wrist and tugged her forward and toward her chair. Coralie continued to shake her head as she sat. "I had ne'er thought to hear *that* voice again."

Pagas' speech had continued, but Gowthaman heard nothing but self-glorifying, verbal posturing. Considering the possibilities for advancing the recording, he tilted his head to study the three disks. He hoped they would be able to replay important sections. Or they might only be able to listen to the message once. He flipped to a clean page in his journal and began to transcribe the speech.

"Good idea," Breanna whispered as she slid the sketchbook in front of her. "I'll take notes too. Hopefully I'll catch anything you might miss. We may only get this one chance."

Her insight and willingness thrilled him and he missed a few words as Pagas moved from glorifying himself to a brief description of how the elemental first contacted him. Breanna understood the needs of intellect and worked well with him. In past research efforts, what one picked up on complemented the other to give a more complete picture. In this case he hoped for a complete solution and a successful rescue of the Alfar-Sindhu prince.

Pagas spoke on. And on. Underlying the drone of his proud words Gowthaman detected anger at being used by the elemental. Gowthaman allowed himself to empathize with the other man. But only for a moment. The invasion of another mind without permission remained an unpardonable sin. That Pagas continued to invite and allow the elemental access to his mind was unpardonable. Gowthaman dragged his full focus back to Pagas' words.

"...fool, Lachlan..."

"Daddy," Lucidea whispered. Jayse wrapped his arm around her shoulders and she leaned against him.

Gowthaman's grip on his pen tightened with a flare of primal envy. No. He would focus.

"...left a journal. Ramblings of the Sinhu crown prince." Pagas laughed, currents of evil flowing through the sound. Breanna shivered.

"...able to use single pages to torment the secondary prince. The remainder is hidden in the rough stone wall behind the library. So near to those who would cherish Lachlan's words, yet so far."

Coralie was on her feet in an instant. "I shall go--"

"Wait." Jayse lifted one hand. "There may be more."

Coralie clenched her fists, but remained still, only rising to her toes, ready to rush off at any moment.

The recording device fell silent. Gowthaman glanced up from his writing. Matching frowns around the table focused on the trio of figurines. Finally Lucidea stretched one hand toward them and carefully poked the connected bases. "There must be more. There has to be."

Coralie took a step toward the table. "Aye, more. Please. *Air mo shon.*"

At her words the disks resumed humming, the tones slightly lower and more discordant than before. Breanna made a soft sound of triumph then positioned her pen on the sketchpad and returned to an intense listening silence.

The voice speaking was different, deeper, more commanding and honest. A pleasure to listen to.

"Morghan." Coralie's voice broke and her eyes filled with tears as she slipped back to her chair. Lucidea took her hand.

The recording started in the middle of a thought. Breanna made a quick notation then glanced sideways at Gowthaman. His mouth set in a thin line, he returned the look. Even more than she might ever feel a loss of some of Morghan's words, Gowthaman mourned any missing information. Pagas must have recorded over the words Morghan had already placed there. With luck, they would be able to correlate what they already knew with any new information Morghan may have placed in his message.

"...I have felt the vibrations upon the wind while the waters speak to me. Spurred by these feelings, I take upon m'self a charge. To protect the human world as well as my Sindhu folk.

"Why the human world? I believe this world be the only place he can thin the veil enough to break through."

Morghan took a deep breath. Only the scratching of Gowthaman's pen could be heard in the room.

"As ye ken, Coralie an' I searched long for the incantations used to originally bind the elemental. While we did no' find the exact words, we also discussed the conditions needed for his escape. I believe until recently the elemental did no' ken this knowledge either.

"A conjunction of full moons is needed. No' just any full moon, but the second within a human month. What 'tis called a blue moon. An' no' just a single blue moon, but the conjunction of three blue moons in three differin' worlds. I believe a world where magic is no' so believed in must be home to one of the moons. I am also convinced one must be in the world the elemental wishes to enter. Both conditions are ripe in the human world."

Listening not only to Morghan's words but also to the tones of his voice, Breanna scribbled her notes. Without looking she knew Gowthaman's notes were more complete and infinitely more readable. She sensed him nodding as if the recorded voice confirmed the theories he'd already discussed with her. Hopefully that was true. It didn't sound like they had much time to prepare. The worry in Morghan's voice was nearly palpable and a corresponding urgency rose in her.

"An' I ken the elemental has much of the knowledge I've gathered. Mayhap his understandin' is greater than mine, but I must hold to the truth he does no' ken everythin'. I wish I could speak of this to ye afore my battle with the elemental this night. There is much to say an' too little time. Once I complete this recordin'..."

Morghan paused again. In the silence, Coralie drew a shaky breath.

"Sweet Coralie, *eudail*, 'tis my hope ye and Lucidea be still at the manor and that she has accepted in truth her heritage. Fair niece, the help I can give ye now rests with yer father.

"Time grows too short and I must face the elemental. I set the field of battle to give him no foothold in this world. Luck is no' my companion this night. I feel a chill wind of evil intent. The elemental is strong. Do no' underestimate him or his tricks. He will use any means to gain his desires. This night, an' in the future.

"I offer ye my knowledge, such as it may be. For if ye listen here, ye have the skill. Dinna concern yerself wi' my fate, I do as I must. As ye will. Remember, a message waits for ye with my beloved brother. *Mo air shon*, for my sake, my loves. For the sake of both our worlds, ye must no' allow the elemental freedom."

Morghan's recording ended with an odd, metallic squeal. After staring at the figurines and willing them to speak again, Breanna asked, "You think that's it?"

Coralie nodded. "That sound indicated the end of the magic. 'Twas all he had to say."

Jayse scrubbed his hands through his hair. "Wonder what he said before, what Pagas recorded over."

Bree doubted they'd ever know until they were able to ask Morghan himself. And unfortunately, he'd given them less information than they already knew. "What did he mean that the help is with your father?"

Dabbing at her eyes with a napkin, Lucidea shrugged.

Jayse straightened from comforting his wife and gave Bree a terse grin. "I may be able to help there." With attention focused on him, he unfolded the sheet of parchment he'd brought to the table.

Lucidea waved one hand toward the page. "That's a letter Morghan left for me. I've read it so many times. There's nothing... Oh."

Jayse's grin spread. Coralie's eyes widened. Gowthaman cocked his head to one side. Bree felt totally left out of the loop. "What?"

Jayse explained. "There's a line in this letter that we've never been able to figure out. It seemed so out of context. But in the light of Morghan's statement that the knowledge is with Lucidea's father, we might finally understand what he was trying to tell us."

Still confused, Bree tapped one finger on the table. "But, you've never found... Oh, I'm sorry. I don't mean to bring up any more bad memories. But how could something be with your father, when you never found his... uh..."

"It's okay, Bree." Lucidea took the letter from Jayse and lovingly smoothed her hand over the parchment. "Here's the line he wrote. 'Lachlan listens, for the future whispers to his ear'."

Gowthaman straightened with a jerk and dropped his pen. "In the skull?"

Gowthaman winced as a single blow from a heavy hammer punched a small hole in the side of Lucidea's father's head. Tears streamed down Lucidea's cheeks as she carefully picked away the pieces of hard clay exposing a small section of the skull.

"Eww," Breanna muttered. "Is that real? Did you always use a real skull as a base?"

"Of course not. But Morghan needed the reconstruction done so quickly I didn't have time, or means to make a cast. At the time, I figured I'd pull the clay off when I was done. But when he told me who this was... I couldn't. There wasn't anything else left of... my father. Then I was going to give the skull to the Sindhu people so they could perform the rituals to send his spirit to the great sea. But when the time came, I just couldn't. I mean, Coralie magicked a stone replica for the palace, but I couldn't let this little bit of Daddy go." She stroked the side of the bust's cheek. Taking a deep breath, she continued, "But if this will help my uncle..."

Breanna peeked around Lucidea's shoulder at the smooth bone. Withholding a shudder, she sucked her bottom lip between her teeth. Something didn't look quite right. "May I?" she asked.

Lucidea shrugged, stepped aside and Breanna smoothed her fingers over the darkened bone until she touched a slight, sharp point. "Here, what's this?"

"That wasn't there when I did the reconstruction." Lucidea reached around her to touch the tip of one finger to the protrusion. "Oh, Coralie, touch this. I think I feel magic."

Coralie moved closer as Bree stepped back. After touching the point, a soft smile graced her lips and she closed her eyes. "He must have place this here after ye completed yer work."

Coralie stood back as well. Lucidea gave the miniscule protrusion a slight tug. It moved, then slipped from the skull in a long ribbon of curling parchment.

Breanna grinned. "Looks like you won't have to totally destroy your work after all."

The strip unfolded to a sheet about the size of half a notebook page. Lucidea spread it carefully on the table but slid the parchment to Gowthaman instead of reading it herself. "I can't. You look at it."

With infinite care Gowthaman moved the parchment closer and bent over the table to read. "Interesting. It is not written in

Sindhu or English, but in an ancient earth language. A moment please." He studied the parchment silently then leaned back slightly and looked up at the expectant expressions.

"By using a language few are able to read, Morghan protected this information. He gives a series of computations for the rising of the blue moon in a number of worlds. With your permission I will refrain from explaining the complexities of his computations until I compare them with my own."

Nodding, Lucidea said, "Go on. I'm not interested in the computations, as long as there's answers in the end. Does he say anything else?"

Gowthaman pointed to a line three quarters of the way down the page then slid his finger along the line as he continued. "He writes as though he knew he would be taken to the World Between Worlds. According to his reckoning, a simple rescue will fail. Instead, another must... enter... the gray world to find him. The only time this will be possible is two nights prior to the conjunction of moons, for there will be a weakening in the veil." Thoughtful, he paused. "That may be why the only records I've discovered concerning beings sent to the world between world make mention of the days prior to the full moon. Fascinating. That may mean a tidal component to the thinning of the veil."

Gowthaman shook his head to clear his thoughts and gave an apologetic shrug. Breanna smiled and his breath stalled in his chest. She had become accustomed to how his mind skipped from one interesting fact to another while still retaining a connection to the original information. Others were frequently confused by his seemingly random thoughts.

Jayse made a thoughtful sound deep in his throat. "So someone must go into the World Between Worlds."

The parchment blurred. Gowthaman grasped the table edge, squeezing but not feeling the pressure against his fingers and palms. Forcing himself to breathe, he struggled to push back the rise of mental pain and dark, empty memories. The mere mention of anyone entering the World Between Worlds drove him further from the reality of his world. And from caring.

A warm hand covered his with gentle, comforting pressure. He knew the shape of her fingers, and the peace she could bring to him with just a touch. The clarity he needed and longed for. But not now. Perhaps never again. He'd taken too much from her already, and could give nothing in return.

He took a shallow breath and slipped his hand from under Breanna's to reach again for the parchment. If he held the slip the shaking would give away his fear, so he simply rested his hands next to it and continued.

"These computations indicate the rescue party must enter the World Between Worlds in two nights' time. Once there, Morghan must be found before the full moon. On the night of the conjunction, the veil will again weaken and using the incantations to create a stable opening, all will be able to return here."

"What about the fire elemental?" Jayse asked

"Though this parchment doesn't address that factor, I believe this is how the elemental attempted to enter this world, and when unsuccessful, dragged Morghan back with him. Undoubtedly his strength will have been renewed since that time and he will again make the attempt. We can not allow him access. Not to this world, nor any world. He must be permanently contained."

It was a harsh statement. However, he should have made the more appropriate, the more realistic proclamation. Brandr Ur would have to be destroyed. There were some beings with no goodness, who could never be redeemed. Much like he could never return to the man he had been before the attack on his mind.

"There is nothing more on the parchment. Perhaps after comparing the calculations, I will be able to provide more exact theories."

Lucidea stood and flattened her palms against the tabletop. "I'm going. We'll get everything arranged tonight."

"I'm going with you." Jayse stood beside her and wrapped an arm around her waist. She gazed up at him with love and thankfulness then leaned her head against his shoulder.

Breanna closed her eyes against the sight. Jealousy reared an ugly head. How she longed for the kind of love and support these two had for each other. She had no doubt where one would go... Her eyes flew open.

"No."

Startled gazes turned to her. Lucidea opened her mouth but Breanna prevented her speech with a wave of her hand. "You can't do anything dangerous like that."

"And why not?" Jayse asked. "Morghan is her uncle. Who better to--"

"No, you don't understand. She can't. Not now. Not when she's..." Breanna froze, horrified she'd been about to break her promise to Lucidea. "No, I'm the leader of the Alastriona. I've trained for this. I'll go and bring Morghan home safely."

"Breanna. My uncle. My rescue. Of course I'll want to you assist."

Widening her eyes and glancing at Lucidea's abdomen in what she hoped was a meaningful manner, Breanna strained for Lucidea to understand. Lucidea couldn't endanger her child, not when she'd had so many disappointments in the past. When Lucidea simply stared at her in confusion, Breanna made a decision. The safety and healthy growth of Lucidea's child was more important than the promise she'd made. She'd deal with the consequences later.

"I can't permit you to go into the unknown. Not now. Not when you're pregnant."

Jayse jerked and pulled his wife around to face him. "Dea Annie?"

Lucidea frowned and pointed an accusing finger at Breanna. "*She* thinks I'm pregnant." Lowering her hand, she sighed. "I don't know. I have to admit there've been signs, but I ignored them. Jayse, I... You know how hard it's been for us, how much harder each time was." She stood stiff and unrelenting for a moment then let herself be enfolded in Jayse's arms.

He kissed the top of her head. "If there's any possibility, Dea Annie, any chance at all, there's no way you're going to go into the World Between Worlds." He chuckled softly. "I don't even know if I'll let you pass through any portal."

"But I have to save Morghan," she mumbled into his chest.

Jayse leaned back and held her shoulders at arms' length. "At what cost to you? To us? No, Lucidea. I would never deny you a thing. But this. I won't let you endanger yourself and the possibility of our child."

"But it *is* only a possibility."

Breanna shook her head and blew out a breath, stirring her bangs. "Each of you has trusted me with healing a wound.

Have I ever failed you?" She rested her gaze on each in turn. And received slow head shakes in return. Except from Gowthaman. He sat, head bowed, refusing to look at her. She couldn't take time now to examine his behavior; she had to convince the others of what she knew. Of the happiness that awaited them in a few months.

"When I allow myself, I see the colors surrounding each of you. I see soulfire rising strong and bright between Jayse and Lucidea. And in that soulfire is a another color. Pale, but strong. Centered and sparkling around Lucidea's womb. Trust me, you've got a baby in there. And Jayse, it's long past the time when she's miscarried before. I don't believe this child will leave you."

At Lucidea's sharp intake of breath, Bree lifted one hand to forestall her speech. "Unless you do something stupid. Crossing into the World Between Worlds is a fool's errand at any time since we know so little about it. You will not risk it. If I have to pull rank on you, I will." She smiled to soften her all too real threat.

"As shall I," Coralie stated firmly. "Ye shall no' endanger yer family in any way. I shall go in yer stead. 'Tis my right, mayhap more than yers. Ye have yer love to hold. I shall bring mine home." She turned her gaze to Breanna, eyebrows lifted in question over her determined expression. "If that is permissible, lady Alastriona."

"I welcome your help." There would be no way to keep Coralie from joining in her lover's rescue. Bree glanced at Gowthaman, understanding the intensity of Coralie's feelings.

"But--" Lucidea started.

Jayse covered her lips with his for a brief, hard kiss. "They'll be fine, love. We'll be here for the planning and to hold down the proverbial fort. I'm sure we'll all have our parts to play in Morghan's rescue. Just remember what I said." He tapped his finger on the tip of her nose. "Here. This house. This world. Oh god, Dea Annie, I love you." He rested his hand over her abdomen. "Both of you."

Blinking back tears Breanna left the workroom followed by Gowthaman. She returned to her seat in the kitchen and fiddled with the sketchpad. Gowthaman waited a moment then began adding the new information to his journal. When Coralie scooted her chair close, Bree studied her. "Coralie, I think we'll need at least one other to go with us. I know we don't have much time to make the decision of who would be best suited. I'd really like your opinion."

The other woman nodded. "Agreed. But first, since we've heard m'lord Morghan's words, we should listen to what Gowthaman has found. With both together, we shall have more basis for our decisions."

Gowthaman jerked at the mention of his name, his fingertips scraping over the journal page. Breanna ached to take his hand again, to offer nothing more than calm reassurance. He needed her touch, his soul called out for her healing. She reached one hand toward him, but he flinched and she drew her hand back to her side. One day he would realize how much she loved him and how deeply they needed each other. *One day.* Holding back a sigh she looked past Coralie and out the window overlooking the loch. She was tired of waiting for one day.

When this mission was complete, with Morghan home and in Coralie's arms, Bree vowed she'd find a way to make him face his demons. And her.

Flushed and smiling, Jayse and Lucidea returned to the kitchen. Gowthaman took a deep breath and after digging though his carry sack set a few scrolls next to his journal. Bree dipped her head to hide her grin. He didn't need the scrolls except to create a secure wall of knowledge to hide behind. He knew the information the scrolls contained, or had at least copied the relevant parts into his own notes. His mind amazed, intrigued and delighted her. His intellect was one of the many things she loved about him.

Gowthaman looked briefly at his notes then began. "An hour or two should be all I need to determine the exact time when the veil will allow passage to the... World Between Worlds. We need to determine the incantations needed to part the veil for both the transition from here and when you are ready to return."

Coralie reached for the sketchbook. "There were a few chants Morghan discarded afore his battle against the elemental. I shall write them out for ye. Mayhap 'twill be of assistance."

Gowthaman smiled at Coralie, though Bree noticed how tightly he gripped his pen. "Thank you. I believe comparing those to other recorded incantations will bring us the correct words for our purpose."

"If you can get us there, that will be enough." Breanna put more confidence into her words than she felt, and the look Gowthaman flashed her said she hadn't fooled him. "Okay, maybe not enough, but it will be a start."

Morghan bent double, scrambling over low, jagged rocks. He peered around a narrow ledge into a level, open area at the top of a conical hill. Now that he'd found his mind... He shook his head fiercely and speared his fingers through his hair chasing the mist and forgetfulness continually attacking his consciousness.

He would not lose himself again.

A massive temple complex had once stood centered on the vast plain. He scanned the tumbled ruins. Surrounded by the remnants of smaller buildings, the arches and broken walls of the ancient temple reached majestically toward the gray sky.

Empty. Morghan frowned. Wearied of tormenting him, the fire elemental had retreated to his temple.

Sinking to sit behind a tall stone, Morghan supposed that retreat had been a mixed blessing. While ending the constant taunting and battle had been a relief to his exhausted soul, the lack of stimulation had led to his dulled mind and--

The muffled crunching of feet upon stone rose from across the plateau. Morghan stilled his breathing and allowed his lips to stretch to a smile. The movement and stretch of unused muscles felt odd. He increased the width of his smile. Mayhap he would now treat the elemental to torments of his own.

Morghan eased close to the ground and peered around the rock. Brandr Ur stomped up the narrow stairs toward the three-sided structure topping the temple. Once the elemental stood before the stone throne he'd claimed, he turned and stared in Morghan's direction.

The heat of Brandr Ur's scrutiny touched Morghan. Awareness crawled across the back of his neck. The elemental tilted his head and lifted his hands chest high. A ball of flame burst into brightness between his palms. He held the churning gray fire and moved his hands to increase and decrease the size of his show of power.

Morghan rose and stepped from behind the rocks. No need to hide his presence. The elemental had sensed him and now sought to disable his renewed spirit. Morghan tossed back his head and laughed.

Brandr Ur answered with a growl and his flame ball burst into fiery fragments that smoked in the dry air.

The physical touch of the elemental's glare sparked memories of their first battle. Morghan fought the rise of anger and lifted one shoulder to ease the tension tightening his neck.

He hadn't been defeated yet. Neither had the elemental won. Both were trapped here in this gray world. Letting despondency take him had been a mistake. He would not again fall prey to meaningless posturing and threats.

From the blatant show of power and the elemental's posturing, Brandr Ur knew as well as he, a conjunction of moons approached. A conjunction signaling renewed battle.

Morghan tossed off a cocky salute and turned his back on his enemy. No matter the cost to him, the fire elemental, Brandr Ur, would never leave the World Between Worlds.

Such was his vow.

Anticipating how she would tell her parents she was leading a rescue mission to the World Between Worlds was one of the most difficult things Breanna had ever encountered. When she finally got the words out, their reactions surprised her.

"It's part of the duties you took on as the leader of the Alastriona, honey," her mother said calmly. "Your dad and I have every confidence in your abilities. Oh, don't worry, I'm going to stress over every moment you're in that nether world. But you worrying about how we feel isn't going to help the mission." Her shoulders lifted in a casual shrug, but a shimmer of tears glistened on her lashes. "I suppose it's not a whole lot different any time mothers send their children off to war, is it?"

Mom had hit the nail square on the head. Bree was going off to war. Not against the people or politics of another nation, but against a world, a place. "No Mom, it isn't. I can't promise everything will be fine."

"I know, honey. Just be safe. Have you told your granda?"

Bree shook her head and grimaced.

Her dad chuckled at her unwilling admission. "Da will be envious. He's often spoken of exploring different worlds."

"Maybe he'll get a chance once all this is over. Gowthaman has some interesting theories on how worlds connect. We may be able to find portals to some of these places without having to pass through the World Between Worlds." Bree shared her granda's excitement for adventure and exploring. Despite the dangers inherent to any mission into the unknown, the thrill burned within her. Although she wouldn't be the first to experience the World Between Worlds and return, none of the others she knew of had embraced the experience by choice. If only there was a way to share her excitement with Gowthaman.

"How is Gowthaman?" her mother asked. "He hasn't shown up to many family gatherings lately."

"He... he's withdrawn. He won't let me help and it's been too long. He's unsuccessfully dealing with the recurring horror and pain alone."

"He's a proud Faerie, Bree."

"I know, Dad."

"And it's difficult to ask for help."

"I know that too. I hurt for him, seeing him suffer when he doesn't need to."

Her mother's eyes darkened for a moment and Bree knew she relived the dark moments of her own past. "Maybe he does, honey. It's a part of healing."

"But to hold on to that pain for a lifetime? He's got to come to terms with what happened. Work through it like you did. With help. No, Mom. It's some stupid... oh, I don't know. After all this is done, I've got to find a way to make him talk to me. About us."

Her parents shared a look she didn't have to interpret and Breanna blew out a breath filled with frustration and a bit of humor. "I've got to run. We'll cross into the World Between Worlds tomorrow night." She gave them each a hug. "Love you both."

After another round of somber hugs, Bree smiled, waved and left the house. She leaned back against the brightly painted door and closed her eyes. All around her were couples so filled with love for each other it was amazing they didn't burst with the joy.

She shook away her thoughts. This was not the time for daydreams and romantic notions. This was the time for preparation and action. Eyes open, she stared unseeing into the park across the street. There wasn't much time before the action would consume all her attention.

"Sis?" Chance eased around a tree.

She gave him half a smile. "What do you want? I don't have time to--"

He crossed his arms in a belligerent pose. "I'm going."

"Where?"

"With you, stupid. To the World Between Worlds."

"No, you're not."

"Come on, Bree. What have you been training me for if not to stand by your side in battle? So I'm not *mature*. So I'm not a full Faerie warrior. So? I need this, Bree. I need to do something important."

She didn't have the patience for his young man bravado or angst and pushed away from the door. "You've got plenty of time for importance."

"No, Bree. Listen. I've got this... No, I can't be like my father. I've got to prove..."

"What are you talking about?"

Chance glanced around and moved a step closer. Breanna tensed. *What was he playing at?* But the look he gave her, the dark, haunted dullness in his normally clear blue eyes reminded her so explicitly of Gowthaman's pain she reached out to him and rested her hands on his shoulders. "What is it?"

After swallowing heavily and looking around again, he spoke in a harsh whisper. "It's like, there's a voice. Inside my head. Suggesting things, telling me things... stuff I don't want to hear." His whisper morphed into a ragged chuckle. "Nah,

I'm not schizophrenic or anything like that. I'd know. Hell, Sis, you'd know. It's like when Feidhlim tried to contact me, to control and use me when I was a baby." He shuddered and she gripped his shoulders tightly.

"He's dead. It can't be him."

"I know." Frustration flowed from Chance in waves. "Sorry. I know it can't be him. I said it was *like* him."

"How long has this been going on? Why haven't you said anything before now?"

A ruddy color crept up his neck and stained his cheeks. He shook off her hands, but didn't move away. "Only a couple days ago. That might not seem like much, but it won't stop. The voice is always there in the background. Most of the time, I don't understand the words, but I feel them. Like a constant hum. White noise. It's driving me crazy."

Breanna squinted and calmed her mind to study her brother's aura. There *was* a dampening of his color, an odd gray tinge surrounding his head. So this experience really bothered him. But she saw no intrusion, no evidence of some force attempting to psychically assault him.

"I don't see any attack. But you are dull."

"So you've told me many times. Geez, you believe me, don't you?"

"Yeah. I've got tell Granda about the mission into the World Between Worlds, then stop in Faerie before I head back to Scotland. Come with me and we'll find time to talk. You can tell me what you think this voice thing is saying to you."

"I don't think. I know. It's telling me to go with you. Well, maybe not exactly that. I just know I need to go with you." He frowned and fell silent.

They'd made their way next door to their grandfathers' home. Bree mounted the steps then paused when Chance stumbled to a stop behind her. "I'll, uh, wait on the porch," he mumbled.

"Chicken."

Breanna made short work of her story, relieved her granda, the former leader of the Alastriona, agreed she was the appropriate choice to lead a small force into the world beyond worlds. Pop-pop on the other hand, fussed over her until all three broke into laughter. She was still smiling when she closed the front door and nudged Chance with her toe.

"That must have gone well," he said, rising to stretch until his tee shirt slipped from his jeans, exposing his abdomen. Breanna's eyes widened at the well-defined muscles. Her baby brother had grown up. Maybe Granda was right and he would be an important addition to her group. If it helped him work through whatever bothered him, that would be even better.

"Yeah, it did. Granda gave me some good suggestions too. He agrees I should ask Searlait to come with us. She spent a long time in the World Between Worlds. But, I don't know if she'll be willing to go back."

"She doesn't have the same kind of problem Gowthaman has, does she?"

"No. Still, she doesn't talk much about her time there. Even if she won't go, any information about the place she can give us will be invaluable."

Silent, they passed through the rose trellis portal in Jaye's backyard to the Faerie Otherworld. Each took a deep breath. Breanna closed her eyes and let the clear, untainted air fill her lungs. It was a blessing, a way of cleansing her body after the much-breathed air of the human world. Not that she'd ever deny her human half, but she did love the clean, fresh air.

Chance cleared his throat. "So, what are ya gonna do about Gowthaman? When all this is over, I mean."

A shrug was the only answer she could give right now. Her heart screamed for her to pursue him ruthlessly, make her love and intentions as clear and honest as the Faerie air. But doing so would only make him withdraw further into himself. Somehow, there had to be a way to convince him it was time to live again. And time to love. To love her.

Eyes glinting with mischief, Chance looked ready to pursue his question so she adroitly changed the subject. "Granda gave me another suggestion that I think was pretty right on."

"Yeah?" He'd given in easily so he must not have been interested in teasing her about Gowthaman. Something truly bothered him to miss such an open opportunity.

"Yeah. He had another suggestion about who would be good to have on my team."

Chance shoved his hands into his pockets and hunched his shoulders. "Who?"

Breanna decided to draw out the moment, let him stew just a little longer. "Someone I've been working with a lot lately, training, that kind of thing. Granda thought this person would both benefit from the experience and have a great deal to offer to the mission."

His shoulders hunched higher when he stared at the ground. "Makes sense."

She couldn't stand the physical expression of her normally cheerful brother's despondency so she slapped him on the shoulder.

"Geez, Sis. What's that for?"

"You, stupid." She laughed at the odd, dumbstruck questioning expression he gave her. "You're the one Granda suggested. No, I didn't tell him about the voice," she rushed to say when Chance's eyes widened in dismay. "I think he considers this mission as some sort of right of passage. For both of us."

Chance planted his fists at his hips. "What about you? Just because Granda suggested me, doesn't mean you'll give me a place on the team, does it? You still think I'm some kid. Okay, so I'm not twenty yet. That doesn't mean--"

"Of course you're coming with me. Thankfully Granda said he'd let Mom and Dad know, so I don't have to face them again."

"And you called me chicken." Chance grinned, straightening his back and setting his shoulders in a strong line.

Breanna caught her bottom lip between her teeth. When *had* Chance grown up--at least physically? His teasing was still child-like and for the most part innocent, much like the tricks played by those of Korin's winged fairy race. She eyed her brother critically. Actually, she kind of liked the combination of strength and innocence.

"Nope, not chicken, just relieved to pass the buck. Mom and Dad were okay with me going, I don't know how they're going to react to you following in my footsteps."

"No way, Sis. I plan on making my own footprints."

She tugged him into a hug. "I know you do, little brother. And you will." She released him with a stern look and shook her finger. "You will follow my orders. I am the head of the Alastriona and the leader of this adventure."

He gave her a brisk, military salute. "Yes, sir... ma'am... sis."

"I need to talk to Searlait and have her meet us at the loch tomorrow. We'll leave from there. I don't know what kinds of weapons will be useful in the World Between Worlds, but I know Searlait kept a long sword at her side. Probably that kind of traditional weapon would be best. There'll be four of us, and we'll supply a weapon for Morghan as well. Will you gather what we need for five from the armory while I talk to Searlait?"

"No problem. Then I'll meet you at the loch."

"If you beat me there, ask Gowthaman to fill you in on what we've learned so far."

"Gotcha." Chance turned away, froze and spun back, a plea in his wide eyes and open palms. "Sis?"

"I didn't forget. This evening we'll find a quiet corner and you can tell me about what you've been hearing. Just so you know, that's part of the reason I agreed to you coming along. There has to be some reason why you're being drawn to enter the World Between Worlds. And I'm sure it's crucial for the success of this mission."

Gowthaman worked rapidly, annotating his notes with new information and possibilities. He penned precious thoughts onto the pages, making his theories as clear as possible. He would insist Breanna take the journal with her. Much would still be left to the whims of fate, but he planned to give the rescue party any advantage he could discover.

He glanced at a small timepiece set at the corner of the desk. His breath caught painfully in his chest. *The hours flowed too rapidly.* Even with the journal he would never be able to impart all the needed information and make sure each member of the team understood and would be able to remember. The slightest difference of pronunciation in an incantation or an imprecise movement could mean disaster in their mission.

Failure was not an option. He snorted softly, lay his pen aside, and pressed the heels of his palms against his tired eyes. Hadn't he heard that line in some movie Breanna had made him watch with her?

Cupping his elbow with his opposite hand he twisted, pulling to stretch tight muscles. He repeated the stretch on the other side then rolled his shoulders and arched his neck until he heard a muffled crack. "Ahh." A neck rub would sooth the tightness. He sighed. Breanna always used the exact pressure needed to ease his stiff muscles.

Breanna. She soothed and eased his discomforts in so many ways, but beyond a curt thank you, he'd never let her know how greatly he appreciated her efforts. Nor how he appreciated her. Now instead of telling her, he was helping to send her into the most dangerous, loathsome place he could imagine. Resting his forehead in one palm, he leaned over the table and closed his eyes. He didn't have to imagine. He had experienced the World Between Worlds.

Already despondent from the trauma of a fey witch invading his mind and attacking his memories, he had wished to remain. No light nor color hovered in his soul, his mind had been overcome by gray. Why shouldn't his world have been the same? But Bard and Searlait had forced him to return to Faerie.

Upon that return Breanna had touched him. Barely five years old, she had touched his mind in a way so gentle and loving for a moment he'd forgotten the violence that had ripped through his intellect. At the last moment he'd realized what the child was doing and erected a thick mental wall around the potent, disabling memory of the mind rape. She'd even smiled as she helped him construct the barrier. He didn't know if Breanna realized how many times since then he'd had to shore up the failing protection, hiding the pain he would never let her see.

Gowthaman released a slow breath. Determined to impart as much knowledge as he was able in the allotted time, he turned back to the journal. His efforts had to be enough. Even if Breanna's team wasn't able to find Morghan, they would require the means to return.

The pen slipped from his fingers and rolled across the table. He stared at the word he'd just written but the fine lines blurred. When he rubbed his eyes, his fingers came away damp. They had to return. *She* had to return. Deep, hidden in his heart, was the acceptance he would not survive were Breanna lost to him. He could not express his love to her as he wished, but still, selfishly, he needed her near. Needed her desperately simply to survive.

Not expecting any of her team to have arrived at the manor yet, Breanna stumbled to a stop at the sight of a tall, gray-haired man speaking earnestly with Jayse just outside the heavy front door. Catching her lower lip between her teeth she tilted her head to one side. Something familiar about the figure spoke to her but she couldn't fix a name or recognition to the man.

Before she moved closer, she paused to study the man's back. Slim, yet with the hint of powerful shoulders. Long legs were encased in tight jeans showing muscular thighs and calves. She couldn't hear his voice, but the cadence, the rise and fall of words was comforting and familiar.

He threw one hand sideways in an expansive gesture. "Honey, please."

"Nightshade," she cried and rushed forward. He turned and caught her in a tight embrace that she returned fiercely. She grinned. Whenever Nightshade was around, everything always worked out. He'd been a secure presence her entire life, saving Pop-pop when he'd been kidnapped, then providing an escape from Chance's evil bio-father for her family just after her brother's birth. Nightshade had always been there for them and she loved him for it. "What are you doing here?" she asked, her question muffled against his chest.

He held her at arm's length, a solemn light filling his eyes. "Nightshade had a feeling, little girl."

"Little girl? You haven't called me that in ages."

"Honey, you'll always be a little girl to me."

"Yeah, you and my folks. Wait a minute." She shrugged out from under his gentle hands. "Did they send you here to check up on me?"

A wounded expression blossomed on his face and he covered his heart with one hand before staggering back. "*Moi?* Checking up on you? Honey!"

"Yeah, you." She laughed at his dramatics and as tension flowed from her muscles, realized she'd been riding a wave of intensity over the past hours and needed to relax. "Oh, it doesn't matter. I'm glad to see you."

"And I you, little girl." He bowed deeply.

She swatted his arm. "Stop that."

Jayse joined in their laughter then excused himself by explaining Lucidea was with both the Faerie healers and those of the Alfar-Sindhu. She hadn't wanted him in the room during the magical examinations, just in case they were disappointed yet again. He grinned and pressed a kiss to Breanna's cheek.

"I know they're not going to find anything different than what you told us, Bree. Thank you." With that he turned and she could tell the effort it took for him to walk away when he wanted to run to Lucidea's side.

She sighed, then caught Nightshade's smug, knowing expression. Not wanting to invite back the tension by delving into her feelings, she asked, "What did you do to your hair?" Reaching up, she ran her fingers over his short-cropped hair. "And what's with the color? Do you have a new lover who likes this better?" For as long as she'd known Nightshade, her entire life, he'd worn his bright auburn tresses long, despite any current rage or fashion.

He patted a disrupted, ragged wave back into place. "Don't you like it?"

"It's... different." Studying the thick, soft hair, she circled him. "Yeah, I do."

"Truthfully, honey, I got tired of it. All the styling, the coloring--"

"This isn't colored?"

Nightshade took her hand and they wandered into the manor. Turning to the right he led her almost to the end of a long hallway to a pair of overstuffed chairs facing a view of the loch out a wide window. "Honey, this is me... *au naturale*. I've had stone-gray hair my entire life."

"That's odd. Even as a child?"

Settling into a chair, he nodded. "Even so." When she sat, his playful expression turned serious. "Are you sure you need to do this?"

Breanna leaned back, closed her eyes and blew out a long breath. "I knew it. Mom and Dad did send you."

"They have no idea where I am. I'm here of my own volition, honey. Didn't I say Nightshade had a feeling? I learned long, long ago to trust my feelings. At least this type of feeling." He fell silent and stared out the window.

A quick study of his profile revealed nothing, even though the way he'd said 'long, long ago' held significance for him. Her curiosity piqued, she wondered how long ago he was talking about. Nightshade had changed over the years. The flamboyant drag queen from her childhood had morphed into a serious... Her thoughts faltered.

Sometimes she found it extremely difficult to merge the opposing aspects of his personality. Chameleon-like, he could go from soft and flighty to primal warrior in less than a heartbeat. He remained an enigma. Yet, even with aspects of his personality firmly settled on both ends of a spectrum, his caring and protective nature never changed.

No, he never changed. Except, she realized with a start, despite his now steel gray hair, he hadn't seemed to have grown any older. In fact, with his new short haircut, he looked younger. She shook her head and he turned to look at her, questions in his hazel eyes.

"What is it, little girl?"

"How old are you?"

He lifted one hand and pressed the back to his forehead. "Where's mah smellin' salts?" He peeked at her from under his hand. "Honey, don't you know never ask a lady her age?"

"Cut it out, Nightshade. Call me dense, but I've never thought about how you still look the same age as you did when I was five."

His fingers flew in a zigzag triple snap. "I *am* a fairy, honey."

"Give me a break. I'm serious. How old are you?"

Nightshade leaned forward and took her hand. "Take a look at your own father, Breanna. What about your pop-pop, Tommy? Allyn? They're all full-human, and have aged imperceptibly over the years. I've been a friend of this clan for longer than your daddy's been alive. Why shouldn't I benefit from time spent in the Faerie Otherworld as well?" He lifted his eyebrows to punctuate his question.

Of course, he was right. Humans who had contact with the Faerie Otherworld enjoyed longer lives due to a much slowed aging process. So, obviously, his aging had been slowed as well. But, for how long? She opened her mouth.

"Don't even go there, little girl. My age is my business and no one else's."

She nodded her acceptance. Someday she'd figure him out, but not today. "So, did your feeling tell you why you needed to be here?"

He shrugged with a graceful, elegant lift of his shoulders. *Almost regal,* she thought, and added this new facet of his personality to her list of the incongruities that made up Nightshade.

"What are your thoughts on this... adventure?" she asked.

Elegant hands resting over the ends of the armrests, Nightshade gazed out the window. He remained silent for so long, Breanna was about to ask again when he turned to face her. The tightly controlled warrior had emerged. "Honey, I think this is going to be most dangerous thing you'll ever attempt. I also believe that you're more than capable and have chosen appropriate companions."

"How do you... nevermind, you talked to Granda, didn't you?"

"When I mentioned my *feeling* to Derek, he provided a few specifics. I'm most concerned over your decision to include Chance. Are you sure he's ready?"

That was the question she'd been asking herself ever since leaving her brother in Faerie. "He's trained enough and is ready physically. Mentally... he's young. So am I, if you want to be honest about it. There haven't been any situations remotely like this, nothing to test my ability or leadership either. Thankfully, no one's voiced any concerns about that fact, yet. I think Chance's positive attitude will be a great help, especially when we have to deal with seemingly hopeless situations. Oh, yeah. I know we'll have those situations. This whole mission could be viewed as hopeless."

She remained silent about her concerns with Chance's emotional state. She didn't understand what he'd been experiencing, but wouldn't discount his feelings. Once in the World Between Worlds he would have to discover his own answers. Morghan's rescue came first.

Leaning forward, Nightshade clasped his hands between his knees. "If you're worried about Chance, you could deny him--"

"No, I can't."

Nightshade nodded. "I understand, honey. Loyalty means a lot. Don't sacrifice your team in misguided loyalty. Be sure of what you do."

A hint of sadness tinged Nightshade's eyes, and his mouth set in a firm line. Somewhere in his past, in those parts of his life he kept hidden behind a flamboyant character, he'd lost something. Or someone. In the name of loyalty. She understood that without knowing his past, without looking into his aura. She took a deep breath.

Nightshade lifted one eyebrow. "And what about Gowthaman?"

"What about him?" She winced at the sharpness in her voice.

"No need to get your hackles up, honey. I was just wondering what his part is in the grand scheme." He chuckled and winked suggestively.

After blowing out a harsh breath, Breanna leaned forward, mimicking Nightshade's pose. "With the extent of his research, and his personal experience, he knows more about the

World Between Worlds than any of us. Maybe even more than Searlait. But I'd never, ever ask him to go there again. Nightshade, he won't let me help him." Realizing she'd slipped from business to personal she collapsed back in her chair. Nightshade elicited confidences and maybe if she vocalized some of her own pain and helplessness, she could leave those issues behind for the duration of the mission.

"I can see the effects of his pain, even without tapping into his aura. It's in his eyes, in the way his shoulders slump when he thinks no one is looking. His hands... his hands tremble." She covered her face with her hands, muffling her words. "I don't know what to do. How to help."

"When he's ready, he'll ask."

She dropped her hands to her lap and glared at him. "You sound pretty sure of that."

"I am." He flourished a grand gesture, finishing with his fingers splayed over his heart. "Nightshade knows love, honey."

"I'm not so sure he loves me... not the way I want him to, the way I need him."

Serious, Nightshade took her hand between his palms. "If nothing else, little girl, I'm observant. I see how his eyes follow you, how his expression fills with longing. He's got some hang ups about age and propriety. Fool. More important, he doesn't want to saddle you to someone who's not whole. He considers himself damaged."

"How would you know? Oh, nevermind. I've been fighting the age thing forever. It's always been between us. Like you calling me 'little girl' I don't believe he knows I've grown up."

"Oh, he knows, honey, he knows. He just doesn't know what to do about that knowledge." Nightshade laughed softly. "When you get back, I'm sure you'll be able to... convince him figure to it out."

Bree cast him a doubtful look. "Thanks. If you say so."

"I do, honey, I do." Keeping her hand safe and warm in his, he rose with an easy, fluid motion. "Now, I've got a *feeling* Jayse and Lucidea will be making their announcement soon. Let's get a front row seat."

Breanna chuckled. "Let's." She stood, slipped her arm through his and rested her head against his muscular upper arm. "Thanks. Just talking to you helps. It always has."

He patted her hand. "That's what Nightshade is here for, honey. Now, head up. Back straight. Exhibit your strength and confidence."

"Showtime?"

"Showtime."

There. He felt the veil thinning. The conjunction had begun. Brandr Ur smoothed his hands through his hair and smiled with satisfaction. Over time he had lost the locations of the openings to various worlds. Now the connecting points were revealed to him. Not long, and he would be free.

Brandr Ur strutted back and forth before the thinning veil. It didn't matter what world this opened on to. Once he was free of his gray prison, he would easily find his way where he wanted to go. He wanted the humans.

The parents of Dea Anu had been human, or what passed as human at that time. He snorted. For a frail race, humans had survived long eons, rising many times only to fall prey to either the whims of the prevalent gods or the planet itself. Or their own foolish delusions of grandeur. Ah, how he would use those delusions.

The human world was ripe for his plucking. The fragile humans needed a powerful new god. He was that god. A god to control, to deliver them from foolish ways and into worship of only him.

Brandr Ur threw back his shoulders and snapped his fingers. A hunched, cowed being of indiscriminant origins crawled to his side and fawned at his knees.

The elemental smiled benignly down on it. "You have done well and I feel generous this day. You shall have the world beyond this veil. When I am done with it."

The creature's eyes widened. "Th-th-thank you, lord. I am h-h-honored. H-h-how else m-m-may I serve?"

"I command you to watch another. The one who returned with me when I last split the veil. You know the one?"

"Y-yes, lord. Do you w-w-wish me to b-bring him to you?"

Brandr Ur thought a moment on the various possibilities before him then slashed his hand down across his chest. "No. Not yet. Watch only. He feels the weakened veil, knows the time for our confrontation approaches. I would not have him escape my wrath when he may yet be useful. Bring to me word only if he attempts to part the veil. Watch well, please me, and your reward shall be greater than a world to rule as you will."

"Yes, m-m-my lord."

The creature scuttled away in a swirl of mist. Smiling still, Brandr Ur watched the moving gray settle into heavy stillness. The anticipation was nearly as pleasing as using a woman's body. Lust slammed into him, hardening his body, bringing his breath harsh and fast. He needed one of the females trapped in the gray. Perhaps he could even find a female who still had a fighting spirit. A challenge, the chance to overpower, suited his mood.

He drew his brows together. No female in the World Between Worlds was as pleasing as Dea Anu, but any would suffice when his need was strong.

As it was now.

He lifted one hand to summon a minion, then changed his mind. He would pursue his own prey. The hunt would postpone the satisfaction, making his release all the more powerful.

Power. Those without it called power an aphrodisiac. Fists clenched he threw his hands into the air, arched his neck and shouted. Vibrations pooled in his groin, the throb of his blood burning to more powerful lust. Soon his voice would carry across many worlds. *As it should be.* As it would have been, if not for the triple spawn of Dea Anu.

Lowering his arms, he growled in frustration for the millennia wasted, confined in the World Between Worlds. The burning raged along his veins, filling his body. All who remained with a single drop of blood from any of those descendents would be destroyed. By his own hand.

Brandr Ur strode forward, the mist flowing from him as if fearful of his anger. The flaming vow filled his heart. By his own hand.

"That's enough."

In the midst of the sudden silence, Breanna rose from her seat and caught the eye of each person in the large family room. Much to her surprise and delight, even Gowthaman set aside his pen and watched her, questions filling his dark eyes.

"We've talked and argued this mission to death. We need a break. Each and every one of us. Tomorrow will be soon enough to get back to training and planning."

Coralie lifted one hand, palm outstretched. "Do ye--"

"Nope." Bree shook her head.

Chance pointed at Jayse. "Jayse and I are--"

"Not tonight, baby bro."

Gowthaman reached for one of his precious books. "There is yet much--"

"I said no more."

He tried again. "But, I must--"

"Not tonight. Everyone..." She glared at Gowthaman who dipped his head, then moved her glare to her brother. "Everyone is going to relax and not worry about what tomorrow night might bring."

A slow clapping rose from one corner and Bree smiled at Nightshade's show of support. After the flow of chuckles eased around the room, she pointed down the hall towards the media room. "Gowthaman and I are going to watch a movie."

He sat back and frowned. "We are?"

"Yes, we are. And, I expect everyone to join us."

Jayse leaned over to whisper to Lucidea and Chance, then eased from the overstuffed couch, holding one hand out to Lucidea. Chance eased to his feet and bounced on his toes.

"Movie sounds great, sis. We'll need popcorn and sodas. Since it's your idea, you get to help me with the snacks."

Jayse gently pushed Lucidea toward the door. "Come on, Dea Annie. If we get there first, we get to choose the movie."

Bree had expected more arguments, but was gratified her idea met with limited complaints. One glance at Gowthaman showed her the brunt of the resistance. Ensconced firmly in a hard desk chair, his palms flat against the curved arms, he stared back at her, defiance etched on his features. The man might as well be tied to his books. Disliking the feeling of pulling rank, she took a deep breath.

Nightshade moved silently behind her and whispered, "Go with Chance, honey. Coralie and I will make sure our librarian joins us. Look."

Coralie stood beside Gowthaman's chair. When he opened his mouth in protest, she silently shook her head. Then with one hand she carefully closed his journal. Still without speaking, she rested her palm on the book and jerked her head toward the hallway.

Knowing how Gowthaman disliked interruptions, Bree held her breath. *Would he leave his work willingly?* She couldn't see Coralie's face, but imagined the woman's determined, no-nonsense expression. During those years Coralie had home schooled her, she'd faced that expression many times.

Bree knew the moment he capitulated. Her heart wept at the soft slump in his shoulders, although he did offer Coralie half a smile.

Nightshade prodded her shoulder to angle her toward the kitchen. "He'll leave his work more easily if you're not watching." Louder, he continued, "Bring extra salt with you."

She took a step then turned back to watch Nightshade twine his arms around both Coralie's and Gowthaman's shoulders. "More salt, honey," he called back.

Watching for a moment, Bree sighed. Gowthaman had let himself be led away easily, but it would be difficult to keep him settled through an entire movie. Hopefully Jayse would pick a video that might hold her love's attention, at least for a while. He'd effectively used his books to shut her out.

Smelling the warm, homey scent of popping corn, Bree hurried into the kitchen. Chance was notorious for overcooking popcorn and although he seemed to relish gnawing on the hard kernels, she hated the black flavor of burned.

Chance was another concern. She would never regret her decision to have him on her team, but she hadn't had time to confront him on his personal issues. Maybe now, while they finished up the movie snacks, he could help her understand.

While he reached for colorful bowls, his back was to the door. Ringing pops slowed from a heavy pan on the stove. As usual, he wasn't paying attention. She hurried across the wide stone floor and lifted the pan from the flames.

"I knew you'd rescue the popcorn, sis." Chance set a huge, deep bowl next to the stove. "How many batches to you think we'll need?"

"Knowing you and Lucidea, at least three." Bree dumped the fluffy kernels into the bowl, replaced the pan on the stove and started the next batch. "Butter?"

"In the microwave. You wanna finish the popcorn and I'll get the sodas?"

"Yeah. I'd like to be able to eat it. Uh, Chance?"

"What?" He'd turned away casually for a tray but the tightness of his movements belied his calm tone.

Now that the moment was there, she discovered she wasn't ready to bring up his reasons for insisting he be a part of the mission, so she searched for something else to say.

Chance reached around her and gave the popcorn pan a brisk shake. "Don't do my trick. It's okay, Bree. I know we haven't had time to talk, and that's okay. Really. Since I've gotten here, I've hardly heard... the noise. Tomorrow will be soon enough for us to talk about it."

He moved to the huge stainless steel refrigerator, mumbling under his breath. "Never'd be soon enough."

Dumping the second pan of popcorn, Bree sighed. Was it a guy thing to want to talk and not want to at the same time? The final batch of kernels sizzled in a bit of oil before she said, "Thanks for bringing the weapons from the armory."

His shoulders jerked. A bronze red covered the back of his neck. Bree frowned at his unusual reaction. Still, he smiled when he turned and saluted her with a bottle of soda in his hand.

"I only brought part of what you wanted. Searlait said she'd bring the rest when she joins us tomorrow."

The blush deepened to stain his high cheekbones. He hid something from her. Why he'd always attempted to keep secrets from her was beyond her comprehension. Even without tapping into his aura, she'd always known. She opened her mouth to pry--

And closed it again. Hadn't she been the one to call a stop to talking about the next night's mission? Mentioning the odd voice in her brother's head would only bring them back to Morghan's rescue. While she couldn't stop anyone's thoughts, hopefully relaxing with a movie would keep the anxiety at bay. *At least for a short while.*

Clearer minds would be more aware and open to possibilities. No dramas for them tonight, hopefully Jayse picked a light-hearted movie, a comedy or musical.

"I'm ready."

She started at Chance's bright words then gave herself a mental shake. Getting her wayward thoughts under control before the mission needed to be her priority. She couldn't let her mind wander when she needed to be fully aware of everything around her.

"Geez, sis. You're burning the corn." Chance laughed when she jerked the pan from the flame. Carefully lifting the lid to avoid the steam, she inhaled deeply but didn't smell any over-cooked kernels.

"Got ya. Come on, you're the one who decreed we need to not think about tomorrow."

"Nope, got you there, bro." She dumped the pan of perfectly popped corn into the bowl then poured the last of the melted butter over the heaping mound. "I wasn't thinking about the mission. I was thinking about tonight's movie."

"Uh-huh."

"Okay, and how I shouldn't be thinking about tomorrow."

They laughed together. Bree gathered the over-full popcorn bowl in both hands and followed Chance with his heavily laden tray of drinks. Before leaving the kitchen she stopped, leaned sideways and snatched the salt shaker from the table.

Gowthaman slouched in one corner of a well-worn loveseat, staring at where his hands lay idle on his thighs. Idle. There was no time for idleness this night. He leaned his head against the high cushioned back and stared at the dark ceiling. The wealth of information held in his brain left little room for his personal concerns, but the knowledge did little good if it was not transferred to a form others could use.

Casting his gaze sideways without moving his head, he glanced at the others. Jayse and Lucidea cuddled in the second loveseat. After depositing him here, Coralie and Nightshade had taken the two single chairs. He tipped his head slightly to see the doorway. Perhaps after the movie began, he could use the cover of darkness to slip from the room and return to his task.

Laughter preceded Chance into the room. He set a heavy tray on the sideboard, glanced around the room, nodded to Jayse then flopped to his stomach on a pile of thick pillows. Breanna followed her brother and added an overflowing popcorn bowl to Chance's offering. Then she turned and scanned the room.

"What happened to the rest of the chairs?"

Jayse looked away and cleared his throat, but Lucidea answered. "I've been in the mood to redecorate. The chairs were comfy, but boring. I'm having them recovered."

A tiny frown marred the smoothness of Breanna's forehead and she peered at the floor. Gowthaman followed her gaze to the sets of parallel lines crossing the carpet to a closed door. So that's what Jayse had been doing when they'd entered the room. Moving furniture. Creating less seating.

Realization slammed into him at the same moment Breanna's gaze lifted to his. Her bright blue eyes sparkled. Watching him, she spoke to Lucidea, her tone dry. "I'm sure you've been planning to redecorate for a long time. Good thing there aren't more of us ready to enjoy a movie."

The light in her eyes dimmed and Gowthaman imagined he saw a plea for understanding. He managed the start of a smile and was rewarded with her visible relief.

Turning her back, Breanna filled a smaller bowl with popcorn. "So, now that you've rearranged, what movie did you pick out for us?"

"I didn't have anything to do with this one," Jayse said.

"That's right." Lucidea laughed. "This is my choice. It's a movie we've seen many times. It's good for tonight, full of hope for overcoming what appears insurmountable, with plenty to laugh over."

Breanna lifted two sodas in one hand and showed them to Gowthaman. He nodded approval. She brought the bottles and the popcorn and sat next to him. "Sorry about their little trick," she whispered. Situating the bowl between them, she said, "So, what movie?"

"Give you a clue. 'Never give up, never surrender'."

Breanna chuckled, the sound warm and hopeful. The tight band of worry around Gowthaman's heart loosened. He didn't understand Lucidea's vague reference, but then, he seldom found time for the frivolity of movies. And then only with Breanna's encouragement. If she believed this exercise to be beneficial, he would hold his thoughts and not argue.

But with the seating arrangements, neither would he be able to leave. Mourning the loss of valuable time, he couldn't hold back a sigh.

"Ready?" Lucidea held up the remote and made a show of pressing two buttons, lowering the lights then starting the movie.

In the few seconds of darkness before the screen lit, Bree leaned over the popcorn bowl and whispered, "Relax, Gowtham. Enjoy. Everyone needs these moments."

Her breath stole across his cheek and he fought to remain still and not lean the mere fraction of an inch to touch his skin to her lips. Want blazed through him, pure, unadulterated lust for the woman he loved. He sensed her hesitation before she settled back with the bowl a flimsy barrier between them.

Glad of the near dark and shifting to a nominally more comfortable position, he struggled with the intensity of his reaction. Yes, he loved her, and an honest component to love was desire. He could not allow himself to act upon neither the love nor his desires. Never before had a physical reaction to her nearness been so--instant. So intense. *Had it to do with the danger she would face the next night?*

The opening scenes of the movie flickered on the huge screen and he blinked at the odd, science fiction images. Bree gave half a chuckle. "I love this movie." Then she leaned close again. "I can't believe I've never made you watch this with me." The low, sultry tone of her words vibrated through him like a song. A fey angel's song. Breanna's song.

He turned his head and bumped her nose with his. She gulped back a gasp but didn't move away. He could kiss her now, in the movie darkness. But not the kiss he wished to bestow upon her; how could he, when he was undeserving?

Tiny frown lines marked the downturn of her lips as if she knew his thoughts.

"We should..." he started, then cleared his throat of the words hovering there.

"I think a better..." Bree said at the same time.

"Shh." A wadded napkin landed on Bree's outstretched arm. Chance's movements rustled from the overstuffed floor pillows. "You're the one who said we've gotta watch a movie, so be quiet." He laughed, spoiling his stern reprimand.

"Okay, okay. I'm watching the movie." Bree rolled her eyes as she sank against the back cushions. She lifted her soda can in a sarcastic salute after Chance focused on the screen. "Brat."

The interruption had been timely. Unsure exactly what Chance had interrupted, and vaguely angered with the young man, Gowthaman stored his erratic thoughts away and after a quick glance at Bree, determined to watch the movie. No thinking, no action, just mindless drivel to take him away from his concerns.

After all, that was what his Breanna wanted. *Wasn't it?*

The distraction worked--for a short while. He even found himself identifying with one of the characters. Until the actors portraying actors arrived on a real space-going ship modeled after the vessel on their television show. Until his hand bumped Bree's in the popcorn bowl when they both tried to keep the bowl from tipping. Until she twined her fingers with his, moved the bowl and scooted closer, resting their joined hands on her thigh.

Without turning his head, he glanced sideways at her. A tiny smile accented the fullness of her lower lip. The tip of her tongue swiped at a shiny spot of salty butter at the corner of her mouth. Gowthaman clawed the fingers of his free hand into the furniture arm. The aching need to kiss her, to show her his love rumbled deep in his chest. He released a slow breath, the roar of movie battle covering the low sound of his indiscretion.

Perhaps if he did kiss her, he would be able to take control of his wayward emotions. He glanced at her again. Seeming oblivious of his internal struggle, she laughed at the movie actors.

He *should* kiss her. He would after the movie. One kiss then he could return to his journal and complete the preparations needed to send the mission off successfully. *Just one kiss.*

After all, that was what his Breanna wanted. *Wasn't it?*

Sitting on the deck railing, Breanna watched Gowthaman escape through the workroom door. She held on to the cool wood and leaned back to stare into the dark, star-filled sky. Frustrated, she pounded one fist against the rail. Yep, she was frustrated all right.

Gowthaman had allowed her to hold his hand through the last half of the movie. He'd kept possession of her fingers as they left the media room and strolled to the deck. She'd been amazed he hadn't rushed right back to his journal once she'd released everyone from her well received yet imposed relaxation.

They'd stood in the silent night staring at the loch's dark waters. Alone. Bodies close. She hugged herself. The moment had been quietly romantic. Then he'd turned her to face him and taken both her hands. The memory alone was enough to shift her breathing to that sense of anticipation, of longing. He'd looked at her. For once, she felt he really looked at her, a man gazing into the eyes of a woman.

The shadows had hidden the darkness of his eyes, but his expression had filled with heavy-lidded desire. It had. And that expression had drawn her closer, until she'd held their hands at her hips. A tremble passed from him to her, settling low in her body. He'd been ready to kiss her. Finally.

She snorted and slipped to her feet. *Yeah, right.* Tricks in the moonlight, tricks her mind played on her, showing her what she wanted, not the true expression filling his face the second before he'd turned and practically run away. She'd wait forever for Gowthaman to come to his senses about her. Now he confused her too much.

Chance peeked over the railing from the land side of the deck. "Well? Did he finally--"

She shook her finger at him. "You planned this, you and Jayse. Don't act so innocent around me, little brother. I smell your stink all over the popcorn ruse and reupholstering fiasco."

"Yeah, well, he needed a push. Did it work?"

"I'm standing in one of the most romantic spots at the manor. Alone. What do you think?"

"Geez, sis. A little help from you--"

"Would get me nowhere. Now, for this little stunt, I think you need some early morning sword practice. Say six?"

"Me? It was Jayse's idea." Chance lifted himself over the rail and crossed his arms. Not the least bit repentant, he lifted his eyebrows and tilted his head at her.

"I'll get him up, too. You can cross swords together. I'm sure he needs the workout."

"Great. I'll go tell him the good news." Chance's shoulders slumped and his expression drooped. "Bree, we really didn't mean for you to get upset."

She slapped at his shoulder. "I know. And I'm not really mad. But you still can use the practice before we encounter the World Between Worlds. Don't worry. I'll be there, too."

Chance sidled closer and touched his shoulder to hers then kissed her cheek. "Love ya, sis. I'll tell Jayse and Coralie, sword practice at six."

He paced through the doorway, waving over his shoulder. She called to him, "Make it seven, Chance. Sleep well."

Morning came much too early and Bree opened just one eye to stare at the alarm clock. The outrageous noise continued until she uncurled from the comfort of the soft bed and swatted the clock to silence. A groan preceded her tossing the light quilt aside and standing. Once on her feet, she stretched her spine then smiled.

There'd been the sound of movement and conversation in the manor house long after midnight, so she'd known Chance and probably Gowthaman had been up too late. She didn't worry about Gowtham, but her brother had a hard day-- perhaps many difficult days--before him and should have been resting. She'd work him to near exhaustion this morning, then insist he rest the remainder of the day.

Before she hit the shower, she paused. The clash and clang of steel against steel made her tip her head in confusion. It was only 6:45. Why had Chance or Jayse started practice without her?

She rushed through her shower, skimmed a comb through her towel dried hair. Dressed in comfortable jeans, she trotted from her room. With his love of renaissance faires and reenactments, Jayse had created a practice area just off the parking area so she headed out the front door and across the rough gravel drive.

Lucidea sat on a stone and metal bench at the edge of the clearing, a heavy mug in her hand. She shouted encouragement to Coralie, who held a short, slender sword and sparred with Nightshade. Breanna moved to stand behind Lucidea and watched silently. She'd had little occasion to test Coralie's skill with a blade. Now, she found nothing to complain about nor any suggestions to add to Nightshade's running commentary. Although how he knew so much about fighting with a sword... she shook her head and turned her attention to Jayse and Chance.

The two men fought with an intensity that surprised her. Chance never fought that seriously when she challenged him. *Maybe this mission would be good for him.* She sat next to Lucidea and leaned forward, elbows on her knees.

"How long have they been going at it?"

Lucidea took a sip from her coffee mug. "Hmm, Coralie and Nightshade started almost an hour ago. She said its been too long and she wanted to regain a comfortable, working knowledge of the blade. The guys, not so long. Maybe half an hour. We decided to let you sleep."

"I assume Gowthaman's inside somewhere with his nose in a book."

"You'd be assuming wrong."

Startled, Bree glanced sideways at Lucidea. "I am?"

"He's just gone to bed. Was up all night--with his nose in a book. Jayse practically had to rip the pen from his hand and force him at sword point to lay down on the couch in the study." She chuckled. "Don't expect him to stay there very long, though."

"I'm sure he won't. Besides, he's never seemed to need a lot of sleep."

"He's worried about you, you know."

Bree scrubbed her hand over the back of her neck. "I know."

"I wish you two would--"

"I know that too. But I can't push him, I can't force the issue."

"And why not?" Lucidea waved one hand. "I know now's not the time. But once you're back and Morghan's here, there must be some way to get him to focus on you. And only you. Then you'll be able to help each other to help him."

Unable to decipher what Lucidea was talking about, Bree blinked. "Huh?" She needed caffeine.

With another wave, Lucidea turned her attention toward her husband. "Nevermind. Your mind's somewhere else. We'll talk when you get back." She bent sideways and lifted an insulated carafe. "Coffee?"

"You've been holding out on me. Give. Maybe with a little stimulation I'll be able to think."

"Hmm, but I just said Gowthaman's asleep." Lucidea laughed and handed her a mug of steaming coffee. "Sorry, Bree. I don't mean to make bad jokes or innuendoes, I'm... I'm excited, nervous, scared stiff. This, what you're doing, where you're going... it means so much to me."

"Oh, Lucidea, I understand. I'm glad I'm able to do this for you." She took the other woman's hand. "We'll do all we can to bring Morghan home. Your uncle's safety and return is my primary concern."

Tears filled Lucidea's eyes. "I know it is. But then, after he's home, then promise me you won't give up on Gowthaman, will you?"

Bree's lips felt quivery when she tried to smile. "I'll never give up on him, Lucidea. No more than you'd give up on Jayse."

"Good. Now, I'm going to go in and wash my face before Jayse sees me. I can only blame hormones for so much. I'll bring out more coffee. And water for our combatants."

Nodding, Bree turned her attention back to the two pairs on the practice field. Coralie and Nightshade stood talking, the wide sweeps of Nightshade's hands illustrating his points. Bree grinned and turned to watch her brother.

There was something different about his fighting style, an odd, awkwardness usually found in his movements. She tipped her head in confusion and found herself watching the tip of his weapon rather than his body's movements. *Why did his actions look so strange?*

A few slashes and thrusts later, she frowned. He was practicing with a claymore a good foot longer than his personal weapon. *What the hell was he thinking?* They had no real idea what dangers they might face in the World Between Worlds. He needed to be comfortable with his weapon. With *his* weapon, not some sword he picked up for the heck of it. Just because he wanted to. Just because he was named Chance didn't mean he should take chances with an unfamiliar sword.

Coffee sloshed over the edge of the cup when she jerked to her feet. She glared at the brown stain covering the stone seat. Needing calm, she took a deep breath. Confronting her brother already frustrated wouldn't help. So she stood a moment longer staring as the coffee dripped to the ground.

"M'lady Alastriona?"

Only members of the defenders of mankind called her that, and then only in the most official or serious of moments. The coffee she'd drunk settled bitterly in her stomach and she turned to face her second in command.

"Macaire?"

He ducked his head, angling so he didn't meet her eyes. The lump in her stomach fell, pressing firm and hard against her apprehension. The simple gesture, the lack of eye contact--there was something wrong. Seriously wrong, for Macaire never hedged, never actually dragged his toe through the dirt to avoid looking at her.

She took a deep breath. "Is there something wrong in Faerie? With my family?"

His eyes lifted quickly to hers, then dropped again and he scuffed the other toe in the dirt, lifting a small stone to the surface. He shook his head. "Nothing such as that, lady Alastriona."

"Then what?" His refusal to meet her gaze didn't bode well for anything other than devastating news.

"Lady--"

"You know better--"

"Aye, I do. But as the bearer of tidings you will not wish to hear, I thought it prudent..."

She forced a bark of dry laughter. "Prudent? Just tell me. What can be so bad that you have to resort to unwanted titles?"

"It is Searlait."

The hard, sour lump sank low enough to feel as though it settled against the base of her spine. A shiver crawled from that place of origin and dread tightened her throat. "Is she... ill?"

"Not in the sense you mean. She is ill at heart, for she fears she has failed you desperately."

After placing her coffee mug on the bench, Bree wrapped her arms around herself. "Failed me how?"

Macaire's gaze focused somewhere in the distance over her shoulder. Then his dark eyes returned to her, pleading for understanding. "She has tried. I have been with her, and she tried until she could no longer... I swear to you, Breanna. I swear..." His gaze drifted away.

"Macaire. Look at me." Each second longer than the one before, she waited until his focus returned to her. "I think I understand, but I need to hear."

"She tried." He spread his hands, his long fingers splayed and curled with entreaty. "She was able to open the portal to join you here, but she could not cross. She can not, she will not, return to the World Between Worlds."

Macaire collapsed to the bench and, ignoring the drying coffee spill, Bree sat next to him and took his hand. "I'm really not all that surprised. Her participation in this mission was a lot for me to ask after she'd already spent a lifetime there."

"She fears... she would not be able to return to this world, that she would be trapped there once again. This time with no means of escape. Without the anger or one such as your mother to watch over, she knows she would not survive. She would not return to me as a whole being. Her mind--even if her body returned--she fears her mind would not."

The cold tremor tumbled down her spine. Unfortunately, she did understand. Years of observing and attempting to help Gowthaman honed her sensitivity to his plight. And Searlait's.

Macaire sighed. "She wanted to come, to support this mission. But when she tried, she collapsed."

"Is she okay?"

"Aye, in a physical... She fought herself, tried so desperately. Even now, I fear for her mind. Her soul."

"Return to her, and tell her it's okay. That I understand. Tell her... tell her I appreciate everything she's been able to tell us over the years, how she's willingly shared her knowledge of the World Between Worlds. That knowledge, along with what Gowthaman has provided, will keep us safe and return us home. Successful. With Morghan."

Macaire cast her a knowing look. "You hide your concerns well, lady Alastriona. You will do well in the World Between Worlds. I will return now to my love's side, if there is nothing here I may do for you?"

"Chance said--"

"I brought the weapons your brother set aside for this mission. I... I apologize for not being able to do more."

"It's enough for me to know the Alastriona, and you, are my backup here."

Rising to execute a low bow, Macaire offered a small, sad smile. "It shall be as you wish, Breanna. Go carefully. Fight bravely. Return safely."

Bree watched him form a portal and pass back into Faerie, his head bowed, his shoulders slumped. Searlait had always been one of the bravest women she'd known, an experienced warrior, often the first in the line of battle, real or practiced. For her to fall prey to her own fears confirmed for Bree there was more to fear in the World Between Worlds than physical enemies.

At least Searlait allowed Macaire to give help and support. And his love.

Lucidea returned and rested a tray of bottled water on the bench. "Was that Macaire?"

Nodding, Bree rose and cupped her hands around her mouth. "Practice is over. I need to see everyone inside as soon as you get cleaned up."

When the four sets of eyes turned to her in question, she called, "Hurry it up. I'll fix breakfast."

Lucidea gave her an appraising look and handed water to the others as they passed silently on their way to the manor. After Jayse shut the door behind him, she turned to Bree.

"Not good news?"

Bree shrugged at the tension riding her shoulders. "No, but it'll work out. I'll tell everyone over breakfast. I'm in the mood for scrambled eggs, hope you've got plenty."

"Good job at evading my question, kiddo. Yep, plenty of eggs. Some bacon, ham and, oh, whatever else you might like to put in them. I'll give you a hand--and not ask any questions."

"Don't bite your tongue too hard trying to keep silent." Bree chuckled. "We'll let Gowthaman sleep until everyone else is gathered. Then he'll need to hear what I've got to say, too."

One arm thrown over his eyes, Gowthaman feigned sleep when Lucidea peeked into the study. He wasn't yet ready to face the members of the team, especially Breanna herself. The way he'd left her, alone on the deck, waiting for his kiss, shamed him. A kiss he'd nearly given her, a kiss of promise. He sat and rubbed his face. Why did a simple kiss--no, the mere thought of a simple kiss--cause him such distress? Why was he so unable to act upon his wishes, his needs?

Shaking his head, he rose, brushed at the weary wrinkles in his clothing and moved to the window. The study was at the front of the house, so the wide window overlooked the area where mock battles disturbed the early morning silence. His gaze found Bree unerringly and he frowned. She spoke with her second in command and their body language told of unpleasant news. He watched for a few moments, wishing he could hear their words, then turned away. *What new problems did Breanna face now?* The team would enter the World Between Worlds in too few hours, allowing her no time to deal with other issues.

He focused on the neatly stacked books he'd left beside his journal, ready for his renewed efforts. The desire to return to them faded to a cold lump in his chest. During the last hours of the night, the only information he'd found had been no different than what he'd discovered previously. Delving further into useless references would be of no assistance. All such a pursuit might do would be to increase his frustration. And helplessness.

The empty hollow of his stomach rumbled and he pressed the flat of his hand to his abdomen. Last night's popcorn had not made a nutritious, nor long lasting meal. He managed a smile. After their workouts the travelers would need nourishment. He would prepare breakfast.

Morghan woke with a start and stared into the bleak gray. His mind remained clear of the haze that had taken residence over the past, long uncounted time. Cautious, he sat and looked around. A change was coming. Once standing, he lifted his head and scented the lackluster breeze. There was difference, a lightening of the very air. *Definitely a change.*

A slight movement, caught from the corner of his eye, made him jerk toward a low rise of building-sized stones. "Who's there?" he called, not expecting an answer.

And he didn't receive one. He squinted into the gray, maintaining his position until the intruder moved again. Then he leapt, scrambled over the stones, and captured the small creature around the neck.

"Hold still, ye beast. Hold or breathe yer last."

The creature froze. The muscles in its scrawny neck vibrated as it swallowed then took a deep breath.

"P-p-please. I did not m-m-mean to disturb."

Morghan chuckled. "Ye mean ye dinna mean to be discovered. Yer a nauseous thing. What d'ye want?"

"N-n-nothing, kind sir."

Morghan moved his grip to the creature's shoulder and clawed his fingers into the tight flesh. "Speak true, or die."

"Leave him."

Clutching the creature before him, Morghan turned to face the imperious voice. Arms crossed, legs spread, chin tilted at a haughty angle, a figure stood upon the tallest stone. Morghan knew the man, but before that knowledge settled into his mind it slipped away.

The figure blurred, became clear then blurred again. Ah, a hallucination. The longer he remained in this place the more Morghan had unwelcomed visions of people and places. Once he had come to understand, he had accepted them as his temporary companions.

He released his grip and the creature escaped, scampering up the rocks to stand beside the tall figure. Morghan fought himself for a brief moment, knowing he should care. The physical presence of the insect-like creature had been real. Slumping to the ground, he sat and stared at his hands.

Why hadn't he been able to hold the creature? To hold on to reality? What happened to his determination? The clarity of only moments before? He shrugged. Didn't matter. He shrugged again. *Did it?*

His head felt heavy but he lifted his chin to look up at the figure on the rocks. The leathery creature perched on a stone like a carrion bird, watching. Haloed by the brighter patch of gray indicating a sun, the tall figure moved lower on the hillside.

The air grew warmer, drier. Morghan took a deep breath and frowned. Warmth. No, heat. No... fire. In the space between one breath and the next he knew his foe. Truly knew and fully remembered. He rose slowly to his feet, staring at the fire elemental. At his enemy.

Brandr Ur straddled a low rock, rested one elbow on his knee and cupped his chin in his palm. He watched Morghan silently, an appraising glint in his eyes. With a slow smile he nodded then spoke. "So, in your confusion you believe you know me. Shall I tell you then how I will breach the veil? You shall not stop me again, prince of waters. However misguided, you fought bravely. Perhaps you might enjoy the tale of my victory."

Morghan solidified his stance, crossing his arms. The position, although lower than the elemental's, gave him a sense of power, the sense of *being* he'd not felt for a long, long time. In that moment he rediscovered his power, touched his magic. Knew... his soul. As his *self* returned, the confusion flowed away like water released from a dam. He reveled in the realization the enemy did not know he was once again Morghan. Drawing back the triumphant sneer threatening his mouth, he lowered his gaze.

"Tell me?" he mumbled. The elemental would never resist bragging, and perhaps he would learn something to benefit his efforts to finally defeat the evil being.

"You wish to know?" The elemental seemed genuinely surprised at his response.

"I think I do?" Let the lack of surety show. Let the elemental feel he had the upper hand.

Brandr Ur straightened. "Good. I shall enlighten you. Times and opportunities have come to me--by right--and I have found assistance in many worlds beyond this place. Most worlds I care little for. I will leave them under the control of my loyal followers.

"Ah yes. Weak minds are so easy to control. Yet there were others, not so weak. Still, I controlled them, with promises of powers gained, of titles. Promises." Brandr Ur snorted. "It was so easy for them to believe in promises. Do you realize, prince of waters, that you only need discover the mind's deepest desire? Once you hold that knowledge in your hand..." He held his palm flat and open then slowly squeezed his fist closed. "Yes, once you hold another's desire in your hand, it is but a simple matter to exploit it."

The elemental fell silent, staring at his hand. A blank expression filled his face. Yet his eyes twitched as though he watched something in the distance. Carefully, Morghan glanced sideways to match the elemental's stare, but could discern nothing but the endless gray of the World Between Worlds.

Morghan narrowed his eyes. Perhaps this was how Brandr Ur appeared when he 'spoke' to beings outside this place.

Feeling the heat of the elemental's gaze, Morghan turned his attention to his foe. Brandr Ur smiled.

"I know you have questions. Perhaps my words will answer them. Perhaps not." His shoulders lifted. "You desire to know who aided me in your world, prince of waters?"

Helpless anger crushed the air from Morghan's chest. He didn't need to be told who the elemental had used. Or how empty promises of power had controlled his high chancellor. He'd known, yet he hadn't acknowledged that knowing. Because of his lack of action, he'd placed his world, and the human world, in danger. Those he loved... his shoulders slumped lower as he fought the renewed guilt and memories of failure.

"You don't remember what happened before." The elemental made the bland statement and looked away.

To maintain outward calm, Morghan bit the inside of his cheek. He would not show how much he did recall. The anger, sorrow, determination... and now, amazingly, Coralie's love. He softened his lips to a smile.

"Hmm, perhaps you do."

Morghan jerked, pulled back the delightful, loving memories of Coralie and glared at the taunting grin spread across Brandr Ur's face.

"Your brother..."

Morghan clenched his teeth. The muscles of his thighs tightened, quivered with the need to launch himself at his enemy.

"Ah yes, your brother would have done well as my underling. He was stronger than you." Eyebrows lifted, the elemental watched him expectantly.

"He was." Morghan would give no more than that. Not an admission of his own weakness, but a statement of honor for his beloved brother, Lachlan.

"Had he listened, had he followed me, I would not have taken his life as sacrifice. I... find I rather liked your brother. There is another, perhaps one now..." Brandr Ur waved one hand. "It is of no consequence. But perhaps you'd be pleased with the victim of sacrifice at this conjunction. I have heard humans say there are no coincidences. That may be true, it may not. And I... I did not know. I did not have a hand in the moment."

Brandr Ur shook his head in mock dismay. "So, see how the worlds have taken Pagas and contrived to open the way for me once again? It is truly my time of power and glory."

Satisfaction his high chancellor no longer lived--no matter what the reason--straightened Morghan's spine. "Ye shall no' pass me."

A distain-filled snort answered Morghan. "Yes, yes. I understand. You will fight me... once again. And you will lose... once again. The difference in this time will be that I shall be free of this cursed place. You... if you live, you will remain here." He shrugged. "I care not what happens to you."

"Ye shall no'. Ye shall be the one destroyed. Ye shall no' enter another world."

"Empty threats, blood of my blood. There is nothing to prevent me. In your dullness, you do understand my words, do you not? None shall stand in my way. I will be free. I will rule as is my right. Defy me and die."

"Try then. Try now to destroy me. I defy ye." Fists at his hips, Morghan tossed the challenge into the dry air.

Brandr Ur laughed. "You are not worth my effort, little Al-far. If you wish battle so strongly..." He snapped his fingers and his waiting minion jumped from its rocky perch and cow-ered before him. Placing one hand as if in blessing upon the creature's head, Brandr Ur said, "This being will do battle in my stead, prince of waters. Be wary, for it has existed long in this place and is anxious for freedom. I have not yet decided whether to give him your Alfar world, or the world of the hu-mans. Either way, he greatly covets his prize."

Morghan remained silent. He'd held the creature before, felt the wiry strength. And an odd weakness born of stealth and conniving. He would need to gain the upper hand quickly or the battle could turn long and ugly. He flexed his fingers. With a sword, he would make short work of the vile being.

Shoving the creature away, Brandr Ur turned on his heel. "Finish him. Kill him. Bring me his..." The elemental paused, turned back and smiled. "...his heart. The rest, do what you will."

The creature licked the edges of its thin-lipped mouth. "Y-y-yes, lord."

When the creature turned a broken-toothed grin on Morghan, he shuddered. Then he relaxed his stance, rolled his shoulders, and leaned forward on the balls of his feet.

The creature was on him before Brandr Ur disappeared over the hilltop. Snarling and spitting, it clawed at Morghan's face, trying to poke long digits into his eyes or curl wicked talons around his ears. Morghan protected his face and defended against the creature's frantic actions, studying his opponent.

A rip of hot pain coursed down his arm and Morghan cried out. A warbling chortle of glee from the creature spat saliva onto his face. The tiny droplets stung with the burn of venom. He'd not accounted for poison. Glancing at the ragged flesh and gaping tear in his upper arm, Morghan steeled his mind against the pain and jerked the creature's talon from his arm.

Fresh pain staggered him. He collapsed. Rocks tore into his knees and shins. He held fast to his opponent, pushing the dripping fangs from his torn skin. He fell forward pressing the smaller creature beneath him. Pokes and jabs from boney knees forced the air from his diaphragm.

He dared not curse the creature, so wasted no breath on words or unreliable magic. When the creature scrabbled for a handful of dirt, Morghan turned his face, but instead of tossing the dry earth into his eyes, the creature ground the dust and tiny, sharp rocks into the wound on his arm.

Unable to muffle his agony, Morghan turned the creature's unobservant glee to his advantage. Before the echoes of his cry dissipated in the heavy air, he'd twisted, capturing both of the creature's stick-like wrists in one hand. The other hand, slick with blood, he curled around the scrawny neck.

He paused, and the creature laughed. "The l-l-lord said you c-c-c-could not kill." Wide, surprisingly intelligent eyes stared up at him, glittering with malice. "B-b-but I can."

One of the creature's hands slipped from Morghan's grasp and the long fingers wrapped around the wrist of the hand Morghan had encompassing its neck. It twisted and lifted Morghan's hand.

Morghan shook his head, clearing the path to older memories. With a jerk, he angled his upper body and brought the creature's own arm across its neck. Pressing his weight against the forearm crushed the creature's fragile windpipe.

Its eyes widened and it attempted to gasp air into deflating lungs. Twice it tried, twice the long, frantic fingers clutched at Morghan's arm. With a silent snarling curl of thin lips, the creature died.

Morghan struggled to his feet, clutched his upper arm and backed away. He blinked. Shook his head. Fresh agony seared his belly. In all his years, he'd only twice before willingly killed another. He stared at his fingers. And never with his hands, only with a sword.

He was no warrior.

Heaving breaths filled with physical pain and mental anguish, he watched the dead-eaters slink from whatever holes they inhabited to drag the body away. He shuddered and glanced toward the distant plain, watching the elemental's retreating form move toward his temple.

He was no warrior, but this Morghan did vow. The elemental would not pass him. By whatever means given him, the elemental would be denied entry to any world. Palm pressed to the slowing drain of blood from his arm, he turned away.

A hot touch filled his mind. *::Perhaps I chose the wrong brother after all.::*

The well-stocked kitchen was a pleasure to work in and Gowthaman took advantage of the silence to quickly gather and arrange ingredients for breakfast. Something simple, yet nourishing. He froze holding a container of brown, speckled eggs. *Would the rescue party carry food with them? Had any-one considered that need?* He hadn't been--there--long enough to know hunger. He set the eggs on the counter and reached for a small bowl. Had he remained, he didn't believe he would ever have felt hunger. Felt anything at all.

Concern over missing a possibly important factor washed over him. Straightening his spine, he shoved at the concern, dislodging it only slightly. Searlait had addressed this. He closed his eyes to visualize a page in his journal. No nourish-ment nor liquid were necessary to maintain life. However, he would suggest carrying water and protein bars. If for nothing more than to maintain a semblance of normality in a place where normal was an emptiness of nothing.

He pulled a cutting board from a low cupboard.

"Well now, that's what I like to see. A man who knows his proper place."

He froze at Lucidea's droll statement, then took an oddly-shaped Faerie knife from a wooden block. "I thought to make myself useful."

"You're supposed to be asleep," Breanna said. Delighted with the sound of her voice, he closed his eyes to let the melodious tones flow over him. Just her voice could heal him--if he would allow.

The women moved further into the kitchen until they hovered behind him. "You may set the table," he said. "It will not be long until breakfast."

Bree leaned over his shoulder and he inhaled the spicy floral scent of her hair. The aroma skated along his senses, tugging at his heart.

"Oh, good," she said as she turned back to Lucidea. "He's making scrambled eggs. Unless..." She touched his shoulder and he held back a sigh of longing. "Unless you're fixing omelets."

He cleared his throat. "Which would you prefer?"

"Plain old scrambled eggs, please. Of course I still want all that stuff you have out on the counter in them."

"Of course." Gowthaman managed a smile. Breanna had an almost passionate love of scrambled eggs. Such a simple thing and yet she found such joy and delight with each bite. Passion filled her, spilled out into everything she did. Frustrated with himself for recognizing her passions yet refusing to allow her to share with him, he whacked an egg on the side of the bowl, shattering the shell.

Holding his breath for a moment calmed the disturbed churning in his chest and belly. It was not the egg's fault he was a fool.

Breanna chuckled. "I guess I will set the table. Doesn't look like you're working to well with an audience this morning. Want me to magic the shells out of the bowl for you?"

"Thank you, but no. Such is a frivolous use of magic that would be better used elsewhere."

Breanna patted the counter next to the bowl. "I know. Just make sure you get all the shells out. You know I don't like crunchy eggs." Her chuckle filled the kitchen as she moved to gather plates and silverware.

Bereft of her warmth, Gowthaman methodically and carefully removed the broken shells from the bowl then finished cracking the eggs. Ignoring the busy sounds behind him, he completed his preparations and moved the bowl and piles of ingredients to the stove. By the time a platter of scrambled eggs studded with ham, bacon, vegetables and cheese graced the center of the table, the others had found their ways into the kitchen.

The early meal was congenial. No one spoke of the coming night's mission or the World Between Worlds. Grateful, Gowthaman willingly moved back to the stove to make a second platter of eggs.

Although Chance still munched on thick, toasted bread slathered with berry jam, the others pushed their plates away. Gowthaman focused on one of his concerns. "Will you be taking provisions?"

Coralie nodded. "I've packed food and water already. Even though 'twill no' be physically needed, we'll care for our bodies. Each will carry a careful day's amount." She grinned. "An' mayhap a bit more. Especially Chance."

"Hey."

"Ye are the strongest among us, are ye no'?"

"Just because I'm a guy. Geez, Coralie, you're as bad as Bree."

Breanna leaned back and crossed her arms. "Now it's my turn to say 'hey'."

Coralie rose and reached for plates to clear the table. "'Tis no' such a bad thing to be a man, young Chance. In truth, since we are no' used to campin', we shall all feel the weight of our packs. An' in truth, I believe we may wish them heavy far longer than the weight remains."

"I don't doubt," Chance grumbled then shoved his finally empty plate toward the stack Coralie piled at the edge of the table. "Bree? Shouldn't Searlait be here by now?"

Gowthaman wondered the same thing, but hesitated to mention the passing time. Now he turned his expectant gaze to Breanna. She sat with her head bowed and palms flat against the table. In the silence, she shook her head then lifted a sad gaze to the gathering. She looked at each in turn, but her brilliant blue eyes fell to him last and she held his gaze.

"I spoke with Macaire this morning. Searlait... well, she won't be coming with us." She paused and the pain of what she had not said filled him.

He cleared his throat and nodded once. "She is unable to face the World Between Worlds. She can not find the strength within her to enter again."

Breanna's focus remained on his face as though she drew strength from him. Remaining silent, he gave what he could, offering all his damaged soul to assist her.

"No, she can't. Macaire said she tried, but fears if she goes back, she will never return--that somehow she would trapped there. Forever this time."

Chance shifted in his chair. "How does this affect the mission, sis?"

Straightening her shoulders, she answered. "Only in that we will be one person less."

"But what about everything she knows about the World Between Worlds? Might we get stuck there?" Chance leaned his chair back on two legs, the casual position belying the seriousness of his questions.

"We'll just go with what we know. She's given us plenty of information in the past. And Gowthaman's been supplying so much more. We'll be... we'll be fine, Chance. You, Coralie and I will bring Morghan home."

The offering of his journal seemed insignificant now, but it was all Gowthaman had to give. "You will take the journal with you. My research may not be as helpful as someone directly able to answer questions, but with luck, the answers will be there."

"Take the journal?" Breanna's eyes grew wide and curious.

He'd surprised her with the offer. "Yes. Why else would I have compiled the information in a portable form?" He winced, the words had sounded so ponderous and self-important. He angled to face her. "Breanna, I have done this for you."

She took his hand, the warmth of her soft palm offering more than he could ever have to return. "Thank you, Gowtham. I've tried to memorize what I felt was important, but there's just so much to know. With the journal we'll be fine." The pressure from her fingers caused him to look down at their joined hands. "Thank you."

He read a wealth of feeling into the two simple words and understood her gratitude was for much more than just a simple journal. He covered their hands with his free hand and returned the pressure. A simple gesture. An easy thing to do.

Yet it was difficult to maintain the contact when he ached for so much more.

Bree closed her eyes to savor a few moments of physical contact with Gowtham. Captured between his larger hands, hers felt small, delicate, cherished. Warmth seeped into her fingers. Had the stress of the last hour chilled her skin? Such a thing was possible she supposed.

The pressure against her fingers lessened. She released a soft breath. If he was true to form, the comfort Gowtham offered wouldn't last much longer.

To her surprise, he lifted his hands slightly and turned the bottom one until their palms touched, keeping the joining hidden beneath his right hand. His fingers curled between hers.

"I wish I had been able to accomplish more."

Meanings beyond the simple words, meant only for her, tumbled through her mind. To have the leisure to explore those meanings would be bliss. To discover Gowthaman's true feelings... ah, her heart skittered in her chest.

Scowling like a schoolboy sent to the principal's office, Chance dropped the chair back to four legs with a clatter and slouched low in the seat. "So, we're minus Searlait but we've got the book. Where does that put us in terms of the mission? I mean, what's changed?" He glanced sideways at Coralie and grimaced. "Other than the fact I've got to lug a bigger pack."

Jayse chuckled and slapped him on the back. "You'll be fine." Then he looked at each of them in turn. "You all will be. We're so confident, Dea Annie and I have already begun planning the coming home party. How does... popcorn and a movie sound?" He gave Bree a wink. The men of her extended family loved to tease.

She shook her head. "I was thinking more along the lines of everybody leaving the manor to Coralie and Morghan. For their own homecoming."

Bright red flamed over Coralie's cheeks. "Oh, nay. Lucidea is no' allowed to travel the portals. I will no' chance her child fer my own..." She sighed, clasped her hands together, then smiled. "My own desires."

"We can take the car, you know," Lucidea offered. "It's been awhile since we've traveled the Scottish countryside." She glanced at Jayse from under her lashes. "Remember that bed and breakfast up on the northern coast?"

"Oh, aye. That I do, lassie." Jayse scooted his chair closer to his wife. "And do you remember that little glen hidden deep between the rocks? There was barely room for us to--"

"Jayse." Lucidea slapped his arm.

He waggled his eyebrows. "I see you remember. I think our visit there would be a wonderful homecoming for your uncle. After you've had the time for proper hellos and introductions of course. I've never met the man, though I feel I know him well. I'm sure we're all anxious to overwhelm him with a Zeroun clan welcome."

"Overwhelm is right," Chance said. "But to be here, to be home, I can't imagine he'll mind. But that doesn't answer my question. Does lacking Searlait change our plans in any way?"

Gowtham squeezed her hand but when she glanced at him, he turned to stare out the wide kitchen window toward the loch. She treasured that silent show of support more than any boisterous word from another.

"I don't think so. We know what we need to do. Enter the World Between Worlds." Gowtham's fingers tightened painfully around hers for a moment. When he relaxed his hold, he trembled. Bree made a rapid, silent vow. Once home, she'd never speak of the World Between Worlds around him again. There would be no need.

She continued to the others, "We find Morghan. I know there are many different landscapes and areas there, however, none of them are extremely large. Unless Morghan discovered how to move from one to the next as Searlait did, I'm hoping he won't be too far from where the veil will open. I'm sure he'd realize that any rescue would come from the same location as where he was pulled through.

"Once we find him, we watch for the elemental and bide our time until the full moon. We've got two nights. Searlait said, and I believe Gowthaman's research supports the notion, that time there will flow with the same speed as here. So, two days. Then we'll reopen the veil and come home."

Chance gave her a droll lift of his eyebrows. "In other words, we're winging it?"

She threw him an exasperated glare. "It would be great if we didn't have to deal with the fire elemental, but I can't imagine he'll be too far from our point of entry either. He'll probably try to use our magic to weasel his way to this world. That will not happen. We will end this now. Brandr Ur will be controlled. One way or another."

A tiny catch at the base of her throat stopped her impassioned words. She didn't like killing, didn't relish even the thought of destroying another being. But she also knew *this* being, this fire elemental, would be stopped no other way. If he was not destroyed, their family might never be rid of him.

She glanced at her brother. Just like another powerful being had plagued the Zeroun clan for centuries, ending in Chance's conception. Her gaze skipped to Jayse and Lucidea.

They had destroyed that being, literally cutting the evil faerie in two.

"Uh, I need to take a walk." Without another word, Chance rose and left the kitchen. Bree rose to follow but Gowthaman's gentle pressure on her hand held her in place.

Nightshade spoke softly. "Leave him be. He's got to work out his own issues, little girl. You trust him enough to bring him on this mission? Extend that trust to him now."

She glared at Nightshade, then sighed. "As usual, you're right." Plopping back to her seat, she slipped her hand from Gowthaman's and hugged herself, rubbing her shoulders. "I'll give him some time. But we all need to discuss our final strategies this afternoon."

"Even though it is early in the day, you must rest." Gowthaman made the declaration in a low voice.

"I don't have time--"

"You will make time."

"But there's..." She turned in her chair to face him. The stony look he gave surprised her, the tight squaring of his jaw, the thin set to his lips. The normally soft, tortured chocolate brown of his eyes had firmed to deep, black ice.

Her shoulders drooped. "You're right. We'll all need to rest. But now I..."

Gowthaman shook his head. "I know you will not. Even if your body is at rest, your mind will work frantically at what you perceive as problems. Come, while you relax we will discuss the information in the journal. The lord and lady will make sure Coralie and Chance rest as well." He canted his head toward Jayse and Lucidea. "Will you not?"

"Of course," Jayse agreed. "And even though we don't need to, we'll double check that Coralie thought of everything the group might need."

Coralie gave a soft snort of mock disgust then joined Nightshade in laughter.

"I see I'm completely outnumbered," Bree said. "Okay, Gowtham, lead on. I'll try to relax while you fill my brain." Secretly she was delighted to spend time alone with him, even if it was while he lectured to her. She glanced back as she followed him from the kitchen. From the smug looks on the four remaining faces, her delight wasn't so secret after all.

Gowthaman's hand was a warm comfort around hers and Breanna cherished each second he let the contact remain. When they reached the library, he led her to the couch.

"I'm not going to be able to sleep, you know."

"Yes, I know. This will be more comfortable than sitting at the table. I doubt you will find much of comfort in the..." He swallowed heavily. "Where you go... no." He swallowed again as if finding the strength to speak the name. "In the World Between Worlds. So take your ease while you are able."

Beads of sweat formed on his forehead, but even without a physical reminder, she knew how much effort just saying those worlds cost him. That he would speak the name of a place he dreaded held deep meaning--for both of them. Before she could say anything, he turned to cross to the table and re-trieve his slim leather journal.

He returned with the book and sat close to her. Their thighs touched. She held her breath but he didn't adjust his position and remained close as he opened the journal on the coffee table before them.

Pressing both palms flat against the pages, he sighed. "I believe you already know what I've placed upon these pages. The challenge will be accessing the appropriate information quickly. I do not know how much time you will have should a... a problem arise. I regret I can not offer you more."

She leaned forward and rested her hands over his. "It'll be enough, Gowtham. Don't worry."

"But, I will worry." He turned his face toward hers. Inches only separated them. His voice dropped to a harsh whisper. "Each moment until you have safely returned."

"We will return. With Morghan." She lowered her voice as well. "I promise."

Silent, he angled, almost facing her. Emotions played across his features, and she wished he would allow her to understand and to know him. He held her gaze while a long moment passed. Sensing movement, Bree glanced down to where he lifted one hand then returned her gaze to float in the searching chocolate dark of his eyes.

The tip of one finger touched her jaw, just below her ear. Her breath caught at the base of her throat. With infinite slowness, each fingertip touched her face, his thumb finally resting just below her chin. He barely touched her yet heat charged through her, awakening the desires she'd kept wrapped safely away from the world. From him.

Bending his fingers, he skimmed his knuckles along the curve of her cheek, back and forth, softly drawing her closer. Tingles followed his touch then her skin flushed hotter. She drew a shaky breath.

Light as a feather's touch he pressed one finger to her lips and slowly shook his head. Lost in the intense glitter of his dark eyes, Breanna waited. In the depths of her mind a tiny voice laughed in delight. The world really did slow. Time really did pause. Nothing existed for her but Gowtham's tender expression, his touch, his breath...

His kiss.

Warm and firm, yet with tentative pressure, his lips brushed hers. She closed her eyes to savor the gentle caress. Her being burst to life, every cell alive, affirming, aching for more. But she held still, kept her hands in her lap, unwilling to break whatever spell had eased through at least one layer of Gowtham's self-imposed solitude.

The only contact between them remained their lips and the tips of his fingers against her cheek, yet he held her there as surely, as permanently as if she were bound. She held no desire for escape.

Gowtham eased back, but only a wisp of air separated their mouths. His breath flowed over her skin. She ached to open her eyes, to see his expression, yet fear of what she wouldn't see kept her in darkness. His fingers moved, joined by the sensual touch of his other hand to caress and stroke, as if memorizing the structure of her face.

She smiled. Gowtham took a sharp intake of breath then tunneled his fingers through her hair, gently tilting her head. His lips... oh, when his lips captured hers, she sighed. He took advantage, as she'd hoped, and slowly ran his tongue along the parted seam of her lips.

Needing support to keep herself upright and coherent under the onslaught of sensations spinning out from Gowtham's kiss, she lifted her hands to his shoulders.

As if her touch signaled her surrender, he pulled her closer, deepened the kiss and took sensual possession of her mouth. He tasted of dark desert honey and desire. She wanted more. Needed more. Knew she would forever crave more.

Breathless when he eased them apart, she cherished her amazement at the intensity of their first kiss. With a tiny start to her scattered thought process, she realized this had been their first real kiss, a kiss of equals, of adults. Of lovers. She smiled and opened her eyes.

A myriad of emotions flashed through Gowtham's eyes before he drew a deep, uneven breath and returned her smile. Still hovering in a sensual daze, she refused to catalog those emotions, fearing she would precipitate his solid return to his hidden pain-filled self. She leaned back, slipping her hands back to her lap.

He took another breath, lowered his hands to cover hers. He drew a third breath to speak.

"No, Gowtham," Bree said softly. "Don't apologize."

Startled, he stared at her for a moment then lowered his gaze to their hands. She held back a sigh. If he continued anyway and apologized for kissing her, for giving her a taste of his passion, she'd fall apart. She'd cry... and she hated crying. She had no time for any foolishness such as that.

Gowtham curled his fingers through hers, then lifted one hand to press his lips against her knuckles. "Yes, I was about to apologize. But not for what you suspect." For a moment the pain normally haunting his expression disappeared. "But, as you wish, I shall not speak of it now."

Bree drew her brows together. What would he feel the need to apologize for if not for kissing her? Reluctant to do so, she still felt the need to create space between them or she'd embarrass herself completely before sorting out her feelings.

"Then we won't," she said and winced inwardly at her sharp tone. She pulled her hands from his slack fingers and rose. Turning toward the wide window, she stared unseeing at the practice field. A few steps carried her to the window where she leaned heavily on the wide, stone sill.

Movement just beyond a low hedge caught her attention. Alone at the edge of the forest, Chance flowed through a series of exercises, the long sword an extension of his arm. Studying her brother allowed Bree to push aside her stormy, confused feelings. Yet while she critiqued Chance's occasionally awkward movements, she relived every second of Gowtham's kiss. And her reactions.

She'd waited a long time for their first kiss and at times had completely despaired of the romantic moment ever happening. Now, when he'd pulled further from her than ever before, when he repeatedly refused her offer of healing, when she was about to embark on the most dangerous mission she could imagine and there was no time to explore their feelings... now was when he chose to kiss her? She sniffed, appalled at the wet sound and the damp coating her eyelashes.

Chance took a misstep and landed on one knee. Even with the distance between them, she felt his frustration. And more. Strange, different emotions she wasn't able to identify, something he was keeping hidden from her. She knew even touching him wouldn't allow her to see past his defenses. A shudder tripped down her spine. What was he truly fighting?

"I need to go to him," she said and turned, colliding with Gowthaman who had moved behind her. He wrapped his arms around her and shook his head.

"He would not appreciate your intrusion at this time."

Bree glared at him and twisted away from his embrace. "What would you know about it?"

Silent, Gowtham studied Chance. "I know nothing of it, Breanna. Still, I understand there are times when a young man may not appreciate the advice of a sister. Has he not always come to you when he needed counsel?"

Reluctantly, she nodded and crossed her arms. "Yeah, so?"

"So, when he needs to speak with you, he will."

"And when are you such an expert on human communications? Or any communications."

He glanced away. "I am not."

She hadn't meant to hurt him, to so blatantly attack his pride. From the stiff, angry set to his shoulders, she'd pushed too far. "Gowtham, I'm--"

He lifted one hand to silence her words then turned toward her, the faint smile on his lips not dimming the hurt in his eyes. "No apologies, remember?" Then he gave an elegant wave toward the window. "Besides, another has reached his side before you. Allowing you to return to your rest."

Slightly suspicious of his odd attitude and the coincidence of someone else talking to Chance, she returned to the window. Even though Nightshade stood next to her brother, hands flowing with his normal expansive gestures, Bree was unable to let go of her conflicted emotions and relax. She tapped her fingers against the windowsill.

Gowtham's hand hovered over hers, then lowered to stop her irritated movements. "Perhaps it is the strain of the mission making you feel out of sorts."

She glared sideways at him before relenting. Maybe that was the reason. Part of the reason anyway. His unreadable, unpredictable behavior of just the past few minutes didn't help either. Another kiss might though. Catching her reflection in the wavy glass, she pulled her dreamy smile into a frown.

But he'd seen, and if she understood the male psyche even half as well as she believed she did, he recognized her smile, and despite his own confusion, was quite pleased with himself. The pleasure faded to a neutral expression then she faced him.

He held out one hand. "Come. You did promise to rest."

"Yeah, I did." She shrugged one shoulder and let him lead her back to the couch. He sat angled comfortably in the corner and tugged on her hand until she sat beside him. "I wish you could hold me," she whispered then gasped as she realized she'd spoken out loud.

Frozen like a lead statue, she dared not look at him. He circled her shoulder with one arm and settled her against him. She glanced at him from under her lashes. He closed his eyes for a moment and the neutrality faded. She wasn't sure what emotion tightened his lips, only that it was a pain of a differing kind than he normally carried. Before she could ask, he cupped the back of her head and guided her to rest her cheek against his chest.

"Rest, Breanna. Do not think, at least for this short while." Tucking her legs to the side, she wrapped her arm across his firm abdomen and snuggled closer. With his fingers stroking her hair, she slept.

The past hour had been filled with blissful agony. The soft warmth of the sleeping woman cuddled against Gowthaman brought too many dangerous thoughts of what could be. He eased to a more comfortable position and rested his out-stretched hand on the inward curve of Breanna's waist. She sighed, stretched then relaxed with her head on his lap.

Gowthaman swallowed against the sudden dry anticipation in his throat and shifted again. But this brought his splayed fingers higher on her side and he snatched his hand away, holding his fist in the air. There was no safe place for his hand. He released a shallow breath then cupped his fingers against her skull, delighting in the soft tickle of her hair.

He fingered a short, silky strand, wondering what it would feel like, long and sensuous, against his skin. Gulping back a groan, he began silently reciting an ancient, boring... and long genealogy. But as if with a sensual need of their own, his fin-gers continued to stroke and caress her hair making his recitation only marginally successful.

Breanna stirred, tensed, then released a long breath. "That feels wonderful, Gowtham. Oh, don't stop," she said when his movements froze.

Knowing the dangerous folly of the actions, Gowthaman resumed the caress.

Incredibly, Breanna snuggled even closer and tucked her hand under her cheek to curve over his thigh. "You know,

I've been considering letting my hair grow long again. What do you think?"

Think? He could not think. If he thought, he would not react. He wanted to react, to act. He drew his hand from temptation. He wanted... her.

"Gowtham?" Breanna pressed lightly on his thigh and sat. Her touch burned through his light trousers, an invisible brand marking him. He shoved her hand away and, expecting to see the burning imprint of her palm, stared at his thigh.

Disappointment flowing from her in vibrant waves, Breanna jerked to her feet. Gowthaman lifted his gaze and willed her to look at him. She did, both pain and love revealed in her eyes. The pain sliced through him like sharpened steel, while her love offered healing. Who was this woman who held him so surely even when he denied her?

Rising, he took her hand and pressed her palm to his chest over his heart. "I have always..."

An expectant light glimmered in her eyes. Ending his denials would take only words, simple words, a few short syllables. What would her eyes show if he said what truly resided in his heart? He could not bear to know. "...liked your hair longer."

Breanna's brows drew together for an instant over the dimming joy in her eyes, but then she smiled and laughed. "Then when I get back, I'll be sure to let it grow. Maybe I'll even ask for a touch of frivolous magic to make it grow faster." She drummed her fingers against his chest then tried to move away, but he held fast to her hand.

"Gowtham?" Her whisper focused his attention on her lips. He should never have kissed her, for now he knew the taste of her, the delights of her mouth against his. He leaned forward to experience again.

"No, look." Breanna nodded toward their hands then lifted their entwined fingers. "Oh."

A crimson aura, dark as blood, pulsed over her hand. She slipped her palm from his, but kept her hand hovering near his. Then he saw bright gold surrounding his hand. Never having experienced his own magical aura, Gowthaman watched in fascination as the color danced and played over his skin.

Breanna moved her hand closer and arcs of his magic shot toward her. Red lightning burst from her aura reaching for him. Merging, the colors swirled in a sensuous display, stealing the breath from his lungs.

Soulfire.

Breanna snatched her hand back and hid it behind her back. "We'll talk about this when I get back, Gowtham. That will give you a couple of days to come up with some lame excuse to deny we belong together."

Still staring at the wonder faintly glowing in the air between them, he barely noticed the knock on the door. Nor when Breanna moved away to talk with the intruder. Nor the excitement of a new arrival at the manor.

There was no denial.

Soulfire.

Bree shoved her hand into her jeans pocket and berated herself for hoping. Wishing was for children and fools... Oh, but she was a fool where Gowthaman was concerned. Wasn't anyone in love a bit of a fool? Still, she knew deep in her heart, he'd almost said he loved her. She knew it.

Maybe it was honestly better he hadn't spoken of love. The glow and sparkle of their soulfire had certainly rattled him into speechlessness.

She curled her fingertips against her palm. Confined in her pocket, the heat faded to a mild, slightly scratchy sensation. Drawing her hand from the pocket, she scrubbed her palm against her hip but the soft denim did little to relieve the longing or the odd tactile reminder of her love's touch. Something changed between them while she napped. She and Gowthaman touched often and while she occasionally sensed a flicker of soulfire from his reactions, she was convinced he never had. She felt the same, so the change had to have been in him to produce soulfire now.

Hearing voices in the kitchen, Bree squared her shoulders and stepped forward quickly. She wouldn't forget. She and Gowthaman would talk in two days. No way he would get away with avoiding her this time. Putting on a public smile, she tucked her personal life away and entered the kitchen.

"Catori, it's great to see you." She greeted Coralie's sister with a hug then grabbed a bottle of water from the refrigerator and leaned her hip against the counter to take a sip.

Tori smiled then grew serious and took Coralie's hand. "In a dreamwalk I saw you leaving. I couldn't let you go without my support."

"I dinna think, 'tis been a hectic time, for we dinna realize how limited the time was. We must leave tonight or we lose the opportunity."

Tori nodded. "I know. That's why I'm here. And I'll be here when you get back. I wanted to talk to you anyway."

"Aye?" Coralie gestured absently then tucked an indefinable packet into the pack set beside her chair . "An' it could no' wait?"

"I would have thought so, but a shadow figure in the dreamwalk said I needed to be here now, to tell you before you go."

Bree straightened. "Well, we should let you get talking then. I'll go--"

Tori caught Bree's sleeve. "No, I'm supposed to tell everyone. I don't understand why this is important, but it is. Please. I won't take long, only a few moments. I know your time is precious. I don't understand how this has any bearing on what you plan to do. I've learned, though, not to question the guides I meet on dreamwalks."

"Nor would I ever expect ye to, m' sister." Coralie rose to hug her then stepped back. "Tell us, then. If we do no' now understand what import there may be fer Morghan's homecoming, then we shall when that time is upon us."

Tori grinned and Bree stared at the matching expressions on similar faces. As often before, she fought amazement at how alike they were. Sisters, definitely, but raised in totally different worlds. Coralie had been a ward of Morghan's father, the king of the Alfar-Sindhu, while Catori had grown up in a human, native American society. Whether it was fate, fortune or magic that brought the sisters together, none would dare step between them again.

As if summoned, the rest of the family gathered quietly in the kitchen. Bree glanced at each person as they settled into their chosen places then gave a soft snort. How long had it been the tradition for families to gather around the hearth? No matter what race or upbringing, everyone always came here.

She shook her head and rolled her eyes behind closed lids. That was an interesting, random thought. Not appropriate to the time or gathering. Or, perhaps it was. This widely inclusive, accepting family, while gathering for another reason, was also here for support.

Gowthaman paused at her side, then moved past her to take a seat at the table. The low murmur of individual conversations halted and Tori spoke.

"Dreamwalks have been difficult for me to interpret lately. Even when I factor in the disturbances that might stem from the World Between Worlds..." She sat and slapped her hands on her thighs. "I'll do my best, but I can't promise accurate answers."

Coralie touched her shoulder. "Aye, we ken. 'Tis never an easy thing to unravel mysteries, even if they be only yer dreams. Nay, before ye give ma another lecture on listenin' to my dreams, I shall tell ye, sister mine, that I dinna need yer lectures. At least no' now. Now we need to hear what yer guides have told ye to say."

"I'd never lecture you, Cor."

At Coralie's lifted eyebrows, the sisters dissolved into giggles. The oppressive atmosphere filling the room lightened and Bree breathed a sigh heavy with relief. So caught up in Gowtham and her own feelings, she had momentarily lost touch with the others. Not a good thing. She'd have to keep her personal life separate while on this mission, otherwise...

But one glance at Gowthaman, who listened intently to Tori's description of her dreamwalk, and her heart raced, her body felt languid and jittery at the same time, and she couldn't focus on anything but him.

She adjusted her stance, crossed her arms and gave herself a pinch. Pay attention.

Letting Tori's lyrical voice hold her attention, Bree kept her gaze locked on Gowthaman, gauging his reactions.

"So you see, the overt meaning of the dreamwalk is really self-explanatory. You go, find Morghan, and come back."

Nightshade leaned back in his chair and lifted one eyebrow in Bree's direction. "I'm sure Bree is gratified your guides predict success for the rescue. But honey, what haven't you told us?"

Tori made a self-depreciating face. "I hesitate to say anything now, because I don't see how this has squat to do with the rescue. It's just that the information came to me during the same dreamwalk and I was instructed to tell all."

"Then ye must tell us, Tori, dinna ye think? Ye ken, even if what ye say may no' make sense to us now, perhaps at another time such information may prove vital."

Bree smiled at Coralie's words, exactly what she had drawn breath to say herself.

After a short nod, Tori continued, "As you all know, ever since Cor and I found each other, we've been searching for more information about our parents. Since Cor was raised in the Sindhu royal palace, and I discovered later I have the, uh, talent of breathing under water, we assumed we share an Alfar-Sindhu father. We discovered the truth of that assumption ten years ago. But we still have no ideas about our mothers. Their identities have remained hidden. I always thought my mother was human, a Native American, and that's why I was placed with a tribal family."

"So, did yer guides tell ye of our mothers then?" Coralie leaned closer to her sister, an expression of rapt interest filling her face.

"Even though my Alfar half is drawn to water, I never really gave much thought to why it's so easy for me to enter a dreamwalk. To float through the air of possibilities and flow with the breezes until I reach the dawning of understanding. It's like--flying."

Leaning back, Coralie tilted her head to look out the wide kitchen window. "Yer thinkin'--"

Tori nodded.

Chance slapped his hand on the table jarring Coralie's unpacked collection of containers and startling Bree from her mental lists. "Are you gonna share with the rest of us?"

Clasping the young man's shoulder, Nightshade said, "She means her mother probably wasn't human."

Chance shrugged. "So?"

"But who she may have been, or of what race, is the important issue, honey."

Chance ignored Nightshade, and rose from his chair to stalk to the sink. He turned to face the table with his hands fisted low on his hips. "So, was she Faerie?"

Bree turned her concentration on her brother, attempting to read deeper than his surface emotions. He'd been skittish all day, one moment his normal, cheeky self, at others brooding and distant. Now he was argumentative and angry. She had to get him settled down before they left tonight. There wasn't time to baby him along, nor could they afford any mistakes.

Tori slowly shook her head. "It's always possible, since I've the feeling she held a great deal of magic. But Faerie..." Lips pressed into a tight line, she continued shaking her head.

"No, I don't think so. The atmosphere where I was led felt--different. And I've been to Faerie often enough to sense such differences. I think, maybe--no, probably--my mother was also Alfar."

At the edge of Bree's vision Nightshade gave a barely noticeable jerk and straightened from his loose, relaxed pose. Drawing her brows together she watched him, more interested in his reaction than in Catori's revelation. Why did the possibility that her mother might be Alfar make him literally sit up and take notice?

Tori continued, "It doesn't feel right that she was Sindhu, so she must have been Domovoii or Andras."

Coralie hugged her sister. "'Tis wondrous news. When we return with Morghan, ye an' I shall discover the truth of yer mother. Then perhaps we shall find a clue to my own."

Tori kissed her sister's cheek. "That sounds like a plan, Cor. A good plan, after you have some time with the returnee, of course."

A bright pink blush covered Coralie's face and she dipped her head to hide a smile. Bree mentally slapped her forehead. Only recently she'd come to realize the depths of feeling Coralie had for Morghan, learned that they'd become lovers only days before Morghan disappeared. Even though Coralie had hidden her love well, once she became an adult herself, Bree should have at least suspected. A lump of heavy doubt settled in her chest. She'd been trained to be observant. Her own family, and she'd missed something really important.

She cast a glance at Gowthaman. He was why. Either she was so blinded by her feelings for him she didn't notice other relationships or though happy for others like Jayse and Lucidea, she avoided thinking about those relationships because it hurt. Because she didn't have that connection with Gowtham, that love.

They did have soulfire. He had to at least acknowledge the sparkling gold and crimson swirls of their soulfire.

Silently she slipped from the kitchen. Doubting anyone but Nightshade realized she'd gone, and knowing he wouldn't say anything, she continued to the manor's front door and out across the driveway to the woods beyond. A quick run would clear her mind so she could face the important task ahead. To face the World Between Worlds.

Gowthaman lagged behind as Breanna led her small party toward the outcropping a short distance from the manor. Concern for the rescue party lay like a stone weight in his heart and dragged his footsteps at a slow, contemplative pace. Some vital piece of information had been missed. A key to success. If the team was able to find Morghan and return the prince to this world, his worries would be unfounded.

He tried, but couldn't believe that possibility to be true.

And now the time was upon them. In minutes the waxing gibbous moon would rise, followed in two nights by the full moon. There would be no triple conjunction of blue moons including the human moon for another three hundred years. Not long in a Faerie's lifetime, for he was older than that by two times over. Nor for one of the Alfar-Sindhu race. But the young ones, Jayse, Lucidea, and younger still, Breanna and Chance, had yet to live even the length of one human life span. Without the patience and calming experience of long years, they were eager for action. Perhaps too eager.

His fingers jerked against the journal's leather cover. Here he recorded everything he had discovered about the World Between Worlds, including the incantations needed to open the veil now, and again in two nights to return them to this world. He could do no more.

None of those participating in the rescue had asked him about his experience within the World Between Worlds.

Gowthaman supposed they'd not wanted to cause him increased distress. Or perhaps Breanna had forbidden them to ask. Either way, he was glad. It was difficult enough to face the demons of his past when there were no outside demands, when it was only his own mind he had to fight. He could only hope he had put enough information in the journal. Given more time, he might have been able to organize his notes a cohesive set of instructions and theories for their journey of rescue.

But with less than a handful of days, he'd only been able to record what he thought would be most beneficial. In any case, his memories of the World Between Worlds were as misty and gray as the place itself. At the time of his brief incarceration there, he'd only been aware of the pain and emptiness caused by the witch's rape of his mind. He had not wanted to live, let alone escape from a place that didn't require him to feel. He would have languished there still had not members of Breanna's clan physically returned him to Faerie. Had Breanna not innocently taken his pain that first time...

He stumbled to a halt to watch the backs of those who chose to rip through the veil this night. Breanna walked the narrow, rocky path with calm purpose, her back straight, head held high. She hid her tension well, developing into an excellent leader. Although he did enjoy those rare occasions when her frustration had become too great and she would come to him, tense and irritable, and make him watch old science fiction movies. Fantasy for one who was fantasy. A smile tempted his mouth. She was his fantasy. No, she was his life.

His life. And she was entering a dangerous, unknown place accompanied only by two unseasoned warriors.

Searlait should be with her. The tall Alastriona's duty was to stand at Breanna's side, to guard her back. Searlait knew each varied landscape of the World Between Worlds and the creatures inhabiting those forlorn places. She had protected and encouraged him during his brief time there.

But neither he nor Searlait had ever desired to relive time in the World Between Worlds. Their experiences had never been truly been spoken of between them, only hinted at in vague conversation. Although surprised by the warrior's fear, he understood her inability to face entering the place where she had been imprisoned for so long. Still, he could think of few others he would choose as competent enough to do battle beside Breanna.

He was also surprised by Coralie's firm insistence she be included in the rescue party. The petite Alfar-Sindhu hardly gave the appearance of a warrior. However, Morghan had been her lord, her peoples' ruler before he disappeared. Her manner, an easy gentleness belying great strength, would be a calm, comforting force within the group. She had helped Morghan create the original spells for the first battle with the fire elemental. An altered form of one of those spells would open the veil for them this night.

Coralie paused at the base of the outcropping and glanced toward the horizon. Gowthaman followed her gaze. Only a bare lightening over the distant hills indicated where the moon would rise. Then she hefted her pack loosely over one shoulder and began her assent to the brae's flat crown. Gowthaman frowned, wondering briefly if he should suggest she wear shoes.

Chance followed Coralie, his soft pack bulging. The young man wore a sword at his hip but had also strapped a long, plain scabbard to the pack. Gowthaman studied the leather wrapped grip then the scabbard, calculating the sword's length to be even longer than the weapon Chance attempted training with that morning. Why Breanna's brother carried an extra, awkward weapon hinted at the faulty judgment of an untried warrior.

Although Breanna had exhibited wise decision making in past Alastriona affairs, she had agreed to allow her brother to accompany her on this dangerous mission. Gowthaman watched the young man's broad back. Chance swaggered with the indestructible pride of youth. His skill at weaponry exceeded that of many seasoned Alastriona, but lack of determination and experience showed in his mock battles. This rescue should not be undertaken as a learning experience or a right of passage for the young man. Gowthaman added another failing to his list. He should have reasoned with Breanna about her decision to include Chance.

The others had climbed to the top of the brae but still he held back. Until he accepted the strength of his emotions and the evidence of a soulfire he tried to convince himself he didn't understand, he'd never be able to let Breanna go. If only he had more time. If only he'd told her that afternoon. Warmth still tingled his skin where she had rested against him and slept. Even though hours had passed, the drug-like after effects of the sweet passion in her kiss scalded through his body. He clutched the journal tighter, his knuckles tight with the strain.

From that day when she was but five years old, when she had stated she was going to marry him, she had resided deep in his soul. Now, as a woman, the young girl's innocent love had blossomed, changed, grown. Now, he loved her as that woman.

A shadowy presence spoke from the dense thicket of trees lining the path. "You should have told her long before now."

Knowing Nightshade only voiced the crux of his inner debate, Gowthaman still straightened his back and denied. "Told her what?"

Nightshade stepped from under the cover of the tall trees and shook his head. "You are more a fool than I thought."

Gowthaman took a deep breath and released it slowly. He discovered no anger in response to the man's statement, only acceptance of his own failures. "Perhaps."

"No perhaps about it, honey." Nightshade studied the sky. "Time's short. Coralie is making ready to begin the chant. You've ignored your chance. Again." He glanced back and tapped a hard knuckle against the journal. "You'd best be getting that into Breanna's hands."

"Yes. Of course."

Nightshade stalked up the steep path. Gowthaman heard him mumbling but ignored the words he knew were true. He was a fool. Now, he would pay a price for that foolishness. He started forward deliberately. No, not foolish. Fear-filled. He stumbled, righted himself and continued. He was afraid. Of feeling. Anything. For any person. His thoughts, memories, and emotions had been stolen once and used to endanger an entire family. The clan who had accepted him despite his unwilling part in Feidhlim's planned destruction.

Despite the evidence of soulfire burning his skin, he would not again endanger Breanna by loving her.

A faint glow, reminiscent of reflected flames, shadowed the dips and valleys of the low-lying clouds. The eerie nighttime sky brightened. Clouds parted, revealing a rounded, glowing circumzenithal arc, the lower edge of the nearly full moon.

Bree pressed one hand against the churning in her belly. Her earlier run had calmed her enough she'd been able to gather the team and get them here on time. Still, her mind never ceased working rapidly through her list of mental lists. Any action to bolster her refusal to listen to the insidious little voice claiming there would be no success, that she'd fail, and worse yet, doom the others to remain in the gray.

She reached the outcropping, climbed the steep hill and turned to survey her small team. Jayse had refused to allow Lucidea anywhere near the possible danger of opening the veil. In order to keep her safely in the manor, both he and Tori remained behind as well. Nightshade and Gowthaman would report their successful entry into the World Between Worlds.

Here on the outcropping, Coralie stood calm and silent, staring into the sky, looking as though she was simply out for a stroll on a calm, midsummer evening. Breanna sighed, wishing she could share that calm.

As she expected, her brother bounced on the balls of his feet, filled with nervous energy. His gaze darted toward the moon, around the flat hilltop and over the loch's dark waters. He cocked his head to one side as if listening. Then he closed his eyes, wrinkled his forehead and a flash of pain tightened his features. She was about to cross the rocky path to him when he opened his eyes, blew out a harsh breath and resumed his energetic bouncing.

Whatever demons pursued her brother would have to wait. He seemed in control and she fervently hoped he was. She didn't have the energy to worry about him.

Bree turned toward Coralie. The Alfar-Sindhu nodded.

"'Tis time," Coralie said.

Morghan brushed a shock of hair from his forehead and frowned. Since coming to himself, he'd done little but watch the elemental. He touched his face, feeling the deep furrow between his brows. How long has it been? Days? Months? Mere hours?

He pressed his fingers to his eyes, a firm touch to rub away the confusion. After he blinked, it took a moment for his eyes to focus. No matter how long he remained in this cursed land of gray, he would not return to the confusion. For he had an enemy to watch, an enemy's actions to gage, analyze and ultimately end.

Taking a deep breath he angled one shoulder to rub against the thick gray bark of the tree at his back. A sharp pain stabbed needles into his upper arm and he adjusted the torn strip of cloth he'd wrapped around the bite. 'Twould heal. He gave a soft snort. At least he no longer felt the need to hide his actions from his nemesis. The elemental's magic allowed him to know--Morghan scraped the itchy spot again--to know where Morghan was and what he did.

A foul magic that.

Yet, mayhap it was a good thing, for the magic had given Morghan a sense of knowing as well--when he made the effort to search his mind for the point of intrusion. However, there was little to do in this dry landscape and if maintaining a watch on Brandr Ur would help him focus his thoughts and find a way to defeat the elemental, then watch he would.

Angling onto one buttock, Morghan brushed away a sharp rock then settled again with his back to the tree, his knees bent so his feet rested flat on the ground. He balanced his wrists on his knees and stared across the plain. Brandr Ur sat in a ruined temple on a throne of stone, centered on the rubble-strewn dais. Distending his nostrils, Morghan huffed out a breath.

The distance was not great, so the elemental's face and expressions were clear to him. And puzzling.

If there had been another being before the elemental, Morghan would be convinced Brandr Ur spoke then reacted to a returned bit of conversation.

A shudder crept across Morghan's shoulders. Brandr Ur was speaking to another. Momentarily thankful he wasn't the focus of the elemental's mind-talk, he filled with anger that anyone should have to experience the touch of another within their mind.

Morghan clenched his fists and fell into a memory. He remembered the page he'd found torn from his brother's journal, a single page that spoke of feeling another being invading his mind, of the fear of insanity and hopelessness that drove his brother from their lands. Morghan straightened his fingers, then clenched them again, his ragged nails digging into his palms. He had felt that same invasion. From the same being.

He'd fought the foreign presence there in the false security of his two worlds, and then for a time after he'd been brought here. He frowned. Had the elemental simply ceased invading him, or had he lost enough of himself he had no longer cared? How long had he spent walking in madness, allowing the elemental to manipulate him?

Closing his eyes, he pressed one hand to his belly. Without even the need for food or drink, how did one track the days? He failed to understand how, after his initial hungers had passed, his body had been sustained. He was not dead. This one thing he knew for fact.

How had his people fared during his incarceration? He found a smile at the rediscovered memory of Lucidea's determination that she would not need to rule. Ah, she'd be a fine ruler. He rubbed at the wound. More competent than he, and more willing to accept assistance. Dark thoughts skittered across his memory and a growl rumbled in his throat. If Pagas had done anything to harm Coralie or his new-found niece...

The air surrounding him warmed. Uncomfortably. He blinked to clear the dry air blur from his vision then jerked to his feet.

Leaning forward casually, Brandr Ur sat on a low stone near him. Watching. A faint smile tilted his arrogant lips.

At the sound of a Morghan's second, focused growl, Brandr Ur chuckled. "Relax, child of my descendants. I am not here to fight you. This time." He stared into the distance and Morghan fought the impulse to turn and follow his gaze. Ignoring the elemental, Morghan set his shoulders and searched his memory for words he should know, words his Coralie had given him before for the battle. But the words were hidden from him so he planted his feet firmly in the dry earth, shrugged to release the tightness of his shoulders and fisted his hands in preparation for a physical battle.

"Settle yourself." Brandr Ur curled his lip in a mocking sneer. "I do not deign to fight you at this time." He glanced again into the distance. "Don't you feel it? Are you so dulled the ripples in the veil elude you? Reach out, prince of waters, weak though you are, for you are still blood of my blood. Even your meager abilities should allow you to know that which surrounds you."

Morghan eased his stance. Curious about the elemental's strange behavior, he cocked his head to one side and listened. The elemental smiled and leaned back, crossing his arms and giving a sharp nod.

"Good. Follow the pathway of what you feel, foolish prince. Follow and know the time grows short. We shall join in battle once again before the veil. I shall triumph."

"Ye shall no'."

Brandr Ur's smile widened. Heat pressed against Morghan, burning his cheeks, flushing the skin of his forearms, burying coals of pain deep in the jagged wound. He refused to move, to show any reaction to the elemental's attack. Lifting his chin he bared his teeth. "Fight me, blood of my blood. Now."

After a moment of strained silence, Brandr Ur broke into laughter. Gasping, he pointed his finger at Morghan and spoke between harsh breaths. "You... amuse... me. Perhaps I... should... not destroy... you."

"If ye do no', ken ye this, I shall destroy ye. I have no qualms in killin' ye now. Ye will die."

"No. I will survive and you will die. Eventually. Perhaps I should keep you temporarily, for you lighten my day."

Flexing his hands, Morghan strained, angling his upper body toward his foe. "I shall lighten yer head from yer shoulders, like ye had done to m' brother. Yers would be a more fitting sacrifice to my mind."

Brandr Ur waved one hand in dismissal. A vision popped into Morghan's head, blazing with the heat and crackle of invisible flames. He saw himself bound by a chain wrapped thrice around one ankle. A multi-tipped cap sat low on his head, the bright colors burning to vision accustomed to the gray.

Brandr Ur lounged upon a velvet-lined, gilded throne, twirling the free end of the chain. He spoke. "Pagas did not wish to entertain me. He saw no glory in such a position at my side. You, blood of my blood. How say you?"

Tearing the belled cap from his head, Morghan shouted, "I will no' be toyed with, ye pretender god."

"Pretender god?" Brandr Ur lay one hand on his chest. Then he rose, stretching to his full height and tugged the chain until Morghan sprawled at his feet. "There is no pretense in me, prince. I shall return to the god-form I held so long ago, return and claim my true place. The place you and your kind denied me." He tossed the chain to the side and gave Morghan his back. "Get up, fool. I came to you this day to give you the opportunity to worship me. Not that I believed you would."

The elemental, the throne, the chain disappeared. Morghan opened his eyes to the muted landscape, and Brandr Ur's back as he stalked away. But the elemental's voice echoed still in his head.

::Remember my words, blood of my blood. Listen. Feel. I think you may be pleased with the happenings. Or... perhaps not. Either way, I will not again stand before you until the night of my liberation. Two nights, prince. Two nights for you to use as you will, until one way or another... you are mine.::

Sudden silence brought Morghan no comfort, for the elemental's words confused him. What should he listen for? There was never anything new, nothing worth listening for. Yet, in the silence, a vibration tickled the back of his neck. He chased the tickle with his palm and turned from Brandr Ur's valley. The awareness crawled over his scalp to the center of his forehead, drawing him toward his own claimed area of the World Between Worlds. Listening to a hum building in the air, he allowed the pull to move him forward. The hum called to him in familiar, dulcet tones. He paused, shook his head but couldn't clear the rising chant from his mind. Someone was...

"Nay," he cried. "Nay ye must no'." Panic rose with sour bile in his throat, strangling the breath from his lungs. His heart pounded a ragged, staccato beat. The cold sweat of dread coated his skin and he shivered. "Coralie, ye must no'," he choked out. "Do no'!"

Finding strength in his fear, he ran.

Sixteen

The trio gazed at each other in silent communication before Chance and Breanna moved behind Coralie to form a loose triangle. Gowthaman eased closer to Breanna. She acknowledged him with a faint smile when pressed the journal into her hands. "I'll bring this back safely to you."

He ached to shout, to cry to the rising moon he didn't care if the book were lost, torn to shreds, disintegrated. He didn't care about a book. He cared about her safety, her return. To him. Instead he swallowed heavily and said, "I know."

They stood, hands touching over the leather cover. He knew she was distracted, her mind racing to make sure she'd discovered and dealt with every conceivable contingency. Say something. Tell her. "Breanna? I..."

Expression clear, she focused her bright blue eyes on him. Words stalled in his throat. His declaration of love would potentially be another burden for her to carry into an already too dangerous mission. He couldn't. Tell her.

Coralie's low chant flowed with increasing intensity and a musical trill. He curled his fingers around Breanna's, lifting one of her hands from the journal. She held the book close to her chest with the other hand and tilted her head in question.

Tell her. Coward. Yes, he was a coward. Looking into her beautiful eyes he sighed then spoke in a whisper. "Be safe."

With another of her soft, sad smiles, Breanna leaned closer and pressed her warm lips to his cheek. Heat burned through him and a brief spasm tightened his hand around hers. All he needed to do was turn his face, take possession of her lips and kiss her as he had before. As she was meant to be kissed. A simple act to show her the strength of his love.

"We will," she whispered then turned away and his opportunity dissolved.

Wind tossed the surrounding branches with a cacophony of creaks and rustling. Breanna took a step forward, tightening the triangle. Her heart thumped with heavy doubt and sadness. She should have told Gowthaman how much she loved him... at least one more time. The empty cold at her back told her he had moved away, back to the safety of this world. Caressing the leather journal, still warm from his hands, was a way to hold him close to her heart. When they returned, she'd make sure he knew exactly how important he was to her. She shook her head as old movie lines sang a countermelody to Coralie's chant. ...is another day... just a day away... always tomorrow.

Please, let there be a tomorrow for us.

With the strength of will she'd seldom had need to call upon, Breanna tucked away her love and concerns to focus on her companions. Whether it was because of Coralie's chant or some other force from beyond the veil, fierce, windy blasts kicked up waves on the normally placid loch. A faint, lighter patch of gray expanded in the darkness, hovering low over the water. Mist swirled in spirals within that gray, parting then closing in a silent, mesmerizing dance. Each time the spirals parted the mist the faint opening grew larger, closer.

She gasped as though the air was being sucked from her lungs. Forces pulled at her, drawing her closer to the veil, tugging on her heart and lungs. It hurt to breathe.

Breanna glanced at her brother. Appearing unaffected by the forces manipulating her, Chance continued to bounce on the balls of his feet, eager and ready to go. His face had settled into that odd, listening expression but his eyes were focused on the veil.

Coralie's chant continued, whispering past her lips, yet raging over the loch to the veil, bringing the swirling mist closer still. Her eyes were fierce and intent, but the softness of a smile remained on her lips.

An echoing roll of rumbling thunder crashed across the loch. With a grinding rip the fabric between worlds rent asunder, spilling the mist and dead silence over them. Coralie's chant dissolved into the silence and she lowered her arms.

"'Tis time. Go."

Breanna took a deep breath and counted to five slowly as she released the air from her lungs. The edges of the narrow disturbance fluctuated, rippling with the wind, but the opening remained stable. Taking a step to the side, she bumped shoulders with Chance.

"Ready?"

"You know it."

"On the other side then?"

He tilted her a smile and sketched a mock salute. "The other side, sis."

Hand gripped tightly around his sword hilt, Chance leaned back on one foot then leapt forward, easily clearing the few feet between the edge of the brae and the hovering opening. In the space of a breath, his hand appeared at through the veil, giving the signal it was safe for the others to cross.

Coralie touched Breanna's hand, nodded then followed Chance's leap, slipping through the tattered opening. The hem of her skirt fluttered briefly in Scotland's clear air before disappearing into the World Between Worlds.

Breanna waited a few seconds watching the steady sway of the opening then glanced back at Gowthaman. Silently she sent him a message filled with hope and her abiding love.

His stricken expression faded and in its place he offered her an encouraging smile. Had he felt her thoughts, or was he merely sending her off with his hard won encouragement? She held fast to the thought he'd understood her message of love, clasped the journal, fought to keep from closing her eyes and leapt.

Hands steadied her when she stumbled forward on hard, rocky ground. Straightening, she turned in a slow circle. Searlait had explained the gray of the World Between Worlds, but the words hardly prepared her for the utter lack of color. Even the clothing they wore had faded to a drab camouflage of gray. She spread her hands and looked down at herself wondering if she looked the same to the others as she did to herself.

Breaking the heavy silence, Chance cleared his throat and asked, "Sis? Where's Gowthaman's book?"

The book? She'd held the journal tightly in her hand when she jumped through the veil. Whipping around, she stared back at the narrow opening. The veil hadn't totally repaired itself and she peered through the thickening membrane to the human world.

"Oh no," she cried. Behind the gauze-like veil the thin leather journal lay on the scuffed ground at the rocky edge of the outcropping. She took one step forward.

Chance clutched her arm. "Why'd you leave it?"

"I didn't." Breanna pushed against the world-separating veil with one hand. Like a rubbery balloon, the membrane bulged outward at her touch, but she couldn't break through. The more she fought against the force, the more the magic thickened and pushed back.

"Ye'll no' be able to get through. 'Tis said to be part of the punishment--to be able to see but no' escape."

Bree leaned her shoulder into the solidifying mist but turned her face toward Coralie. The Alfar-Sindu gnawed on her thumbnail, an action Bree found strangely disconcerting. Bree straightened. "We're not being punished, Coralie."

"Aye, I ken. 'Twas just somethin' Morghan said afore he no longer could reach me in my dreams. Forgive me. 'Twas no' important."

Slapping her hands against her side Breanna voiced her frustration. "No, it's not. How am I going to get Gowthaman's book? I don't remember everything he told us. What if I do something wrong? How will we get back?"

Chance curled his fingers painfully into her shoulders and turned her to face the veil again. "Bree... look."

Gowthaman closed his eyes a second before Breanna entered the World Between Worlds. He couldn't bear to witness her disappearing into the gray nothingness. She was too vibrant, too alive to be trapped there. His heart was breaking.

Nightshade clasped his shoulder in a firm gesture of support. Unable to look at the edge of the outcropping Gowthaman turned away before opening his eyes. He would wait there on the hilltop until she returned in two night's time. Longer if need be. No matter how long it took.

"Something's wrong," Nightshade stated in a harsh whisper.

"No." Gowthaman jerked, turned and took a single step toward the thin veil. Shadows moved on the other side, the forms of those who had just passed through. But the veil had almost completely healed itself. He moved closer and tripped over a loose object.

He frowned at the obstruction then widened his eyes in disbelief. His journal. Why had Breanna dropped the journal? Did she not understand she needed the information recorded there, information he had not the time to impart to her? Echoing cries of anguish filled his brain yet somehow he kept from voicing his pain to the darkness. She had to have the journal.

With Nightshade at his back, he moved as close to the edge of the brae and the still swirling pattern of the veil as he dared. Four feet of empty space separated him from the magical portal. Striving for objectivity, he studied the churning mass of gray. The opening was closing in upon itself, healing the tear. But he could see through the World Between Worlds, at least well enough to recognize Breanna standing just on the other side, her hands outstretched, pressing against that unforgiving fabric.

A tiny flash of relief stole his breath. She was trying to reach through, trying to get back, to retrieve the journal. He bent, grabbed the slim volume and held it out. Leaning precariously over the cliff edge, he pressed the book against the thin, swirling fabric of the veil. There was no give, no indication anyone or anything had recently passed through.

A low growl of panicked frustration rumbled in his throat and he leaned into the book. One foot slipped off the loose rock. Nightshade wrapped his hand in the back of

Gowthaman's shirt preventing him from falling into the dark loch. When Nightshade pulled him back, he violently shrugged off the other man's hands and stretched forward again, willing the book to slip into the World Between Worlds.

At the other side of the veil Breanna attacked the barrier with her sword, but when he flattened his palm against the spot not even a single vibration indicated her hits. Renewing his determination with a curse, he shoved the journal against the unyielding veil.

Nightshade grasped his arm and yanked him away. "That's no good, man."

He shook with combined fury and anguish. He slapped journal with the flat of his hand. "They need this. They won't be able to get Morghan... to get home. Breanna..."

"The World Between Worlds will not accept your journal."

Gowthaman jerked away and glared at the vague gray patch in the night air. Their magic had been constructed so that this simple evidence of the veil should remain in place for two days, allowing the party to return after Morghan was found. If they succeeded in opening the veil before Morghan was with them or before the appointed time, the next chance for rescue wouldn't come for over three hundred years. Breanna didn't know of his suspicions. "I have to get this to her. It's imperative. I couldn't tell her everything."

"Think, Gowthaman." Nightshade took a step sideways and peered at the veil. "They aren't fighting the magic any-more. They understand they can't open the veil again for two days. If they come back now to try and get your book, their mission has failed."

"It will fail anyway and we'll lose them. They need this." Gowthaman shook the journal at Nightshade. "Don't you understand--"

"I understand. And I understand that the World Between Worlds has rejected your notebook. You need to accept the alternative."

"There is no alter..."

Nightshade stood with his arms crossed over his chest, speculation filling his face.

"Alternative." Gowthaman dropped his journal and stared at the splayed pages. "Yes, there is one alternative."

"You know what you have to do."

Gowthaman winced at the powerful conviction in Nightshade's voice. "I know," he retorted with a strange rise of righteous anger, then repeated softly, "I know."

If the journal was ejected by the World Between Worlds, there was only one way for Breanna to have all the information contained on the linen pages. Only one way.

He would have to follow her... into the World Between Worlds.

"Hurry, man," Nightshade urged. "The opening is gone, but the veil looks thinner there in the lower left edge of the swirl. No time to think. Go."

If he stopped to think, he would not be able to face his fear. Gowthaman bent and found the area Nightshade indicated. Even if the veil allowed, there would be barely enough space to crawl through. The area shrank as he hesitated.

"Move."

He bristled at Nightshade's order then focused the anger into momentum. Bending low, he aimed for the last bit of thinned veil, held his hands before him like a diver and jumped. The membrane-like surface stretched. His legs flailed in the open air. Spray from the wave covered loch chilled his skin. He was falling. He had failed.

Smooth suction held his arms and shoulders in place, keeping him suspended above the dark water. Then the membrane flowed down his back, sucking at his skin. Solid gray formed beneath him and he crawled forward as the veil sealed behind him.

A slight, moist pop sounded when he pulled his foot free. Curled into a ball with his eyes closed, Gowthaman collapsed on the gray, dusty earth of the World Between Worlds.

Nightshade tapped Gowthaman's journal thoughtfully. He took a step back from the drop off at the edge of the brae and watched the swirling clouds settle into little more than a misty blur in the night sky. For good or for ill, four people now faced an unforgiving world, a little known foe, and those things, known and unknown each held within themselves. He scrubbed a hand over his face. If the few tales he'd heard of the World Between Worlds were true, the principle battles would be those waged within.

Shaking off the feeling that by not giving in to the protective impulse to jump after Breanna he had somehow missed a strange opportunity, Nightshade turned back to the manor. Those waiting there would be anxious to hear how the night's events culminated.

Even though Jayse and Lucidea expected an immediate, full report, he ambled along the path. The electric buzz skimming the back of his neck when the veil was open disappeared and he knew the magical portal was gone. In two nights he would join the others here on the brae and wait for the rescue party's return.

"Be safe, baby girl. Don't make Nightshade have to tell your folks you're gone."

He ran his thumb along the edge of the journal. Gowthaman was stronger than the librarian thought himself. The rescue party would be fine. Bree and Gowthaman would be fine. Maybe this was the kick needed to bring baby girl the happiness she deserved.

Yet, with that hopeful thought hovered a measure of dread.

Nightshade paused at the edge of the loch and stared across the surface of the black water. Few bright stars reflected and danced upon the water, adding to his unease. Like those who entered the World Between Worlds, his most diabolical enemy was himself. And his past.

He'd grown tired of this incarnation of Nightshade. While his old friends Derrik and Tommy had never questioned him, he saw a wealth of inquiries in their granddaughter's eyes. This time, Breanna wasn't going to let go until she knew the answers, until she really knew him.

Perhaps it was time. He snorted back a dry chuckle. Time to come out of yet another closet.

"Nightshade, that you?"

The subtle command in Jayse's voice reminded Nightshade of his brother. He smiled despite the memories crowding to the forefront of his mind. Tonight, at least, there was no time for memories. He had important news for Jayse and Lucidea.

"You know it is, honey."

"Everything... okay?"

That was a loaded question. "Give me a moment, honey. I'll tell you everything there is to know."

"Lucidea's--"

"Impatient?"

"Understatement."

Nightshade sauntered into the circle of light highlighting the manor's front door. Jayse stood under the deep overhang, his pose casual, his expression intense. His gaze darted past Nightshade's shoulder. "Where's Gowthaman?"

Nightshade remained silent.

Shaking his head in disbelief, Jayse said, "He's not going to sit up there on the hill until they get back, is he?"

"Worse than that, honey. Or, maybe better."

"I don't have time nor patience for your word games, Shade."

Nightshade clasped him on the shoulder. "Then let's go inside and I'll tell everyone all about it."

Lucidea rushed forward as soon as they entered the family room, then hung on Jayse's arm while she stared silently at Nightshade, expectation glowing in her eyes. Tori hovered slightly behind them reminding him of the trio opening the veil. He smiled, unable to make them wait any longer.

Sinking onto an overstuffed chair, he waved one hand. "Coralie experienced no difficulty in calling the veil then opening it. Although, their access point didn't remain open and accessible as long as we'd hoped. They all got through just fine. I could see them, dimly, like through a fog, for a short time before the veil closed off completely."

Lucidea perched on the ottoman. "Did they have any trouble getting through?"

"The veil opened, oh, maybe four feet from the cliff edge of the hill so they had to make a jump. No problem for any of them."

"Any... any sign of Morghan?"

"Not that I could tell, honey. But then, I could only see about six feet into the World Between Worlds. And that not clearly."

She leaned against Jayse when he sat beside her. "I know. I was just hoping this whole thing would be easy. You know. He'd be standing there waiting and they could turn right around and come back without waiting the two nights. That would have been good."

"That it would, honey. That it would."

Lost in their own thoughts, they fell silent. Until Tori leaned over the back of Nightshade's chair. "What did you do with Gowthaman?"

"I did nothing with the man except encourage him to admit his feelings to Bree." Wishing that answer would suffice, Nightshade held his breath for a few seconds then shook his head. "Didn't work. However, more significantly, when Bree crossed into the World Between Worlds, his journal remained in this world."

"Explain."

Nightshade cocked his head at Jayse's peremptory tone then continued. "Gowthaman gave her the journal just before she made her leap. She had it tight in her hand. Once she was through, the journal lay on the ground in this world. Gowthaman attempted to shove it through to her, but the spell was breaking down and the veil repairing itself. Even if it had been open wide, I don't believe the journal would have passed through."

"Any idea why not?" Jayse asked.

"I'm afraid, my darlings, that I do not. I'm sure you must all realize how frantic our good librarian became when his knowledge was denied to the woman he loves."

"So what happened?" Tori touched the journal, disrupting the delicate balance where he'd rested it on his thigh.

"He went through."

Jayse frowned. "Gowthaman? Through what?"

Nightshade leaned forward. "Gowthaman, despite his fears, knew the team needed information he'd not had the time to give them. Information compiled only in his journal, and in his brain. So despite his fears, Gowthaman forced his way through the closing veil and into the World Between Worlds."

"Oh my God," Lucidea stammered. "What if being there really snaps his control, his mind. What if..."

"Don't be borrowing trouble, honey. There's more to Gowthaman than we realize." Nightshade chuckled. "And definitely more to him than he knows."

"Still..."

"He'll be fine. They will all be fine. And back home with us in two night's time." The determination in Jayse's words was a balm to the worry binding Nightshade's heart. With luck, the mission would be a success. But he wouldn't trust only to luck.

"So, my darlings, we have two days and nights to prepare ourselves for their triumphant return. I suggest we leave nothing to chance on this side of the veil."

"So, Shade," Jayse rose and stretched before offering his hand to his wife. "What do we do?"

Easing to his feet, Nightshade held up Gowthaman's journal. "I don't know about you, honey, but I've got some reading to do."

Breanna's warmth kneeled beside him. Gowthaman flattened his hands against the crumbly earth. He would find the strength to function, to serve this mission with the best of his knowledge and ability. He curled his fingers capturing dirt against his palms. And if he died in this place, at least he would be at her side. Cool fingers brushed his forehead.

He rolled to his back, took a deep breath and opened his eyes. Flat and cloudless, the gray sky showed only the barest hint of a sun--or moon. No more than he expected. He shook his head, reprimanding himself. No, not what he had expected. The other time, when he'd wished to remain, he had been held in an area Searlait later explained was reserved for judgment, a place of swirling mists and a mind-shrouding fog.

He had been told there was variety in the World Between Worlds. Not of color, but of landscapes, as if the area had once been a world itself, then was blown apart to fill the gaps between other universes. He knew that. But had still expected, and perhaps hoped, for the Watcher's fog.

Even dulled by the odd gray coloring, Breanna's face was beautiful when she filled his vision, blocking the sky. "Gowtham?" she asked softly and brushed the hair from his forehead. "Why did you follow us?"

Unable to bear the strange, frightened light in her eyes, he turned his head to stare at Coralie's bare feet and Chance's well-worn athletic shoes. He chuckled at the contrast then caught the laughter at the back of his throat to contain a rise of hysteria. Pushing against the ground, he sat.

"Gowtham? Are you... okay?"

He could not lie to her again. He closed his eyes. "No, I am not. But, I will survive."

"Why?" Hesitantly, she cupped his cheek and he pressed against her palm. The simple contact was a balm to the churning of his mind, the pounding of his heart. He choked back another rise of laughter. She asked why he had followed them? She knew, she had seen their soulfire as well as he. Yet, she needed the words. In all honesty, so did he.

"I love you."

The thick air muffled the sounds of the others shuffling away. Breanna's hand trembled and he lifted his hand to cover hers. Even though her crystal blue eyes now shone a light gray, the sparkle of tears hovered on darker lashes. "Why now? Oh, Gowtham, why now? I know. I've always known. And you know how much I love you. You should have waited, told me when we get home. Not put yourself through..." She waved her hand vaguely indicating their surroundings. "Through this."

"No, I could not. You do not have the journal. You do not know all you need to understand. Perhaps all you need to do to come home safely. I could not leave you here. I could not allow this place to take you from me." He touched his forehead. "You need what I hold here. No fear, no... place, could keep me from providing..."

She'd leaned back, her smile growing and he paused, wondering at her reaction.

"You finally said you love me."

Gowthaman stared to one side, the rocky terrain undulating into the distance until it faded into a gray haze. He was unable to determine a horizon. "Yes," he said simply.

"This is gonna sound like some movie line, but you picked a fine time."

"I know." He risked a glance at her then was unable to turn away. Joy radiated from her, even in the drab surroundings, she sparkled. For him. Humbled, he lowered his gaze.

"Look at me, Gowtham."

Slowly, he lifted his head.

"Do you regret your words?" Her expression had grown sad. He could not bear the loss of her joy.

"I do not. I love you, Breanna." Lifting both hands, he invited her into his embrace. She accepted his touch, accepted him. He did not understand how, or why, but she did. Perhaps questioning was no longer necessary.

They held each other and he drew strength from her acceptance, from the soft assurances muttered close to his ear and from the power of his own love for the glorious woman she was.

He opened his eyes, meaning to draw back slightly before kissing her. Not far distant, clambering over a towering cairn of boulders, a figure rushed toward them.

The abrupt stiffness in Gowtham's body alerted Bree to danger at the same moment Chance said, "Sis, someone's coming."

The harsh whisper jerked her into action and she drew her sword as she rose and turned. Gowthaman scrambled to his feet and she moved slightly in front of him. Her gentle love had no weapon, but no foe would ever reach him as long as she lived. Chance moved in, shoulder to shoulder to indicate his readiness, then took a step sideways to give her room. She'd trained him well. Coralie eased next to Gowthaman, a long dagger held comfortably in her hand.

"Chance, watch behind us."

"No worries." He angled to easily shift his focus in either direction. Gowthaman moved parallel to Chance, watching their other flank. Satisfied with their reactions, Bree focused on the advancing man.

Once past the rocks, the intruder slowed and his shoulders drooped. He eased his arms from his sides, palms facing them, showing he held no weapons. He paced steadily forward, his expression hidden by a shock of hair falling over his face.

"Oh," Coralie gasped and shoved past Bree then paused, leaning forward on her toes. Both Bree and Chance reached for her, but she shook them off, dropped her dagger and shot forward.

Skirt snapping behind her, she ran, leaping into the man's arms. They twirled in a circle until he lowered her, held her face between his hands and kissed her.

"Must be Morghan," Chance stated dryly.

Morghan tore his lips from hers and stared into the brilliant depths of Coralie's eyes. He dropped his hands to her shoulders and gave her a slight shake. "Ye should no' have come here."

Silent, she smiled at him and tilted her head. Ah how he'd loved that angle, that perfectly kissable position. Unable to resist, he bent again to kiss her, dancing his tongue along the softness of her inner lip, losing himself in the sensual memory. This could not be one of the visions of his madness. She was too real, too warm, too much his sweet Coralie.

"Eudail," he groaned when he could put any distance between them.

"Morghan," she sighed and nestled against him, her cheek resting over the pounding of his heart. "Really 'tis ye, at last."

"Ye should no' be here."

She smiled up at him. "An' where then should I be?"

"Safe. As ye were. Safe."

Her smile broadened. "An' safe I shall be, with ye when we return home."

How could he tell her he could not return? Not with the elemental's continued threats. Now that he was himself again, he would no' let Brandr Ur pass the veil into any other world. In doing so, he knew he would be destroyed as well. But death was a better fate for him than failure. After all this time, he could no' tell Coralie such things.

"How long?"

Coralie drew her lower lip between her teeth and watched him a moment. Did she see the madness lingering in him?

"A bit over twenty human years."

"Ah. I could no' tell the passage of time once the elemental destroyed the water an' I could no' longer talk to ye."

She nodded. "I ken. Has been longer than long for me. An' I could no longer wait. 'Twill be longer still afore another opportunity rises with the full moons. So we came for ye now."

Morghan's heart lurched. Not only was she here, but others as well. Must his failings always include innocents?

"I could no' be here without them, so have no concerns for them. They will help us open the veil in two nights an' we shall all go home."

He'd witnessed the protectiveness of these others when they gathered before Coralie, then attempted to keep her from running to him. Mayhap there was a chance. He strained to see through the haze distorting the short distance. "I do no' recognized these warriors."

"Nay, an' ye would no'. The young man was no' even born when ye... came here. The woman is his sister, an' the leader of warriors called Alastriona."

"The name is no' familiar."

"An' now, do I ken somethin' that ye do no'?" She chuckled and Morghan gave in to his need and drew her close for a breath-stealing kiss. When he released her, she trailed her tongue across the fullness of her lower lip but stepped back before he could catch her to him again. "There will be time for us later, milord."

He lifted one eyebrow and her cheeks blushed a deeper gray. At that moment, he hated this World Between Worlds with a ferocity that startled him. All because he ached to see the pink rising in her cheeks, and the sparkle in her sea-green eyes.

She took his hand. "Remember how Lucidea understood the concept of parallel worlds?"

How could he have forgotten Lucidea? "How fares m' niece? Our people?"

Coralie nodded to herself, as if satisfied with something he'd said. Then she answered, "Lucidea is well. Her mate would no' allow her to join us in yer rescue because she carries a child within her."

"A child? Happy and blessed is the Sindhu who--"

She laughed, the sound seeming to lighten the gray around him. "Oh, 'tis no Sindhu who caught her love. An' afore ye say anythin', no human either. But one of another race, of another world parallel to the humans. A world they call Faerie."

He cast her a skeptical look.

"An' milord Jayse is ruler of his folk as Lucidea is of ours. An' half human as well. The three ye see there are of his race."

"I do no'--"

Coralie tugged on his hand to lead him toward the trio closely watching him. "Come, Morghan. I shall introduce ye. Two nights lie afore us, then we will be able to open the veil an' go home. There shall be time enough for tales until then."

He remained solidly planted so she turned back and caressed his face. "Come now, my love, Air mo shon."

For my sake. Words, spoken in a loving whisper, he could not refuse. Hand in hand, they crossed the plain then stood before the others. The two blondes grinned at him, but the darker man's expression was contained and neutral. Morghan recognized something in the man's eyes, a reflection of himself, of thoughts he didn't wish to examine. The man's expression altered and a flash of surprise settled into acknowledgement.

Coralie released his hand. Emptiness returned to bind his soul. Then she touched his arm and life flooded through him. He'd been so dead here. And now he was alive, all because of his treasure, his Coralie. He smiled at her then turned his smile on the others.

Coralie inched closer as though she couldn't resist touching him. Good, for he never wanted her to stop. Never again would he let her go.

"If ye have no' guessed, this is Morghan."

Back pressed against a smooth, tall boulder, Gowthaman watched Chance start a small fire of gray wood. The tiny flame rose, trailing a thin wisp of smoke. Intellectually, he knew the World Between Worlds stole the colors from life, but he was still startled by a flame snapping and crackling the dry wood in shades of gray. He chuckled and Bree turned worried eyes on him.

He indicated their location with a wave of his arm. "Do you remember the comedy you encouraged me to watch, about the legend of a doctor creating a man from parts of others?"

Her brows drew together. "Yes?"

He touched his chest then held his hand out and waggled his fingers. "Do we do not look the same as the actors in that movie?"

Chance elbowed Breanna. "Hey, that's cool, Gowthaman. We can just pretend we're in an old black and white movie. And you were worried about him." The young man moved away to rummage through his pack.

Bold words Gowthaman didn't believe. His observation had not been made to make their surroundings more acceptable, though if that were a benefit of his words, then so be it. But he had not spoken to ease the others. He had spoken the outrageous thoughts to keep from sinking into the depths of his frozen mind.

Breanna continued to watch him with cautious concern. He wanted to smile, to reassure her, but from the tightening of her expression realized he'd failed. What grimace had he given her, how much had he been unable to conceal?

Looking down at his hands, he forced himself to relax the tight curl of his fingers. Even if he were successful in hiding his emotions from the others, Breanna would know. She'd always known. Perhaps... no, he shook his head... that was one of the things he loved about her. One of the many things.

The others gathered around the small fire so he rose to join them, sitting by Breanna and earning her terse smile. She leaned close to whisper, "I'm glad Morghan found us so soon. It gives Coralie more time with him."

"She kept the depth of her feelings well hidden until recently." He understood how difficult that could be. Although perhaps containing the outward evidence of love was simpler when the object of one's affection was not often close. Now Coralie happily let her love shine.

A knot, a jealous tightening in his chest made him look away and focus again on his hands. He had admitted his love to Breanna, but he could not yet show that love before the others. Lost in a fresh litany of failings, he listened half-heartedly to the conversation around the fire.

"Ye really did no' need a fire," Morghan stated. "An' now that ye are here, ye will no' need the food ye carried with ye."

Coralie made a tsking sound and set a battered metal pot near the flame. "So it may be, but we decided to maintain a normal routine. An' I must heat water to cleanse the wound on yer arm."

Morghan covered the dirty strip of cloth with one hand. "'Twill heal without yer fussin'. Like everythin' else here, there be no need."

Coralie held out a gauze bandage, keeping the roll steady until he took it from her. With a soft smile, she untied the cloth and washed the nearly healed bite. When she finished her ministrations she said, "Even bein' here only two days, we did no' wish to chance the doldrums affectin' us. Too much is at stake. With all of us together, we shall keep our sense of reality and purpose intact." She smiled at Morghan, then reached out to cup the side of his face with her palm.

"Then normal we shall be. Ye did no' happen to bring--"

Chance held up a crinkly, cellophane bag. "Coffee?"

Gowthaman found a grin for the Sindhu's obvious delight.

"Although, it is instant," Chance continued.

"'Tis no matter. I... Oh, for a few moments..."

Breanna reached into her pack and handed around energy bars. "I'd like to talk about what's going to happen when it's time to leave."

Gowthaman drew a deep breath. This was why he was here.

Morghan nodded. "Ye shall do what ye need to do an' return to where ye belong. I must remain to prevent the elemental from followin'."

"Brandr Ur," Breanna stated flatly.

"Aye. Even here territory is important. While I chose this patch of inhospitable ground as m' own, he had chosen a much grander place a short distance from here."

"Then we should post a guard."

Morghan shook his head. "Nay, I dinna believe 'tis necessary. He said--"

"And you trust him?" Chance exploded.

Gowthaman focused on the young man, curious at the force of his outburst. A note of fear tainted Chance's bravado though he glared boldly at Morghan.

"Water's ready," Coralie stated calmly. "I can offer ye coffee, or tea."

Chance's shoulders dropped and he spread the finger of one hand, offering a half-hearted, "Sorry."

Breanna released a slow breath. She dug in her pack then held out a plastic mug. "Thanks, Coralie. Coffee for me." After she sent silent thanks for diffusing her brother's odd behavior, Coralie glanced up and winked. Bree could swear there were times the soft-spoken woman read her mind. Shouldn't surprise her, each of them around the fire held secrets and magics the others knew nothing about. Her brother's secrets... She held back a sigh. She needed to make time for him.

Later. Everything was always later. She needed a good dose of now.

Morghan made a contented, satisfied sound in his throat and lowered his mug. "Ah, nectar of the gods. I had forgotten."

Bree let everyone enjoy the warm beverages in silence. When the contents of her own mug were half gone, she straightened and began laying out the plans for their return to the human world.

Eighteen

"Uh, sis," Chance interrupted an hour later.

Frustration huffed the breath from her lungs and she turned to Chance with a scowl. Although Morghan had long showed signs of wanting to end their discussion, undoubtedly to allow him to slip away with Coralie--not that she blamed either of them--but there was so much more she needed to know. "What?"

Chance blinked then squared his shoulders and set his chin defiantly. "You'd better take a look at Gowthaman." Then his eyebrows rose and he jerked his head toward the spot where Gowthaman had moved away from the fire. She'd felt him drawing away mentally, long before he physically left her side.

Setting his mug on the ground, Morghan leaned forward. "He has been here afore." Not a question, an astute observation.

Bree paused a moment before answering. "Yes. Actually, twice. But only in a place where there was no landscape, no anything but gray mist. He's never said much about the experience."

With a single nod Morghan eyed the space behind her with frank speculation filling his expression. "An' he followed ye. Despite his fear."

Heat filled her face, and Chance chuckled. "They'd follow each other anywhere. But neither of them will admit it."

Morghan lifted Coralie's hand and kissed her fingertips. "I ken. Ah, how well I ken. I ken as well how he fights his feelin's an' fear of this place." He stretched forward until his face hovered close to the fire and lowered his voice. "I also ken he needs ye."

Startled at the intensity of Morghan's statement and prepared to deny his words, Bree sat back. But Coralie caught her attention, rose gracefully and motioned to that same spot behind Bree.

"'Tis been a long day, an' night. I need... rest." The look she gave Morghan spoke blatantly of other needs. Morghan returned her look with equal passion and stood, gathering her close to his side.

"Aye, a rest, my sweet love. Even I must rest." He tucked a strand of Coralie's curls behind her ear, fingers lingering at her hairline.

Coralie's eyes opened wide with mock innocence. "I have somethin' else for ye, milord."

He winced at the honorific then cocked his head to one side. "Do ye now, eudail?"

Holding his gaze, she crouched and pulled a large plastic bottle from her pack. Morghan peered at her curiously while she slowly twisted the cap. She held the open bottle under his nose.

He inhaled and his eyelids drifted closed. "Seaflowers."

"Aye."

"Ye brought water from the loch."

"Aye."

Breanna couldn't help but grin at the sparkle in Coralie's eyes, as if stars twinkled there. The intimate moment twisted in her heart and she ducked her head. She would never begrudge Coralie any happiness she and Morghan could find in this dismal place, for they'd been waiting a long time. Bree understood waiting.

"Come," Morghan said softly. "Shall we find then a place for our rest?" After Coralie's suddenly shy nod, he turned to Breanna. Heat and the twinkle of stars lingered in his eyes as well and she wondered at the possibilities.

"'Tis safe enough, an' we shall no' be far." Morghan's gaze drifted toward Gowthaman then back to her. "Another secluded grotto lies in that direction, should ye need... privacy."

Although his comment should have embarrassed her, there was something in his tone that redirected her thoughts toward serious matters.

Morghan and Coralie slipped between a pair of towering stone pillars. Bree took a deep breath then Chance touched her arm. "Really, Bree. Gowthaman needs you."

She shook her head. "Maybe, but that doesn't mean--"

"Stop right there. Don't say anything." Chance poked her shoulder. "You haven't even looked at him in the past half hour. He. Needs. You. Now. I'm going to keep watch. Despite what Morghan says, I'm not trusting that the elemental won't try something."

The increasingly familiar distracted look crossed his expression when he paused to take a breath, but cleared rapidly. "No, I'm going to keep watch anyway."

"Okay, I think that's a good idea. If you want to take the first--"

He poked her shoulder. One jab punctuated each word. "Gowthaman. Needs. You.",

She grabbed his finger and twisted.

"Ow. Geez, sis. Turn around and see for yourself. I'll be..."
He pointed back over his shoulder. "Up on that ridge."

After an indecipherable grimace, he turned, scooped up his
pack and both swords and stalked away. Bree watched him as
he climbed the ridge and settled into the shadows of the rocky
ledge. Then, bracing her scattered emotions, she turned.

Knees drawn tight to his chest, Gowthaman sat unnaturally
still just beyond the reach of the firelight. No, she amended,
not still. He rocked nearly imperceptibly in the gray night.
Arms locked around his legs, spine arched until his forehead
pressed to his knees, the man she loved suffered in the bonds
of mental torment.

How much had she contributed to his pain? After he had
spoken of love, she had turned to other matters and purposely
ignored him.

"Oh, Gowthaman."

Even lost in memories, Gowthaman knew the moment
Breanna turned her attention to him, but it was too late. No
longer could he restrain the powerful images or fight the rush
of the past. Emotions and events he'd forced himself to for-
get--as much as he was able--demanded his attention. All
now. All powerful. All agonizing.

If he could have moved away, found that secluded place
Morghan had spoken of, away from the others, he would have
slunk there, crawled on his belly, and hidden until the past
receded once again.

But he could not. The past held him as surely as the mana-
cles had bound him in that dank, Faerie dungeon. And no less
gently.

The air of the World Between Worlds, thick and cool as
the touch of silk upon his skin, swirled over him when Brean-

na knelt. Unable to meet her gaze, he kept his head lowered. Such was a proper position of shame.

She leaned close and her words whispered across his cheek chasing the chill. "I'm going to help you. Now. Please don't try and stop me this time."

His automatic denial died before reaching his lips. As repugnant as the thought of her discovering the complete truth of his past was, intellectually he knew he was of no benefit to the mission in this condition. Perhaps he could accept a small comfort, enough to allow him his usefulness for two days.

"I know what you're thinking, Gowtham. That won't work. It's all or nothing this time. I will not accept nothing. It's not just for you. I need to do this for everyone. We need to get home, and you hold the key to the knowledge we need."

Her words were spoken softly like a lover's whisper, yet even through the dark haze of his mind, he heard the determination. She would not allow him to prevaricate, to hide his torments from her. This time, she would have her way.

With aching slowness he nodded, but did not lift his head. "It shall be as you say."

She curled her hand over the back of his head, softly stroking his hair. "I love you, Gowthaman. That's the main reason I have to do this. I've never... never been able to stand watching you fight and suffer for the happenings in your past. Knowing I could help. Knowing you refused me."

"I will not refuse you. I... trust you." Once the horrific internal struggle to force the words past his lips was conquered, a measure of weight lifted from his heart.

"I need to touch. Here." Caution filled Breanna's voice when she moved her fingertips to his temple.

"I know."

"There's no one..." Breanna paused then continued, "No one to see. Morghan and Coralie have gone somewhere private."

"I know."

"Chance is keeping watch, but he's--"

"I know." Gowthaman lifted his head. "It does not matter if any witness. Could the healing be any more revealing than what I have become here? By the desert sun, Breanna, my sundarii, I must be able to think, to function." He lifted his hands, wincing at the uncontrollable tremors. "I will not add to your concerns."

She cast him a weak smile and settled cross-legged before him. "You've always been my concern. You always will be. This... this I can do something about."

Clasping his hands at his shins, he whispered. "I know."

"I'm not going to hurt you. I won't let this pain, or your memories hurt you like this again."

As she lifted her hands to his face and lightly rested her fingers against his temples, he closed his eyes. He lingered in denial for a moment, then surrendered to her touch and the opening of his memories.

"I'm not going to hurt you."

Under her gentle touch his brow wrinkled with his frown. She had said those words before, as a child. When he'd returned from the World Between Worlds the first time. In this now, smooth comfort eased from her fingers and into his mind. This time, he let her follow the path of his humiliation to discover the past he'd hidden.

Another woman's cool fingers had pressed lightly, just above his eyebrows. "If you fight me, this will be painful," the seeker, Petulia, had whispered in his ear.

Tendrils, light as the newest growth of a Faerie vine had curled inward from each of Petulia's fingertips. He had seen them, felt them as she inched deeper and deeper into his consciousness. One by one, the tendrils wrapped around the stones of his mental barriers, easing between the tightly mortared construction, and tore them down. With the tearing away, a scream had ripped from his throat.

He swallowed heavily against the strain and dryness, reminding himself Breanna's fingers touched him now. With his permission. With his full belief she could help him. She crooned to him of that healing, but the memory remained, demanding acquiescence.

Each deconstructed stone had become a scream, followed by his captors' wild laughter. Unable to stand, he'd hung by his wrists, gouging deep tears in his abused skin. He hadn't felt the pain or the hot blood that ran down his arms. His shoulders popped with remembered strain. His throat burned. Unable to escape the seeker's touch, he thrashed his head.

"Shh. It's me, Gowtham. Let me take the hurt."

Breanna's touch.

Anguish returned. Petulia's tendrils had withdrawn, leaving a void that filled slowly as his mind returned to him. She had taken but somehow the contents of his mind remained intact. She knew--good and ill--knew all he knew, all he'd done, all he was. Petulia had stolen honor and dishonor both as she'd sought through his mind.

He had failed to keep the Zeroun clan safe. There had been nothing left for him. At one point, he had begun to hope. To hope the evil ones would kill him.

But members of Breanna's family had rescued him, although that rescue had taken him to the World Between

Worlds. Twice he had entered the gray and twice had he been forced to leave the place where he may have been able to forget the violation of his mind. New anger simmered, skittering from Breanna's healing touch.

Her touch called to him and the anger dissipated in the welcoming comfort.

Her touch. So different from the seeker's. He relaxed and felt Breanna's gentle, mental smile. "That's it, Gowtham. Now, we need to break down the walls you've constructed around those memories. Please. Allow me to help you."

With a reflexive ruthlessness he barely understood, he reinforced the barriers around his frozen heart. Ah, but the aching of his soul far exceeded any pain his physical being had ever suffered. As he had then, he longed to slink away, make his way back to his beloved desert and disappear. Or, perhaps wander off in this foreboding place to dwell in the emptiness... like the wounded animal he was.

"Gowthaman?"

Trying to deny the voice--a musical combination of Breanna then and now--he shook his head.

"Gowthaman?" Breanna the child. A memory then.

Releasing a long breath, he tried to smile. "Yes, little missy?"

"I'm glad you're here."

Now that the golden-haired child had seated herself firmly in his mind, his memories coalesced around her and the comfort of her innocent smile. With a groan, he fully opened his mind to Breanna's healing.

"Somebody hurt you, didn't they?" The cherub's voice intruded again on his thoughts.

"Yes, little missy, someone did." Why should he have denied the fact when the marks upon his body vividly showed the physical abuse. He had hoped none would discover the rape and torture of his mind.

"Here, too." She touched his temple, a twin of her older self's touch. A cool wave of comfort eased into his mind. He tensed at the invasion and the child jerked her hand away. "I'm sorry. I'm not supposed to do that without asking you first if it's okay. But you hurt so bad."

He frowned. A child could not know of that pain. At her serious expression, he attempted a smile. "Do not worry about me, little missy."

She giggled and patted his cheek. "Why d'you call me that?"

"Because you are so young, yet still I honor you."

"Oh, like you're old." She giggled again.

"But I am, little missy. Older than you can imagine." Had he smiled at her then? He could not remember.

"But, you're Faerie, so you'll live a long time."

He had wished then that the fact were not true, for how could he live with his actions for the length of such a lifetime? He had no choice then, and no choice now. "Yes, that I shall."

"Don't be sad. I'm gonna marry you when I grow up."

Despite the pain, and surprised at her confident statement, he chuckled. "Are you now? Why would you wish to marry an old librarian like me?"

"You're not old. And because that's what people who love each other do. Just like Daddy and Mommy."

In the stillness of the World Between Worlds, he heard the echo of her words from Breanna's lips "...who love each other."

Breanna's grandfather, the then leader of the Defenders of Mankind had crouched beside them.

Breanna frowned up at him. "Granda, Gowtham's hurt bad. But I can fix him."

Gowthaman stared at the young girl. None had used a shortened form of his name, not since he was a young faerie lad, not much older than the child was now. Warmth filled his chest. She was... a peculiar child.

The adult fingers at his temples shifted with Breanna's soft snort but the gentle memory continued.

"Did ye ask him, Bree? What did yer da tell ye?"

Counting on her small fingers, she answered by rote. "Don't heal without permission. Don't heal when people who don't understand are around. Faerie healing--"

"Aye," the Alastriona laughed. "Ye remember well. So, did ye ask him?"

She turned a crystal-blue gaze on Gowthaman. Her earnest expression returned the smile to his face. What harm could there be to humor her? Perhaps any fledgling talent she held would ease the physical aches.

"Gowtham, may I heal your hurts?"

After a quick glance at her grandfather's tolerant grin, he nodded. "As you wish, little missy."

Bright joy suffused her face and she shook her finger at him. "My name's Breanna, silly."

Now he whispered her name, "Breanna," and received such a powerful wash of love and heat he gasped. His inner vision burned with entwined gold and red then faded again into his memories.

Pressing her small hands to his chest, the child closed her eyes. Calm, cool waves engulfed him, easing the burning pain of his physical injuries. One by one, he watched as he bruises healed and the skin knit over cuts and scrapes. She carried more than a fledgling talent.

A pale pink glow surrounded her hands. Tinged with hints of deep red and gold, the glow pulsed softly with the beating of his heart.

No. How could that be? This was not a part of his memory. He had not seen soulfire then. Soulfire never appeared in one so young. The magical expression of... love... would not... could not... despite her foolish affirmations she would marry him. No, the haze had to have been a remnant of confusion within his tortured mind.

When he lifted his gaze to her face Breanna the child opened her eyes. The brilliance of her smile held him still while she lifted her hands and touched his temples softly. Her adult fingers trembled then remained firmly in place. As he had then, he did now, opening his mouth to beg her to stop, for he could not pull away from her touch.

::I'm not gonna hurt you, Gowtham. I'd never hurt you.::

Whose voice? The child or the woman?

Then the soft pink entered his mind, hovered in the darkness of his abused memories before taking the form of small hands that lifted bits of his protective mental wall and pieced them together, slowly rebuilding his shields. Finally with a touch light as the kiss of innocence, the child retreated.

"Oh, no," Breanna said quietly. "I'm sorry, Gowtham, I did that without knowing how difficult it would be for you. I shouldn't have. I... I didn't understand the extent--"

He lifted his hands to cover hers. "I know. Now, I understand many things. I must breach those reinforced defenses, for they do not shield me from pain, but hold me captive. The walls you constructed are strong. Breanna, will you help me? I do not know if I can do this alone."

"You're not alone. You're never alone, Gowtham." She leaned forward and pressed a kiss to his forehead. "Let's fix what I did out of love so long ago."

Gowthaman took a deep breath and returned to the memories haunting him for so long. Deep, passionate red surrounded him as he tore stone from stone, tossing the pieces as far as he could in every direction, so they would never be found and brought together again. Angry, violent winds howled around him trying to contain that which he released.

Whenever a memory pressed too close, Breanna was there, binding the pain into submission. Until only one final, solid lump remained: the cold, hate-filled touch of the mind-seeker. With a mental battle cry, Gowthaman smashed the memory. The weak, ineffectual wail as the pain dissipated made him smile.

The beautiful red caressed him then flowed away. He opened his eyes.

"You will still have the memories of that time," Breanna said.

"I know. I shall have the memories, but they shall not have me. You have returned the control to me."

"Good." She lurched forward and wrapped her arms around his neck. "Good."

"Breanna, I..."

Shaking her head, she hugged him tightly. "No, you don't need to say anything." Then she leaned back. Tears shimmered in her eyes, but her smile was a bright as the faerie sun. "When we get home, I'm going to go right up to Granda and say 'See, I told you I could fix him'."

Brandr Ur squirmed, attempting to find a comfortable position on the hard dais that had been his chosen place of watching for so very long. He grumbled under his breath. After the ages he'd spent here, he'd expected the rocks to conform to his needs, to ease his body as he waited. And planned.

A slow smile followed by the cracking roll of his neck and a deep shrug helped. The planning was complete. All that remained was the waiting of two meager nights and he would be free once more. Free to determine the fates of worlds. Free to deliver his ultimate revenge upon those who'd sent him here.

Dispassionate, he gazed across the wide landscape, empty but for rocks. Rock. Nothing but gray rock. Not even a tree to flame remained in his valley. He reached to pick up a fist-sized stone and concentrated but the stone would not burn. After tossing the rock as far as he could, the elemental eased back to prop himself on his bent elbows. Lighting flame to something... anything would be a relief.

He paused to consider why he had never completely destroyed the small section of this cursed place his twice-cursed descendant occupied. There had been great joy in burning away any hint of moisture and blocking the prince of waters from communicating with his world.

But once that joy dissipated, Brandr Ur had found no need, no desire for additional destruction. What were a few scraggly trees or bushes?

A scent drifted past him on the dry, hot breeze. He jerked upright, inhaling deeply. Then he shook his head, rubbed his nose with his palm and inhaled again.

Fire.

Small, insignificant. But fire.

He chuckled then laughed loudly. None who resided here felt the need for the comfort of fire. So the builders must be those who had entered this night, intent on rescue. How--he rested one hand centered on his chest--touching. Let them have their image of comfort and security.

He had told the prince he would not near the weakening veil until the time of his escape. As he was a being of his word, he would not physically interfere with the scheming of the near-mortals.

Focusing on the small group gathered a few leagues away, he skimmed over the uninteresting minds until... Ah, yes. This one. One mind among them held his interest. One mind he'd touched before. One mind held possibilities.

Finding a comfortable nook within the young mind, he watched, listened, and studied the complexities of this new species. He discovered a taint, an ancestor perhaps, that with a gentle nudge, opened the mind wider to him. The taint reminded Brandr Ur of others he had used in the past, but there was no lust for power elsewhere in this mind.

Accepting the challenge of bringing this being, this possible follower to him before the veil opened, Brandr Ur slowly receded from the mind's depths and lingered on the surface, listening.

"...I'm not trusting that the elemental won't try something."

Communication opened with a simple twist of his thought. ::I said I shall not approach the prince until the time of our final battle. In two night's time, when the veil weakens, then shall you see me. Then shall you know my glory.::

Chuckling at the useless attempts at shutting him out, of building puny mental walls, Brandr Ur remained seated firmly in the other's mind.

The young one spoke out loud. "No, I'm going to keep watch anyway."

::Watch if you wish. You will not see me until the time of my glory is at hand.::

::Get out of my head.::

::In time, my young friend. I find you... interesting. There is much potential in you, potential to increase my glory. And your own.::

::Get. Out. I won't listen to you. I'm here to defeat you, not to become your pawn.::

The rippling defiance delighted the elemental. Until a solid bubble of indigo shoved at him, blocking him from the young one's mind. He thought to return an undeniable pressure, then let himself slide away with only a hint of resistance.

::I shall return, my young friend. Then we shall see who is to be defeated. And who will hold supreme rule. Two nights, young one, we meet face to face.::

::Fuck off.::

Brandr Ur's thought essence returned to his body. Dark, heavy laughter rang from the temple, echoed from stone to stone, filling the gray valley.

Halfway between midnight and dawn, Nightshade set Gowthaman's journal aside and turned off the bedside lamp. He'd opened the heavy drapes to let the night in through the wide window and now he lay back, hands clasped behind his head, to watch the sky. An untrained eye would miss the faint haze lingering at the edge of the stone outcropping. A human's eye.

Letting his eyelids drift closed, he waited for a sleep he knew would not find him. Too many thoughts, possibilities, recriminations... too much rumbled through his head until he had lost primary focus. After a few minutes he threw back the blankets and stalked to the window.

Cool air surrounded him, raising chill bumps on his naked body. Had he become so used to comfort that a little cold made him shiver? He snapped his fingers in a precise 'Z'. "Honey, get over yourself."

After slipping on silk pajama bottoms and a crumpled tee shirt, he snagged the journal, left the bedroom and sought the comfort of the huge kitchen.

Only the soft light over the stove illuminated the room, that and the last of the moonlight reflected on the loch. In a few hours the sun would rise over the distant hills and another day would begin.

Nightshade took a bottle of milk from the refrigerator, a box of heavily-sweetened cereal and a glass from the pantry and sat so he could see out the window. After pouring the milk, he tipped the box, cascading a small pile colorful circles onto the tabletop. He opened the journal.

While munching on the crunchy cereal, he stared at the pages covered with fine, precise script and well-marked diagrams. Although his eyes saw the words, his mind wandered elsewhere.

He'd been too long in this life. Too much of who he was had slipped from beneath his flamboyant facade. Always in the past he'd moved on long before now, leaving a mystery and little else. Twice he'd tried to leave, to disassociate himself from this place, these people. Twice he'd returned.

He drew in a deep breath then released it slowly. He was tired of moving on, starting over, deciding who he would be. The closest he'd ever been to his true self, he liked who he was now. Liked his place in the world. Maybe he should consider...

But not now. There was too much on the table already for his adopted family. Once everyone was safely home, once the drama this family constantly found themselves in was over, maybe then. He crunched slowly, swallowed, then took a long drink. He would come clean with them.

Or disappear.

The sounds of someone scuffling over the stone littered ground woke Gowthaman from an exhausted, oddly peaceful sleep. Without moving he glanced around, wondering when he'd fallen asleep. The sweet memory of Breanna holding him brought him to sitting as he looked around for her.

Chance was the only one visible at their tiny campsite. When the young man noticed him, Chance dropped the pack he rummaged through and hunkered down beside him.

"As far as I can tell, it's still a couple hours until whatever passes as dawn."

Gowthaman nodded and took the water Chance held out to him. Chance studied him while he drank greedily, but the frank perusal did not cause him distress as it had so often in the past. He lowered the bottle to his knee and looked around. The landscape was still the same bleak gray, yet it seemed less oppressive. He would survive.

"Where... are the others?"

Chance tossed him a cocky grin. "The... others. Well, Coralie and Morghan are off that way somewhere." He waved over his shoulder then looked expectantly at Gowthaman.

Shaking his head at the young man's impetuous nature, Gowthaman obliged. "And Breanna?"

Although the smile remained in place, the teasing glint in Chance's eyes faded. His gaze skittered to one side then back. "Said she needed a little private time."

Breanna's brother had no talent in prevarication. Tight, dense terror sucked at Gowthaman's breath. "Why?"

"Sometimes... Oh, hell, Gowthaman. She healed you, even I can see that. Can't you just leave it?"

The terror took a jagged bite into his heart. He clasped Chance's arm. "Tell me what you mean."

Chance studied him for a few seconds, gave a sharp nod and sat. "She'll kill me for this, you know. But, maybe it's time. It's like this, Gowthaman. She heals."

"Yes, we have established that."

Waving a hand to prevent Gowthaman's further speech, Chance continued. "She heals two ways. Physical and emotional. The physical's easy. She takes the hurt, the pain and somehow it dissipates. Somewhere. I don't think she understands the process either. It's just something she does. We've both benefited from the physical healing. To her it's no big deal. But the other."

"The pain of a mind in torment."

"Yeah. Look, I have some idea what you went through, how much baggage you've carried around with you. I'm glad two finally got all that taken care of."

The urge to shake the young man strained Gowthaman forward. Chance must have read his intent, for he leaned back and said, "Okay. But she's really gonna kill me."

"And if she is reluctant..." He gave a small smile to soften his threat. The worry remained, but without the burden of negativity, he had opened his heart to a world, to many worlds, of possibilities. Possibilities he would explore with Breanna once Chance told him where she hid.

"Only a few people know about this. Mom and Dad, Granda, Jayse. I suppose you'd find out sooner or later anyway, seeing as how... well, nevermind that. I only know because I followed her once when she told me not to." He ducked his head. "I made it worse because she tried to hold back."

"Hold what back? Chance, tell me where Breanna is."

"In a grotto over that way. The place Morghan mentioned earlier."

Gowthaman tensed his muscles to rise, but Chance pressed down on his shoulder. "Wait. Before you go running off, I've got to tell you more. Unlike when she heals physical injuries, and the pain just kinda flows from her and drains away, when there's emotional pain involved..."

Grasping Chance's wrist, Gowthaman growled a low threat. A knot formed in the pit of his belly. Bitter acid filled his throat. He knew, but needed to hear the words. "What are you avoiding telling me?"

Now Chance's eyes dimmed, a flash of tortured denial spoke more to Gowthaman than any words. "The pain, she takes it inside herself. It doesn't just float away. She carries your agony with her until she has time, a private place, somewhere where she can let them go."

"But when she was a child--"

"She doesn't understand that either. Maybe it didn't bother her then because of a child's innocence. That's been the best theory we've been able to come up with. Once she understood the scope of emotional pain, she was unable to simply funnel it though herself."

"Are you saying she is out there somewhere trying to rid herself of my torment? That I did this to her? Gave her my pain?"

"Hell, Gowthaman, you didn't do anything to her. She took from you. And willingly. She'd do it again in a minute."

"I must go to her."

Chance grabbed his shoulder again. Gowthaman resisted the need to shake off the unwanted pressure and rush into the murky gray to find his beloved. Chance held his gaze, a fierce light in his eyes so similar to Breanna's, Gowthaman's heart stalled. "No. She wouldn't want you to see."

The heavy beat of his heart resumed with his determination. "I must go. She will see me."

Chance held up his hands in mock defeat. "I've made my token resistance. You tell her that. She does need you now." He reached blindly to one side and snagged a blanket. "Take this, she'll be cold."

Gowthaman rose, took the blanket then paused. Perhaps he should not intrude upon her.

Chance scrambled to his feet and gave him a not too gentle shove between the shoulder blades. "Go. Don't think. Just do. Geez," he muttered as Gowthaman stumbled away. "Who'da thunk I'd be giving relationship advice."

Hands covering her face, Breanna collapsed to her knees. She'd barely reached the tiny, hidden grotto before her legs gave out and she could go no further.

How had Gowthaman carried such a tremendous weight of guilt and pain every day? He was so much stronger than she'd ever imagined. If only she had known the extent of the damage he kept hidden, she would have insisted on this healing long ago, and never given up until he relented and allowed her to help. How different would his life be, or her life... their life together?

Bending forward until her forehead pressed against the ground, she gasped for breath then coughed when the dry dust coated her throat. She lifted her head slightly, scraped her fingers through her hair.

The pain of biting her lip failed to contain her sobs. Dry as the land around her, the sounds of an intense healing echoed in her ears, trembled through her chest. Gowthaman's healing. Chains, cold and burning like ice wrapped around her heart, crept agonizingly along her veins, invaded her mind. Clinking silently against the memories of the pain she'd eased from Gowthaman, the bindings threatened to pull her inexorably into those memories, to hold her there. To replace Gowthaman's pain with her own.

She struggled to straighten her back and face the coming release upright. But her muscles refused to respond and tightened, keeping her frozen in tortured agony. Years he'd carried this with him. Years she could have given him if she'd only known. But her naïveté... she shook her head violently. No, at five she had been an innocent child, believing she helped. Repercussions now helped no one.

She pounded her fists against the ground in rhythm to the sobs wracking her body. It hurt. Oh gods, it hurt.

Hurts.

She tasted blood but bit her lip harder to keep from crying out. The force of her fists raised a cloud of dust that settled over her. Violent coughs battled with her dry sobs. As though she had run miles, sharp pains punctured her sides. Yet those pains were minor irritants compared to the anguish she fought to force from her mind and soul.

Finally, she pressed one hand to the ground and forced herself to straighten. Rocking on her knees, she wrapped her arms about her waist, and tipped her face to the sky.

Leave me. He's healed. Go away. She accompanied her mental scream with an inner vision of hands pushing away a tangled, writhing mass. As she shoved, thin, ragged-edged tentacles stretched out to wrap around her arms, digging deep into her flesh, holding, binding the mass to her. A deep groan broke the seam of her tightly compressed lips. Her groan eased to his name.

"Oh, Gowthaman."

The soft warmth of a blanket wrapped over her shoulders. "I am here."

Breanna jerked fully upright, shoving the fleece to the ground. "Go away."

"I will not." Gowthaman knelt before her and rewrapped her in the blanket.

Frantic, Bree looked from rock to shadowed rock. Was anyone else nearby?

Gowthaman touched her cheek with the tips of his fingers. "Breanna, I am alone. I am here for you. As you have always been for me. This..." He brushed the dust from her forehead. "This that you suffer now is because of me."

Sinking back to sit on her calves, she jerked her face from his touch. "Please." Her voice wavered. "Don't look at me now. Please, just go away."

Somehow, she had to make him leave. No one could ever see her like this, especially not him. Not him. Unable to control the tremors coursing through her, she knew only moments remained before the full impact of her struggle was made known. He shouldn't see her like this. Not now. He couldn't.

How might he react when subjected to the memory traces, the lingering evidence of his memories? Would he take those memories back upon himself and return to the tightly hidden pain? She would not risk that happening.

"I need to be alone." The dead tone of her words strengthened her determination to protect Gowthaman.

Gentle, he caressed her face. With no hesitation in the simple contact, he brought his face close to hers and pressed his lips to her forehead.

Breanna gasped. Then burst into tears.

White-hot pain shot through her mind. She bit her abused lip to contain her moan. The aftereffects had never been so intense. Cold sweat covered her. Shivering, she tried to draw away.

"No, sundarii, do not refuse me. Do not let the past stand between us again. How many years have I refused you?"

Her single bark of harsh laughter faded rapidly in the heavy air.

The comforting strokes of Gowthaman's fingers wiped the tears from her face. "Yes, far too many. For that, I beg forgiveness."

"P-please go. I c-can't stand for you to s-see me this way."

"I will not leave you. TvaaM me priyatamaa."

The intensity of disintegrating memories, the ripping away, tore her from Gowthaman's touch. Arched her back. Cramped her muscles. Froze the cry in her throat. Battered, torn, her senses blinked into darkness.

One breath, ragged, barely filled her lungs. Exhale. Inhale. Again. Tentative, she searched the darkness for any glimmer, any clue, any hope. There. Breathe. Again.

Faint, shimmering gold against velvet black. There. Dancing red. There. Ah. Soulfire.

Breanna opened her eyes.

Twenty

Bree woke cradled against Gowthaman's chest. He had settled cross-legged and held her in a gentle embrace. He carefully wiped the still falling tears from her face. Cocooned in the blanket, she cried, long and hard. The aftershocks of the healing had dissipated, and now she cried for Gowthaman, all he had suffered, all he had lost.

When finally she could cry no more she pressed her palm to his tear-dampened tunic to ease from his embrace. He held her more securely. Lips close to her ear, he whispered, "For too long I fought to keep this from you. I believed I had to hide what happened, how I felt. From you, from all who knew me."

"I'm sorry. I shouldn't have... not like that. Not when I was so young. I had no idea--"

The gentle press of his finger to her lip stopped her speech. "Hush, little missy. This is my time to speak."

More than his touch held her in silence. Glorious delight chased remnants of darkness from her when he moved his finger to trace the curve of her lip.

"There is to be no blame, no recriminations for that time. You were too young to understand I needed to face those memories to heal. I was too overcome with my own perceived failings. Neither of us knew, nor understood the process. Ah, my Breanna. It may be that even had we known, the past and this present would still be no different than they are. For too long I thought keeping these memories repressed was the only way I would survive. But this night, if it is night in this damnable place, you have freed me from my self-inflicted curse."

She held his gaze, studying the changes in his eyes, wishing she could see the deep, dark chocolate brown. If he knew the gray hid his reactions, his feelings, might he return to denying her?

Shaking his head, Gowthaman offered her an easy smile. "Your face tells me much, sundarii. You worry still. Perhaps, you always shall. As I shall worry about you."

She heard his words, but her mind had halted, holding on to a single word. "What does that mean?"

"No matter how either of us feels, we shall--"

"No, I know that. What does that word mean? Sundarii? You've said it before."

The tone of the skin covering his high cheekbones darkened. Curious, she smoothed her finger over the spot. He pressed into the touch of her open palm. "It is an ancient human language, one I have long felt a kinship with."

"Oh." How long had she ached to be able to touch him like this, without him pulling away and rebuking her? By not shrinking away, he welcomed her touch, so she untangled her other hand from the blanket and captured his face. The arm holding her tightened and she sighed.

"Beautiful woman."

"What?"

"The word means beautiful woman."

"You think I'm beautiful?"

Surprise lit his face. She traced the lifted arch of his eyebrows then drew a fingertip down the length of his nose.

Spearing his fingers through her hair to cup the back of her head, Gowthaman held her gaze. Her exploring fingers stilled. "Yes," he said, and kissed her.

No simple kiss, he brought them together with an intensity that startled her. Heat flared through her body, chasing the lingering chills, settling in her breasts, at the apex of her thighs.

When he paused, she tilted her head to one side and Gowthaman obliged by tracing his fingers down the column of her neck. Reaching the tender spot where her neck met her shoulders, he moved his thumb in slow circles. Then he lifted her closer and pressed his warm lips to the same spot. The moist heat of his tongue tickled her skin. She sighed and snuggled into his embrace.

Gowthaman stroked her hair, smoothing the short strands from her face. "You should not have kept this hidden."

Sniffing, she shook her head, dislodging his gentle touch. "You're a fine one to talk."

His tight smile was hidden when he dipped his head in acknowledgement. "You would bear this alone?"

Remnants of pain tightened to a ragged knot in her chest. "I always have. It's a part of what I do."

Gowthaman lifted his head and held her eyes for a long moment before his gaze dropped to her lips. The pain-filled knot dissolved into tight expectation, delight and heated desire.

"No longer."

She pushed at his chest, a weak, half-hearted struggle, but before anything else was said, he had to understand. "I won't stop healing. Even if this is the price, it's worth a few moments of pain to help someone." Her voice lowered to a whisper. "It was worth it for you."

"You have mud upon your face."

"What?"

"The dust and your tears have made muddy tracks over your cheeks." He took a corner of the blanket and wiped her face with gentle, precise strokes.

Confused at his reaction, Bree stilled his hand and repeated, "I won't stop healing."

"I know, Breanna. Such is a part of you I would not wish to change. However, no longer will you be alone when you face this after time. I shall be with you."

"But..."

"Now is not the time for this discussion."

He wasn't going to get away with avoiding her any longer. Nor would she let him evade her questions. "Now is as good a time as any. I don't--"

Gowthaman captured her words with a kiss. She would not let the issue rest until she understood he would not dissuade her from healing, only that he wished to assist her when she faced the release of pain. Sliding his lips over hers, he teased until she relaxed against him and returned the kiss.

He dipped his tongue into the heat of her mouth, tasting the lingering salt of her tears. Layered beneath the rising of her passion lay the essences of tart apples and sweet honey mead. A heady combination he pulled into himself with the slow, twining dance of their tongues.

Tight, heavy, his body responded, the ache of long denial melding with the heat low in his body. As long as he'd denied his love for this beautiful woman in his arms, he'd denied himself. He moved his lips from hers to chase the flicker of her pulse at the hollow of her throat, drawing a gasp and a sigh from her. Slipping one hand beneath the blanket, he spread his fingers over the crumpled cotton of her tee shirt, then shoved the material aside to touch the skin low on her back.

Electrical awareness prickled his palm. Breanna arched and rolled her back like a cat to press into and encourage his touch. Unable to resist returning to the sweetness of her mouth, he gathered her soft, wordless cries with his kisses while tracing designs on her skin with his fingertips.

The press of her hip where she rested cradled between his legs captured the rise of his erection. He gulped back a groan. This was neither the time nor the place for kaama, for the physical expression of their love. Yet only her wish, her denial would stop this moment.

Breanna touched her cheek to his and whispered, "Please, don't think. Please, I need you. Love me."

"TvaaM kaamayaami, Breanna."

Captivated by the gray sparkle in her eyes and the damp glistening of tears on her lashes, he finally understood how lost one could become in another. How lost and yet now completely whole. He took her hand and pressed her palm over the beating of his heart. "TvaaM kaamayaami. I love you. I do not need to think to know this. You are my soul."

"TvaaM kaamayaami," she repeated carefully. "I like how that sounds. It means I love you?"

He nodded and unwrapped the blanket from her shoulders. Nuzzling her neck, he spread the blanket over the cold ground with one hand then lowered them to the makeshift bed.

She sighed when he splayed his hand on her flat belly, then slid her tee shirt up over her breasts to expose the white cotton of her bra. Sadness assailed him but he smiled. She should be dressed in the finest of Faerie silks, not this plain, serviceable garment.

Brushing his hands over her, he removed her shirt then leaned down to trail, hot wet kisses over her collar bone. She tangled her fingers in his hair, exerting slight pressure, but he denied her the satisfaction of her silent entreaty.

This time, this moment, might be the only one they would have. If a sacrifice were called for, Gowthaman accepted he would be the logical choice. If such a sacrifice were called for, he would have this memory to sustain him. Despite her determination he did not believe all of the rescue party would return safely from the World Between Worlds.

Breanna tugged on his hair, the tiny, sharp pains returning his full attention to her. "What're you thinking about?"

To give himself a moment to clear his mind of concerns, he stripped off his tunic then lifted his gaze to hers. "You should be lying upon a pillow strewn bed, hidden in the shadows of a colorful awning at the oasis. The finest of silks would adorn you." He flicked a finger over the firm peak of her cotton covered nipple making her gasp. "Never should such common materials touch your golden skin."

His hand slipped lower, to the fastening of her jeans. "Warm desert winds would caress you, and I, I would follow that caress, my lips against your skin, tasting sunshine and desire upon you. The sweet sounds you make for me would dance to the song of the water over the smooth, rounded rocks."

Watching his eyes, Breanna lifted her hips and he drew the denim from her body. The warmth of his hand skimmed up her leg and curled over her inner thigh. "Moonlight will bathe you. The orchids will withhold their fragrance, for no aroma should compete with the scent of your skin, the honey musk of your arousal."

Only Gowthaman's light trousers remained of their clothing. Bree stroked his chest, both patient and frustrated with his slow touch, his words, his seduction, hardly daring to believe his words or the reality of his touch.

"And I, sundarii, in that place, I would worship you. With my hands. My mouth. My body. My love."

"And I you." She arched into his palm, catching her lower lip between her teeth at the spiral of joy and desire tightening beneath his teasing explorations of her breast.

Clutching his shoulders, Bree allowed herself to sink into the sensations Gowthaman aroused, until her body ached with need, demanding his touch, the joys of release. At last the gray worry receded, and all she knew, all she felt, was him. When at last he removed his trousers, settled in the cradle of her thighs and smiled down on her, tears of relief burned her eyes. Almost.

He caught a tear on a fingertip then brushed the backs of his knuckles along her jaw. "You are so soft."

She tilted her hips and his length twitched against her belly. Her low sensual laugh vibrated along her skin and she gasped, "You're not."

"Breanna..."

"No more, Gowtham. Please, don't make me wait any longer."

"No, no longer," he whispered against her lips. Holding her gaze, he rose above her and encouraged her to lift one leg over his hip. Strain showed in the tight set of his jaw, yet he smiled and slowly joined their bodies.

"Gowtham," she sighed. He'd filled her and now held himself still as her virgin body softened to welcome his. He pressed his forehead to hers, then with another smile, brought their mouths together. His tongue dueled with hers, twining and stroking, mimicking...

He withdrew slowly then returned, each time a little faster, or firmer, or at a new amazing angle. Pleasure rippled through her, again and again. Building. Growing. Stirring her senses higher, until she could no longer contain the rising. Yet she clutched at the feelings, tightened her hold on him, strangely reluctant, expectant...

"Gowtham."

The force of his thrusts increased and she caught her lower lip between her teeth. Too much, the feelings... too much. His breath burst past her ear, timed to the building pressure within her. Capturing his face between her hands, she traced his lips with her thumbs. He caught one in his mouth and suckled it deep into his heat.

A burst of crimson sensation shattered her control and she cried out her delight. Hips pressing her hard into the ground, Gowthaman shuddered, whispered her name and collapsed. His weight against her brought a sharp wash of golden joy.

Then his lips found hers and she believed.

Twenty-one

Fingers entwined, Bree and Gowthaman returned to the tiny campfire. He waited until she sat then crossed to the packs, found water and energy bars. Sitting at her side, he handed her an opened bottle. "Drink."

She did. Although she felt no thirst, she drained half the bottle. Healing not only drained her emotionally, but the physical demands on her body needed repair. Especially in this place. Amazed the glorious moments of loving hadn't depleted her further, she cast Gowthaman a shy look.

His smile touched his eyes and the worry hovering there lessened. "Is there anything I may do for you, sundarii?"

"Don't stop loving me." Eyes wide, she bit her lip. She hadn't meant to say that out loud, to voice her fears that somehow, someday, he'd take back the words he'd spoken and the love he'd shared with her in this dismal place. That his actions had only been from a sense of duty or obligation... or because that's what she expected.

In a fluid motion Gowthaman rose to his knees and wrapped her in his arms. "I will not."

"But you..." Burning tears nibbled away at her resolve and she blurted, "But you stopped loving Kaelea."

Gowthaman sank back on his calves and shook his head. He stroked her upper arms. "Although I believed I loved her for some time, I did not love her as I do you, Breanna. Yes, I believed it so, but after Bard arrived, I knew my feelings toward her were those for a friend." He smiled ruefully. "Not that I did not attempt to deny that fact, and wrongfully pursued her for too long. She is, and will always be, a dear friend. But only a friend."

Silent, Breanna watched the emotions play across his face. She would take joy in his expressions now that he no longer held such a tight grasp on his emotions. At this moment he appeared no more than a man coming to terms with a decision.

Finally he took a breath and asked, "Do you remember the day you found the cave at Lucidea's manor? And the wall of water contained within it?"

Setting the bottle aside, she studied her hand while she gathered her thoughts. Why was he asking about that? Kaelea hadn't been at the manor then, so this couldn't be about his feelings for Kae, could it? Since no one had mentioned the incident in years, Bree had almost forgotten it. "Yes," she drawled. "I got in so much trouble that time, disappearing the way I did. But my explorations had a positive effect in the long run."

Waiting for him to make some comment, she took tiny bites of the dry, crunchy energy bar. She grimaced, carefully rewrapped the bar and set it beside the water bottle. Dusty tasting enough in the real world, eating it here was like trying to chew sand. And this was supposed to be good nutrition? The least manufacturers could do would be to make the thing taste like chocolate.

"Do you, Breanna?" Gowthaman's low voice intruded on her musing. "Do you remember my words to you that day?"

She attempted to dredge up the incident, knowing even though the effects of Gowthaman's healing had dissipated, the memory could be doubled in her mind. Strangely, the time remained hidden. "I can't remember."

"You were young. And undoubtedly more concerned with the punishment promised for your unthinking actions than with the words of yet another distraught adult."

"I do remember that being one of the few times I was ever seriously grounded. I had to serve out my entire sentence. I didn't think that was fair." She gave a dry chuckle. "I was pretty good at weaseling my way out of pranks and mischief, wasn't I?"

"You were." He took both of her hands and clasped them between his. "On that day, when none could find you, the minutes seemed as hours, the hours a lifetime. On that day, I believe I knew, I understood. On that day, I named you my soul. And for the second time, witnessed the glow of your magical aura."

"The second time?"

He stroked his thumb over her wrist. "The first incident was when you healed me upon my return from... this place. Palest pink and faint enough I was able to excuse the observation away as a remnant of my ordeal. I would not believe I could see the presence of magic within you. The manifestation of an aura does not normally appear in one so young."

"Pink? But in the library, I saw red... and gold."

"And you are older now, a woman of passion, no longer an innocent child."

Her face burned. And no longer an innocent woman either. She stared at their joined hands. "Could that have been soulfire?"

In the silence that followed, she knew he was thinking, so peeked at him from under her lashes. His eyebrows were drawn low over his closed eyes and she imagined the tireless working of his mind. A moment later his brows lifted and he looked at her.

"I do not believe so. Such would be unprecedented in a child. As it was, the evidence of your aura, and Chance's before Fiedhlim was destroyed, are extremely rare. Even though soulfire, and the color or colors produced are influenced by one's magic... ah, Breanna. Now is not the time for learned discussions. Know that in my heart, in my wounded soul, even then I knew, but dared not acknowledge, how important you would become to me. Do not doubt me, or my love, Breanna. For you are my soul."

There were no words adequate to respond to his declaration. Simply saying 'I love you' didn't seem enough. He watched her, newly released emotions flitting through his eyes. She wiggled the fingers of one hand until he released her then cupped her palm to his cheek.

"Gowthaman, I loved you even before I understood what love was. You are my soul." Guiding him nearer with her fingertips, she met his lips softly at first then with firmer, demanding pressure. Want and need rose from low in her body, swirling to settle in the places he'd loved not that long ago. Hoping his kiss would always affect her so powerfully, she sighed into his mouth.

A throat clearing registered through the slow, sensuous assault of Gowthaman's kiss. She moaned a denial when he dropped three feather-light kisses against her lower lip then drew away. He angled his head to look over her shoulder. "Yes, Chance?"

Bree blew out a frustrated breath. Leave it to her baby brother to ruin a mood. She swiveled to face his cocky, unrepentant grin.

"Hey, sis."

Standing loose-limbed, one sword unsheathed in his hand, the second strapped to his back, he looked every inch the self-assured warrior. Except for a brief glimpse of uncertainty in his eyes. Bree frowned, shook off Gowthaman's restraining hand and rose to face her brother. "What are you doing?"

"Going on a bit of a walk-about."

"You need to rest."

"What? Are you my mother now? All I've done the last five or six hours is sit around. Although..." His grin returned. "There were some mighty interesting things going on from time to time."

Nothing felt amiss, but she had been distracted. First by her post-healing trauma, then--she released a satisfied breath--then by Gowthaman. But if Chance had noticed anything out of the ordinary, maybe she should reconnoiter with him.

Chance sheathed the sword and leaned the upper half of his body toward her in a conspiratory manner. "You know, the Sindhu must have something like soulfire."

Not what she expected, so his low whisper threw her mind into a confused tangle. "Soulfire?"

"Sure. Every once in awhile last night, there was this burst of tiny lights, like stars, over where Coralie and Morghan were. In this gray place, I can't say if there's any color like our soulfire, but the stars are certainly indicative of something."

"Aye, 'tis magic."

At the rumble of Morghan's voice, Bree grabbed Chance's forearm and jerked them both to face the tall Sindhu.

Morghan crouched to add water to the battered pot and set it near the fire. Coralie stepped from behind the rocks and when she touched his shoulder, he covered her hand with his. "Aye, magic that comes only from the lovin' of the one who is yers alone."

Gowthaman tossed him the packet of instant coffee. "Very much like our Faerie soulfire. Although soulfire manifests as color."

"Boy, does it." Chance chuckled and gave Bree a soft punch in the shoulder. "Deep crimsony-red swirling with gold."

Bree turned to stare at Gowthaman. He met her look with silent questions of his own. Both turned to Chance, although with her face burning hot, Bree avoided meeting her brother's teasing gaze.

"Yep, quite spectacular."

"How... how do you know?"

"I told you, I was keeping watch last night. But there wasn't anything to watch..." He waved one hand toward Morghan and Coralie. "...except stars and soulfire. Couple of times, it was like stereo, like watching two fourth of July displays at the same time."

She started twice before finally managing, "But the colors?"

"Saw them, bright and glowing against... the... gray. Whoa, Sis. I didn't think about that. I shouldn't have been able to see the color of your soulfire here, should I?" He spun in a circle and spread his hands looking up into the sky. "Whoa, this is so cool."

"Chance..."

He lowered his hands and his gaze. A proud smile made him look even younger. "You did it. You and Gowthaman. No," he said when she frowned and took a breath. "Okay, so I mean that too, but look, you two brought color to a place where there isn't any. That's got to be significant. I mean, really important, don't you think? So... while you guys think about it and talk it to death, I'm going to look around."

He lifted one hand and shook his head. "Nope, don't say anything. I mapped out the area for myself during my watch last night. I can find my way around. I'll be back..." With one toe he drew a line a short distance from a tall rock then indicated the faint shadow sprouting from the base. "I'll be back by the time the shadow reaches that line."

After touching one finger to his lips, then giving her a mock salute, he turned and sauntered away.

Twenty-two

Bright dawn glinted through the kitchen window. Nightshade rubbed his eyes then shoved the empty cereal box to one side. After a long, but productive night, he had a few ideas he needed to run past the others. The manor was silent in the early dawn so he assumed he'd have a bit longer before anyone joined him for breakfast.

Breakfast. He grimaced at the cereal box. He needed protein. The refrigerator yielded ham and eggs but a common meal wasn't what he was after. In the pantry he found an unsliced loaf of bread and inspiration.

An hour later, with a French toast casserole baking and thick ham steaks waiting for the grill, he tapped a pen against one of the yellow legal pads Coralie loved so much.

Two readings of Gowthaman's journal finally brought some cohesion to the scattered entries and theories. Pieces had fallen together like a puzzle; unfortunately, somewhere along the line, the box had been shaken and a number of key pieces were missing. Turning to a page marked by a thin strip of yellow paper, he scanned Gowthaman's words, halting at a strange notation in the bottom margin.

Ring a ring o' rosies.

Why had the librarian made note of a children's rhyme. A game?

A quick flip of pages brought him to another yellow strip. The prophecy that years ago had led to the destruction of an evil Faerie who had long haunted the Zeroun clan.

At first reading he'd assumed Gowthaman had included the two verses because of the reference to the children of light and darkness--Breanna and Chance.

"Hey, Nightshade, you're up early. What is that wonderful aroma?"

"Morning, honey. The ladies up yet?"

Jayse ambled to the coffee pot and poured himself a mug. "Lucidea's still sleeping, but Tori's already been out for a swim, so she should be here shortly. You've been cooking?"

"Breakfast is the most important meal of the day."

"Since when are you mister nutrition?" Jayse sank onto the chair across from Nightshade and shook his head. "Eh, I'm sorry, Shade. Don't mean to be grumpy. I don't think any of us slept well. Won't until everyone's back safely."

Nightshade grunted a response, rose and peeked at his casserole. "I was up all night with Gowthaman's journal."

"Any insights?"

He paused, then shook his head and turned on the flames under the indoor grill. "Almost. Right now I've got more questions than possibilities. Set the table, Jayse. We'll get the discussion going over breakfast."

The men worked in silence, acknowledging Lucidea and Tori's entrances with nods. Once his grand breakfast filled the table, Nightshade had settled on a theory--as long as the others could help him connect a few dots.

Jabbing his fork toward Nightshade, Jayse turned to Lucidea. "Do you know what he did?"

"I have no idea."

"Ate my new box of cereal."

Lucidea patted his cheek. "Poor baby."

Nightshade patted his other cheek. "Honey, the sugar helped me think." No longer hungry, he pushed his plate aside. "Now, we already know most of the information in here, but there's a few entries in Gowthaman's journal that caught my eye. And although they don't appear related, I have a feeling..."

He paused to take a deep breath. "We'll worry about feelings later. Any clue why Gowthaman would make a notation about a child's game?"

Blank looks met his question.

"Or what about the prophecy?"

"What prophecy?"

Drawing back in surprise, Nightshade blinked at Jayse. "What prophecy? Honey, have you forgotten your past so soon? The verses that helped defeat Feidlhim."

Shaking his head while he chewed, Jayse held up one hand to silence Nightshade. He swallowed. "No, I haven't forgotten, but it's the past. What's an ancient verse got to do with today?"

"That's the question now, isn't it?"

Contemplative silence followed. Tori waggled her fingers toward his notes and he shoved the pad across the table to her. She ran a finger lightly over the page, tapping twice at a couple of entries. "How many times do you think Gowthaman made reference to three?"

Lucidea said, "A lot. You know what I want?"

"No darlin', what?" Jayse rested his arm on the back of her chair.

"Kumquats."

"Cravings?" Jayse leaned closer to kiss her cheek.

"No. I don't know. Maybe." She chuckled. "Kumquats just sound good."

Nightshade gave a dramatic wave toward them. "Don't mean to break up this moment, but--"

"We've got way too many things to figure out," Jayse agreed. "So, what are you thinking about the prophecy?"

"When looking at it like from the standpoint of a normal day, I would assume it's been fulfilled and all's right with the world. But that doesn't feel right. And Nightshade learned long ago to trust his feelings."

"So, what does it feel like at this point in time?" Jayse prompted.

"Now... I believe that the prophecy as it reads now has been fulfilled."

"But didn't you just say--"

With a single, sharp nod, Nightshade agreed then went on to explain. "The whole situation feels incomplete. As though there's a part of the prophecy missing. As well as part of the solution to our situation."

Lucidea gave a startled exclamation and scooted her chair back with the squeal of wood against stone.

Panic claimed Jayse's expression. Matching trepidation clawed into Nightshade's chest. He rose as Jayse reached for his wife.

"Darlin', what is it? The baby?"

Tori swung her arm to the side and halted Nightshade's progress around the table. He glared down at her and she shook her head. "It's okay," she whispered.

Lucidea batted at Jayse's hands as he tried to press his palm against her forehead, hold her hand and cover her belly protectively at the same time. "Stop it. I'm fine. Baby's fine. I just... just remembered something."

Jayse continued to fuss, until Lucidea grabbed his shoulders and shook until he lifted his hands in surrender. "Now, unless you're on your way to find me some kumquats, sit down and listen." She gave Tori a long-suffering wife look then sighed. "I am okay, Nightshade. You sit down, too. I can't stand all this hovering. If I want anybody hovering, you three will be the first to know. Now, what I was going to say is that I just remembered a passage in one of Coralie's books. She showed it to me not that long ago. I didn't think much about it then, but since you mentioned that old prophecy..."

"Do you remember which book?" Tori asked. "My sister has a few, you know."

Nodding, Lucidea caught her lower lip between her teeth and thought a moment. "I remember it was very old, bound with sea-turtle leather, then wrapped in sealskin. She took it to the palace at Gowthaman's suggestion since the air here was causing the pages to deteriorate."

"That doesn't help much now, honey."

Tori grinned. "I'd love another quick swim. I've been getting to know Na-h-Ulie and a trip to the palace would give me a chance to interact with her again."

"Great. I'll write out official 'orders'." Lucidea glanced at Nightshade. "But, I don't really want to bring the book here. Coralie would kill me if something happened to it."

Giving her a negligent shrug, he brushed at imaginary lint on his sleeve. "If a copy could be made of the pages you remember, that should be good enough for now. With the caveat that if we need further information, the book may have to rise to the surface anyway."

"Agreed. It shouldn't take too long. What I'm remembering is only a page or two." She reached for the legal pad,
turned to a clean sheet and wrote quickly. Then she handed
the folded page to Tori. "The pages I'm thinking of are near
the front of the book. No more than a quarter of the way in."
She closed her eyes. "One page had a poem, or a verse of
some kind." She opened one eye and tilted her head toward
Nightshade. "Like the prophecy." Closing both eyes again,
she took a deep breath. "The facing page had..."

Waiting silence hovered around the table.

"What?" Jayse asked, taking her hand.

She turned to look at him. "You're not going to believe
this. A diagram. With three... somethings... a thick bar with a
different something on the other side. There may have been
more to the drawing, it's been awhile."

"That should be easy enough to find. I'll be back in a
flash."

Nightshade stared after Tori, peering down the empty hall
until he heard the soft splash of her dive into the loch.

Then he focused on Lucidea. She cast her gaze at the ceiling.

"Before you ask," she said, "I didn't think of this before
because nobody mentioned any kind of prophecy. It's not
even a part the information Gowthaman talked to us about, so
why would I even think of it?"

"Don't get your dander up, honey. Even I don't understand
where all this will lead. Yet. Until Tori gets back..." He
yawned. "I'll be trying to find a bit of that beauty sleep I lost
last night."

"We'll call you."

Nightshade rose and waved over one shoulder. "Don't worry. I'll know."

He smiled, then chuckled softly at Lucidea's next words. "And you, Jaysson Allan Zeroun, go find me some kumquats."

Obsessed with plans of ruling and revenge, Brandr Ur paid little heed to the shift in air currents. It mattered not if an unwelcome creature entered his current domain. Not much longer and this place would not even be a memory, for he had the future to look to. The air shivered. A scent flowed from beyond his temple. The stick in his hand stilled and he smiled.

Ah, the young one came to him. Delightful. And so easy. He didn't look up when the boy stood before him.

"Elemental."

Such bravado from one so young. He inhaled, testing the boy's scent. "Human."

Taking another sensing breath, Brandr Ur stared at the marks and doodles he'd incised into the dirt. The young one was not totally human, but he didn't recognize the source of the magic.

His smile returned. The make-up of the young almost human made no difference. He would be used--as long as that use served Brandr Ur's purpose. He lifted his gaze.

"So. Young human. You have chosen to invade my territory. I would know why."

One hand tightened around the hilt of the sword at his side. The grip of a second blade extended over his shoulder. Brandr Ur let his grin widen. The young fool thought mere steel weapons would defeat him. Ha. Such bits of metal wouldn't even slow his march through the human and Alfar worlds. But, in the hands of such a warrior the weaponry might be useful.

"So, human, what is it you wish?"

A growl sounded from low in the boy's throat. "Stay out of my head."

Brandr Ur leaned back on one elbow. "No." ::This pleases me.:: Sending the connection deeper before the boy could raise additional defenses, Brandr Ur searched rapidly for the source of the odd scent. His effort was little more than a thought, but the boy broke a sweat and his face contorted with strain... and agony. He pressed one palm to his temple and Brandr Ur laughed.

Then spoke with both words and the mind touch. "I shall do as I desire. Sit and we shall speak as men. Tell me your name."

Groaning, the young one released his grip on the sword, clasped his second hand to his temple and dropped to his knees. His lips firmed to a thin line of physical refusal. Brandr Ur laughed at the futile rebuff.

"Come, come," he said, cajoling. Let us speak as equals. At least for this moment."

Silence continued the boy's rebellion. Brandr Ur pressed his mental probe deeper and found a name. "Chance. You are Chance. An odd name."

A surly growl reverberated from the boy and the elemental laughed again. He hadn't had such an enjoyable time for ages. Eons perhaps. Then he fell silent as well, watching the one whose skin stank with the need for battle. A battle Brandr Ur was more than willing to give him, except for the stupid promise he'd vowed before the prince. Still, another pleasure might come from this meeting.

"So, young Chance. You wish to fight me?"

"No." He shook his head slowly. "Not really. What I want is for you to leave Morghan and his people alone."

"Ah, then you come to me as their champion."

Chance snorted. "Hardly. But if fighting and defeating you will achieve my purpose, then so be it."

"Your purpose?" Brandr Ur leapt to his feet, drew himself as tall at the boulders surrounding him and slapped his palm to the center of his chest. "Your measly purpose means nothing to me. The future awaits. My future." He spread his arms to indicate the land around him. "This nothingness is merely a delay."

"A permanent delay." Chance rose and, fists clenched, took a step closer.

Lifting one eyebrow, Brandr Ur stared at the young man's face. Determination had hardened his jaw; tight corded muscles strained his neck and shoulders. Only a glimmer in the pale eyes showed any fear. Yet, the child desired a battle. "Think you so?"

Chance stepped forward again. Brandr Ur called upon the heat flowing through his body and the air around him shimmered. But the boy did not retreat. He leaned his upper body through the heat and gave a cocky grin. "I know so, old man. Yeah, I know you're an all-powerful elemental. Control fire and all that. Ages old plans." He angled back and gave a slight nod. "Those grand plans haven't come to fruition yet, have they?"

Startled by Chance's sarcasm, Brandr Ur remained silent. There was something more to the challenge hanging heavy in the air between them, more than words had yet spoken.

Frowning, he pressed deeper into the young one's mind. ::Let me in and I shall show you my plans. Show you your place--::

::No!::

Projected with the force of magic and the scent Brandr Ur didn't yet understand, the mental cry shoved him from his comfortable avenue of invasion. Pain, a soft wave of pain... How could this be? He was impervious to pain. The unusual sensations made him lose the last of his focus and the connection with the boy disintegrated.

A cock-sure smile twisted the boy's lips before he gave a mock salute and a shallow bow. "So, elemental. Until tomorrow. Rest assured you won't get past me to any other world. And you will leave Morghan and the Alfar alone." Spinning on one foot, he gave the elemental his back.

Astounded at the boy's audacity, Brandr Ur stared at the retreating swagger. He inhaled deeply, capturing the oddly familiar sense of magic. What power did the boy keep hidden within him? As a god, he would know this power. And use it.

A faint tickle started at the center of his forehead. He lifted a finger to touch the spot and a presence exploded into his brain. ::And stay the fuck out of my head, bastard.::

Twenty-three

There was nothing to do. Bree leaned against a smooth stone, staring into the distance. When asked, she'd said she was watching for Chance, but in reality she let her vision blur to stare into nothing. Inaction ate at her, churning in her belly, making her doubt.

They had entered the World Between Worlds with the extra days before them to aid in their search for Morghan. But they'd landed practically on his doorstep--she smiled to herself--if he'd had a door. They knew of no way to open the veil any earlier than the blue moon the following night. As background noise to her musing, Gowthaman and Morghan continued to discuss every avenue of possible escape Morghan had attempted when he'd first been brought here.

Tapping her foot raised a cloud of dust. She cast a quick glance sideways to study the shadow of a neighboring rock and the line Chance had drawn. If the shadow would only move a little faster and meet the line, she'd have an excuse to go look for her brother. At least it would be something to do.

A human shadow moved next to her and Coralie knelt at her side. "Come an' join us at the fire, Breanna. Yer doin' no good sittin' here by yerself. Chance will return when he is good an' ready."

A retort burst to her lips and she bit back her snarl then sighed. "I know. I'm just out of sorts."

"Ye mean this situation is out of yer control."

Bree gave Coralie a sharp look before sighing again. "Yeah. It is. I didn't realize I was such a control freak."

Coralie patted her arm. "Oh, yer no'. But ye are concerned for the lives of our little group. An' how we are to return. 'Tis naught we can do but wait until the appointed time and do what we planned. The magic will either work, or 'twill no'."

Stunned by the complacency in Coralie's tone, Bree asked, "Don't you want to get home?"

"Ah, ye ken..." After a pause Coralie gazed at Morghan and a soft smile curved her lips. The sour bile of jealousy settled in Bree's stomach at the love shining there. "Ye ken wherever he may be, that be my home. In the human world. In Alfar waters. Here. 'Twill always be so."

If only she could allow herself the luxury of love. Bree firmed her resolve and looked at Gowthaman. As though sensing the touch of her gaze, he turned to smile. Her heart leapt but she tamped down the loving elation. She offered a half smile in return then looked away from Gowtham's quizzical expression.

Coralie touched her elbow. "I do no' understand ye, Breanna. Afore this night past, ye did no' hide yer feelin's from the librarian. Now that he openly returns yer love, ye will no even speak with him?" She shook her head. "I do no' ken."

"Neither do I. I want us to be like I've dreamed for so long. But now... here... I can't."

"An' ye would give away yer chance for happiness?"

"Happiness? Here?"

Disappointment filled Coralie's expression. Bree's stomach lurched lower. She might as well find a piece of paper and start making a list of her failures. She wanted to be a loving mate, ached to be, but her relationship with Gowthaman had changed so rapidly. And after the violence of the post-healing release. How could she go on from that moment, living her dream as though he hadn't seen her in the throes of weakness? Would he have given her comfort or offered her love in another place? At another time? The desperation of the World Between Worlds might cause any of them to act or react differently than they would in their comfortable, well known worlds.

The thought tumbled round and around in her brain. Thankfully Coralie remained silent. Bree didn't have a clue how she would answer any more questions from her astute friend.

Action would clear her mind. With a soft 'humph' she understood why Chance had gone to explore. And Searlait's warnings against letting the doldrums settle in the mind.

Resolved to shake off the gathering lethargy and despair, she scrambled to her feet and held one hand out to Coralie. "Let's go see what our guys are talking about, shall we?"

Morghan paused in explaining his theory when Breanna and Coralie moved toward them. Gowthaman relished the silence that gave him a moment to watch Breanna's easy stride, the soft sway of her hips. She was troubled, but after he'd caught her staring at him, she appeared to have hidden those troubles away. Now her smile was relaxed, yet he sensed the tension tightening into tiny lines at the corners of her eyes.

He didn't know whether to honor her silent plea and not acknowledge her concerns, or take her in his arms and kiss away whatever troubled her. He settled for taking her hand and drawing her down beside him. He kept her fingers curled against his palm and stroked the side of her thumb with his. A flash of--ah, he'd spent too long ignoring or denying the emotions her eyes showed so clearly, now he wasn't sure what he'd seen. While Coralie settled in the cradle of Morghan's crossed legs, Gowthaman tugged Breanna closer and whispered, "Do not doubt. I do love you."

Her eyes glistened before she turned her face from him. "Thank you," she mumbled.

He kept his voice soft. "No, sundarii, it is I who must offer thanks for all you have given me. For the years I did not understand, the times I pushed you away."

The dimple in her cheek deepened before she faced him with a true smile. "We'll talk about that when we get home. You've got time to make up for."

The teasing glint overlaying the worry in her eyes lessened some of his concerns. He would gladly give her that time, now and forever. "Yes, there will be much to say."

"Say? Yes, that too."

Breanna glanced at the designs Morghan had drawn in the gray dust. "So what were you guys talking about?"

Morghan cleared his throat. "While Gowthaman told me of the legends an' tales he'd discovered about the blue moon, I remembered a drawin' I'd once seen. Long ago when Da was tryin' to teach m'brother an' me to lead our people. 'Twas in one of his old books. I fear at that time, I did no' care to learn anythin' but what was of interest to me." He gave a short chuckle then continued. "I believe the book was among the collection Da gave ye, sweet Coralie."

Coralie poked him in the chest. "Aye, an' what would ye have learned then instead?"

He grabbed her finger and brought it to his lips. Gowthaman cast down his gaze, knowing he should be able to so easily shower the woman he loved with simple affections. Their relationship was too new, and the time too desperate to find the moments to become lovers comfortable with each other.

Breanna squeezed his hand and leaned her shoulder into his. He accepted her silent understanding with yet another personal vow to discover the ways to treat his Breanna as the love and soul she was to him.

"An' mayhap, sweet Coralie... No, I will no' think of what might have been. Much of my life was wasted. I accept my faults an' the repercussions of m' actions."

Morghan had stated simple concepts in words Gowthaman knew he should be able to vocalize, though the reasons may be vastly different. The increased pressure of Breanna's hand continued to grant him understanding. She had always understood and forgiven him. How could one woman be so true?

Breanna asked, "What was this drawing? Is it something that will help insure our safe return home?"

"That, I am unable to answer. In truth, my recollection is dim, at best. But, this illustration consisted of three circles separated from a fourth by a thick line."

He fell silent. The tiny fire cracked and snapped. Gowthaman stared into the gray flame. He did not remember seeing drawings similar to the one Morghan described, but his access to Alfar knowledge had been limited. Morghan had sketched a simple drawing in the dirt, one that would seem to hold no special meaning. Yet he felt an importance deep in his bones.

How was it that the simplest puzzles were often the most difficult to solve?

Morghan lifted a strand of Coralie's curls, twisted it through his fingers, then began to plait the length. He hummed as he worked.

Gowthaman tilted his head to listen. The soft notes danced in a rhythmic pattern he could almost grasp. Similar to another... no, to a game. A game human children often played. He glanced at Breanna. As a child, she had charmed him into joining her in that game.

Straightening with a jerk, he closed his eyes to visualize a page from his journal. In the lower corner was an odd notation he'd made without understanding why. The name of that game. Ring o' Ring o' Roses.

"What are you humming?"

Breanna asked the question he was about to speak. Gowthaman opened his eyes to give her a grateful nod. Once again she anticipated his intellectual need.

His pulse throbbed. Slow heat filled his veins then settled low and heavy in his body. Another need flushed through him, burning hotter at the easy wink she gave him. This need, this she would anticipate as well.

Morghan continued to hum until he completed the thin braid. Resting his hands on Coralie's shoulders, he leaned back with a thoughtful expression. "A children's song. A game. I do no' ken why I think of it now. Feels as if ages have passed since I last watched children at play."

Gowthaman pointed at the rough scratching in the dirt. "Do you believe there is any connection between the drawing and the song?"

Cuddling closer to then lifting his arm to wrap around her shoulders, Breanna said, "I was just going to ask that." She chuckled, then stared at Morghan. "Well?"

He shrugged. "Who can say?"

"Hopefully we can. The tune reminds me a little of Ring around the Rosie. I just loved that when I was little. Especially the falling down part. Remember?" She gave Gowthaman a gentle jab with her elbow.

"Yes, little missy. You made me join your game many times." He smiled and touched the tip of his middle finger to her nose, just as he had when she was a child.

She grabbed his finger, pressed a kiss to the pad then continued, "But, you know, the song wasn't just some nonsense for kids. The rhyme was originally created so people remembered the black plague."

A shudder crawled along Gowthaman's spine. Although his Faerie home had been far distant, the threat of the Black Death had kept the portals closed and well-guarded. Young and daring, he had risked exposure many times in the name of illumination and knowledge. Long before his risks had led to the stealing of his mind.

Warmth from Breanna's simple caress steered him from the still tender pit of his loss and memory. He glanced at her face; she stared past Morghan's shoulder, searching the distance.

Coralie sighed. "Aye, that was a terrible time. The Alfar seldom rose to the surface in those days. We were susceptible to the disease as well." She glanced sideways at Morghan. "Yer Da once told me he believed my parents died then."

"Did he now? Was there more he told ye? Afore--"

"He did no'. We shall speak of such things when we do no' have more important discussions." Coralie caught Breanna's attention. "So, yer thinkin' our Alfar song may have a similar hidden meaning?"

An elegant shrug lifted her shoulders. "It's worth a thought anyway. The timing of Morghan's remembering the song, along with his drawing, feels like it should be important. Great, now I'm sounding like Nightshade and all his 'feelings'."

Morghan scratched his head. "Ye wish me to remember words from my childhood?"

"Oh, come on Morghan. Surely you're not so old." Bree glanced from his face to Coralie's grin and back. "Or are you?"

He gave her a long, appraising look and said, "No' so much older than yer man. Though ye are a wee bit of a young one."

"And I remember the games I played. So..."

"So," he repeated. "Coralie, ye must help me. Yer memory far outshines m'own."

"Compliments? Aye. Will ye hum it again?"

Bree leaned close to Gowthaman while Coralie teased Morghan into the song. "I wish Chance would get back," she muttered.

Gowthaman stroked her hair. She loved his hands in her hair. She would grow it long again--when they got home. Pleasure relaxed the tense muscles of her shoulders. His fingers danced down the side of her neck, tickling the tender spot below her ear. "Soon, sundarii. The shadow has not yet met his mark."

The sharp sound of Coralie's clap chased Chance from the top of her list of concerns. "What?"

"I remember the game we played, but no' yet all the words. First we would join hands and spin in a circle while we sang. I think... aye, we did often tumble to the ground."

"Yep, just like our Ring around the Rosie. Anything else?"

Concentration drew Coralie's brows together. "I... um... aye, at a certain phrase one of the players jumped to the middle of the circle an' we had to hold him within. We were no' supposed to allow the center child to break apart our hands. No matter how hard he tried."

"Now that sounds like a game we had called London Bridge. Someone got 'locked up' when the bridge fell down. That was the fun part--trying to break free and getting tossed around."

"Oh, an' in our game no matter how many children played, there was ne'er more than four in each group. Three for the circle an' one inside." Coralie kissed Morghan's cheek. "Do ye remember the words yet?"

"Soon, eudail. Hush now an' let me think."

Reaching for the stick Morghan had dropped, Gowthaman traced over the designs the Sindhu had drawn. Bree watched the slow movement. The sound of dry wood against the even drier earth screeched like fingernails against a blackboard. She shuddered and Gowthaman's movements stilled.

"I am sorry. I did not mean to--"

"Hush. The sound just grates on my nerves. I know you're thinking."

Nodding slowly, he laid the stick aside. "While I do not sense anything familiar about this diagram, there is meaning for us. The need to know settles in my chest, and at the center of my intellect."

"Three circles. Hmm. All through your research into rescuing Morghan, the number three has played a prominent role."

"Three is a holy number for many civilizations. Perhaps it is no more than that."

"You don't believe that, do you?" Bree took his hand, curled down his thumb and little finger then indicated the remaining fingers. "What do we know about the number three in this case? Speaking a spell or incantation three times? Morghan tried that before with limited success. He prevented the elemental from escaping but was brought here as well."

"There must be a conjunction of second moons within a month's span. A conjunction within three worlds."

She stroked his long, elegant fingers, lost for a moment in the texture of his skin. Desire sparkled between them. Gold and crimson. She gasped. "Can you see this?"

Gowthaman leaned to touch his forehead to hers while they stared at the colors dancing about their hands. "Yes. I see our soulfire."

"The colors?"

There was a smile in his voice. "It would appear Chance was correct. Even the gray of the World Between Worlds can not dampen the colors of love."

"I remember." Morghan's soft spoken words drew Bree's reluctant attention. He tapped his temple. "Here in the World Between Worlds, 'tis too easy to forget, an' even easier to forget to care. But, with my thanks to ye, I remember."

After a moment of silence, he began singing quietly. "Once from water, once in air, again for land, challenge an' dare. Dance to sing. Sing to close. Forever bind, forever hold. Air an' land, deep water too, now we sing this dance for you."

Coralie began nodding part way through Morghan's song. When he finished, she wrapped her arms about his neck and kissed him full on the mouth.

Heat crawled up Bree's neck to fill her cheeks. She stared at her feet. Why should a kiss between two people she cared for embarrass her? She was delighted Coralie and Morghan were finally together. A gentle finger lifted her chin and she met Gowthaman's tender, knowing gaze. A slight pressure drew her closer. The warmth of his breath flowed past her cheek. Her eyelids drifted closed.

"Hey sis, what's up?"

Dust from Chance dropping to the ground filled her nostrils. She sneezed, rubbed her nose and opened her eyes, turning from Gowthaman's resigned expression.

Obviously well pleased with himself, Chance grinned. "What have you guys been up to?"

"Singin' the songs of children," Morghan answered.

"Uh, sure. Yep. Looked like it to me. Uh-huh, more like you were all thinking about making children."

Face burning, Bree slapped his shoulder. For all the teasing in his tone, he was close to the truth. And he knew it.

"Geez, Bree. Just kidding. Sorta," he finished under his breath.

Before she found a proper retort, Morghan asked, "Did ye discover anythin' of interest on yer walk?"

Guilt flashed through Chance's expression and he shook his head. "Nothing but a lot of gray."

Studying the tic just below her brother's ear, Bree bit back the need to call Chance on his lie. From the corner of her eye she saw Gowthaman give a barely perceptible head shake. So, he detected the falsehood as well.

"An' ye'll ne'er find more than that here." Morghan waved a hand toward the ground at Chance's feet. "As ye have returned, an' ruined my drawin', mayhap ye can assist us in findin' the meanin' of the children's rhyme."

Chance glanced at the partial circles remaining sketched in the dirt and scuttled back a few inches, further obliterating the drawing. "Oops. Sorry."

Slipping the scabbard from his back, Chance laid both swords behind him then stretched and crossed his legs at the ankles. He wiggled his feet up and down reminding Bree of when he was a little boy, innocent and mischievous at the same time. What would she ever do without him to brighten her life?

"So, what's all this about kid's songs?"

Gowthaman answered. "We were discussing the importance of three, attempting to determine how best to insure our escape."

"Okay, nothing new about that. What's up with the songs then?"

Gowthaman shrugged and Bree frowned at the odd reaction. But then he smiled. "I have heard it said the things we remember best are the songs and games of childhood."

"Sure, that makes sense. So, you're thinking that there may be a clue to help us get home in some children's song?"

"Yes."

Chance thought for a moment then glanced at Morghan. "And the drawing?"

"Somethin' I remembered from an old book. Here, I shall show you. An' we have no' determined if there be a relationship between the song and the drawin'."

"But there might be?" Chance arched his eyebrows and waited for Morghan to answer.

"Mayhap."

"Cool. Let me see."

Coralie handed Morghan the short stick while Chance scooted back a bit further then rose to his hands and knees to watch Morghan draw. Bree studied her brother in silence. In spite of his lie, he appeared more relaxed and focused than he had before he went on his walk-about. Something had changed within him. Something important. And she needed to know. "Chance?"

"Shush. Let me think about this." He waved one hand before leaning forward, intent on the tip of Morghan's stick. "Can you sing the song for me, too?"

Coralie's light alto filled the small camp while Morghan completed the crude drawing. At the end of the simple tune, everyone turned to watch Chance. Proud of her brother's interest, Bree held her breath waiting for his first comment.

He leaned back and settled cross-legged again. "You're messing with me, right?"

"Messin' with ye?" Morghan asked.

"Sure. Seeing if the kid can figure this out. A test."

"No, Chance," Gowthaman said. "Here we present a true conundrum to you. As of yet, we do not understand either the song or the drawing."

Chance laughed. "You're kidding, right?" After a moment of stunned silence while he looked at each of them in turn, he asked, "Want to hear what the kid thinks?"

Bree nudged his foot with hers. "Of course we do."

"May I?" Chance held out his hand for the stick. In a showy move learned from their dad, he waved the stick like a magic wand over the three circles then touched the thick bar. "This is keeping the single circle from the others. Easy." He tapped the single circle. "Brandr Ur."

"But what about--"

"Shush. Let's leave the drawing for a moment and study the song."

Thinking that her brother sounded a bit like Gowthaman in a lecturing mode, she explained, "Actually, Coralie said it was a game. Like Ring around the Rosie or London Bridge."

His grin spread. "Even better. Now it make's complete sense."

"What does?"

"Look sis, there's three things mentioned in the song. Air, water and land. Also the words forever bind." He paused and looked at them expectantly, eyebrows arched high. When no one spoke, he shook his head and continued. "You must be too close to the problem. Air. Water. Land." He touched the three circles then made the mark of a letter as he indicated each again. "Sindhu. Andras. And... I keep forgetting the name of your earth-dwelling cousins." He glanced at Morghan.

"Domovoii."

"Right. Domovoii. So. There's your three. The drawing and the song both tell us it took all three Alfar races to bind the elemental and hold him in the World Between Worlds."

Grinning, Chance leaned back on his elbows. "Simple."

Twenty-four

"And while I was in the library, I heard children playing in the gardens," Tori said after she spread the sheet with a simple drawing on the patio table. "Normally I wouldn't think much about it, but they were playing a singing game that called to me as though I had heard it before. A long time ago."

Nightshade nodded. "The games of children are pretty much the same no matter where or when you go, honey."

She leveled her gaze on him. "I know. But this was different. I don't remember words, but I'm almost positive my adoptive grandmother hummed the tune when she put me to bed. Then... then I took a couple of minutes to glance through the book after I copied the drawing and found this." She slipped a second sheet from the waterproof carrier and unrolled the page, laying it over the drawing.

Nightshade angled the page to read in the dim, early evening light. The day had been long, and their discussions fruitless. He'd sent Jayse and Lucidea off to rest an hour ago. He snorted softly to himself. At least he hoped they were resting.

He read the short poem twice, then letting his questions show in his expression, glanced up at Tori. She'd grabbed a snack from the chest inside the workroom door and joined him at the table. She pointed with a tiny wedge of cheese. "Those words, that's the song the children sang while they played."

"Once from water, once in air, again for land, challenge and dare. Dance to sing. Sing to close. Forever bind, forever hold." The words triggered his own memories. Of being tossed back and forth while trying to escape the circle of his brother and cousins. "Air and land, deep water too, now we sing this dance for you."

After swallowing her bite of cheese, Tori nodded. "I looked out the window to watch. There were four children. Three held hands and circled around the fourth who tried to break through their circle. Nightshade, I think this is what we've been looking for. I think this is how we keep Brandr Ur contained while the rest get home."

"A game?" Even as he said the words, he knew she was right. A heavy shadow surrounded his heart. There was no turning back now, whatever decisions he'd made in his life had brought him to this point in time. To this family and their quests. He closed his eyes and sighed deeply.

"Is something wrong, Nightshade?"

"No, honey. Nightshade's fine."

"Hmm, I don't think so. You didn't rest today, did you?"

He swung his arm in an expansive gesture and tried for a flippant grin. "Who needs rest when there's a puzzle to solve?"

"Doesn't work with me, honey."

"Tori..." He leaned forward and pressed his hands flat over the papers. "Do you think you could contact our travelers during a dreamwalk?"

Her eyes widened at his request and she sat back with a soft release of breath. "Not what I expected," she muttered.

Satisfied he'd thrown her off his case, at least for a short while, Nightshade continued. "If I remember correctly, and of course Nightshade always remembers, when Morghan first disappeared he was able to communicate with Lucidea and Coralie as long as he could find water. They assumed that when he no longer visited their dreams, he could find no water. Coralie packed extra bottles of loch water with her in hopes of communicating with us should a need arise."

"I didn't know that."

"You didn't take a look at her bulging pack, did you?" Nightshade chuckled. "But even though they could hear Morghan, Coralie doesn't believe he could ever hear them. So it was only a one way conversation. Maybe if we initiate the contact here--"

"Great idea. And in a dreamwalk, I'll have more control. Maybe the drumming will get their attention faster."

"So I'm hoping. When will be the best time for you to try?"

"At moonrise. What am I going to tell them?"

He held the silence for a long moment before speaking. "That instead of reciting the spell three times, we believe three voices are needed to simultaneously create the magic to keep the elemental contained."

"If you're going to try something like that..." came a soft voice from the doorway. Nightshade turned to face Lucidea and she continued. "I think the best place to try is at the water wall in the cave below the manor."

"Chance, I would like to speak with you." Leaving the others arguing over whether Breanna had the strength to heal the wound on Morghan's arm, Gowthaman followed the young man a short distance from the campfire.

Chance's shoulders stiffened, then with a deep breath he rolled one then the other, looked back over his shoulder and said, "Sure. Let's wander this way just a bit further, okay?"

Holding back a smile at the young man's nervousness, Gowthaman nodded. He watched Chance's back as they moved away, noticing the rapid shifts from tense to relaxed. Something bothered Breanna's brother. Perhaps if given the opportunity, he would confide. Realizing he would accept and relish the fact someone could again confide in him, Gowthaman paused.

Chance stopped in the shadows of a tall rock and looked out over the distant plain. He gave a satisfied nod then motioned Gowthaman nearer and leaned against the stone. "So, what did you want to talk about?"

Matching the casual pose, Gowthaman considered the cold stone at his back. No sun shone in the gray world to heat the stone, but the heavy, arid air burned his nostrils. This was a place of sameness, with many contradictions.

His first visit had taken him to a place of mist, gray and impenetrable. A place of judgment, yet the Watchers who resided there had not judged him. He had judged himself, allowing himself to exist in a world he knew, yet had allowed to become as colorless as the landscape surrounding them. Just as Breanna brought color to the World Between Worlds, she had gifted him with the colors of their soulfire. Now there were as many contradictions in him as in the World Between Worlds. There would be much for him to remember, much to study when he returned home. If he returned.

Ruthlessly shoving away his concerns, he bent one knee to plant his foot flat against the stone behind him. "I am impressed with your deductions and solution to the song and diagram."

Chance gave a start, then chuckled. "Thanks. I really thought you were testing me. I can't believe any of you, especially you, didn't figure that out a long time ago."

"Sometimes the simplest answers are the most difficult to find."

"I guess so."

"You have a sharp mind--"

"That I don't use often enough, as my sister likes to remind me. I'm really glad you two finally got together. Teasing aside, Gowthaman, it's about time."

"Yes, it is. I was too proud."

"Hey man, I understand. At least you finally came to your senses. I got tired of her moping around over you."

"Moping?"

"Yeah, you know..." Chance slouched to one side, opened his eyes wide and stared at the sky. He heaved a huge, noisy sigh. Then he grinned and stood straight. "Like that."

"She did not."

"Not when you would see, no. But when she was alone, when she didn't think anyone was around." His grin faded. "I hated seeing her like that... loving you when you didn't seem to care. Or simply even notice her. If your idiocy would have gone on much longer I was considering forcing a man to man talk with you." He dropped his gaze to his clenched fist. "She would have kicked my ass if I did, though."

"I do not doubt she would, and done a thorough job. I thank you now for your concern, for the love you bear your sister."

"Hell, Gowthaman. I like you. You're the best man for Bree, no question about it. Just took you long enough."

No response needed, they fell silent. How he'd earned the right to be a part of such a family, Gowthaman was unsure. Days ago he would have denied the existence of that right. Today he was the luckiest of all Faerie, for Breanna loved him. Him... despite his failings and denials. She loved him. Here in this loveless, colorless place he had found love and acceptance. Miracles.

Chance fidgeted, scraping his foot in the dirt. He squirmed, rubbing his back against the stone creating a dry, rasping that set Gowthaman's teeth on edge. "Gowthaman, I lied."

"I know."

"Not about you and Bree, about when I was scouting."

"Yes, I know. As does your sister. I am sure she will corner you and wish to discuss it with you later."

"Can you talk to her for me?" He sounded as young as he was, pleading for a champion. But his eyes shone with age and hidden wisdom. Like the World Between Worlds that held them, Chance was full of contradictions.

"Tell me your lie." Gowthaman wouldn't make a promise without knowing the stakes. Standing between Breanna and her brother would not be wise.

"I went to see Brandr Ur."

"You what?"

Chance made hushing motions with his hands then peered around Gowthaman to see if the others had heard the outburst. Gowthaman stared at him, unable to believe the seriousness-- the foolishness--the utter... "Chance, explain."

"It's kind of a long story."

"We have time." He straightened to block Chance's view of the others--and his escape. Folding his arms over his chest, Gowthaman waited.

"Hey, for a librarian you're pretty formidable when you want to be."

"No stalling. Explain."

Chance lifted his hands in surrender then sank back against the stone. His face settled into serious lines. "Even before anyone talked about this being the time to rescue Morghan, there was this voice in my head. Whispering just beyond what I could hear most of the time, but there. It reminded me of my bio dad, of how Fiedhlim repeatedly tried to invade my mind when I was a baby. Before Jayse killed him. Eventually, I did some research."

Gowthaman arched his eyebrows.

"Okay, so maybe it was more like snooping. Anyway, I heard about how the elemental had invaded minds when he tried before to escape. Then I knew what was in my head. Like that was a key I started hearing and understanding what he had to say."

"What--"

"I don't want to get into that now. Let it suffice to say it wasn't pretty. Oh, he offers a good deal, but I'm not stupid enough to believe him. That's why I wanted to come along. Had to come here. That's why I went off on my own today. To confront him."

"You were successful in your confrontation?"

A half-smile lightened Chance's expression. "Yeah. I was. I forced him from my mind. I don't think he was happy about it. I challenged him, too, but he said he'd made a promise to the prince--I guess he means Morghan--not to fight until tomorrow night."

"You believe him to be a creature of his word?"

"Yeah, strangely enough, I do. What I need to tell you is that when I encountered him, he had a stick and was drawing in the dirt. Like Morghan. And, Gowthaman, he'd drawn the same bar and circles."

"You are positive the drawing was the same?"

"Essentially, yeah, but the elemental's looked more like random doodling than Morghan's precise drawing. And once he started taunting me, he scuffed it over like it wasn't anything but scratches in the dirt. I don't think he knows the significance."

"But it is significant he drew the same diagram."

"So you gonna tell the others?"

Gowthaman studied Chance and the young man met his gaze solidly. He clasped Chance's shoulder. "Not as of yet. I must think on this. I shall keep your secret until it proves necessary to expose your activities." He gestured toward the campfire with a cant of his head. "Come, it sounds as if our meal is prepared. I shall attempt to keep your sister occupied so she has little time to question you."

"I'm sure you can think of something." With a waggle of his eyebrows, Chance straightened from his slouch and nodded. "I'm ready."

Pale gray embers glowed in the banked campfire; the occasional spark danced into the air with a soft snap. Breanna sighed, imagining color and sparkle instead of gray. The slightly duller shadows of night had come to the World Between Worlds and once again, nothing had been solved.

Not true, she told herself. After an evening's discussion they believed they knew how to prevent the elemental from escaping with them through the open veil. Chance's insight proved the turning point in their thoughts.

Now Chance curled under a blanket on the other side of the fire. His soft snores testified to the young man's ability to sleep anywhere, despite the lingering concerns and the dangers of tomorrow.

Restless, she shifted but Gowthaman followed, snuggling her close to his body. Maybe they should have wandered away like Morghan and Coralie, and returned to the privacy of the small grotto. Maybe she should follow the desires curling through her body and forget her worries for a short while. One night to savor and share with Gowthaman.

Instead she had opted to remain here, fighting her thoughts and still discovering no way to win. If what they believed was true, it was impossible--

"Sundarii," Gowthaman whispered close to her ear. "You must rest."

She shook her head.

"There is little we can do this night. Perhaps when it is again day we shall discover a new possibility."

Rolling to her back, she stared up at him. "I don't... it's impos--"

His kiss was gentle, tender, demanding nothing but her silence, her acquiescence. Willingly, she accepted the comfort and love he offered, returning passion in the press of her lips, the dance of her tongue. Yet while her responses grew more heated, his kisses remained soft and teasing.

Then he touched her. He slid his hand under her shirt, warming a path over her abdomen. A gasp passed between them when he cupped her breast and traced his thumb over her nipple. His kisses teased her lips, her cheek, the tender spot beneath her ear. His hand roamed, soothing, delighting and she arched into his palm.

He paused with his lips against her cheek and she felt him smile. She drew breath but before she could speak, he'd captured her mouth and stole her thoughts with the slow thrust and retreat of his tongue. When she stroked her hands over his back he stopped his caresses and rose on his elbow, touching her mouth with a fingertip.

"Shh." The sound ended in a sigh before he took her hands and draped her fingers over his shoulders. "Touch me there only. No more."

Bree frowned, but nodded and after a moment of holding her captured in his dark gaze, Gowthaman returned to his slow seduction. He didn't need to go slow. She was seduced, and wanting. Though she squirmed, tightened her hands on his shoulders, begged with her body, he continued his slow, torturous pace.

She nearly sobbed with relief when Gowthaman pulled a blanket over his head and shoulders cocooning them in a makeshift tent then slid his hand past her belly button and under the waistband of her jeans. The snap popped free and he slowly opened the zipper. She sighed. At last.

His long, wondrous fingers circled, teased, entered to stroke deep inside her. As if he knew the moment her cries ached for release, he covered her mouth with his, sealing the sounds between them. Taking her. So high. So tight. So...

The interior of their makeshift tent filled with sparkling crimson and golden lights. Gowthaman lifted his head, gazed down on her and with one final stroke gave her powerful, shattering release. Bree bit her lip to contain her cry until Gowthaman soothed the spot with his tongue. She sighed and tugged him close for a kiss.

A long, satisfying kiss. Even longer they remained under the blanket watching the colors of their soulfire collide, swirl together and combine. Finally Gowthaman pushed the blanket from his shoulders, rolled to his back and fitted her against his body so her head rested on his chest.

Her breathing slowed as he stroked her back and she listened to the strong beat of his heart.

Another thrumming beat intruded on the languid moments. She lifted her head. "Do you hear that beating?"

"It is only the song of love in my heart, Breanna. Rest, love."

Her breathing relaxed to the rhythm of Gowthaman's heart. She listened to the other insistent beat. The sounds lulled her toward sleep.

Her eyes popped open. She pressed one hand to Gowthaman's chest and sat. "No, listen. Those are drum beats."

Tugging and fastening her jeans, Bree scrambled to her feet. She reached down for Gowthaman's hand and pulled him up beside her. After one quick glance at her brother she turned away. No use trying to wake him when he slept like he was dead to the world. Since the drumming felt more comforting than threatening, she let Chance sleep.

Morghan emerged from between two massive boulders followed closely by Coralie. Meeting at the edge of camp, the four silently scanned the horizon, straining to discover the direction from which the drumming emanated.

"Have you encountered anything like this?" Gowthaman asked Morghan.

"I have no'. Unless there is a new captive, one who has no' yet become accustomed to the silence..."

"No, this sounds more like there's a purpose," Bree said. "It's a consistent, even beat."

Coralie took an eager step forward. "Aye, like the drummin' Tori uses for a dreamwalk. Quickly, I need water. An' a place to make a puddle."

Bree joined Coralie at the pack, grabbing four bottles of the loch water. Gowthaman knelt to scoop out a shallow hole in the dry dirt. When Morghan stood frozen watching the activity, Coralie nudged his side with her elbow as she passed. "Ye contacted Lucidea an' I, remember? By talkin' through water into our dreams. If this be Catori, she is in a type of dream. We need the water. Mayhap we can communicate with Lucidea."

He scratched at his chin. "Who is Catori?"

Corali paused. "Oh, aye, I have no' had time to tell ye about my sister."

"Sister?"

"Aye, now either help or move out of our way."

Morghan chuckled then crouched beside Gowthaman to even out the shallow depression. Bree tossed them a small square of plastic and after they lined the hole, poured in two bottles of water.

Shoulder to shoulder, the four hovered over the small, still puddle. Bree held her breath until Gowthaman took her hand and gave a gentle squeeze. As she released a slow breath tiny impact tremors bounced over the surface, gathered near one edge then smoothed. A slender figure appeared in the distance, moving forward, swiftly growing larger.

"'Tis Tori," Coralie cried.

When her upper body filled the watery space, Tori stopped, smiled, and began to speak. The drumming continued, throbbing in the background, but no sound carried Tori's words.

"We can no' hear ye," Coralie shouted then made an angry sound of dismay when Tori continued as though she hadn't heard her sister's shout. Morghan wrapped his arm about her shoulders.

"Guys, tryin' to sleep here," grumbled a muffled voice behind them. Bree glanced at Chance, but he'd turned over to face away from them.

"Do you think she can see us?" Gowthaman asked.

Coralie waved and Tori returned the gesture. "Aye. Can ye hear me?"

When Tori continued speaking, Coralie frowned, then held one hand cupped behind her ear and shook her head. A stricken expression filled Tori's face. Her image wavered as if seen through a panel of running water then she was gone. The drum continued for five beats, each fainter than the last until the final echo pulled a single circular ripple in the water.

Bree stared at the now still surface and the faint reflections of the four faces bent over the puddle. "How do we get her back?"

"Of more importance, how do we communicate? Share our theories?" Gowthaman touched a fingertip to the water, disturbing the surface.

"We could use hand motions and props," Bree suggested, but then shook her head. "We don't know how much she really could see...only Coralie's face? Her whole body? That would make our game of charades more difficult."

"Aye," Coralie agreed. "An' trying to speak words clearly so that she could read our lips would probably no' work any better. The ripples cause too much disturbance on the surface."

Silence enveloped them. Bree sat, winced then leaned sideways and brushed a sharp stone from beneath her. Although they had discussed Morghan's early communication, and Coralie brought water along in hopes of doing the same now, Bree had never really considered the possibility or implications of communications to other worlds. They had simply planned to enter the World Between Worlds, find Morghan and take him home. Simple.

At least it should have been simple. She glanced at the others. Morghan and Coralie sat staring thoughtfully at the water puddle. Gowthaman drummed his fingers against his knee, obviously lost in his own thoughts, theories and possibilities.

"When I was able to contact my sweet Coralie or my niece, I did no' really understand how the connection happened. They were always dreamin'. Is that true, Eudail?"

Coralie nodded.

"Yet none of us here were sleepin' when the drummin' began."

Gowthaman lifted his head, and spoke. "Tori was raised in a Native American culture. She is a shaman and able to walk in dream worlds. I believe this is how she came to us. However, the how of her appearance does not concern me as does the why. Why did Jayse or Lucidea feel the need to communicate with us? What new problem has arisen without our knowledge?"

"Whatever it may be, we'll face it down, Gowtham." Attempting to ease his obvious anxiety, Bree added a determined smile to her words. "I'm pretty sure she'll try again, so let's figure out how we can talk back."

With direction and focus, Bree felt wonderfully alive again. There was something to do. She didn't know what, but something. And that was so much better than sitting around and still not knowing what waited around the corner.

A heavy sigh sounded behind her. "You guys have got to be so glad to have me along."

Caught off guard by the playful egotism in her brother's voice, Bree chuckled. Turning to face Chance, she watched as he stretched, groaned, fought with his blanket then sat up and rubbed his hands over his face. She laughed again.

"Go ahead and laugh, sis. I'll just go back to sleep and won't tell you the answer."

She broke off with a squeak and Chance grinned. "Okay then. In the movies--"

"Chance--"

"Hang on. Let me finish. In the movies whenever anyone needs to communicate with someone else, and all the so called normal avenues are unusable, what do they always fall back on?"

He watched her expectantly, then slid his gaze to each of the others, shaking his head. "It's like how the countdown always stops at one."

After blowing out a frustrated breath, Bree pointed at him. "Just. Tell. Us."

"Nightshade would say, 'Use the code, honey.'"

"Code?"

"Dense tonight, aren't we? The code. Morse code. If we could hear Tori's drumbeats but not her voice, and she couldn't hear Coralie, then it stands to reason she would be able to hear drumbeats from our side. Find something to make a drum out of and use the code. Nightshade did say it might come in handy one day when he made us learn it, didn't he?"

With that, he flopped to his back then turned on his side facing away from the fire. After pulling the blanket over his head, he waved over his shoulder. "Geez, Bree, you're slippin'. Leavin' the answer up to the kid again."

Twenty-five

Tori listed sideways. Nightshade narrowed his eyes watching until he was sure her spirit had returned from the dreamwalk, tapped a few more beats on the drum then rested his fingers lightly on the taut skin head. Keeping his anxious thoughts contained, he remained silent while Lucidea supported Tori.

Finally the dreamwalker gave her head a shake, straightened and frowned. "They couldn't hear me."

With the drum wobbling on his knee, Nightshade leaned toward her. "Start from the beginning..." he glanced toward the ceiling, "...trite as that sounds."

As he'd hoped, a smile touched her lips although her dark eyes remained shadowed with worry. "I had no trouble finding my way once in the dream. The veil parted for me easily. Maybe too easily."

"Don't second guess yourself, honey."

She gave him a grateful look. "Thanks, Nightshade. Anyway, I was in the World Between Worlds and I found them right away. But when I tried talking to them, they couldn't hear me. But, they must have heard the drumming. Otherwise I don't know why they would have made a connection through water."

"You're sure there was water involved?" Lucidea asked.

"Yeah. What I saw was like looking out from under the surface of the loch. When I realized they couldn't hear me, I lost focus and was thrown back here."

Lucidea rose from her crouch, helping Tori to her feet as well. "So, we know we can get there. We just need to figure out how to communicate so they know what we've figured out."

"We don't have much time." Tori spread her hands.

"A day is long enough," Nightshade said. 'After this first contact, they'll either be waiting for us to try again or try from their side. I'd suggest we stay here until we make contact--or it's time to go back out to the hill to welcome everyone home."

Tori nodded. "The water wall really helped focus my dream energy. I'm pretty sure that's why I found Coralie and Morghan so quickly."

"Hmm." Lucidea nodded absently. "I've tried to see anything beyond the wall many times since we originally figured out how to use it. But I've never been successful. Maybe I should be a little jealous of your success."

"Oh, I didn't--"

"Oh hush. I'm glad I thought we should be here and that the wall did seem to help. If anyone can find a use for this thing, I'm delighted. Jayse?"

He appeared from the shadows at the edge of the room. "Darlin'?"

"You haven't said anything."

He shrugged. "I'm feeling really out of my element here."

She crossed to him and wrapped her arms around his waist. "Poor baby."

Nightshade turned from the loving couple, stretched his legs out in front of him and asked Tori, "When should we try again, honey?"

Morghan found a mostly hollow tree trunk and dragged it back to the campsite, angling the short length close to their water puddle. While Breanna drew the coded alphabet from her memory, Gowthaman composed a concise message. There might not be much time to pass on information, if they were even able to contact the human world.

Forcing doubt from his mind and replacing the lack with determination, he straightened. Contact between the worlds had been made. Once made, the action could be repeated. Whether they initiated the contact or Tori walked again in a dream world, did not matter. The only thing of importance was the passing of their message.

After altering a bit of wording to make the message more concise, he pictured the words in his mind, committing them to memory. Then he simply sat and watched Breanna.

A tight furrow marred her forehead and she'd compressed her lips to a thin tight line while she tapped a series of patterns against the ground. Occasionally Chance would shake his head, and move his finger against her forearm. She repeated the pattern until they were both satisfied.

Once again he was surprised at Chance's knowledge and abilities. The young were often underestimated. He was as guilty as any for seeing only the man's youth and carefree attitude. He had developed a tunnel vision where others were concerned. Gowthaman shook his head. No, not concerning others, only himself. In that lack of vision, he had overlooked much.

The time had come to make up for that lack, for his losses. The lives of others moved in a slow dance around him, but he had not even taken the moments to listen to their music. To understand. To know. In believing himself damaged and at fault, he had wrapped himself in thick, invisible cocoon and hidden away in his beloved library.

Ah, the library. Hidden beneath the desert sands, deep, distant chambers scattered along seldom explored hallways held the knowledge of ages. Of both Faerie and the human worlds. If only he'd had more time. Perhaps the answers needed here were contained in some forgotten room. Perhaps the legends and tales, histories and daily records of other worlds existed in the unexplored dark. Perhaps...

Perhaps instead of hiding in the past he should step into the present. Watching Breanna tap out letters filled him with longing. The present guarded his future.

She glanced at Chance who nodded in satisfaction then beamed at Gowthaman. His heart, his breath, his world froze for the flash of a brief moment. By the gods of the desert, she was his future.

Many times, she had seen him in pain, had taken the brunt of his angry denials, and gone beyond those moments. Even after experiencing the pain of his healing... Unable to do else, he held out his hand.

Impossibly, her smile brightened. If any being could bring color and life to the World Between Worlds, it would be her. For had she not already brought life... and the wondrous colors of their soulfire to him?

Ruffling Chance's hair, Breanna stood, then walked toward Gowthaman and took his hand. Her touch sparked the beating of his heart. He could breathe again. She bent and kissed a spot near his ear then whispered, "I know. I love you too."

Dah dit dah dit dah

Nightshade jerked from his slouch and stared at the water wall. Something woke him from his light doze, a call he strained to hear repeated. Silence. He glanced around discovering Jayse and Lucidea curled in sleep on the couch. Tori was nowhere to be seen. Perhaps she'd left and her movements had broken into his dreams, waking him.

Returning his attention to the waterwall, he studied the continual flow of water over the smooth rock surface. Twenty years ago visions had overwhelmed Lucidea when she touched the water, but since that time, the wall remained only a softly gurgling water feature with no discernible source. Fighting a memory, he sank back into the overstuffed chair and willed himself to rest.

Dah dit dah dit dah

On his feet before the soft reverberations ended, Nightshade paced to the wall and tentatively flattened his palm against the flowing water. The sound repeated, throbbing up his arm to settle in his chest.

Behind him, he heard the rustle of papers then Tori moved to stand beside him. "What are you doing?" she whispered.

"I heard something."

"And you're touching the wall because...?"

He frowned. "I'm not sure, honey."

Dah dit dah dit dah

"Did you hear that?" He glanced at Tori and she nodded. "Drumming."

"Are you sure? There's only been a couple of short bursts, nothing like what you use for focus." Nightshade inched his hand from the water, shook his head and replaced his palm. "Come on... again."

As if in answer to his command, the faint beats sounded.

Dah dit dah dit dah

Tori stepped closer. "That sounds... familiar somehow."

It was familiar. How had he not noticed immediately? Nightshade threw back his head and laughed.

Mumbled complaints came from the sleeping couple but they hurried to join Nightshade at the wall. "What?" Lucidea grouched, then cast him an apologetic glance.

Turning toward the others, and keeping a serious expression on his face, Nightshade said, "It's them. We need paper and your drum. Now."

While the others scurried to fill his demands, Nightshade reached through the water to touch the stone behind the flow. He closed his eyes. "That's my girl," he whispered.

Jayse moved back to his shoulder. "So what're we doing?"

Dah dit dah dit dah

"Don't you recognize that?" Nightshade asked him.

"No," Jayse drawled as he shook his head.

"Oh, so Nightshade's lessons are forgotten so quickly? Honey, it pains my heart." He rested his free palm against his chest and closed his eyes in mock despair.

"Cut it out, Shade. What's going on?"

Nightshade arched one eyebrow. "It's our rescue party. From the World Between Worlds. Trying to get our attention. Morse code, honey. They're using the code."

Jayse drew his brows down into a frown. "Oh." Then he straightened and grinned. "Oh."

"Do you remember the code well enough to help while I beat the replies? With any luck they'll be able to hear Tori's drum if we can hear theirs."

"I-I think so."

"Good." Nightshade took Jayse's hand and flattened his palm against the flow of the water wall. "This should help magnify the sounds."

Lucidea inched closer to her husband and held her hand next to his. "I don't know Morse code, but I can help listen."

"Tori, would you write down the message as Jayse calls out the letters?"

She waved a pen and small notebook. "I'm ready."

"Okay, let's do this." Nightshade reached for Tori's small drum then sank cross-legged to the floor. Closing his eyes for a moment he paused, hoping he was right, then tapped a series of beats on the drum.

~

"Come on, come on," Breanna muttered before tapping out the start message signal yet again. "Come on, hear me."

Gowthaman rested his hand on her shoulder. "Patience, Sundarii."

"I know," she grumbled. "They may not be able to hear this at all. They might not realize we're trying to communicate with them or what we need to convey. Lots of variables. But this has got to work. It has to."

"If it does not, we shall find another way."

She glanced up at him, surprised by the confidence ringing in his soft voice. When he'd scrambled through the opening in the veil after them, she'd been startled and amazed. When he lay tightly curled in upon himself she'd nearly cried with anguish and despair. She had feared for his sanity, his life, then buried that fear deep within herself. She had needed to be strong. For him. For herself. For all of them.

When he'd allowed her access to his memories and his pain, she hadn't had time to appreciate the strength he'd needed to release the pain to her. That strength continued to surprise and please her when he'd comforted her during the release of the healing pain.

In an amazingly short time he'd changed. Her face heated as he stroked his finger along the side of her neck. Changed from a reticent man whose denials had turned him inward with anguish to a demonstrative, confident lover. She'd only known him in pain, was this the man Gowthaman had been before?

"Try again, Breanna." Gowthaman let his hand slip from her shoulder and stood back. The loss of his touch, of the warmth of him at her side made her fumble with the stick. Blowing out a frustrated breath, she snatched the makeshift beater from the ground and tapped out the signal.

Pay attention, Bree. Think about Gowtham later, when there's time.

Dah dit dah dit dah

The fading reverberations of her beats lingered in the air and she sighed. This had to--

Dah dah dit dit dah

G. A. Go ahead.

Chance whooped and twirled Coralie in a circle. "It works," he shouted. "It's them." Then he left Coralie in Morghan's arms and crouched next to Bree.

"Ready, sis?" he asked as he smoothed the dirt in front of her then picked up a short stick. He looked at her expectantly.

She nodded. "You?"

"Yep."

After a pause, but before she could start their message, beats from the human world continued. Chance wrote each letter in the dust and the others moved closer to read over his shoulder.

"Three to speak spell open veil stop Ur."

Gowthaman spoke in the silence at the end of the drumbeats. "So, they have come to the same conclusions."

"Not quite," Chance said. "They don't mention who the three need to be. Bree?"

Nodding, she began the message Gowthaman had drilled with her.

Chance whispered the words as she completed them. "Keep Ur here need all three Alfar clans. With Tori have two. Hope faerie voices substitute."

The long pause stretched and tension shivered across Bree's shoulders. Had they heard? Did they understand?

Nightshade tapped the numbers one and three. Understood. The high of contacting those in the World Between Worlds rapidly sank to the pit of his stomach. He'd never considered the possibility of the combination of specific races, though why he'd failed to recognize the significance drove his mood lower.

Tori suspected her mother was an Alfar-Andras but if those suspicions rang false, they had only a combination of Sindhu and Faerie voices. And human. If they couldn't find enough power to contain the elemental...

Knowing the others watched, he physically shook off his concerns and managed a loose grin. "Looks like they'll be on their way home tonight."

Lucidea bent until her nose was bare inches from his. "Don't. Do not even say everything will be all right. How can it be when we don't have a damn Domovoii." She shook her finger. "None of your Nightshade optimistic chatter. We've got to figure out how to make up for the fact that no one's heard anything from the Domovoii for thousands of years."

She straightened and turned away. "I don't even have a clue how we might go about finding... and there's no time anyway."

Jayse moved to wrap his arms around her shoulders. "We've got to stay strong, darlin'. There'll be a way. We haven't come this far--"

She shoved him away. "Stop it. Just... stop." Tears trailed down her cheeks and she dashed them away with the back of her hand. "I'm sorry. Must be hormones." After a watery smile, she let Jayse cuddle her close again.

"I know," she continued in a weak voice. "I know we can open the veil, and we will. That's our part of bringing everyone home. I have confidence our spell will work. After all, we got them into the World Between Worlds."

Paper crinkled as Tori set her notebook aside. "We have to extend that confidence into believing the truth that my mother was Andras. Belief is half the battle. And if we believe the magic of Faerie will compensate for not having a Domovoii, then the magic will work. Our family will escape and Brandr Ur will remain imprisoned in the World Between Worlds."

"I know..." Lucidea sniffed. "Maybe I just need to get all this doubt out of my system before I can gear up for battle again. Twenty years is a long time to plan for something... and still have roadblocks constantly falling in your way."

Her despair settled over the small cavern. In the silence Nightshade explored options but could discover no alternatives. But one.

"We have until moonrise," he said.

Lucidea straightened, brushed her hair from her forehead and nodded. "I'll be ready."

Resting his hand on her shoulder, Jayse said, "With me at your side, darlin'."

"And me," Tori added.

When they all turned to look at him, Nightshade buried his doubts behind a broad, flowing gesture. "Honeys, Nightshade wouldn't miss this for the world. Any world."

Each hour of the day dragged more slowly than the one before. Messages had passed to and from Nightshade, and plans had been fine-tuned to Gowthaman and Morghan's approval. Coralie had stuffed their gear into the packs and made a small pile near where they hoped the veil would open.

Breanna watched Chance run through drill after drill with the unusually long sword he'd brought with him. Morghan watched as well, giving the occasional comment or instruction. She was pleased Chance took to the older man's instruction so well, when he would have argued with her. This mission was good for him.

Taking the shorter sword from the jumble of packs, Gowthaman drew the weapon, replaced the scabbard and advanced on Chance. Morghan backed away.

Bree frowned. What was Gowtham doing? When he took an offensive stance, she blinked. What was he doing? She'd never known him to willingly take up a weapon, preferring the battle of words to physical conflict. He saluted Chance and attacked.

Heart in her throat, Bree rose to her feet intent on stopping the farce of a battle. Chance would easily overpower Gowtham, and one, or both of them might be hurt. She took a step forward.

A hand landed heavily on her shoulder. She turned and twisted from Morghan's hold with a grumbling negative response.

"Do no' interfere," he said. "Watch. Yer brother and yer man both have fine skills. 'Twill be excellent practice for the young one."

Skill? Gowtham? He was a librarian. After a moment's hesitation, she turned back to the mock battle, ready to ignore Morghan's admonishment and stop the farce.

But the easy rhythm of Gowtham's attack and defense held her in place. In awe. His movements flowed like a dance, showing the smooth evidence of the ease of long practice.

Weak-kneed, she sank to the ground. Morghan and Coralie joined her. Together they sat silent, watching, listening to the clang and scrape of metal upon metal, the soft grunts of effort, the taunts and laughter of success.

After a prolonged volley of thrusts and parries Chance took a step back and held up one hand. "I yield."

Gowthaman lowered his weapon, then lifted his shirt hem to wipe the sweat from his face. "Guard your left, Chance. After attack you drop your shoulder."

Chance tapped the flat of his blade against his thigh. "Yeah, Always have. Bree gives me grief about it too."

Gowtham clasped his shoulder. "We would prefer you experience grief at our observations rather than at the hand of an opponent."

"I'll remember."

The combatants turned toward their small audience. Breanna studied Gowtham's easy stride, the way he held his sword loose, but ready, his satisfied smile. She'd never imagined he would have skills with a sword... or with battle. Who was this man she loved?

She'd loved him forever, loved him despite the way he hid from life, his physical and emotional pains... would she still love him as the man he'd been before the mind rape? Of course she would, and enjoy every moment of discovering the Gowtham she had never known.

Her breath caught and she lifted one hand to her throat. Would he still need her? Still love her?

After he sheathed the sword, Gowthaman turned toward Breanna. He had seen the surprise in her eyes when he challenged her brother. A bead of sweat trickled from his temple. The physical exertion had filled him with joy and the exhilaration of his muscles remembering. There was much Breanna did not know of him--in fact, few in her family knew. He had not had direct contact with the Zeroun clan until he imagined himself in love with Kaelea. Closing his eyes he let a moment's memory fill him. He smiled. After so long, he discovered an honest memory, untainted by the mind stealer's touch.

When he opened his eyes, Breanna's expression over-flowed with doubt. She ducked her head, hiding her eyes from him. Ah, now she feared she did not know him. He under-stood for he barely remembered himself. She was concerned the changes in him would cause him to no longer love her.

While he wiped his face again, Morghan and Coralie moved away from Breanna. Waiting until she looked at him, Gowthaman studied the top of her head. Even in gray, the soft silk of her hair called for him to touch, to fulfill the aching need to tangle his fingers in the short strands, to hold her still for his kiss.

She had worked more magic than either of them realized when she healed him. Her magic allowed him to return to himself. Somehow he would find the way to help her under-stand, whether in pain or as a whole being, he loved her. He would always love her.

He moved closer and cupped his hand against her hair, sighing as the strands tickled his palm. She shivered under his gentle touch. He knelt at her back and rested his chin on her shoulder. "Sundarii, soulfire does not lie."

A second tremor shook her body. Staring straight ahead, she asked, "What do you mean?"

Tempted by the smooth, delicate curve, he nuzzled her ear before answering. "I mean, caarutama, most beloved, despite how we may change as we live our lives, or appear to become different in some way, those changes will be of no conse-quence to us. Nothing can destroy our soulfire. Nothing either of us may do or say, nothing another may attempt will destroy the destiny that brought us together."

She sighed when he sat, and turned to face him. Capturing her restless hands, he brought her fingers to his lips. She resisted, trying to pull away but he kept her hands in a gentle hold. "Why do you wish to cast a pall over the love I have finally admitted?"

Breanna jerked her gaze to him. "I-I don't..."

"You have not known me as anything other than damaged. You are concerned now that I am able to manage the memories, I will not love you."

She shook her head.

"Ah, so it is that you fear yourself, your love. That you will not love the Faerie with a mind made whole. Or perhaps you wonder if your love was born only of the need to heal."

Wide, her eyes glistened with the threat of tears. "How... how did you know?"

He caressed her cheek and brushed away a single errant tear. "Am I truly so much different? Yes, there is much you have yet to discover of me, of my life. I am, by human standards, very old. I have had experiences, lifetimes, such as you do not yet know or understand. But, my beautiful one, we now have our lives, our time together to discover what we do not yet know of each other. Does not every couple, every relationship encounter such times?"

Her ragged breaths tugged at his heart, but he waited for her to speak. Finally, she nodded, shook her head, then nodded again. "I guess for all my life, for all my loving you and wanting to heal your agonies, I never thought about you. Who you were without the need for healing. Who you would be once the pain no longer dominated your life."

The evil touch of a long known comfort of pain rose in his brain. Confidence fled from the maelstrom as his mental defenses shook, the pieces threatening to return to a solid wall. Being who she had known would be so easy. Too easy.

Breanna gripped his hand. "No, don't do that. Don't give in. Don't go back. Gowtham, stay with me. I'll be okay. We'll be okay."

He blinked, struggled with the internal force of his memories, and found the strength to laugh at the mental winds. The warmth of Breanna's body when she leaned closer destroyed the last of the insidious temptation and he let his shoulders relax.

"Such is my battle, Breanna. The darkness will always be there, just within reach. However, I am no longer willing to allow evil to succeed, to dominate my life. Be my constant, my anchor. When I slip toward despair, assist me to return to me, to remain me. You are the light to my darkness. I need... please, do not question my need for you."

The brightness he ached for shone in her teary smile. "And you've got me, Gowtham. Forever."

Forever. Even with the long ages of a Faerie lifetime before them, he liked the sound of forever.

Twenty-six

"We've got company."

With Chance's bland pronouncement, followed by Morghan's rumble of anger, Breanna knew exactly who approached the camp. Reluctant, but with a determined kiss, she eased from Gowthaman's embrace, stood and brushed the dust from her rear. When he flowed to his feet beside her, and rested his hand over the curve of her bottom, she leaned against him. For a moment she accepted the comfort, then straightened.

This was it.

Confrontation.

Battle.

Panic swept through her, swirling, building, making her muscles weak and trembling. Her Alastriona training had prepared her for battle, but she had never really expected to face a foe as menacing and world threatening as this ancient fire elemental. The urge to turn and run twined with her panic.

Gowthaman wrapped his arm around her waist. Damn, now she couldn't run. If only the trembling would stop. Maybe then she could think.

Granda would be so ashamed of her.

The elemental stopped a few hundred yards from them, smiled broadly and pointed to the faint circle of lighter gray half way to the horizon. Then he shook his head in mock sad-

ness and found a low stone where he sat, crossed his arms and
cocked his head regally to one side.

"What's he doing?' Bree whispered.

A second low growl rumbled from Morghan. "A creature
of his word, so he says. He will no' come to fight until 'tis
time for the veil to open. Until 'tis time for him to make his..."
He paused and increased the volume of his voice. "Attempt..."
another pause, then in a more normal tone, "...to escape."

"So, you really don't think he's going to fight us now?"

Morghan shook his head. "That one has a misguided sense
of himself, an' what actions he decides to take. I do no' ken
why he holds his own word in such high regard."

"So, he's just going to sit there and watch us?"

Chance moved from his position at the edge of the camp.
"Looks like it."

Worry for her brother gave Bree a focus, something other
than misgivings over her own preparedness. "Has he tried to
get in your head?"

"Nope. Don't think he'll give it much of a try either. He
doesn't need to control any of us since what he wants is within his grasp. Or so he thinks."

Control? A fresh wash of fear settled like a lump in her
stomach. "Did he, did he ever..."

Chance gave her his usual cheeky grin. "Never. At first,
when I had no idea what was going on, he may have tried.
Give me a little credit for some strength of character, will ya,
sis?"

"Chance, I wouldn't--"

"I know. And no he never did. Without really trying I must
have found the way to block him before he had the chance to

dig in. Maybe that ability was left over from our battles with Fiedhlim. So, no worries about me, sister mine."

But she would worry about him. Both because he was her brother, and because he was a part of the team. A team she was supposed to be leading.

She stiffened her spine. Gowthaman gave her waist a squeeze then stepped back, close enough to offer moral support, but far enough to allow her to make her own decisions. She closed her eyes. Please let me make the right decisions. "We'll wait, as long as he does. Watch him. If he moves..."

"Aye." Morghan paced three steps forward, lifting his fists higher with each step. "I'll watch the... creature. 'twill no' be long until time to begin. I know the words, have repeated them innumerable times o'er the years here. Ye watch the time. I will no' let the elemental disturb yer final preparations."

He strode to the edge of their campsite, found his own stone and sat facing Brandr Ur. Crossing his arms, he rubbed at the bandage on his upper arm then matched the elemental's pose.

The insane urge to laugh crawled up to settle in Bree's throat. Stand-off, World Between Worlds style. "Okay," she breathed. "What's left to do?"

Coralie shrugged. "Wait."

Bree glanced at Gowthaman. He lifted one shoulder. "We shall each review the incantation and prepare in the event the others are unable to split the veil."

"Agreed. Chance?"

"I'm just gonna sit over here. I'll help Morghan watch, go over the words. And there's a couple other things I need to take care of." He sat on the ground, his long sword balanced across his knees.

In the end, they all sat, lost in the silence of their thoughts. Waiting.

Shortly before moonrise, Jayse led his small party to the brae. Nightshade lagged behind but his thoughts raced as he scuffed along the dirt path.

After the last communication from Breanna they'd each drifted into their own thoughts, though he was sure all those thoughts centered around one thing. All three branches of the Alfar race were needed to successfully hold Brandr Ur in the World Between Worlds. He wasn't convinced the magic of Faerie participation would fill the Domovoii void. But perhaps it would slow the elemental enough to allow the rescue party's escape.

He didn't relish the idea of telling Breanna's parents she and her brother weren't coming home.

Giving himself a shake, he increased his speed and climbed the steep path to the outcropping's level crown. He moved immediately to the edge overhanging the loch and stared out over the dark water.

In the distance the loch disappeared into the cobalt of the advancing night. The moon would rise from the darkness, a moon over-full with meaning and magic. A similar moon would rise in at least two other worlds, enabling the elemental to traverse the veil and enter one of the opened worlds.

To terrorize this human world.

Nightshade took a fortifying breath. He would do anything and everything within his power to prevent that from happening.

A bank of dense clouds hovered in the distance. The lower edge glowed silver as each layer of churning clouds captured moonlight then reflected the iridescent shine further into the sky. It was an ethereal moonrise, one he would have appreciated fully in another place, at another time.

He watched until the moon's curved, gilded edge eased into the night sky. Then he turned to the others, spread his hands and snapped his fingers.

"Showtime."

Brandr Ur stretched. This day was interminably long. Yet he was willing to wait a bit longer, considering his reward.

Freedom. Freedom from this forsaken place. Freedom to do as he wished, to take all he desired. To rule.

He'd never bothered to study the minds he'd been able to touch throughout the ages. Now he pondered what he would discover in the world of weak humans. Would they be much different than those who long ago worshiped him, and his brethren?

The low sound of unrestrained anger rumbled through his chest. Existence had been good all those millennium ago. Fewer beings populated his world then, but they had worshiped him. Closing his eyes he savored the memory of adulation and offerings. Soon, he would again receive his due. That which his brethren had taken from him so long ago.

What fools his fellow Elementals had been, choosing a form of oblivion in another dimension when lesser beings fell to their knees before them. He'd made his stand, refused to retreat with the other gods. Another angry growl vibrated along his spine.

And because he'd refused, had chosen instead the adulation, his brethren imprisoned his fire deep beneath the sea.

A witch who imagined herself as powerful as a god, had discovered the way to breach his prison. Allowing him to break free.

To a world with god-pretenders and only two worshipers. Two who would not bow to him. A stirring of pleasure settled in his groin and he shifted. The most pleasing memories he carried were not of worship, but of their child as a woman grown. Of Dea Anu.

Of the times he'd taken her. Only thrice, but what pleasure.

Movement from the camp destroyed his memory and he frowned. The prince of waters had risen and paced from one side of his camp to the other. And back to his stone.

Brandr Ur blew out a disgusted breath. Blood of his blood. A poor showing of a descendant. Had Dea Anu and the worthless godling she'd chosen over him allowed him access to his offspring, this prince of waters would be a far different creature.

Or perhaps not. Time had a way of diluting the power he would have nurtured in any descendant willing to worship him.

The morose thoughts faded as he stared toward the horizon. The weak sun that lightened the gray, touched the horizon. Soon he would be free. To burn with the power of the sun. Glorious flames. Free of the dull, lifeless gray.

His skin tightened, hot with the anticipation of increased power. In this moment it didn't matter which worlds were home to the rising full moons. His plan was set, the motion begun, and nothing would prevent him from taking his rightful place.

As a god. The only god.

Morghan studied the elemental with the intensity of remembered purpose. The feeling pleased him. Existence in the World Between Worlds was one of deprivation. No color, no interaction, no... Coralie. He'd been nearly lost to the lack of sensation. Mayhap only a few more hours and he would have been beyond caring. Beyond rescue.

Thank Sindhu, thank the blessed waters of the great sea, Coralie had been on time.

Now he had that purpose, and a reason to remain alert and caring. He would see the others safely home. Even if he faced the sacrifice of remaining here.

The elemental stretched and altered his position to watch the barely visible sun lower toward the horizon. Little time remained. And so many thoughts to think.

His niece, his darlin' Lucidea, had ruled well in his absence for Coralie spoke nothing but praise for Lucidea and her husband. Morghan glanced at the young woman who led the party to rescue him. If Lucidea's man was of the same race, of the same quality as Breanna, he was satisfied. This Faerie race bred strong, determined folk. Much like the Sindhu.

He frowned a moment before Coralie came to him. If his sacrifice were called for, how could he watch her pass through the veil, returning to their worlds without him?

"Yer thinkin' very loud, m'lord."

"An honorific?"

"Yer expression was one of royal thought, Morghan."

"Aye, heavy thoughts for heavy times, eudail."

Coralie stroked her hand over his shoulders. Delight followed her touch and he leaned back to increase the pressure. She bent to whisper. "We shall all return home together. An' if we do no', I will stay here with ye."

"Ye shall no'." He shook his head and twisted his shoulders but she wouldn't move away. Instead, she caught his face between her hands and kissed him.

"Oh, I shall. Never would I choose a place such as this for livin'. But, Morghan, ye are my life. Where ye are is where I must be. I would no' survive if I must be separated from ye again."

"No, sweet Coralie, I would no' allow it."

Taking a step back, she fisted her hands at her hips. "Ye would no' allow it? I say ye would have no choice. 'Tis my decision to make. An' I choose ye, my love. I have, an' I always will."

After a quick glance to ascertain the elemental had not moved, Morghan held out both hands to her. "Come here, woman."

She tilted her head to one side, contemplating him. Then she smiled and swayed toward him. Once he held her on his lap and nuzzled her hair, he sighed. "I would not have ye here, but if 'tis to be, then I shall be pleased to have ye here with me."

"Pleased?"

"Oh aye, more than pleased." Yet as he kissed her he was unable to keep his fears contained and the kiss melded into desperation. If they could not stop the elemental--

Coralie stiffened and pulled away. "Listen."

Holding his breath to still the panicked beating of his heart, Morghan strained to hear what held Coralie's attention. She pressed on his shoulder and stood facing the far side of the small camp.

Then he heard--the rising rumble of voices in the distance.

Twenty-seven

Dogs barked in the distance. Desert dogs voicing displeasure. Gowthaman shook his head to clear the fancy. But the sound continued. After a moment grim satisfaction brought a tight smile to his lips. Not dogs. The chanted incantation, blessed voices from the human world.

He glanced at the elemental. Brandr Ur straightened and turned his head, listening, but gave no indication of interest other than to cross one ankle over the opposite knee.

Gowthaman snorted softly. The elemental did not need to broadcast his intentions. They knew his plans well enough. Well enough for Gowthaman to know they weren't truly prepared to do battle with such an ancient creature.

Turning his gaze from the lounging elemental, Gowthaman took a moment to study his friends.

Friends. For far too many years he'd had acquaintances aplenty, but friends? He had not realized how lonely life had been. Others who studied ancient texts, who occasionally inhabited the dim halls of Alexandria's Fey library had once been enough. Not true companionship, but the meeting of like minds, the comfort of knowing there were others nearby-- others who, like him, neither wanted nor pursued attachments.

He had been content. Or so he had believed. The short time he had thought himself in love with Kaelea brought him into the Zeroun family circle.

Not a single one of these who came here bore the name or the blood of the Zeroun clan, yet each was as much a part of the whole as any. Even the Sindhu prince, whom none had yet met, would be welcomed and named family.

The bitter realization he had been so welcomed even after nearly causing Bard his life, and Kae her happiness, welled in his chest, cutting off his breath. One person perhaps could forgive his actions--but an entire family? How did such acceptance happen? He was not worthy of the honor bestowed upon him.

The mumbled chanting grew clearer, the words nearly intelligible. Though the elemental had not yet risen from his stone perch, his eyes glittered with malice. Evil intent strained the cords of neck muscle, deepening the outward expression of Brandr Ur's focus. Only moments remained before the elemental would burst into action.

Gowthaman tightened his determination and reached for the sword he had used in the mock battle with Chance. He would fight beside this family, stand with the woman he loved and the friends he never thought to have.

When he had so rashly followed Breanna into the World Between Worlds, he had believed his purpose to be as a sacrifice. Only two days ago he had thought such a sacrifice was his to make, both to assist with Morghan's rescue and to purge himself of his self-pitying pain. How wrong he had been.

Wrong about so many things. Shame and regret burned across his cheeks, heating his skin unbearably. He no longer wished to sacrifice himself. Found the very idea repugnant. Blindly reaching to the side, he captured Breanna's hand, brought it to his lips then released her. The small caress was enough to show her his love, then allow her the space to perform her duties as Alastriona and leader of this mission.

She leaned against his side, and he found comfort in the warm pressure. He would fight at her side and neither of them would become a sacrifice to the elemental's plans.

The chant separated into three distinct voices. Only mildly surprised to hear Lucidea's clear tones joining with Jayse's deep rumble and Tori's alto, Gowthaman narrowed his eyes, watching Brandr Ur for indications of the elemental's next move.

Brandr Ur smiled benignly and slowly rose to his feet. He gave a courtly bow in Morghan's direction then took a step forward, speaking syllables in a language so harsh and guttural they seemed to rip the Alfar spell from the air.

Morghan moved after the elemental, joining in the distant, human world chant. Coralie added her voice but a moment later.

Gowthaman felt Breanna take a deep breath. She straightened, nodded and they stepped forward together, angling to put the elemental between them and Morghan. When the chant began again, with their voices forcing the words into the World Between Worlds, magic rose around them.

The explosive swirl of powerful, unrecognized magic caused Gowthaman to stumble over the words. He breathed in the essences, tasting the powerful flavor of the Alfar, then expelled the magical intent with his power-filled chanting.

Brandr Ur took a heavy step forward. Chance moved directly before him, the long sword held loose at his side. The young man's fervency when he joined the chant and a sharp indication with the tip of the sword, directed the power to form a tight swirl rising from the elemental's feet to curl about his body.

Laughing, Brandr Ur shook off the magic like a wet dog, shoved Chance to the ground and strode past him. Breanna tensed, then relaxed as her brother righted himself, continuing to speak in unison with the others.

The elemental's laughter broke off in a frustrated snarl. Brandr Ur continued forward, but his movements became a slow motion struggle of arms and legs as though he moved through a sticky, gelatinous membrane.

Gowthaman frowned. Even increasing the force and intensity of their words did not completely stop the elemental. Brandr Ur moved slowly, steadily, toward the spot where his low spoken magic had increased the thinning of the veil.

Using the reasoning someone needed to watch for the unexpected, Nightshade stood to one side of the chanting trio. Facing the sky and the thinning veil, Tori stood in front of Jayse and Lucidea, creating a loose triangle. There had been no convincing Lucidea to remain in the relative safety of the manor house. Jayse's vehement arguments rang with logic which she had countered with fierce determination. She had even used her pregnancy to her advantage--claiming the life they'd created added even more magic to the equation.

Jayse had not been convinced. Nightshade grimaced. Neither had he. Yet she had pushed her way past both men and here she was.

Lucidea calmly spoke words gleaned from the past, words intended to bring about Morghan's return. Despite the serenity in her expression, she clasped her husband's hand with a white-knuckled grip. That same anxiety exerted a tight grasp on Nightshade's heart. He moved a step closer and frowned.

When they had breached the veil two nights previously, the barrier between this world and the World Between Worlds had fought the magic before tearing open. Tonight, it was as if the veil peeled away, each layer bringing them closer to Morghan's return. Nightshade glanced at the rising moon, shivering as the power of the full, shimmering globe rained down on him.

Trepidation tingled across his shoulders and he attempted to shrug it away. But the odd feeling settled between his shoulder blades, a dull knife of anxiety threatening to pierce his skin.

Another layer of the veil dissolved and he saw the wavering movements of shadowy figures. One, taller and broader than the rest moved closer to the veil. Even distorted there was no mistaking the elemental. Nightshade stepped sideways, closer to Jayse and Lucidea.

The elemental shoved someone from his path. Chance, Nightshade decided. The young man was brash enough to openly challenge Brandr Ur. After stepping past the challenger, Brandr Ur strode forward. His presence grew larger, filling the area surrounded by the thinning veil. He pressed against the magical membrane until the fabric stretched to outline hands, face, a triumphant smile. Burning, arid wind poured from the World Between Worlds.

Lucidea's chant faltered. She gasped then whispered, "It's not enough. He's going to come through."

"Keep going, darlin'," Jayse shouted over the rising whine of wind. "Never give up."

Nightshade closed his eyes. Their efforts weren't enough. Their attempts slowed the elemental, but could not stop him. He took a deep breath. Never a believer in destiny, in one heartbeat he accepted his long life had led him to this family. To this point in time. Giving a soft snort, he opened his eyes and focused on the straining veil. He rested his hands on Jayse and Lucidea's shoulder.

The words burst easily past his crumbling resistance. No flamboyant lilt, no affectations. His voice--strong, deep--rose with the others. The ground trembled, shivered in response.

Tori glanced back at him, the questions in her dark eyes fading as the power surrounding them grew and stretched toward the World Between Worlds. She smiled, turned, and placed her hand over his.

"That's it," Lucidea shouted over the wind. She shifted, easing from under Nightshade's hand then joined her hand to his and Tori's.

"The spell... Again." Jayse wrapped both hands over and below the knot of their joined fingers.

A rush of intense magic spiraled from Nightshade's chest down his arm to their joined hands. When their combined voices rose with the chant, the ground shook. Wind swirled around them, gently spinning leaves high into the night sky. Water droplets dashed against Nightshade's skin, pouring from a waterspout hovering at the edge of the dark loch.

Too long. The power... nearly too much to contain. Yet they had more to do. Nightshade clenched his jaw and ground out the word, "Again."

Water, air, earth. Triple whirling ropes of power danced through the sky. Joined into a single tornado, the magic hovered, waiting.

The elemental pushed harder against the veil. Tiny cracks appeared in the gray mist.

Lucidea gave soft sound of dismay and the watery rope slipped from the others. "No," she cried. Her visible struggle to gain control, to raise more power in a weakened state, burned into Nightshade's soul. He could no longer guard his secrets if it meant more losses to those he loved.

Deep in the far reaches of his memories, from long before when he believed he understood his place in his world, he found the key. A single word, taught to him by his father, a magic he'd never understood. Forgotten until this moment.

The three he'd joined with for this battle watched him with question filled eyes. He grinned. "Once more, okay honeys? Just once more."

Squaring her shoulders, Lucidea nodded. Tori leaned forward on her toes. Worry filling his eyes, Jayse gazed at Lucidea. She tilted her chin at him. With a slight smile, he released a ragged sigh. The four drew breath together and began a final recitation of the ancient spell.

The tornado arched toward the veil and the elemental eased back, but did not retreat. Hot, powerful wind whistled through the tiny rips in the veil, battering them. As the last syllable of their spell dissipated in the wind, Nightshade drew himself to his full height and shouted, "Arunz!"

A rumbling tremor shook the brae, tossing them to the ground. Nightshade caught Lucidea, turning them while in flight so his body cushioned her landing. He wrapped his arms tightly around her, shifting as the ground stilled. Sharp rocks bit into his back. He held back a groan.

Jayse jerked to sitting and clasped Lucidea's hand. "Okay? Both of you?"

She covered her abdomen with her free hand. "Yeah, I think so. You probably should worry more about Nightshade." She wiggled and he loosened his hold. Lucidea slid next to Jayse then jabbed Nightshade's shoulder. The pokes were as uncompromising as the stones at his back. "Who are you? What are you?"

Before he could summon an answer, Tori lifted herself on one elbow, then sat, testing her muscles. "Can't you guess?" She grinned and swiped her hair back from her face. "He's Alfar, of course. He's Domovoii."

Staring as if he'd never seen Nightshade before, Jayse leaned closer. In the moonlight his questions were not to be denied.

Nightshade closed his eyes and nodded once. No reason to hide the facts of his birth any longer. Where he'd thought to feel anger or dismay at the revelation, instead relief calmed the churning in his abused belly.

"Shade?" Jayse asked.

"Talk later, honey. Now help me up. Your wife knocked the breath from me."

Jayse peered into the sky then scrambled to his feet and held out one hand. Nightshade grasped the offering and pulled himself to his feet. A fine dusting of earth covered him and he felt a long forgotten sense of welcome... of home.

As Tori helped Lucidea stand she glanced at him and asked, "What was that last word you said? What does Arunz-"

Whining wind stole her speech and pressed the four of them into a tight knot. With sudden silence, the wind died.

"Whoa," Jayse muttered. "What was all that about?"

"I have an idea," Tori answered, trying to smooth wind-blown locks over her head. "Look at the power we raised before."

Whirling magic circled the veil, framing the pale gray spot in the sky. The ropes of earth and air had thickened and wrapped tightly around each other and the veil, the thinner, watery rope held slack between them.

Tori pointed. "When Nightshade and I said that word, the magic rising from our elements got stronger."

All eyes turned toward him. Nightshade shrugged. "Makes sense."

"But why not the water?" Lucidea asked. "While this pretty much proves Tori is Andras, she's also half-Sindhu."

"You say the word," Tori prompted.

Though he and Tori gave rapid coaching, Lucidea was unable to vocalize the word of power. The syllables stuck in her throat, choking her with each attempt.

"That's enough," Nightshade said when she drew breath to try again. "There's no reason why you shouldn't be able to draw upon the magic, but you've been blocked. Maybe it's your pregnancy."

"Great." Lucidea sniffed. "Helps with one thing, denies me another. Just great."

Muted by distance, an angry roar jerked their attention to the sky. Final layers of the veil peeled back, clearing, clarifying, until they looked through a reasonably clear window into the World Between Worlds.

Twenty-eight

Brandr Ur howled. Rage and frustration rang through the thick air. Shivers of dread channeled down Breanna's spine and mixed with a surge of adrenaline. Her muscles flexed, tightened then relaxed. With a nod, she and her team stepped forward, a loose semi-circle of five, to corral the elemental.

While the veil had cleared until she could see the brilliant full moon shining in the human world's night sky, their combined magic had prevented the elemental from breaking through.

A small satisfaction, but satisfaction nonetheless.

The elemental had ranted and beat his fists against the clear barrier before turning and vocalizing his displeasure. Bree stared silently at the elemental while Brandr Ur seethed. She bit back a grin, steam actually rose from his skin, making him look like a demented cartoon character.

Chance snickered, drawing the elemental's attention.

Fists clenched, arms stiff at his side, Brandr Ur stalked forward. "What have you done?"

Morghan leapt in front of Chance to confront the elemental. "Prevented ye from leavin' this place."

Brandr Ur stopped and glared at each of them in turn. "You shall not stop me. None of you has the power."

"Aye, no' alone. But together we have."

With another fierce howl, the elemental shoved Morghan away and stabbed a finger toward Chance. "You. I want you."

"Fight me, then, Elemental."

A cold fist clamped around Bree's heart. "No."

Both Chance and the elemental turned to her. Matching fierceness burned in their eyes until Chance blinked. For a moment he was her baby brother then cold determination return to firm his expression. "It's okay, sis. This is my destiny. The reason I came along." He nodded toward Gowthaman. "He understands."

Brandr Ur thumped a fist against his chest. "You will fight me."

Slowly, Chance moved his focus back to the elemental. "I will. And I will defeat you. You won't find your way into another world nor touch another unwilling mind. It stops here. The insanity stops with me."

Morghan clutched the elemental's shoulder and forced him to turn. "You will fight me."

Brandr Ur laughed. "You? I defeated you once before. I will not waste the time to do so again. I will fight the boy, for he has uttered the challenge. If the young one wishes to die at my hands, then die he shall."

Curling his fingers as if holding a large ball, Brandr Ur faced Chance and grinned. A moment later he stared down at the empty space between his palms and grunted. He switched one hand from top to bottom. The wicked grin spread across his face. But the glee disappeared under a mask of confusion. His hands dropped heavily to his sides.

Odd. Breanna kept her sword at the ready and tried to catch Morghan's eye. The Sindhu frowned and shook his head.

"Gowtham?" she whispered.

"I do not--"

"Lost your powers, old man?" Chance sidled closer to the elemental and tapped him on the shoulder with his long sword. "Kinda sucks, doesn't it?"

"What did you do, human? How--no, you can not restrain me. Fight and I will take the life from you and regain what is mine."

Chance danced to the elemental's other side. "I'll fight you... old man. But you won't get anything but dead."

"Ha. I am immortal."

"Big deal." Chance stepped back and shrugged.

"Chance," Bree admonished. "Don't antagonize--"

"Don't worry, sis. I know what I'm doing." He walked backwards, tugging at the leather strip wrapping the hilt of his overly long sword.

Too many options presented themselves to Bree, the rapid rise of confusion hid any answers for which she searched. Her brother couldn't fight an elemental. She couldn't fight a being as powerful as Brandr Ur and hope to succeed. What was Chance doing? It didn't matter if the elemental didn't have any powers now--what if they came back during the battle? Maybe they could make it through and close the veil before the elemental found a way to follow them.

Before she could rush forward, Gowthaman gently wrapped his hand around her upper arm. "You must let your brother do this."

She turned on him. "What?" No. I can't. What if--"

"This mission is filled with instances of 'what if'. We have faced every challenge." He dropped his gaze a moment. "Each physical and personal challenge, each moment of doubt and concern. Despite odds greatly piled against us, we communicated with our world."

Bree strained toward her brother, intent on being at his side when the elemental attacked. Maybe the two of them...

Gowthaman tangled their fingers together and continued. "A driving factor, an essential source to each success has been your brother. Chance has shown maturity, knowledge and reasoning beyond his years. You can not protect him his entire life. He may not seem a man in years, but, beloved, his heart is strong. See him now not as a sister, but through the eyes of the leader of the Alastriona. What do you see?"

Damn Gowtham for making her look at Chance as anything but her baby brother. Try to rationalize it as she might, she found no fault with Gowtham's astute observations.

Rising dust burned her eyes. Thankful for the excuse to blink back the stinging dampness, she squeezed Gowtham's fingers and turned her blurry gaze to her lover. "You're right. It's just... I've watched out for him since he was born, helped him learn how to push away Feidhlim's evil influence, taught him to fight."

"These strengths you have allowed him to find within himself, as well as the love you bear for him, have led him to discover the man he has become. Let him be that man. He understands the risks, he knows the chance he takes. Of us all, he is the most able to defeat this foe."

Frantic laughter bubbled from her. She caught the distraught sounds in her hand. "A chance for Chance." She laughed again, then burst into tears. "How can I watch him endanger himself?"

Gowtham embraced her. "You shall watch him as Alastriona, as one who has trust in those she leads."

A large hand shoved between them. Thick fingers wrapped in Gowtham's shirt and jerked him away. "Give me your weapon."

Hoping to create enough distance between them to effectively use her sword, Bree shoved the elemental's unyielding shoulder. "Let him go."

Gowtham's shirt tight in his grasp, he rounded on her, fist raised. Harsh breaths expanded his chest and although anger burned in his eyes, no physical heat surrounded him. The lack of his fire concerned Bree; if he should somehow regain his powers the battle would be over.

Slowly lowering his fist, the elemental gave her an appraising look, chilling her to her bones. He kept his eyes on her, but released Gowthaman and opened his hand. "Give me the weapon."

"Come on, Gowthaman," Chance shouted. "Let's get this over with so we can go home. We don't have forever, you know."

Morghan added just as loudly, "No, do no'."

The weight of Gowthaman's gaze on her forced her decision. She gave a short nod. He pressed his sword's hilt into Brandr Ur's hand.

The elemental drew his finger down Bree's cheek. "Perhaps I shall not destroy you immediately."

"Promises, promises," she muttered, turning her face to the side and shuddering. When the elemental moved away, Gowtham cupped her cheek with his palm and she closed her eyes. The swirl of soulfire danced behind her lids dissolving the repugnancy of the elemental's touch.

"Thank you," she whispered. How wonderful it would be to bask in their soulfire, but the reality of the coming battle forced her eyes open. Coralie moved to her side, although Morghan remained a few paces distant. Bree studied the Sindhu's ready stance and focused concentration. As a small group of fighters facing a powerful foe, they were as ready as they could be... for whatever happened.

Brandr Ur weighed the sword in his hand, then tested the balance and swing before stalking toward the flat, open area. And Chance. Bree caught her lower lip between her teeth and accepted--nothing would stop this battle. Both her brother and Brandr Ur sought to prove themselves.

Chance had completed removing the leather from his sword hilt and dropped the long strip behind him. One hand wrapped carefully around the blade just below the curved cross guard, and the other cupped over the pommel, Chance held the sword vertically before him. The tip of the five foot blade touched the gray earth. Eyes closed, he breathed in a slow deep breath.

The aspect of ancient meditation, meant to calm the fighter, worked to ease a portion of worry from Bree's heart as well when she matched his easy exhalation. Maybe Chance did know what he was doing. She had to trust her brother, for that trust was the greatest support she could give him in this moment. Words and arguments would only distract him from his purpose. And distractions could mean failure... for all of them.

Brandr Ur paused, watching the young fighter. Let the child have his brief time of belief. A quick glance over his shoulder showed the veil remained well open. He allowed himself a satisfied grin. Only moments were needed to put the young pup in his place. The others would fall just as quickly despite their belief in their paltry magic.

But the veil... what had prevented him from easily stepping into his new world? The pitiful magic had slowed his advance, though he had expected no less. But the veil... had been a solid force he could not break through.

A sobering thought burst over him. Had the veil somehow taken his magic? Focusing on a tall stone, Brandr Ur called for his fire... insisted the power come to him... cajoled his primal nature... demanded... begged... bargained... found nothing but dim emptiness.

This could not be. These pretenders were no match for his power. A shiver traveled just under his skin raising bumps. He stared at his arm then rubbed the strange bumps and shivered again. He was... this was... cold?

Anger doubled upon itself. That which was his, what made him a god, had been stolen from him. By these puny beings. Clutching the sword hilt in both hands, he drew breath to roar his rage, then pulled back the need and rolled his shoulders. Long ages had passed since he'd held a physical weapon but he remembered the use of such was not assisted by anger.

No matter he was forced to lower himself to this level. If he remained calm and determined defeating these foes would take little effort. Determined, he would regain his due as a god.

Brandr Ur planted his feet firmly in the dry, gray dust and lifted the weapon, his stance eager... ready.

The challenger opened his eyes.

"This is just like watching a movie through a fog," Jayse grumbled. "We see everything going on, but can't do anything about it."

Nightshade commiserated with his friend's frustration. They'd opened the veil, somehow prevented the elemental from breaking through, and now held the passage to the World Between Worlds steady and reasonably clear to their vision. But this was a silent movie, though it was easy to imagine the thoughts of each person.

And like a movie focused on the main action, Chance and Brandr Ur centered their view through the veil. Able to easily see the fierce, determined expressions on their faces, dread deepened in Nightshade's gut as the combatants faced each other. More than with one of his feelings, he knew this was why Chance insisted on joining the rescue mission. Why he'd been so determined to be at ease with a new weapon.

Something about the sword drew his attention. Nightshade took a few steps to the edge of the brae and narrowed his eyes against the winds produced by the triple-strands of power. Lucidea joined him.

"What's caught your attention?" she asked.

He turned his head and grinned. "Can't get anything by you, can I, honey?"

She folded her arms over her chest. "Obviously a lot. We'll talk about that later." She jerked one hand toward the veil. "What about over there?"

"The sword."

"Huh?"

"There's something about Chance's sword."

Lucidea faced the veil and leaned forward. Nightshade shot his arm to the side to hold her back. "Careful."

She nodded and eased back a step but continued to study the scene before them. Chance shifted his hold on his weapon, bringing the blade to ready. A dim glint shone from the pommel, casting faint light on the curving cross guards. Lucidea gasped.

Jayse was at her side in a heartbeat. "Darlin'?"

"That sword. I know it. How did he...?"

Nightshade squinted, and as though the veil wished him to see, a portion of the haft and the fine etching at the base of the blade came into amazingly clear focus.

He recognized the sword as well. "Oberon's."

Jayse pulled Lucidea back from the cliff's edge and shook his head. "Can't be. The sword's safely locked up in the Faerie armory."

"No, Jayse," Lucidea said. "I'm sure that's Oberon's sword. More than just how the weapon looks, can't you feel the power? Even through the veil? How did Chance get it?"

"Probably stole it." At her soft statement, Nightshade turned to Tori. She shrugged. "You know as well as I do there's something going on with him. Bet he knew he'd come to this point and would need a weapon that could possibly defeat the elemental. In any of the worlds we know about, there's only one sword powerful enough to fit that description. Oberon's." She glanced at Jayse. "And it's not like you keep the Faerie armory guarded, is it?"

"I'll make sure." Jayse formed a portal and moved toward the faintly glowing oval.

Nightshade grabbed his arm. "No. All of us need to remain here. If that is Oberon's--"

"It is," Lucidea insisted.

"We need to witness this battle," he continued. "Be thankful Chance had the foresight to take such a powerful weapon." He paused. "I just hope he knows what he's doing."

The air shifted. Thick breeze rising from behind his opponent carried a scent to Brandr Ur, a scent from long ago. The stench of his underwater prison. He glared at the magic-wielding human but the boy showed no indication of anything amiss.

Why did he remember that foul odor? The prison his brethren created for him was long ago demolished. The power had absorbed into him, making him stronger still.

The stench surrounded him, pressing on his shoulders, draining his energy and replacing a numbing cold in his veins. How could this be? Had the boy somehow discovered a remnant of the prison to use against him now? Brandr Ur shook his head. Impossible. What the witch had not destroyed, he had returned and demolished. No binding power remained.

No. His banishment was long behind him. The future lay past this tiny insect of a being. An insect to be swatted aside and destroyed. He shifted his grip and jerked his weapon high above his head.

Twenty-nine

With speed that halted the breath at the base of Bree's throat, Brandr Ur attacked, leaping toward Chance.

One hand wrapped around the base of the blade to shorten his grip. Chance parried and sidestepped. While Bree approved of his stance and easy movements, his cocky grin gave her pause. Hopefully the expression was meant to further antagonize the elemental--rather than being a true representation of her brother's attitude.

She bit her lower lip to contain instructions and comments she knew would only distract Chance. A sister's comments.

Gowthaman stood silent at her side. She cast a quick glance at him, studying the intense concentration in his expression. A welling of love and longing momentarily chased her concerns to a manageable place. The brief seconds of peace and clarity allowed her to return her attention to the duel, set aside the sister and focus instead as the leader of the Alastriona.

After the initial clashes the combatants circled, gauging the other's ability with short strikes and teasing advance and retreat. Each metallic clang echoed, bouncing from the surrounding rocky ledges, creating a cacophony of real and imagined sound. Tempted to cover her ears, Bree winced at each blow.

Retreat. Chance's sword allowed him the longer reach, but the elemental was taller, broader, and quickly gaining skill and confidence with the mortal weapon.

Advance. Taking advantage of a split second when Chance's sword wavered, Brandr Ur swiped his weapon, an awkward, ungainly movement that surprised her brother into taking three steps back. She blew out a relieved breath. He'd avoided a deadly wound.

Advance. Chance's retreat lasted only a breath then he grunted with the effort of swinging his two-handed claymore. The elemental barely caught the thick blade against his quillons. Chance leaned into his sword, pressing, forcing Brandr Ur to retreat the steps he'd gained.

Morghan eased to Bree's side. "We're runnin' out of time."

Now what? Unwilling to move her attention from the combatants, she asked, "Why?"

"The veil's shrinkin'. We can no' wait much longer if ye are to escape."

Ye? She turned to look Morghan directly in the eye. "We're all going home. There's no you or me about it."

Morghan gave her half a smile. "Then we must no' linger."

A resounding clang of weapons made her thoughts stumble. She cast a quick glance at her brother before speaking to Morghan. "You and Coralie move closer to the opening. Whenever you can get through, do it. No matter what's happening here, you get through." At Morghan's rebellious frown, she softened her voice. "This battle is enough for me to worry about. Go home. Now if you can. Take Gowthaman with you."

"I will not go." Gowtham's softly spoken words thrilled her, then burrowed fear deep in her heart. He was barely healed of his pain. What if...

"Do not argue, Breanna. For this is one moment where I will not allow you to win."

Morghan opened his mouth to speak but Coralie covered his lips with her fingers. "Aye, we shall go. Yer man will remain at yer side. As it should be." Bree followed Coralie's gaze when she glanced at the fighters, who stared at each other, still but for their harsh breathing. "Soon, we shall see ye at home. Come Morghan. We need no' give Breanna more to worry upon."

Visibly reigning in his arguments, Morghan's shoulders slumped and he nodded. When he allowed himself to be drawn toward the veil, Bree returned her attention to Chance. She reached for Gowtham's hand to tug softly on his fingers. "You really should go with them."

"I should not."

She heard the smile in his voice and found one for him. "Watch Morghan for me. Make sure they get away. Please?"

"Of course."

A rush of hot air preceded Morghan's return to her side. His eager words stepped over her reprimand. "I remembered. I do no' ken what 'tis, but..." His brow wrinkled in concentration. "Somethin', a word Da taught to Lachlan an' me. So long ago 'tis been buried forever in my memory."

"A word? For what purpose?" She glanced at the fighters. Chance and Brandr Ur remained frozen in threatening postures.

She felt Morghan shrug. "Da would no' say. In truth, I do no' believe he knew himself. But I remember Da said this magic was only to be used in the most dire of need. That would be now."

Gowthaman gently squeezed her fingers. "If this is Sindhu magic, no harm should come to us with its use."

Morghan's frown deepened. "I do no' feel this to be only Sindhu. But somethin' more. Perhaps magic for all Alfar?"

"Good." Bree lifted one shoulder. "Any help we can get. Do what you need to, then get yourselves through that veil."

"Aye. We shall be waitin' for ye. Be quick." Morghan stepped away, hesitated then moved a few paces closer to the veil. Angling so she could see both Chance and Morghan, Bree waited.

"Arunz!"

Nothing happened. At least nothing she could see. A puff of air filled with the sharp tingle of magic breezed by her. The hair on the back of her neck lifted. A tiny dirt devil burst from the veil, then danced across the gray soil to hover a moment over the hollow depression still filled with their scrying water.

The tiny, water-filled tornado moved on, growing until it reached the elemental's knees. He kicked at the damp particles as the whirlwind claimed his body, encasing him in a fine sheen of gray mud. His angry growl reverberated from the surrounding stones. Unable to wipe away the mud, Brandr Ur cursed and stomped in a tight circle, reminding Bree of a child in the throes of a temper tantrum.

The space of three breaths passed as she watched the strange tableau, then Gowthaman said, "Morghan and Coralie have successfully transversed the veil. I see them still, and dim figures welcome them."

Relief swamped Bree's overwrought emotions and she allowed her shoulders to slump for just a moment. The primary focus of this mission was successful. "Thank goodness." Then she firmed her spine, squared her shoulders and softly urged her brother, "Come on, Chance. We don't have much time."

She didn't think he could hear her whisper, but he touched two fingers to his forehead in salute then settled his two-handed grip firmly on his sword. His precise, determined steps herded the still cursing elemental until he had positioned Brandr Ur with his back against a tall, upright stone.

Chance broke his silence. "Time to finish this, old man."

The elemental's expression settled into confusion. The hand clutching his sword shook. Bree kept her gaze fixed on the wavering tip and inched forward, expecting a sneaky attack. Gowthaman refused to let her hand go when she tugged, so she eased back to his side.

"I'm okay."

Nodding, Gowthaman relaxed his fingers. "The passage home is noticeably smaller. We must hurry."

"No sweat, Gowthaman," Chance called. "We'll be outta here in a couple minutes."

The elemental continued to stare at his shaking hand. "What have you done?" He lifted his gaze. "How?"

"Don't know. Don't care." Chance swung his sword in a wide arc, shot forward and impaled the elemental.

Brandr Ur's eyes opened wide, shock and pain evident in his silence. He dropped his sword and clutched the blade piercing his chest. "No. You can not..." Clawing at the blade with bloody hands, he staggered back until his spine pressed against the stone.

"It can not be. I destroyed this power. The well is gone. I can not be held again." Dark blood welled around the blade, stained his skin, spreading down his abdomen to his thighs. "I can... not wounded."

Chance retained his firm grip on the hilt, leaned into his weapon, and push forward. "This ends now, elemental."

"No." Brandr Ur attempted to shove him away then drew a shallow breath. "You... take you with me."

"How you gonna do that?" Chance gave a minute shove, the soft, muted sound of metal against stone loud in the small campsite. Bree shuddered.

"Chance?"

He turned a grim smile to her. "Almost, sis. Get ready to run for home." Forcing metal against stone, he shoved again.

With cut and bleeding hands wrapped around Chance's blade, the elemental struggled to remain upright. His eyes dimmed a moment before a fevered glint sparked in the depths and he began to mumble.

Blue-white flame, startling against the gray world, slithered down the blade and wrapped around Chance's hands, licking up his arms.

"Release the blade," Gowthaman shouted. "A death chant, Chance, let go."

"Can't." Chance groaned as the flames wrapped around his chest and moved to engulf his torso.

Bree shook off Gowthaman's restraining hands to run toward her brother.

"Do not touch him. Breanna. No." Gowthaman captured her only steps from Chance and held her tight against his body. "Do not. Or you may be taken as well."

"What's happening?" Tears burned her eyes and she blinked fiercely. "I've got to help him."

His face frozen in a grimace of agony, the blue-white flames connected Chance to the mumbling elemental.

Gowthaman tightened his hold. "There is nothing you can do."

Horrified, she watched Chance stumble to his knees, hands still grasping his sword.

"I did not believe such magic was possible. A death chant." Gowthaman's shudder settled panic and despair far deeper into her than his words.

"What do you mean?"

Chance's agonized cry ripped at her soul. She fought Gowthaman. "Let. Me. Go."

"If you touch him, you will be absorbed into the magic." Terrified of losing her to an ancient magic he did not understand, Gowthaman attempted to drag her further from the flow of power. His heart lurched in sympathy for Breanna and her brother with each of Chance's deepening groans. But he could not allow her to risk herself.

The elemental was dying, for legends said the magic wielder's dying breaths were needed to call forth a death chant. Gowthaman closed his eyes. Despite the knowledge on which he prided himself, he knew of no way to counter the chant, to save Chance. Once again, he failed his Breanna.

Silent, Breanna continued her struggles. She went limp, surprising him into loosening his hold. She slipped away, skidding to a stop an arm's length from Chance. Gowthaman rushed to her and tried to take her hand, but she shook him off.

Glaring at the elemental, she shouted, "Let him go."

Tinged with pain, Brandr Ur's weak, satisfied grin taunted them.

Chance collapsed, dragging the sword down with him, tilting the blade higher. The elemental paled. "I die. He dies."

"No!" Breanna shoved Gowthaman. "Stay back." She spread her arms then pointed one hand toward the elemental.

Gasping, Gowthaman fell back a step. She called upon unbelievable power, indiscriminately summoning any nearby magic. A physical wave of his magic flowed from him. He reached for her. "Breanna, do not."

Raw power rose and swirled around her, distorting the air like waves of heat over desert sands. She held her hand open, gathering, collecting then tightened her fingers into a fist. "Let. Him. Go."

Distorted power hovered around her. Deep crimson smothered the blue-white flames, then pulsed along the sword, surrounding both Brandr Ur and Chance. Breanna lifted her fists toward the elemental and with a sharp snap of her wrists forced him tight against the stone. A backlash of power skimmed down the sword. A high keening escaped Chance's tightly compressed lips.

"No, Chance." Shaking, she knelt to wrench the hilt from Chance's hands. Her magic pooled with pulsing crimson at the elemental's chest as she rose. One short step at a time, she pushed and the blade slid easily through Brandr Ur's body and into the stone. She leaned into the hilt until the cross guards sank into his flesh.

Frantic with fear for her, Gowthaman struggled against the powerful remnants of magic surrounding her and pried her hands from the sword.

When her fingers slipped away, surprise lit the elemental's eyes. Life blazed. Faded. A single glint flickered. Died. The huge, heavy body slumped forward, held upright against the stone only by the fey metal. Gowthaman shuddered as the lifeless eyes seemed to condemn him. He let the shudders carry the feeling away then relaxed his hold on Breanna. She sank to her knees and he moved closer to Brandr Ur. He needed to be assured the elemental was truly dead.

Unrestrained, Bree crawled to Chance's side and cupped his cheek with a shaking palm. He opened his eyes and tried to look past her to his enemy.

"He's dead, Chance."

"Me, too, sis."

"No, you're okay. I can heal you." She lay her hands over his heart and closed her eyes, calling for her healing abilities. Nothing. Her hands remained cold. Numb. Lifeless. "No, I can do this." Tears spilled down her cheeks.

Trembling, Chance covered her hand with his. "Don't cry, Bree. I can't stand it when you cry."

After a watery sniff, the tears refused to still. She couldn't lose Chance. She couldn't. Gritting her teeth, she demanded the magic come to her.

"Nothin' you... can do. Least we got him. Won't hurt... no more voices--"

"Shh. Quiet, now." She looked around, desperately searching for Gowthaman. She pressed her palms against the empty pain in her belly. "We've got to get you out of here."

Chance shook his head and winced as a tiny shrug lifted one shoulder. "I've dreamed about dyin', sis. Best... best dreams... ever had."

"You won't..." She couldn't say the word.

A faint indigo sparkle lit his eyes and his cocky grin returned. "Hey sis, at least I'm... not wearin'... a red shirt." Chance's eyelids closed. His hand slipped from hers.

Bree choked on a dry laugh. Only Chance would make such an obscure comment when he was-- She screamed in denial. Continued to scream when Gowthaman pulled her away. He shook her, gently at first... then with purpose and brought her back to the horrific reality of now.

Escaping into Gowtham's embrace, she cried. His soft stroking of her hair, the warmth of his breath as he whispered comfort to her failed to intrude upon her abject sorrow.

"Breanna, beloved, we must go. The veil is nearly gone."

"I can't go without Chance. I can't."

"Of course we shall bring him with us. But we must go now. Listen, do you not hear the others call to us from home?"

She clung to his support a moment longer then nodded and he released her. She didn't know how she could ever explain Chance's--this--to their parents. How would she explain her part?

"You'll help carry him?"

"With honor, sundarii. Come."

A disturbance in the dust marked where Chance had lain. Drag marks disappeared into a thick, unbroken gray mist. Bree dashed forward, slamming into a nearly solid wall of gray. "Chance," she cried. Her fists bounced back from the mist as she pummeled the barrier and sobbed.

Gowthaman paused, torn between love and duty. She would never leave the World Between Worlds without her brother's body. To be with her--he stared into the bleak gray mist--he would stay and search with her.

What options faced them? If the World Between Worlds had taken Chance, how would they find him? How would they return to the worlds where they belonged? They could be lost here for eternity.

Jerking his gaze to the veil, he stared at the rapidly shrinking clear oval leading home. There were others, her family, the Zeroun clan, who would help Breanna. Much as she had encouraged him. Each of his rapid breaths seemed to steal inches from their passage to safety. No time. No decision.

"We must go."

Breanna clawed at the mist. "No. You can't have him. Give him back. Damn you, give him back."

Cautious, Gowthaman touched her shoulder. "We must--"

She rounded on him. "No. Not without Chance."

Tears streaked her beautiful face. The agony of her expression nearly felled him to his knees in sorrow. Nearly settled his heart and mind into staying with her in the World Between Worlds.

But faint calls from beyond the veil urged him to decisive action.

"I am sorry, my Breanna. Forgive me." Wrapping his arms about her waist he dragged her, screaming, away from the heavy mist boundary. Ignoring the wide-open, condemning, dead eyes of the once powerful elemental, Gowthaman hefted his struggling love over one shoulder and sprinted toward the narrow opening.

Hands reached for Breanna as he shoved her through to the human world. He glanced behind him. The gray remained surrounding the campsite. Chance was gone. He sighed and dove through the opening. The gods always demanded a sacrifice.

Strong hands steadied Gowthaman as he flew through the last bit of opening in the veil. How different this passage was from his entrance to the World Between Worlds two nights ago. Words of the finest poet could not describe the relief and bittersweet joy washing through him at their safe return. After a deep breath of the fresh, Scottish night air, he searched the outcropping for Breanna.

There. With Coralie and Tori. Nearby Jayse and Lucidea formed a tight knot with Morghan. Nightshade stepped back. "What happened, honey?"

"Chance is... his spirit remains in the World Between Worlds." Conscious of Nightshade's gaze upon him, Gowthaman strode straight to Breanna and took her into a tight embrace.

She shoved him then punched the air from his diaphragm. "Damn you. You left him. Chance. You promised we'd bring him home. You promised me." She slapped at his chest.

He welcomed her anger. He was no less furious with himself but drew a slow breath to speak calmly. "Breanna, you must listen to me. Chance would not have wished you to sacrifice yourself to the World Between Worlds."

"You left him there. You should have left me, too. I had to find him."

"There was no choice."

"I hate you," she whispered then rubbed her hands over her face. "Gowtham?" She collapsed against him.

Relieved, Gowthaman held her gently and spoke to Tori. "Will you bring her parents here?"

"Won't you tell us--?"

"Breanna and I must face Bryce and Carrie with the news of Chance's... death. Then Breanna must rest. Let it be enough for now that we have returned with Morghan."

Without waiting for Tori to respond, he swept Breanna into his arms. She clung weakly to his neck and whispered, "I can walk."

He paused at the top of the steep path descending the side of the brae and smiled at her. "I know you can. But there is no need. Allow me to coddle you for a short while."

She sniffed and rested her head against his shoulder. "I don't hate you."

"I know, Sundarii. I know."

They were nearly to the manor house before she spoke again. "I don't know how I can face Mom and Dad. Not without..." Her voice broke with a watery sob.

All the knowledge of their combined worlds provided nothing to offer for comfort. The joy of Morghan's homecoming, the satisfaction of Brandr Ur's demise, all were tempered with their ultimate loss.

"I shall be at your side. Together we will inform your parents. I will not leave you even when the report of our time there must be given to Jayse and Lucidea."

"Report? Oh, yes." She straightened a bit making him shift his hold. "I am Alastriona. I must report the nuances of this mission. Please. I'd like to walk now."

Behind the sheen of tears, her eyes dulled. Lifting her higher, Gowthaman nuzzled her damp cheek then touched his lips to hers. She allowed his kiss, but her lips were lifeless under his. Setting her on her feet felt like he was letting her go. Forever. The urge to protect her raged powerfully through him. He would, if it were possible, save her from the torment of the coming hours. The days in the World Between Worlds had given him new insights. If Breanna wished to hide from her pain, he would remain at her side, as she had his, encouraging her to face the sorrow.

Muffled, excited chattering announced the others had followed them from the outcropping. He glanced into the sky. The moon's bright, full circle hovered over the trees, far advanced on her nightly journey. Anger stomped through his mind. How easily he could come to hate the cool, silver beauty.

Shaking his head, he pressed his hand to the small of Breanna's back and guided her into the manor. It was not reasonable to hate the moon. Gods and humans, Fey and Alfar, those gave power to the dominant light in the night skies.

Breanna's slow steps led them to a small sitting room. She perched stiff-backed in an overstuffed armchair, her expression blank and lost. For a moment only, he would wrap her heart in a frozen blanket of forgetting. For a moment only, he would share with her numbness he had lived with for so long. But he would not allow her to languish in that moment, for grief cried out for healing. Even for a healer.

As Gowthaman sat on the large ottoman at Breanna's side, Jayse appeared in the open doorway, paused and nodded. Gowthaman drew in a deep breath and took Breanna's cold hand. Jayse would direct her parents to them.

"Too many parents have lost children to war," Breanna's mother had said, bravely blinking back tears. "And you were at war with that elemental. No, that doesn't make losing Chance any easier. But, it's a strange comfort knowing he defeated an evil being."

Her father had pulled them into a three-way hug, but not even the warmth of her parent's love touched the cold, gray ice around her heart. Gowtham had remained at her side throughout this--ordeal--yet she hadn't thought to include him in the family circle until her mother motioned to him and hugged him in a tight embrace.

Everything inside her was dead. Dead as her beloved brother. Her heart. Her mind.

No, not everything.

Her memory flashed the moments to her. Over and over. Making her relive the most horrible time of her life. Making her face what she'd done.

How could she sit here, waiting to give Jayse an official report when everything--when the horrific outcome of the mission--was her fault? She couldn't face any of them. But neither could she leave. This was her responsibility. Her duty. And she always did her duty.

Finally Jayse and the others entered the family room. Gowthaman trailed behind the rest, his arms overfilled with papers and books. This Gowtham she knew, she understood... not the man who forced her from her brother's side. Part of her demanded she accept her earlier words and hate him. She wanted to, but couldn't. Why should she hate him when... if he knew... how could he not despise her?

"Okay then," Jayse started, drawing her reluctant attention. "I've gotten reports from everyone except Bree. Right now, I don't think she'll have significant information different from the observations of the rest of you."

She held back a derisive snort. Little he knew.

"I have a couple of questions," Nightshade said.

"Go ahead."

"Those of us here on this side of the veil did a lot of speculation about what was happening, both there and here. Bree, honey, you and Gowthaman really need to listen to this. Give us your opinions."

He was talking to her because they didn't know. She blinked.

"Honey?"

"Okay, I'm listening." But when Nightshade spoke again she tuned out his words. No one really expected her to respond. Just as well, she had nothing to contribute. Nothing but her pain.

Gowthaman watched Breanna intently, sighing at the moment she mentally left the gathering. He understood her grief, perhaps more fully than any she imagined. There was more to her grieving than her brother's death. In time, he would discover the source of that pain and assist in her healing.

As deeply as he wished to concentrate on Breanna, the conversation around him and his need to record the suppositions and results drew him back to the discussion.

"And that's when Nightshade joined the chant," Lucidea explained. "All this time he's been hiding who he is."

"Seems there are many secrets found in this now vastly extended family." Morghan chuckled and scrubbed a thick terrycloth square over his wet hair. He dropped the towel by the door and crossed the room to squeeze next to Coralie in a large easy chair. "I do no' mean to interrupt. Ah, but I could no' resist the loch another moment. The colors, aye, they near blinded me after so long without them. The water. Na-h-Ulie welcomed me well."

Gowthaman grinned at Morghan's exuberance. Once he had bothered to notice, even after only two days in the gray, the colors here were more vibrant than he remembered. Scents and sounds begged for new explorations. Briefly Gowthaman wondered what effect this would might have on the soulfire he shared with Breanna in the World Between Worlds.

"Hush, ye foolish man," Coralie admonished. Morghan rewarded her with a kiss then shook his head, spattering her with tiny droplets. "Ye'll pay for that, milord."

"I certainly hope so, eudail. But now, I would be serious and know more of this man, Nightshade."

"Ah, haven't told everything yet, honey."

Nightshade basked under the quizzical gazes while Gowthaman flipped to a clean page in the journal he'd begun for this venture. Finally, Nightshade took a deep breath and began.

"Yes, I am Alfar-Domovoii. Had I remained in my world, my position would have been much like Morghan's while his brother remained the crown prince."

"You're royal?" Lucidea squealed.

"Afraid so, honey."

"Why did you leave?"

Somber, Nightshade rose and moved to the window. He stared into the rising dawn for a long moment. "It's been a long time. Maybe Claec, my brother, has changed. Perhaps he hasn't." He turned to face the room, resting his hip against the deep sill. "You see, my dears, while to... my people, it is of no matter who a Domovoii chooses to love, such was not the case for the brother of the crown prince. He was..." Nightshade closed his eyes. "...embarrassed by my love for another man."

He opened his eyes and returned to his chair. "I was young, perhaps foolish. But I could not bear his intolerance. I left. Burned the proverbial bridges. Found my way in this remarkable human world. Oh, and before you ask, honey," he said to Lucidea. "I have always been Nightshade."

"How long ago?" Tori asked.

He shifted his focus to her and grinned. "A new millennium had just begun."

The pen slipped from Gowthaman's fingers and he studied the newly found Domovoii. Nightshade winked at him. "I'll tell you just about anything you want to know, my dears. But some other time."

"Right." Jayse leaned forward, resting his forearms on his knees. "We've pretty much come to the conclusion that ages ago the three races, probably the Alfar progenitors themselves, banded together to contain Brandr Ur in the World Between Worlds. Then by using a children's rhyme to remember their spell casting and a power word known only to the ruling families, insured he'd stay there."

Morghan slapped his thigh. "If we had only understood this sooner, discovered the word they used to bind the elemental, so much might be different."

Head after head moved as each person glanced at Breanna. She didn't notice, didn't respond, and the eyes turned to Gowthaman. He offered only a slight shake of his head. Though Chance's death was horrific enough for her, some deeper pain held her inthrall.

"Gowthaman, would you tell us about what happened with... Oberon's sword?"

He took three breaths then fell into a recitation pattern long practiced by storytellers--and librarians. His telling melded the theories from both sides of the void and added Chance's battle with Brandr Ur. Heads nodded thoughtfully as he finished and took another three breaths. These words he would record precisely in his journal at a later time.

However, there was a piece of the puzzle Gowthaman still didn't understand. "Can you tell me anything of Oberon's sword?"

Jayse shrugged and took Lucidea's hand. "Not much. After Oberon passed into another world, the blade was held in stasis by Wodhan. Underwater." He tugged on Lucidea's hand until she looked at him. "That place, where Wodhan kept the sword, was that the same well where Brandr Ur was held?"

Drawing her brows together, she wrinkled her nose as she thought. "You know, I think I remember that. Oh." Her eyes grew wide. "Also, Oberon forged the blade in the heat and power of that well."

"So," Jayse drawled. "In essence the sword was crafted using residual power from the elemental's first captivity."

"Ah." Gowthaman scribbled a quick note. The intensity of waiting filled the room. He lowered the pen. "I begin to understand. The Alfar words first took the elemental's power, then made him mortal. As a mortal being we could be wounded. Killed. However, Oberon's sword held the same forces that both created and held Brandr Ur. Once the sword pierced his chest, the elemental captured the familiar power and was able to use it."

"Use it how?" Lucidea asked.

Uncomfortable with even the thought of speaking of an evil such as a death chant, Gowthaman shook his head. "This is not easy to say and I will say no more than necessary at this juncture in time. Perhaps when I understand more..."

"In regaining power Brandr Ur found the magic for a death chant. He was determined to drag Chance with him into death. I... do not know how the chant came to be for I have not studied such magic. It is dangerous and unpredictable.

"Connected to Brandr Ur through the sword, Chance was captured by the death chant. Breanna would not allow her brother to be taken. She... I... Again I am a poor resource." How could he explain the intensity of Breanna's pull on his magic? "I do not know what power she called upon to break the death chant. Nor pull the magic back into herself. She freed Chance then..."

Momentarily at a loss for words, Gowthaman paused. No one spoke, breathless anticipation hanging heavy in the room. In the silence, Breanna stood then remained statue-like, dry-eyed, staring into the unseen distance.

"Why didn't you bring the sword back," Jayse asked.

Gowthaman shook his head. "I could not. Breanna's safety was my concern. In any event, Breanna took the sword and drove the blade through the elemental's body, deep into the stone at his back. There it remains."

The collective gasp drew Breanna's attention. With her usual smooth, easy grace she crossed the room to stand before Jayse. Arms held loose at her side, she waited until he handed Lucidea a kumquat from a shallow bowl then looked up at her.

Denial reared in Gowthaman's heart. He had no clear indication of what she was about to do, but he knew... he knew she would make a grand mistake. Hoping to stop whatever she intended, he rose but froze at the sound of her clear voice.

"My lord Jaysson. I resign as leader of the Alastriona, as well as any place I may hold within the Defenders of Mankind."

Thirty-one

Six weeks had passed since... no, she wouldn't think of that. Think happy thoughts. Think since Morghan came home.

The house was quiet, as it should be with the rest of her family gone and only her thoughts and memories to keep her company. Her parents tried, they really did. But they didn't know, couldn't ever know of her part in Chance's death. She caught back a dry sob. She was so tired of crying.

The small room, the sanctuary of her childhood, surrounded her. No one bothered her here. Although fresh pain stabbed through her, she was glad no one cared.

Berating herself, she moved to lie on the narrow bed. That wasn't true. Her family and friends did care. And she cared about them, and because of their love, she couldn't face them with the agony of her soul. They were giving her time to grieve. Jayse had refused to accept her resignation, insisting upon a leave of absence. She sniffed. Macaire was a better leader and should have been appointed when Granda retired. Instead of her.

And Gowthaman. Curling on her side, she clutched her pillow to her stomach and choked on his name. "Oh Gowtham." He'd remained near, always there when he thought she might need him. And she did. Always. But... not if he knew.

She closed her eyes remembering the questions and concerns on his face the day before when she'd asked him to send away the Faerie who had come to her for healing of a simple wound. She hadn't healed anyone since... how could she?

The back door slammed. Light footsteps sounded, climbing the stairs. Now what? She turned her back to the door. Go away.

The bedroom door burst open. How dare anyone just barge in without knocking? But she didn't care enough to turn over and send them away. Maybe they'd think she was sleeping and just go.

"Breanna."

Even through the misery, Gowthaman's voice, the loving way he spoke her name softened her heart. Oh, how she loved him, but she couldn't... shouldn't. "Please leave me alone."

"I will not." The mattress dipped and he slid his arms under her shoulders and knees. He lifted her and settled her into an easy hold. She opened her eyes. He wasn't smiling.

"Put me down."

"No. You will come with me. Now."

Her half-hearted struggle only made him hold her tighter. He carried her down the stairs and out into the back yard. A portal stood open, waiting.

Not wanting to leave her safe haven, she squirmed and wiggled but his grasp was firm. Bree looked into his face from under her lashes. Set in a hard line, his tightly clenched jaw showed his determination, and another side of Gowtham she'd not known. A flutter, somewhere around her heart, made the breath catch at the base of her throat. She would never be able to stop loving him.

"No. I don't want to leave here." Unable to put any strength into the action, her hands flopped useless against his chest.

"In this moment, beloved, I do not care what you want."

"Don't call me that."

He gazed at her and his eyes softened to the color of rich, melted chocolate. "But you are my beloved. Why should I not say the words?" Then his gaze hardened, his eyes black as night and he stepped through the portal.

Into a place so bright she jerked her hand up to cover her eyes. Gowthaman lowered her bare feet to hot sand. When she danced on the burning grains, he slipped off his shirt and folded it on the sand then lifted her to stand on the cooler cotton.

"What are we doing here?"

"I find I am not as patient as you have been, Breanna. I do not wish to wait years for you to admit the pain you carry in your soul. For me, too many days have already passed without your love. Here, now, you will allow me to assist you, to help you heal your grief, until your pain is manageable."

"You can't help me. Nobody--"

"So I avowed many times. So I believed. Until you... encouraged me to put my memories into the past, enabling me to release the melancholy and pain. You opened my heart to the future. With you."

Heat penetrated the cloth she stood on and she stepped from one foot to the other. "Why here?"

"There are no distractions."

"Except the heat."

He shrugged and glanced around. She followed his gaze past the golden, windswept dunes to the bright, clear azure of the sky. "Then we must not dally."

"Take me home."

"I will not."

"Then I'll do it myself." She turned and lifted one hand to sketch the simple symbol to open a Faerie portal. But, that would use magic. Magic she no longer trusted. She closed her fingers into a fist and lowered her hand.

"I see."

She shook her head and stared at the fine, golden sand. "You see nothing."

"Since our return from the World Between Worlds, you have not used the magic residing within you. Even when faced with the pain of another, you would not draw upon your power of healing. Why, Breanna? Why do you deny that part of who you are?"

Setting her shoulders, she chewed on her lower lip until the pain focused her and she could answer in a cold, unemotional tone. "I'm not that person anymore."

"I see."

She whirled to face him, scattering sand over his crumpled tunic. "You don't see anything. I don't know what you're thinking, or doing, or... or... Gowtham, please. Let it go. Let me alone. I--I'm not good for you. For anyone. Not anymore."

Gowthaman crossed his arms and took a step back, studying her. He had not realized how difficult it would be to encourage her to face her demons. Though, he thought with wry self-deprecation, who better to have known? As he also understood how much more difficult this time of realization would be if she were allowed to wallow in self-pity and anger. If she did not come to honor her emotions, such feeling would take on lives of their own. A formidable obstacle he would not allow her to construct between them.

"Don't just look at me. Let me go home."

"No."

Her sad eyes were nearly his undoing. Then a rising blaze of anger flushed her cheeks and made him smile. Good.

"All right. Fine. What do you want me to say?"

"Why do you blame yourself for Chance's death?"

Her mouth dropped open, parting her lips in a delightful, inviting manner. Gowthaman closed his eyes, willing her to answer honestly. There was more they needed to do before this day was done.

She sputtered a moment then said, "Because I was the leader of the mission. It was my duty to see that everyone was safe."

"No."

"What do you mean, no?" She shaded her eyes with one hand, tilted her head and glared at him.

Anger was a step in the right direction. "That is not the reason, although I will allow it plays a role in your feelings."

"Since when do you know so much about my feelings?"

He reached to take her hand and pressed his open palm to hers. Sparkles the color of the glistening sand danced amid fine grains of crimson. He held their palms together until the whirling colors danced up their arms. Silently, he released her.

Freed from the sensual hold of their soulfire, Bree kept her hand lifted for a moment, staring at her palm. Maybe she should be honest with Gowthaman. Maybe she owed him that much. Then he would understand and leave her alone.

Alone. Her heart lurched at the word. The two syllables no longer held the appeal they had even five minutes ago. "Can we go somewhere else?"

"No. Not until this barrier between us is cleared."

Her hand shook so she lowered it and wiped her palm against her jeans. She'd hoped never to have to say the words, but knew Gowtham wouldn't allow her to remain silent. She ducked her head. There was no way she could look at him and say this.

"I killed Chance. I... killed my brother."

"You did not."

She jerked her gaze to him. His face was relaxed, his eyes once again soft chocolate. He seemed so sure of himself, of his words. A mite of hope gnawed at her doubts. "There's no way you can know that."

"Neither is there concrete evidence you caused Chance's death."

"How can you say that?"

He took her hands and she allowed him to caress the backs with his thumbs. Even though she tried to ignore the tingles and worked to push the feeling away, the languid motions played havoc with her nerve endings. "While you have hidden away, I have learned more of the... death chant. Though my knowledge has only increased infinitesimally, I believe I am now able to share my insights with you."

"But the elemental was the one using the death chant."

"Precisely."

"I was trying to stop him."

"Yes. And how was it you made your attempt?"

"I... well, I..." She paused. She'd never really examined the event, so she focused her memory on the moments she drew power to her, not on the aftermath. She furrowed her brow. That couldn't be right. "I called on my ability to heal?"

"You do not need my affirmation."

She added a bit of strength to her statement. "I called on my ability to heal."

"Yes." Gowthaman's smile was relaxed, honest, and... oh, so kissable.

"But... there was a backlash of power. I saw it travel down the sword from the elemental to Chance. When I pushed Chance's hands from the hilt I felt the intensity of the magic. I--"

His long, gentle fingers covered her lips. "No. What you felt was how your healing held back the death chant. I do not understand, for I have found no instances of similar battles in the archives. The death chant killed your brother, your healing prevented the intense anguish the elemental undoubtedly wished upon him."

Shading her eyes again, she studied Gowtham's face. His words... reinforced what she knew. What she'd been using to hide her real fear.

"I called upon my healing power."

"Yes," he encouraged.

"And I used that power in anger. I used it to kill." Covering her mouth with her hands, she doubled over, collapsing to her knees in the hot sand. "I used healing to destroy a living being."

Gowthaman knelt beside her and wrapped his arm over her shoulders. His face close to her ear, he whispered, "Yes, you did. And despite the fact that being was pure evil, had murdered your brother and sought to rain his destruction upon numerous worlds... despite the fact Brandr Ur long deserved an end to his existence... your actions brought you indescribable pain."

She turned her head bringing her lips close to his. "But how can I ever use that ability again? How can I heal knowing I can just as easily destroy?"

"Look into your heart, Sundarii. No evil resides there, no joy of what was done. Your self-loathing was so great, you hid your pain deep behind anguish you found more acceptable."

"How do you know so much?"

His warm breath flowed over her cheek. "I lived in such a way for many years. I used those shields to protect my wounded mind, as you sought to protect your healer's heart. A beautiful woman insisted I see the truth of my life. In doing so, she enabled me to unlock the flow of love in my heart."

The beat of her heart thrummed in her chest. Awareness flowed over her skin. She began to feel. "I will always grieve for my brother."

"As it should be. You have taught me there is no absolute. We sorrow for what we have lost, and at the same time rejoice in our ongoing lives. Because of you I have learned that to love, and be loved in return, is the greatest defense against the pain we submit ourselves to. The pain we hold to ourselves because we believe it to be a comfort or an armor."

"Gowthaman?"

"Yes, beloved?"

"Even after all this, you still love me?"

He groaned, captured her face between his palms and kissed her. Bree leaned into the kiss, planting her hands on the hot skin of his bare shoulders for balance. Much too soon, he drew away.

Silent, he watched her and she wondered what thoughts he hid behind those wonderful dark eyes.

"Breanna. Can you leave your sorrow?"

While she thought, she watched his face. He tried to restrain his reactions, to hide his thoughts from her, but she understood. He was worried.

"I can. I know I spent many long weeks wallowing and only a few minutes ago accepted the truth of what happened. I know how my perceptions colored my thinking. I know it's pretty fast, but you know me."

"Do not take this healing lightly."

"No." She shook her head. "I don't. I just... Gowtham? I don't think I can go back to the Alastriona. I don't want to be responsible for missions or battles. I want to... help you in the library. I need to smile. I need to see you smile."

Gowthaman rose in a fluid motion then held his hand to her. A serious expression lasted a few second then he granted her wish. "Then you shall not return. In truth, your decision eases my heart. Will you come with me?"

At her nod, he drew her to her feet, pulled her close then lifted her in his arms. She stroked the fine sheen of sweat covering the back of his neck. "The desert's pretty hot. Are we going someplace cooler?"

In response he laughed, formed a portal and stepped though.

Cool, damp air caressed Bree's skin. A slight breeze rustled through the palms, setting the tiny bells tied to the branches in musical motion. She sighed. Gowtham's oasis.

"Beautiful. I love the bells. Thank you for making the magic for me."

He gave a soft huff. "I did not. Such would be a frivolous use of magic." His expression soften. "I asked a tribe of Korin's winged fairies to assist me."

"However the bells happened, thank you." Playful, she poked his shoulder. "Since we've obviously been in the Sahara, how about a dip under the waterfall to cool off?"

"I have no wish to cool off."

"Oh? What do you mean?"

The fierceness of his kiss thrilled her to the tips of her wiggling toes. During the mating of their tongues, he lowered her feet to the grass covered ground and she discovered his desire in the press of his body.

"Okay," she panted when he allowed a breath of air between them. "No dip in the pool."

A beatific smile burst across his face. "Good choice."

She arched her eyebrows. "Good choice?"

"May I show you something?" The soft shyness in his voice intrigued her.

"Sure."

"Turn around."

After giving him a dubious look, she did. Suspended from high branches, panels of brightly colored silk rippled in the breeze. Centered between the panels sat a huge, bed-sized cushion draped with more silks and piled with pillows. "It's like something out of Aladdin."

Wrapping an arm about her waist, he encouraged her forward. "This is my fantasy. Even when I denied you, denied my feelings, this was the fantasy I had of you. Of our first time together."

"Instead we had danger, hard gray ground, rocks and an unforgiving sky."

"I--"

"Hush. Don't apologize. It didn't matter where we were. Only that we were. I love you, Gowtham. Not romantic trappings. Not a place."

"But, will you allow me my fantasy?"

She caressed her hand down his chest. His golden skin quivered under her palm. "Yes," she whispered.

"Ah, Breanna. *TvaaM kaamayaami*. He gathered her close, but she stepped back. He moved closer and she retreated. A look of consternation filled his face then he smiled and stepped forward, pushing her more quickly toward the bed.

That suited Bree just fine and she reached for the button on her jeans as she moved. Gowthaman stopped her hands and shook his head. "This is my fantasy."

Willing to discover whatever he carried in his mind, she sat, then lay back and held out her arms. A wicked gleam lit the eyes of her gentle librarian as he crawled over the cushions to half cover her with the delectable heat of his body.

He nipped at her lips, then eased the sting with the slow caress of his tongue and kisses that left her senses reeling. Longing for more, she sighed when he eased away.

He passed one hand above her and her clothing disappeared. Desire darkened his eyes to nearly black.

She giggled. "I didn't think you approved the frivolous uses of magic."

Lowering his head to nuzzle her breast, he mumbled, "Not frivolous. Expedient."

"But... but you're still partially... Oh." The soft texture of his hair tickled her palms as she held his head in place while he teased and delighted her nipples.

Lost in the sensation of his mouth, his hands, the slide of his body against hers, she reveled in his slow exploration.

Breathless, she tried to reconstruct her last thought when he propped himself on his elbow and watched her with a soft, sensuous gaze.

Cool silk caressed her heated skin. He drew the length over her breasts, twirled the soft fabric around her peaked nipples then piled the scarf at the juncture of her thighs. After a much too brief kiss, he tugged another cool scarf along her heated body.

"But, Gowtham..."

He silenced her with a kiss. Bemused, she fought to remain still and silent while he covered her in a multitude of colored silks. Then he sat back on his calves.

"This is how I imagined you. Yet even the finest of silks are not..." Reverence filled his gaze and he shook his head as if searching for words.

The silks caressed her overly sensitive skin and she squirmed, igniting sparks of desire in Gowtham's eyes. "I... oh, don't make me wait longer. Gowtham, you're still partially dressed," she cried in frustration.

With a gesture, his trousers were gone. Bree blew out a soft breath. His body was magnificent. And wanting. Her.

She had to feel him, skin to skin, so held out one hand and started pushing at the silks with the other.

Gowtham stopped her hand. "Please, Sundarii, do not."

He gave her no chance to argue, settling himself between her thighs and drowning her in another wild kiss. The slide of silk between their bodies, the heavy heat of his erection against her thigh, the strange words he murmured between kisses... thought fled. Holding on to the man she loved became her only reality.

Gowthaman trailed kisses down the arch of her neck. She tasted of golden sunshine and sweet honey. Tasted of love and desire and hope. Innocence and desire. He took her silk covered nipple deep into his mouth. Her nails scraped his shoulder and they groaned together.

"Gowtham." A whispered demand.

"Breanna," he replied and cupped his hand over the silks guarding her mound. He lifted his head and watched her face while he stroked and danced his fingers over her. Her lush mouth, those perfectly kiss-swollen lips were soft in an expression of delight and surprise. But her lashes lay in soft crescents upon her cheeks and he wanted to see the brilliant blue of her desire. Wanted to see through her eyes when he entered her.

"Look at me, Sundarii."

She smiled and opened her eyes. As he swept the silk from her body then slowly entered her, she shifted, her eyes wide. No longer able to deny himself, he drew her into an insistent, tension-building rhythm. Her fingers pressed into his shoulders, slid down his back, cupped his buttocks, silently encouraging. Touching, exploring, he discovered what she needed in this moment. No desperation clouded their movements making this their first, truly joyous time together.

Enraptured, Gowthaman watched each ripple of pleasure dance sparkles in her eyes. Her response tightened around him, drawing him deeper, holding him, demanding from him. When she cried out her release, startled oasis birds darted into the sky. Gowthaman followed their flight with his own hoarse cry of soaring, inexplicable pleasure.

Gowthaman eased to Breanna's side and molded her against him. Soulfire sparkled around them, rising into the treetops where gold and crimson danced among the palm fronds. He held out their cupped hands to catch the magic of their love.

The birds returned to their branches, an occasional scolding disrupting the muted chattering. Before his heart slowed, Breanna rose up on her elbow, gazing at him with such love and satisfaction, the heavy beating nearly stalled in his chest. How had such a woman chosen him?

She brushed hair from his forehead and caressed his cheek. "That was some fantasy."

"In the years you waited for me to acknowledge my love for you, did you not dream or create fantasies of our time together?"

She touched a finger to the seam of his lips and nodded.

He drew her finger into his mouth and sucked softly, caressing the pad with his tongue. When she could no longer contain her groan, he smiled and eased away, scraping her fingertip with his teeth. "Then we shall discuss your fantasies and find ways to fulfill them."

"I've had lots of fantasies, Gowtham. Lots."

"My beloved, my Breanna, we have ages of discovery before us."

Deadeaters circled the prone form, slobbering, drooling, long strands of gray spittle trailing from their needle-sharp teeth. The circle closed. They snarled and snapped their jaws with vicious anticipation. Seldom did they fall upon fresh meat and this meal was fine. Young. Not hardened by long ages in the World Between Worlds.

One, the alpha, leapt forward, stretching its long, ragged claws toward the prize.

Yelping, it fell back, scattering the gathered cluster of its brethren. It held one paw out to halt its fellows, jabbering with wet clicks and guttural stops.

A second deadeater separated from the pack, stumbled to a halt then inched forward. Dark claws clacked together, hesitation evident in the challenge and awkward advance.

Inches from the meal, burning agony sliced up the dead-eater's arm. It shrieked in combined pain and rage.

The alpha snorted and pushed it away. "No dead," it clattered to the pack. "Life-pain yet. Bah."

Leaning closer, the alpha sniffed. Pleased, it gurgled low in its throat. "No long. Soon, no life-pain."

The pack jostled each other, snapping and growling before settling in an ungainly pile. The alpha wiped drool from its mouth and sat apart from the rest. Watching the meat. Waiting for the last of the faint life-pain to drain away. Waiting for the meal.

Sudden silence from its pack mates lifted the hair covering the wrinkled skin at the back of its neck. It plucked at the feeling with a claw, a vague bit of memory making it growl. Then it felt--them. Remembered--them. The Watchers.

The growl deepened to a powerful threat. The pack echoed the sound, a crescendo rising to a cacophony of discordant yelps and whines.

Mist hovered above the ground just beyond the meat. Confusion stirred the lesser pack mates to a frenzy, but the alpha cocked its head. It was old, had long eaten the dead of this place, knew the Watchers. Knew they would steal the prize. If they did, there would be no meat.

Joining its snarling, slobbering pack, the alpha clacked and pointed. The meat still lay upon the cloth they'd used to drag it to their territory. Recognition, then knowing the meat still belonged to them ignited slowly in the dull eyes of its brethren. Pushing and shoving they clamored toward the meal.

The mist grew thicker. Descended and moved to cover the meal. The pack screamed in denial. The alpha scrambled toward the meal and fell forward through the cool mist. Shards of life-pain numbed its skin, its cries receding to soft, confused clacking.

The meat. Gone.

ABOUT THE AUTHOR

*lizzie always made up games and stories to keep her company. So, a cunning witch lived in Grampa's weather research station and was only held at bay by waving a certain weed. An ancient road grader morphed into a boat carrying wild adventurers to islands filled with fierce lions and dangerous cannibals, which really looked a lot like sheep. Now, filled with fantasy, love, and romance with a sparkling twist, the stories of her imagination swirl their way into the mundane world. When *lizzie must return to a more routine life, she's *the Lunch Lady* at a private school.

Author and lunch lady~~what a combination!

FANTASY ROMANCE

The Double Keltic Triad
By Keltic Design
Fires of a Keltic Moon
Keltic Flight
Wild Keltic Carouselle
Keltic Dreams
A Faire Keltic Renaissance

Children of the Keltic Triad
Blue Keltic Moon

The Keltic Multiverse
Prince of Dark Ness
(Double Keltic Triad 5.5)

CONTEMPORARY ROMANCE

Birds Do It!

SHORT STORIES
Available as ebooks

At Death's Gates
Dead Lily Blooms
Death and the Dryad

From the Keltic Multiverse
Candy Guy and the Chocolate Brownie

Futuristic Romance
Written in Stone

JOURNALS AND COLORING BOOKS

The Cosmos Journals
Moonstruck
Star Gazing
Fires in the Sky

Coloring Books Coloring Book

For Writers and Creatives
Creating Super Characters
Name Collection Journal for Writers
6 Month Goals and Accountability Planner